THE BETTY NEELS COLLECTION

Betty Neels's novels are loved by millions of readers around the world, and this very special *2-in-1 collection* offers a unique opportunity to relive the magic of some of her most popular stories.

We are proud to present these classic romances by the woman who could weave an irresistible tale of love like no other.

So sit back in your comfiest chair with your favorite cup of tea and enjoy these best of Betty Neels stories!

D0202120

BETTY NEELS

Romance readers around the world were sad to note the passing of Betty Neels in June 2001. Her career spanned thirty years, and she continued to write into her ninetieth year. To her millions of fans, Betty epitomized the romance writer, and yet she began writing almost by accident. She had retired from nursing, but her inquiring mind still sought stimulation. Her new career was born when she heard a lady in her local library bemoaning the lack of good romance novels. Betty's first book, *Sister Peters in Amsterdam,* was published in 1969, and she eventually completed 134 books. Her novels offer a reassuring warmth that was very much a part of her own personality, and her spirit and genuine talent live on in all her stories.

BETTY NEELS

A Gem of a Girl

and

Love Can Wait

HARLEQUIN® THE BETTY NEELS COLLECTION

Recycling programs
for this product may
not exist in your area.

ISBN-13: 978-0-373-60659-7

A GEM OF A GIRL AND LOVE CAN WAIT

Copyright © 2014 by Harlequin Books S.A.

The publisher acknowledges the copyright holder
of the individual works as follows:

A GEM OF A GIRL
Copyright © 1976 by Betty Neels

LOVE CAN WAIT
Copyright © 1997 by Betty Neels

Printed in U.S.A.

www.Harlequin.com

CONTENTS

A GEM OF A GIRL

CHAPTER ONE

GEMMA WAS AT the top of the house making beds when she heard the ominous shattering of glass. The boys were in the garden, kicking a football around, and she wondered which window it was this time. She mitred a corner neatly; news, especially bad news, travelled fast, someone would be along to tell her quickly enough.

It was George, her youngest, ten-year-old brother, who climbed the three flights of stairs to break it to her that it was Doctor Gibbons' kitchen window. 'And I kicked it,' he added with a mixture of pride at the length of the shot and apprehension as to what she would say.

'A splendid kick, no doubt,' declared his eldest sister robustly, and shook a pillow very much in the manner of a small terrier shaking a rat. 'But you'll all have to help pay for the damage, and you, my dear, will go round to Doctor Gibbons when he gets back from his rounds, and apologise. I'll telephone

Mr Bates in a minute and see if he'll come round and measure up the glass right away—perhaps he might even get a new pane in before Doctor Gibbons gets back. But you'll still have to apologise.'

'For a girl,' said George, 'you're not half bad.' With which praise he stomped downstairs again. She heard him in the garden a few moments later, arguing with his brothers as to the sum of money required for the new window pane.

Gemma finished the bed and went, in her turn, downstairs. She was a smallish girl and a little plump, but nicely so. Her hair, hanging down her back in a brown tide loosely tied with a ribbon, was the same soft brown as her eyes and although she was on the plain side, when she smiled or became animated, the plainness was lost in its charm. She was almost twenty-five years old and looked a good deal younger.

She went straight to the telephone and besought Mr Bates to come as soon as he could, and then re-tired to the old-fashioned wash-house adjoining the kitchen, and started on the week's wash; a fearsome pile, but she was used to that; with three boys in the family and two sisters younger than herself, there was naturally a vast amount.

She eyed it with a jaundiced expression; it was a pity that Mandy and Phil had gone to friends' for the weekend—of course she could leave it until the next day when they would be back, but the Easter holidays ended within a day or so and it seemed mean to blight their last freedom with a lot of hard work. Besides, it was a lovely day, with just the right kind of wind. She battled with the elderly washing machine and then left it to thunder and rumble while she went to the kitchen to make coffee. It would be a relief when Cousin Maud got back from her visit to her brother in New Zealand—five weeks, reflected Gemma, of holding down a full-time job, running the old-fashioned house and keeping an eye on her brothers and sisters was just about her limit; thank heaven there was only another week to go—less than a week now, she remembered happily as she went to stop the machine. She hauled out the wash and shoved it into the rinser, set it going and then filled the tub up again. The two motors, working in unison, made the most fearful noise, but she was used to that, merely reiterating to herself the promise that one day she and Cousin Maud would get another washing machine, as she went back to the kitchen to drink her coffee.

She was back in the wash-house, hauling out the first batch in blissful silence, when a faint sound behind her caused her to say: 'James? or is it William or James? take some money from the housekeeping jar and get some sausages from Mr Potter—and don't waste time arguing about going if you want your dinner today.'

She was tugging at a damp sheet as she spoke, and when a strange voice, deep and leisurely, said:

'I'm afraid I'm not the person you think—my name's Ross,' she dropped it to shoot a startled look over her shoulder.

She had never seen the man standing in the doorway; a tall, broad-shouldered individual, with pale hair which was probably silver as well, she wasn't near enough to see, but she could see his eyes, blue and heavy-lidded below thick, pale brows. He had a high-bridged nose and a firm mouth and he was smiling. He was a very good-looking man and she stared for a moment. He bore her look with equanimity, laid a football which he had been carrying on a pile of sacks by the door and remarked: 'Your brothers', I believe,' and waited for her to speak.

Gemma disentangled the sheet and heaved it into the basket at her feet. 'You're from Doctor Gibbons',' she stated, and frowned a little, 'but you can't be the foreign professor who's staying with him; the boys said he was short and fat and couldn't speak English...'

Her visitor shrugged. 'Boys,' he remarked, 'I've been one myself.' He smiled again and Gemma wiped a wet hand down the front of her jersey and skipped across the floor between them.

'I'm Gemma Prentice,' she told him, and held out a hand, to have it engulfed in his.

'Ross Dieperink van Berhuys.'

'So you are the professor. Do you mind if I just call you that—your name's rather a mouthful, isn't

it? For a foreigner, I mean,' she added politely. 'And
thank you for bringing the football. I do hope it didn't
disturb you—the window being broken, I mean.
They all go back to school tomorrow.' She gave him
an unaffected smile. 'Would you like some coffee?
If you wouldn't mind waiting while I load this machine again...?'

His thank you was grave and his offer to hang out
the clothes ready for the line was unexpected; she accepted it without arguing and he went into the large
untidy garden with the basket while she switched on
once more and went back into the kitchen to fetch
another mug.

The coffee was freshly ground and carefully made;
she and Cousin Maud cooked and baked between
them and they both turned out what her older relation called good wholesome food; the coffee she
poured now smelled delicious and tasted as good as
it smelled. Her unexpected guest, sitting comfortably
in an old Windsor chair, remarked upon the fact before asking gently: 'And you, Miss Prentice?'

'Me what?' asked Gemma, all niceties of grammar lost; if the boys had disappeared—and heaven
knew they always did when there was a chore to be
done—she would have to leave the washing and fetch
the sausages herself, which meant she wouldn't get
her work done before dinner. She frowned, and the
professor persisted placidly, 'The sausages bother
you, perhaps?'

She gave him a surprised look. 'How did you know?' She refilled their mugs. 'Well, actually, yes…' She explained briefly, adding obscurely: 'I expect you're a psychiatrist—they always know things.'

Her companion turned a chuckle into a cough. 'Er—I suppose they do, but you did mention sausages…I'm an endocrinologist, myself.'

He got to his feet, his head coming dangerously near the low ceiling. 'I should be delighted to fetch these sausages for you while you finish your washing.'

He had gone before she could thank him, and was back again in a very short time, to put his parcel on the kitchen table and observe: 'There is someone repairing the window.'

'Oh, good—that'll be Mr Bates. I asked him to come round as soon as he could—it's so much nicer for Doctor Gibbons if he doesn't see the damage.'

The professor's lids drooped over amused eyes, but his voice, as he agreed with this praiseworthy sentiment, was as placid as ever.

'I daresay you find it difficult to understand,' she went on chattily, 'but it's impossible not to break a window now and then when there are three boys about the place.'

Her companion made himself comfortable on the edge of the kitchen table. 'I don't find it in the least difficult,' he protested, 'I'm the eldest of six, myself.'

Gemma flung the last of the washing into the

basket. Somehow it was hard to imagine this not so very young man in his elegant casual clothes being the eldest of a large family—and they would surely all be grown-up.

Just as though she had spoken her thoughts out loud, her companion went on smoothly: 'I'm thirty-seven, my youngest sister is not quite eighteen.'

'Phil's as old as that…the twins are thirteen and George is ten. Mandy's twenty.'

'And you are twenty-five,' he finished for her. 'Doctor Gibbons told me.'

'Oh, did he? Would you like some more coffee?'

'Thanks. I'll hang this lot up while you get it, shall I?'

'Well, I don't know about that,' said Gemma doubtfully. 'You're a professor and all that; I dare say you don't hang out the washing at home so I don't see why you should here.'

His blue eyes twinkled. 'No, I can't say I make a habit of it, but then I'm working for most of my day when I'm home.'

It was on the tip of her tongue to ask him about his home and if he was married, but moving very fast for such a sleepy-eyed person, he was already going down the garden path.

She didn't see him for the rest of that day and she left the house at half past seven the next morning, cycling through the quiet country lanes to get to the hospital a couple of miles away.

Mandy and Phil had got back from their weekend late the previous evening; Gemma had called them before she left the house and they would get the boys down for breakfast and off to school and then get themselves away; Phil to her coaching classes before school started—she was in her last term and working for her A levels—and Mandy to the library in Salisbury where she was training to become a librarian. Gemma, pedalling down the road at great speed, was aware that it was a glorious May morning—a morning to be free in which to do exactly what one wished; she cast the thought aside and bent her mind to the more mundane subject of what to cook for supper that evening, the chances of getting the ironing done, whether the twins could go another week before she need buy the new shoes they wore out with terrifying frequency, and behind all these thoughts even though she kept nudging it aside, the wish to see more of the professor. He had been kind and easy to talk to, and Gemma, the plain one of the family and always conscious of that fact, had been aware that he hadn't looked at her with the faintly amused surprise with which those who had already met the rest of the family—all of them possessing good looks—were wont to show.

She rounded the entrance to the hospital and slowed down to go up the neglected, grass-grown drive, casting, as she always did, an admiring glance at the building coming into view as she did so.

The hospital wasn't really a hospital at all; many years ago it had been a rather grand country house with a fine Tudor front, which had been added to by succeeding generations, so that there was a Queen Anne wing to the left, a charming Regency wing to the right, and round the back, out of sight, and a good thing too, was a mid-Victorian extension, red brick, elaborate and very inconvenient. But with the death of the heir during World War Two and crippling death duties, the house had been sold to the local council and had been used as a geriatric hospital ever since. It was, of course, most unsuitable; the rooms were either too lofty and huge and full of draughts, or so small and awkwardly shaped that the getting of elderly ladies in and out of them, not to mention the making of their beds, was a constant nightmare for the nurses.

Gemma propped her bike against a convenient wall and went in through an open side door, into a narrow, dark passage and up a back staircase. There were two Day Sisters looking after the fifty-six patients; herself with twenty-eight old ladies in her care, and Sister Bell, who was housed with the remainder of them in the opposite wing.

Gemma went up the stairs two at a time, changed into uniform in five minutes flat, standing in a cupboard-like room on the landing, and then, very neat and tidy in her blue uniform and starched apron, an equally well-starched cap perched on her bun of brown hair, walked sedately across the landing into another cupboardlike apartment, which Authority allowed her to use as an office. Both the day and night nurses were there waiting for her to take the report, and she greeted them in her quiet voice, bidding them to sit down as she squeezed herself behind the table which served as her desk. The report hardly varied from day to day; Mrs Pegg and Miss Crisp fell out of their beds with monotonous regularity despite the nurses' efforts to keep them safely in—they had both done so again during the night; there weren't enough nurses for a start and old ladies could be very determined. Lovable too.

When Gemma had given up her post as Medical Ward Sister in a big London teaching hospital, she had done so with many private misgivings; it had been expediency, not choice, which had caused her to apply for the post at Millbury House. Cousin Maud, who had looked after all of them for some years by then, was beginning to show signs of wear and tear—and who wouldn't? Gemma had spent all her holidays and days off at home so that she might help her, but it hadn't been enough; once Mandy and Phil were off their hands, things would be easier, but until then, it had become a matter of urgency that someone should help. That was six months ago and although she missed the rush and bustle of the big hospital, Gemma had to admit that she didn't dislike her work; besides, it had made it possible for Cousin

Maud to go to New Zealand for the long-dreamed-of holiday with her brother. Gemma, heartily sick of doing two jobs at once, couldn't wait for her to get back.

The night nurse safely on her way, Gemma and Sally Black, the day staff nurse, separated to start their day's work. The main ward was a long room with windows down its length, overlooking the gardens at the side of the house; at one time it must have been a drawing room, for its fireplace, now no longer in use, was ornate, gilded and of marble, and the ceiling was picked out with gilt too. Gemma trod from one bed to the next, having a word with each of her patients in turn, handing out a woefully sparse post, listening to the old ladies' small complaints, and occasionally, cheerful chatter. Almost all of them were being got up for the day; a ritual which they, for the most part, objected to most strongly, so that the two nursing aides who came in to help part-time were constantly hindered. Gemma finished her round, quite worn out with her efforts to persuade her patients that to get up and trundle along to the day room across the passage was quite the nicest way of spending their day, but she really had no time to feel tired. She took off her cuffs, rolled up her sleeves and sallied forth once more to tackle Mrs Pegg and Miss Crisp, who now that they might legitimately leave their beds were refusing, with a good deal of noise, to do so.

The day went quickly enough. Nothing dramatic happened; the old ladies were dressed, given their meals, their medicines, bathed, chatted to whenever there was time to spare, and then prepared for bed once more. It was visiting time after dinner, but only a handful of people came. After the eager rush of visitors who had invaded the ward Gemma had had in London, she felt sad, even after six months, that the very people who needed visitors seldom had them. True, some of the old ladies had no family at all, but there were plenty who had who could surely have come more often than they did. Millbury House was some miles from Salisbury, but there was a bus service of sorts, and anyway, most people had cars these days.

She made a point of walking round the wards while the visitors were there so that anyone who wanted to inquire about Granny or Auntie could do so, but they seldom did. When the last of them had gone she went to her office and started the Kardex so that Sally would only have the last few details to fill in later on, and it was while she was doing this that she was interrupted by the house doctor, a young man called Charlie Briggs. They discussed the patients one by one over a cup of tea, and because he didn't like her overmuch, he disagreed with everything she had to say; he almost always did. When she had first arrived at the hospital he had heralded her appearance with delight. 'Thank God,' he had said, 'someone under forty at last—now perhaps life will be fun!' He had eyed her at such length that she had coloured faintly and then disliked him forever when he exclaimed: 'Oh, lord—I do believe you're good as well as plain.'

They had to meet, of course, but only during the course of their work. She had often thought wryly that it was just her luck to work with a man who didn't like her at all—a young man, not married, he might have fallen for her, who knew? They might have married... She had laughed at herself for having the absurd notion, but the laughter had been wistful.

She was tired by the time she was ready to cycle home just before six o'clock. Phil would be home, so would the boys, but Mandy wouldn't leave the library for another half an hour. She wheeled her bike round to the shed at the back of the house, called a hullo to the boys as she passed the sitting room where they were doing their homework, and went to the kitchen. Phil would be upstairs in her room, deep in her school books, but she had left a tray of tea ready on the kitchen table for Gemma. She drank it slowly, sitting in the Windsor chair with Giddy, the family cat purring on her lap, before starting on the supper. The boys had peeled the potatoes and seen to the vegetables and she had made a steak and kidney pie the evening before; she went and got it from the fridge now and put it into the oven before going to the cupboard to see what she could serve for a pudding. She had the off duty to puzzle out, too, she remembered; she had brought it home with her and could have a shot at it while the supper cooked. She fished the book out of her cardigan pocket and sat down at the table, conscious that she didn't want to do it at all; she wanted to sit in a chair and do nothing—well, perhaps not quite nothing. It would be nice to have time to sit and think; she didn't admit to herself that what she wanted to think about was the professor next door.

She wasn't on duty until eleven o'clock the next morning; she saw everyone out of the house, raced through the housework and then pedalled through the bright sunshine to Millbury House, wishing with all her heart that she could stay out of doors. By the time she got off duty that evening it would be eight o'clock—dusk and chilly.

Her day was long and filled with little troubles. At the end of it she wheeled her bike through the open gate, stowed it for the night and went into the house through the kitchen door. There was a cold supper laid out for her on the kitchen table and coffee bubbling gently on the stove. She sniffed appreciatively and went on through the kitchen and down the passage to the sitting room where she found the boys bent so zealously over their books that she instantly suspected them of watching the TV until they had heard her come in. She grinned at them, said: 'Don't you dare until you've finished your lessons,' and went across to the drawing room. Phil would be upstairs, working, but Mandy would be there. She was, looking cool and incredibly pretty, and lounging opposite her was Professor Dieperink van Berhuys.

They both turned to look at her as she went in, and the thought crossed her mind that they were a perfectly matched couple, Mandy with her gay little face and curly hair and he with his placid good looks.

Mandy came dancing to her, bubbling over with high spirits, full of the news that the professor had happened to be outside the library when she had left it and had driven her home. She cast him a laughing glance as she spoke, and he, standing with his magnificent head almost touching the ceiling, smiled back at her, murmuring that it had been a pleasure and that now he really should go, for Doctor Gibbons would be wondering what had become of him.

Gemma said all the right things and watched him walk out of the room with Mandy. They didn't shut the door and she heard them talking in the hall and then go into the sitting room where there was an instant babble of talk and laughter. It made her feel suddenly lonely, which was absurd; how could she possibly be lonely with five brothers and sisters, besides the twenty-eight old ladies with whom she passed her days? Perhaps lonely wasn't the right word. She went back to the kitchen and sat down to eat her solitary supper, and presently she was joined by everyone else, crowding round the table to tell her about their particular day, eating a packet of biscuits between them while they did so. She wasn't all that much older, she thought, looking round at them all, but sometimes she felt just as though she was the mother of the family.

They went to bed one by one, leaving her and Mandy to wash the mugs and sweep up the crumbs and lay the breakfast for the morning, and all the while they were doing it, Mandy talked about the professor.

'He's almost forty,' she told Gemma, 'but he doesn't look it, does he? He's not married either, but his sister is—he's got two, the youngest one is as old as Phil, then there's a brother in his late twenties and another one who's in medical school, he's twenty-one.' She added thoughtfully: 'You'd think he'd be married, wouldn't you?'

Gemma wiped out the sink and put the cloth tidily away. 'Well,' she said slowly, 'with so many brothers and sisters, perhaps he can't afford to.'

'His mother and father are still alive.' Mandy perched on a corner of the table. 'He's got a simply super car...'

'Perhaps he hired it.'

'No, it's his, it's got a Dutch number plate.' She smiled suddenly and brilliantly. 'He said I was a very pretty girl.'

Gemma pushed back her hair with a weary little

gesture. 'And so you are, darling,' she agreed. 'We're a smashing lot of good-lookers except for me.'

'We all think you're lovely,' said her sister fervently, 'and depend on it, someone will come along and think the same.'

Gemma ate a biscuit. 'Then he'd better look sharp about it,' she observed cheerfully. 'All this waiting around doesn't do my nerves any good.'

They giggled together as they went up to bed, but presently, in her own room, Gemma sat down on the old stool in front of her dressing table and took a long look at her reflection. It didn't reassure her in the least.

She was persuading old Mrs Thomas to toddle across to the day room when she heard Doctor Gibbons arrive for his round the next day. He came regularly, for several of the patients had been his for years and he still came to see them. Gemma rotated her companion carefully and sat her down in a convenient chair and looked down the ward. Doctor Gibbons always had a chat with Mrs Thomas; she had no family left now and to her confused old mind he had taken the place of a long-dead son.

The doctor wasn't alone, his Dutch guest was with him, strolling along between the beds, saying good morning as he passed the elderlies while at the same time listening politely to Matron, sailing along a pace or two behind Doctor Gibbons doing the honours. Matron was a nice old thing, with mild blue eyes, a ready chuckle and a cosy figure. Gemma could see that the professor had her eating out of his hand.

The party reached her, exchanged greetings and settled down to the confused questions and answers which took the place of conversation with Mrs Thomas, leaving Gemma free to do something else. She went reluctantly, wishing that someone in the party—the professor, perhaps—would ask her to remain. But he didn't, only smiled his gentle smile and turned his attention to Matron, who was explaining about staff shortages, too many patients, the lack of amenities, the lack of visitors, the lack of transport...Gemma, at the other end of the ward, assembling her medicine trolley, could hear the murmur of their voices.

Presently they came down the ward again and Matron went away and Doctor Gibbons started his ward round. They were the high spot of any day and this one was even better than usual, for Professor Dieperink van Berhuys came with them, asking intelligent questions, murmuring in agreement with his colleagues' more profound remarks, and now and again asking her, soft-voiced, her opinion of this or that. It gave her a real uplift when Charlie Briggs came importantly into the ward, to stop short at the sight of her in animated conversation with a man who put him, in every way, quite in the shade. He wasn't near enough to hear that they were discussing the use of water beds for the aged and infirm. She greeted him with dignity and was glad to see that, for once, he was less than his usual cocksure self. Perhaps that was due to the professor's impassive manner and Doctor Gibbons' brisk way of talking to him. Indeed, she began to feel sorry for him after a while, for he was showing off far too much and she strongly suspected that the professor was secretly amused; besides, there was the strong possibility that Doctor Gibbons would lose his patience with him and tear him off a strip. She was casting round in her mind how to deal with the situation when it was saved by the reappearance of Matron with an urgent message for Doctor Gibbons, and she was able to show the whole party to the door. She had closed it behind them and was making for Mrs Thomas once more when the professor came back.

'Er—may I offer you a lift home this evening? I take it you're off at five o'clock?'

She stood looking up at him. He was being polite, of course, afraid that she had minded him giving Mandy a lift. He was really rather nice.

'How kind,' she said pleasantly, 'but I've got my bike here and I shall need it in the morning—thanks all the same.'

She smiled at him warmly and his answering smile was ready enough. 'Another time, perhaps?' His voice was casual, he made no effort to change her mind for her. With feminine illogicality she was annoyed. Her 'Goodbye, Professor,' as he opened the door was decidedly cool.

CHAPTER TWO

COUSIN MAUD CAME home two days later, looking tanned and at least ten years younger—not that she was all that old; a woman in her forties was no age at all; Gemma had often heard Doctor Gibbons telling her cousin that, and had thought it to be a friendly platitude, but now, watching him greet her cousin, she wasn't so sure. She busied herself with welcoming sherry and speculated about that. Doctor Gibbons wasn't all that old himself—in his mid-fifties and as fit as a fiddle as far as she knew. True, he was a little thin on top and he wore glasses, but he must have been good-looking when he was younger—not, of course, as good-looking as his friend the professor. She nudged the errant thought on one side and concentrated on Cousin Maud and Doctor Gibbons. But even if they wanted to marry there were difficulties. He could hardly be expected to house the six of them as well as Maud. Somehow or other, mused Gemma as she passed the glasses around, they would have to manage on their own—after all, if it could be done for six weeks, it could be done for a lifetime. She shuddered strongly at the very idea and then consoled herself with the certainty that it wouldn't be a lifetime. Mandy would surely marry, so, in a few years, would Phil. James and John were clever boys, they would get their A levels and go on to university, and that left little George. Quite carried away, she began to weigh the chances of taking paying guests—with only George at home there would be three or four bedrooms empty, or perhaps Doctor Gibbons would offer George a home and she could sell the house, find a job and live at the hospital. The prospect was even worse than the first one. She frowned heavily and the professor said in her ear, very softly: 'What is it that worries you?'

She hadn't noticed him cross the room. He loomed beside her, smiling his gentle smile, his pale brows slightly lifted.

'Nothing,' she said hastily. His vague 'Ah', left her with the impression that he didn't believe her and she went on quickly before he persisted: 'Doesn't Cousin Maud look marvellous?'

He glanced across the room. 'Indeed, yes. And now presumably you will take a holiday yourself—you have been doing two jobs for the last six weeks, have you not?'

'Well—the others were marvellous, you know,

and it wasn't easy for them; Mandy's away all day and so is Phil, and the boys did their bit.'

'Does Mandy not have holidays?'

She turned a surprised face towards him. 'Of course she does—four weeks each year, but no one could have expected her to stay home...'

'Er—the thought did cross my mind—just a week or two, perhaps, so that she could have—er—shared the burden of housekeeping with you.'

'It wasn't a burden. I—I liked it.'

He had somehow edged between her and the rest of the room. 'That is a palpable untruth,' he observed mildly. 'Don't tell me that getting up with the birds in order to do the housework before spending the rest of your day looking after a great many demanding old ladies before coming home to cook the supper, help with the homework and generally play mother, was something you liked doing.'

He sounded so reasonable that she found herself saying: 'Well, I must admit that it was rather a full day, but I'll have a holiday soon.'

'You will go away?'

'Me? No.' He was asking a lot of questions. Gemma asked rather coldly: 'Would you like some more sherry?'

He shook his head and she need not have tried to interrupt him. 'You will stay here, fighting the washing machine, frying sausages and calling upon Mr Bates at intervals, I suppose?'

She smiled because put like that it sounded very dull. 'Cousin Maud will be here—she's marvellous...'

They both turned to look at that lady, deep in conversation with Doctor Gibbons. Perhaps, thought Gemma, it might be a good idea not to pursue this conversation. 'When do you go home?' she asked chattily.

'Earlier than I had intended. Rienieta, my youngest sister, is ill and at the moment there's no diagnosis, although it sounds to me like brucellosis—her fever is high and she is rather more than my mother can cope with.'

'I'm sorry, it's a beastly thing to have—I had several cases of it when I had a medical ward.'

'So Doctor Gibbons was telling me. You must find the difference between an acute medical ward and your old ladies very great.'

'Yes, I do—but they need nursing too.' She added honestly, 'Though it isn't a branch of nursing I would choose. It's convenient, you see, so near home...'

'You are on duty in the morning?'

She nodded. 'Yes, but wasn't I lucky to be able to get a free day so that I could be home to welcome Cousin Maud?'

Her companion let this pass. 'I'll take you in the morning,' he stated. 'I have something I wish to say to you.'

Her eyes flew to his face, but it was devoid of any

clue. 'Oh—what about?' She paused, remembering
that he had taken Mandy in and out of Salisbury several times during the last few days, and besides that,
she had come across them deep in conversation at
least twice. Perhaps he had fallen in love with her?
He was a lot older, of course, but age didn't really
matter; perhaps he just wanted to discover what she
thought of it. She said matter-of-factly: 'I leave at ten
to eight on the bike.'

'A quarter to the hour, then. That will give us
time to talk.' He moved a little and Phil came over
to join them, and presently Gemma slipped away to
the kitchen to see how the supper was coming along.

It was pouring with rain the next morning when
she left the house, so that she had wrapped herself in
a rather elderly mac and tied a scarf over her head,
which was a pity, for her hair, although it didn't curl
like Mandy's or Phil's, was long and fine and a pretty
brown. But now, with most of it tucked out of sight,
her unremarkable features looked even more unas-
suming than usual, not that she was thinking about
her appearance; she was still puzzling out a reason
for the professor's wish to speak to her—a reason
important enough to get him out of his bed and go
to all the trouble of driving her to the hospital. Well,
she would know soon enough now. His car, an Aston
Martin convertible, was outside the gate and he was
at the wheel.

She wished him good morning in a cheerful voice,

wholeheartedly admired the car and got in beside him and sat quietly; the drive would take five minutes, and presumably he would start talking at once.

He did. 'I shall be going home in a week's time,' he told her without preamble. 'I should like you to return with me and look after my sister for a week or so—they have confirmed that she has brucellosis and she is in a good deal of pain and her fever is high. My mother assures me that she can manage for the time being, but Rienieta is sometimes very difficult—she refuses to have a nurse, too, but I thought that if you would come with me and we—er—took her unawares, as it were, it might solve that problem. She's a handful,' he added judiciously.

'Well!' declared Gemma, her eyes round with surprise while she hurriedly adjusted her ideas. 'I didn't expect…that is, I had no idea…' She perceived that she would get no further like that. 'I can't just leave Millbury House at a moment's notice, you know,' she pointed out at length.

'I had a word with Doctor Gibbons,' said her companion smoothly. 'He seems to think that something might be arranged for a few weeks—unpaid leave is what he called it.'

'Why me?'

'Because you are the eldest of a large family, I suppose, and know just how to deal with the young.'

She felt like Methuselah's wife and said with a touch of peevishness: 'I'm twenty-five, Professor.'

The amused glint in his eyes belied his placid expression. 'I beg your pardon, I wasn't thinking of you in terms of age, only experience.' He slowed down to turn the car into the hospital drive. 'Of course, if you dislike the idea, we'll say no more about it.'

She didn't dislike it at all, in fact she felt a rising excitement. She held it in check, though. 'It doesn't seem fair on Cousin Maud.'

'She hasn't the least objection. Doctor Gibbons happened to mention it to her yesterday.' He drew up outside the side door. 'Think it over,' he said with maddening placidity, 'and let me know. We're bound to see each other during the next day or so.'

His goodbye was so nonchalant that Gemma told herself crossly that nothing, absolutely nothing, would make her agree to his request even if it were possible to grant it, which seemed to her very unlikely. Moreover, she would keep out of his way, he really had a nerve…she shook off her ill humour as she walked on to the ward; it would never do to upset the old ladies. All the same, she was a little distrait, so that old Mrs Craddock, who had been there for ever and knew everyone and everything, exclaimed in the ringing tones of the deaf: 'And what is wrong with our dear Sister today? If I didn't know her for a sensible girl, I would say she'd been crossed in love—her mind isn't on her work.'

It was a good thing that her companions were either deaf too or just not listening. Gemma laughed, told Mrs Craddock that she was a naughty old thing and went to see about dinners. Mrs Craddock liked her food; her mind was instantly diverted by the mention of it. Gemma gave her two helpings and the rest of the day passed without any more observations from the old lady.

It was towards the end of the afternoon that she remembered that she hadn't got her bike with her and the professor had said nothing about fetching her home; the nagging thought was luckily dispelled by the appearance of Doctor Gibbons, who arrived to see a patient very shortly before she was due to go off duty and offered her a lift. 'Ross told me he had brought you over here this morning, so I said that as I was coming this afternoon, I should bring you back—that'll leave him free to go into Salisbury and pick up Mandy.'

Gemma smiled with false brightness. The professor might appear to be a placid, good-natured man without a devious thought in his head, but she was beginning to think otherwise; he had had it all nicely planned. Well, if he thought he could coax her to ramble over half Europe he was mistaken. Her sensible little head told her that she was grossly exaggerating, but she cast sense out. Holland or Hungary or Timbuktoo, they were all one and the same, and all he was doing was to make a convenience of her. Her charming bosom swelled with indignation while she attended to Doctor Gibbons' simple wants with a severe professionalism which caused him to eye her with some astonishment.

Cousin Maud had tea waiting for her, which was nice. Everyone was out in the garden, picking the first gooseberries, and the professor was there too, although long before Gemma had finished her tea he had strolled away. To collect Mandy, Cousin Maud explained with a smile, so that Gemma, on the point of asking her advice about the professor's request, thought better of it. She wasn't really interested in going to Holland, she told herself, she wasn't interested, for that matter, in seeing him again. She could not in fact care less. She looked so cross that her companion wanted to know if she had a headache.

Gemma was upstairs when the professor returned with Mandy. He didn't stay long, though, and she didn't go downstairs until she had seen him get back into his car and shoot out of their gate and into Doctor Gibbons' drive. She could see him clearly from her bedroom window; indeed, she was hanging out of it, watching him saunter into the house next door, when he turned round suddenly and looked at her. She withdrew her head so smartly that she banged it on the low ceiling.

For the time being, she didn't want to see him. Let him come again and ask her if he was so keen for her to nurse his sister, and it was really rather absurd that she should leave her old ladies just to satisfy his whim. She tidied her already tidy hair and sighed deeply. Probably she would be at Millbury House for ever and ever—well, not quite that, but certainly for years. She went slowly downstairs, the rest of the evening hers in which to do whatever she wished, and she was free until noon the next day, too. She wouldn't see her old ladies until then.

She saw them a good deal sooner than that, though. Several hours later she was wakened by the insistent ringing of the telephone. She had been the last to go to bed and had only been asleep for a short time, and it was only a little after midnight. The house was quiet as she trod silently across the landing and down the stairs, not waiting to put on dressing gown or slippers. Doctor Gibbons' voice sounded loud in her ear because of the stillness around her. 'Gemma? Good. There's a fire at Millbury House— they've just telephoned. Matron's pretty frantic because the fire brigade's out at another fire and they'll have to come from further afield. Can you be ready in five minutes? Wait at your gate.'

He hung up before she could so much as draw breath.

She was at the gate, in slacks and a sweater pulled over her nightie and good stout shoes on her feet, with a minute to spare. The house behind her was quite still and the village street was dark with not a glimmer of light to be seen excepting in the doctor's house, and that went out as she looked. Seconds later she heard the soft purr of the Aston Martin as it was backing out of the drive and halted by her. The professor was at the wheel; he didn't speak at all but held the door open just long enough for her to get in before he shot away. It was left to Doctor Gibbons, sitting beside him, to tell her: 'The fire's in the main building, the first floor day room. It'll be a question of getting everyone out before it spreads to one or either wing.' He turned to look at her in the dark of the car. 'The fire people will be along, of course, but if all the patients have to be got out…' He paused significantly and Gemma said at once: 'There's Night Sister, and a staff nurse on each ward and three nursing aides between them—and Matron, of course, as well as the kitchen staff, but I don't think they all sleep in.' She drew a sharp breath and said: 'Oh, lord, look at it!'

The night sky glowed ahead of them, faded a little and glowed again, and now, as the professor took the right-hand turn into the drive without decreasing his speed at all, they could hear the fire as well as see it and smell it. They could hear other sounds too, urgent voices and elderly cries.

The professor had barely stopped the car at a safe distance from the burning building than Gemma was out of it. 'It's my ward,' she cried, 'the wind's blowing that way. Oh, my dear old ladies!' She leapt forward and was brought up short by a large hand catching at the back of her sweater.

'Before you rush in and get yourself fried to a crisp, tell me where the fire escape is?'

Gemma wriggled in a fury of impatience, but he merely gathered more sweater into his hand. As Doctor Gibbons joined them, she said urgently: 'At the back, where my wing joins the extension behind—there's a side door with a small staircase which leads to the landing outside my ward...'

'The way we came the other day, from the centre door—that will be impossible now; the wind's blowing strongly from the centre towards your wing... Is there a fire chute?'

'Yes—I know where it's kept.'

'Good.' He turned to Doctor Gibbons. 'Shall we try the side door, get into the ward and get the chute going from a window at this end? The fire escape is a good way away, I doubt if they can move the old ladies fast enough—if the dividing wall should go...'

They were already running towards the house. In a moment they were inside, to find the staircase intact. 'Get between us,' said the professor shortly, and took the stairs two at a time, with Gemma hard on his heels and Doctor Gibbons keeping up gamely. The landing, when they reached it, was full of smoke, but although the fire could be heard crackling and roaring close by, the thick wall was still holding it back. The professor opened the ward door on to pandemonium; Gemma had a quick glimpse of the night staff nurse tearing down the ward propelling a wheelchair

with old Mrs Draper wedged into it; it looked for all
the world like a macabre parody of an Easter pram
race. There wasn't much smoke; just a few lazy puffs
curling round the door frame.

Gemma didn't wait to see more but turned and
ran upstairs to the next floor where the escape chute
was, stored in one of the poky, disused attics which
in former days would have been used by some overworked servant. The door was locked—she should
have thought of that. She raced downstairs again,
took the key from her office and tore back. The chute
was heavy and cumbersome, but she managed to
drag it out of the room and push and pull it along
the passage to the head of the stairs where she gave
it a shove strong enough to send it lumbering down
to the landing below. But now she would need help;
she ran to the ward door and opened it cautiously.
The professor was quite near, lifting Mrs Thomas
out of her bed and settling her in the wheelchair a
nursing aide was holding steady. He glanced up, said
something to the nurse, who sped away towards the
distant fire escape, and came to the door.

'I can't manage the chute,' said Gemma urgently.
'It's on the landing.'

He nodded, swept her on one side and went past
her, shutting the door, leaving her in the ward. The
beds, she noticed, had been pulled away from the
inner wall and ranged close to the windows, and
there were only six patients left. She sighed with re-

lief as the professor came back with the chute and she went to give him a helping hand.

There was still only a little smoke in the ward, although the roar of the fire sounded frighteningly near. Gemma shut her mind to the sound and began the difficult task of getting Miss Bird, hopelessly crippled with arthritis, out of her bed, wrapped and tied into a blanket ready to go down the chute. The nursing aide had come back; she could hear the professor telling her to go down first so that she could catch the patients as they arrived at the bottom. The nurse gave him a scared look.

'I've never done it before,' she told him in a small scared voice.

The professor eyed her sturdy figure. 'Then have a go,' he said persuasively, and actually laughed. 'I've thrown a mattress down. Don't try to catch the ladies, just ease them out and get help, any help, if you can. And be quick, my dear, for the inner wall isn't going to hold out much longer.'

Gemma glanced over her shoulder. He was right; the smoke was thickening with every moment and there was a nasty crackling sound. She left Miss Bird to be picked up by the professor and hurried to the next bed—Mrs Trump, fragile, heaven knew, but very clear in the head, which helped a lot. She saw Nurse Drew plunge down the chute out of the corner of her eye, and a minute later, Miss Bird, protesting vigorously, followed her. She was ready with

Mrs Trump by now and wheeled her bed nearer the chute and then wasted a few precious seconds dragging empty beds out of the way so that they had more room.

The professor already had a patient in his arms and she was tackling the third old lady when the wall at the other end of the ward caved in with a loud rumble, an enormous amount of dust and smoke and great flames of fire. Gemma, tying her patient into her blanket, found that her hands were shaking so much that she could hardly tie the knots. The professor was going twice as fast now, getting the next old lady into her blanket; she finished what she was doing and went to the last occupied bed—Mrs Craddock, apparently unworried by the appalling situation, blissfully unable to hear the noise around her. As Gemma rolled her into the blanket she shouted cheerfully: 'A nasty fire, Sister dear. I hope there'll be a nice cup of tea when you've put it out!'

Gemma gabbled reassurances as she worried away at the knots. The flames were licking down the wall that was left at a great rate now, and she could have done with a nice cup of tea herself. She was so frightened that her mind had become a blank. All that registered was that Mrs Craddock must be got down the chute at all costs.

The professor, elbowing her on one side without ceremony tugged the webbing tight with an admirably steady hand and bent to take Mrs Craddock's not inconsiderable weight. 'Come along,' he said almost roughly, adding unnecessarily: 'Don't hang around.'

Mrs Craddock was stoutly built as well as heavy, and it took the professor a few precious moments to get her safely into the chute and speed her on her way. They were unable to hear the reassuring shout from below when she got there because the rest of the wall caved in with a thunder of sound. It did so slowly, like slow motion, thought Gemma, stupidly gawping at it, incapable of movement. The professor shouted something at her, but his voice, powerful though it might be, had no chance against the din around them. She felt herself swung off her feet and hurled into the chute. She hit the mattress at the bottom with a thump and a dozen hands dragged her, just in time, out of the way of the professor, hard on her heels.

The next few hours were a nightmare, although it wasn't until afterwards that Gemma thought about them, for there was too much to do; old ladies, scattered around in chairs, on mattresses, wrapped up warmly on garden seats—the fire brigade were there by now and a great many helpers who had seen the fire from the village and come helter-skelter on bikes and in cars; the butcher in his van, the milkman, Mr Bates and Mr Knott, the gentleman farmer who lived in the big house at the other end of the village. The only person Gemma didn't see was Charlie Briggs, who really should have been there and wasn't. She

wondered about him briefly as she went round with
Matron and Night Sister, carefully checking that each
patient would be fit to be moved. Now and again
she brushed against the professor, listened carefully
when he bade her do something or other, and then
lost sight of him again.

The beginnings of a May morning were showing in the sky by the time the last ambulance had
been sped on its way, leaving a shambles of burnt-
out wards, broken furniture and everything else in
sight soaked with water. Those who had come to
help began to go home again while Matron, looking
quite different in slacks and a jumper, thanked each
of them in turn. Presently they had all gone, leaving Gemma and Doctor Gibbons, Matron, the night
staff and the professor standing in what had once
been the imposing entrance, while firemen sorted
over the bits and pieces, making sure that all was
safe before they too left.

It was the professor who suggested that he should
drive everyone to their homes; Matron had been offered temporary shelter with the rector, whose house
could be seen through the trees half a mile away, the
rest of them lived round and about, not too far away,
excepting for one nursing aide who came from Salisbury. He sorted them out, taking those who lived
close by before driving Matron down the road to the
Rectory. That left Gemma and Doctor Gibbons and
the girl from Salisbury; he squeezed all of them into

the car, left Gemma and the doctor at the latter's gate and drove on to the city. Gemma watched the car out of sight, yawned and started for her own garden gate.

'They've slept through it all,' said the doctor as he put out a restraining hand, 'they'd sleep through Doomsday.' He took her by the arm. 'Come in with me and make me a cup of tea. It's gone five o'clock; far too late—or too early—for bed now. Besides, there's no hurry, you haven't got a job to go to now.'

Gemma turned to look at him. 'Nor have I.' She waited while he opened the door and followed him inside; she knew the house as well as her own home; they had been friends for years now. She told him to go and sit down and went through to the kitchen to put the kettle on.

They had finished their tea and were sitting discussing the fire and its consequences when the professor got back. Gemma heard the car turn into the drive and went away to make more tea; probably he would be hungry too. She spooned tea into the largest pot she could find and sliced bread for toast. She didn't hear him when he came into the kitchen, but she turned round at his quiet 'hullo'.

'Tea and toast?' she invited, unaware how deplorable she looked; her slacks and sweater were filthy with smoke and stains, her face was dirty too and her hair, most of it loose from the plait by now, was sadly in need of attention.

The professor joined her at the stove, made the

tea, turned the toast and then spread it lavishly with butter. He said to surprise her: 'How nice you look.'

Gemma stared at him over the tray she was loading, her mouth a little open. 'Me—?' She frowned. 'If that's a joke, I just don't feel equal to it.'

He took the tray from her and put it down on the table again. 'It's not a joke, I meant it.' He bent and kissed the top of her tousled head and smiled at her; he didn't look in the least tired. 'You're a jewel of a girl, Gemma—just like your name.'

He took the tray and led the way back to the sitting room and they drank the pot dry, saying very little. It was when they had finished and she was stacking the cups on the tray again that he said in a matter-of-fact voice: 'And now there is no reason why you shouldn't come back with me, is there?' He looked at her thoughtfully. 'Unless you object on personal grounds?'

Gemma cast a glance at Doctor Gibbons, who had gone to sleep and would be of no help at all. She suddenly felt very sleepy herself so that her mumbled 'No, of course I don't' was barely audible, but the professor heard all right and although his face remained placid there was a satisfied gleam in his eyes. His casual: 'Oh, good,' was uttered in tones as placid as the expression on his face, but he didn't say more than that, merely offered to escort her to her own front door, and when they reached it, advised her to go to bed at once.

A superfluous piece of advice; Gemma tore off her clothes, washed her face in a most perfunctory manner and was asleep the moment her uncombed head touched the pillow.

CHAPTER THREE

GEMMA SLEPT ALL through the sounds of a household getting up and preparing itself for the day, perhaps because everyone was so much quieter than usual, and the professor, keeping watch from his window until Cousin Maud opened the back door so that Giddy might go out, presented himself at it without loss of time, and over a cup of tea with her, recounted the night's events. It was hard to believe, looking at him, that he had himself taken part in them, for he appeared the very epitome of casual elegance, freshly shaved and bathed, his blue eyes alert under their heavy lids. Only when she looked closely Maud could see the lines of fatigue in his face. A tough man, she decided as she went round the house cautioning her young relations to behave like mice so that Gemma might sleep on.

And sleep she did, until almost midday, to go downstairs much refreshed and eat an enormous meal while Cousin Maud plied her with hot coffee and questions. She ate the last of the wholesome cheesc pudding before her, washed up, invited her cousin to come upstairs with her while she dressed, and signified her intention of cycling over to the ruins of Millbury House to see exactly what was to happen. 'Perhaps it will close down for good,' she wondered worriedly. 'What do you think, Maud?'

The older woman sat down on the edge of the bed. 'Well, dear, I should think it very likely, wouldn't you? There must have been an awful lot of damage done and it would cost a fortune to rebuild the place. Doctor Gibbons is coming in to tea if he can spare the time—perhaps he'll know something. He telephoned this morning—he said you were marvellous. Ross said so too.'

Gemma piled her hair neatly on top of her head and started to pin it there. 'Oh—did you see him, then?'

'He was at the back door this morning when I went down, to tell me that you'd only just got to bed.' She got up and strolled over to the window. 'You know, Gemma, it might not be such a bad idea, to take that job Ross suggested. No, don't look like that, dear—he didn't talk about it; Doctor Gibbons told me—I imagine that he thought I already knew about it.' There was faint reproach in her voice.

Gemma was making haste with her face. 'I should have told you—I did mean to, but I wasn't sure— I mean it was only to be for a week or two and although he said he could make it all right with Matron, I was a bit doubtful about her wanting me back. But now I suppose there's nothing for me to go back to.' She went and put an arm through her cousin's. 'I'll go and find out now. Would you mind if I did go? There's an awful lot to do here, you know.'

Cousin Maud, who had been doing it for years, agreed a little drily, 'But it's time Mandy and Phil helped out a little more, and you haven't had a holiday for years—not that this job sounds much like a holiday, but at least it will be a change of scene.'

Gemma mulled over her cousin's words as she cycled along the lanes and forgot them when she saw the charred ruins of the hospital. It really had been badly damaged; true, the Victorian extension at the back had escaped more or less intact, but it had never been used as wards for the patients; the rooms were poky and dark and there were any number of small staircases which the old ladies would never have managed. Gemma propped her bike against a tree and went round to the back and through a door which looked as though it belonged to a church but led instead to a narrow, damp passage leading to the back hall. It was here that Matron had her flat. Gemma knocked on the door and was relieved to hear Matron's voice bidding her go in, for she remembered then, a little late in the day, that she had gone to the Rectory. But Matron was there, all right, in uniform too, looking calm and collected, just as though the hospital hadn't been burned around her ears only a few hours earlier.

She looked up as Gemma went in and smiled at her. 'Sister Prentice, I'm glad you've come. I've been hearing about this job you've been offered—at least one of my staff won't be out of work.'

Gemma took the chair she had been waved to. 'You mean the hospital can't be rebuilt?'

Matron nodded. 'I'm almost sure of it. There's only been a preliminary survey, of course, but any idiot can see that it would need rebuilding completely—what a splendid chance for the Hospital Board, who have been wanting to close us down for months, but of course something will have to be done, the other hospitals can't absorb our old ladies permanently. At the moment they're distributed around the area, but a handful of them will be able to come to Vicar's Place—a large empty house some miles away. I don't know yet, for no one has said anything, but I hope that I shall be asked to go there as Matron until such time as larger premises can be found—probably years. I shall only need two nurses there, for it won't take more than ten patients.' She smiled at Gemma. 'It will take a very long time to settle, Sister Prentice, and I doubt if I can offer you even the prospect of a job.' She added bracingly: 'You could get a post in London very easily, you know—your references are excellent.'

Gemma shook her head. 'That wouldn't do at all,

Matron. This job was marvellous, it meant that I could live at home, you see—there are so many of us and it's not fair that Cousin Maud should have to manage alone.'

Matron agreed: 'Yes, of course. Well, shall we leave things as they are and you could come and see me when you get back.'

It was a little vague, but Gemma could see that there wasn't much to be done at the moment. She agreed without demur and asked after her patients.

'Scattered round half a dozen hospitals, but unharmed, I'm glad to say. Their resilience is remarkable, isn't it? I wonder how many of them realized how near death they were—and several of them owe their lives to you and Professor Dieperink van Berhuys. We are all most grateful to you...'

Gemma went pink. 'The professor was wonderful, but I didn't do much, Matron.' She got up. 'I'm not sure if I shall go to Holland...' She wished she hadn't said that because Matron looked so surprised, so she added hastily: 'I'll let you know, shall I?'

It had been silly to say that, she admitted to herself as she went back home at her leisure, because of course she was sure; she was going. It would be a nice change from the old ladies, bless them. Besides, she was curious about the professor; she wanted to know exactly what work he did and where he lived and what his family was like. She wheeled her bike into the back garden and went indoors, frowning a little. She mustn't get too curious; curiosity was one thing, getting too interested was another.

The professor called round that evening, giving her an affable nod as he seated himself, at the twins' urgent request, at the kitchen table so that he might give them the benefit of his knowledge concerning the more complicated aspects of the algebra they were struggling with.

It wasn't until he had solved the knottier of the problems that he looked up to say: 'I'm returning to Holland in three days' time, Gemma—will you be coming with me?'

She glanced round her. The entire family had found its way into the kitchen by now, each of them apparently absorbed in some task which simply had to be done there, although Cousin Maud was just sitting doing nothing at all, looking at her. All of them were listening so hard for her answer that she could almost hear them doing it. She said 'yes', and then, because it had sounded rather terse: 'Thank you, Professor.'

'Thank you, Gemma,' he answered gravely, and then with an abrupt change of manner, added cheerfully: 'How about all of us gathering round the table for this?'

They had all talked at once after that; they were a united family and each member of it considered that he or she had every right to add their say to the matter. It was the professor who made sense of and produced order out of the spate of suggestions, speculations and improbable advice which was offered. Over cups of cocoa and the total disintegration of the cake which Cousin Maud had only just taken out of the oven, it was decided that Gemma should go to Salisbury in the morning to get a visitor's passport and replenish her wardrobe, but when she mentioned going to the bank to get some Dutch money, the professor pointed out that that would be quite unnecessary, for she would be paid a salary and he would advance any money she might need when they arrived in Holland.

'How much are you going to pay her?' George wanted to know, and was instantly shushed by his elders.

'Exactly the same as she receives here,' the professor told him. He looked across at Gemma. 'That is if you find that an agreeable arrangement?'

'Yes, thank you.' She tried to sound as business-like as he did, but instead her voice sounded a little ungracious, but he didn't seem to notice, only smiled a little and presently got up to go.

As he sauntered to the door he turned to say carelessly over his shoulder: 'I have business in Salisbury—I'll give you a lift. Will nine o'clock suit you?'

As soon as he had gone, Mandy made a pot of tea and they all gathered round again. Gemma hadn't been away for a holiday for a long time—true, this trip to Holland wasn't exactly that, but it was abroad, and as such, an event. Her wardrobe was discussed at length by her sisters and cousin while the boys pored over an atlas, offering occasional unhelpful advice as to what she should take with her. Her sisters had more to say, though: Gemma had nice clothes, but not—they were emphatic about that—enough. Living in a small village with not much opportunity of going out, she tended to buy serviceable, even if nice, things and make them last far too long. She was quick to take Phil's point that the professor's family might live in the middle of a town and be most frightfully fashionable, in which case she would feel quite out of things. The matter was clinched by Mandy's dreamy: 'He wears the most super clothes himself, you know, and I bet they're wildly expensive—you must have something new, Gemma darling.'

Gemma poured more tea. It was true enough, his clothes had an understated elegance which betokened money, but that didn't mean to say that he had a lot of it or that his family had either; it was a pity she didn't know. She had asked him once where he lived and he had told her that he had his own home and that his parents lived within an easy distance. What was an easy distance, anyway? and he hadn't said where.

'I saw a denim jacket and skirt in Jaeger's,' she said thoughtfully, 'sand-coloured. I could get some cotton sweaters and a couple of blouses—they had some the colour of a seashell—and I suppose I'd better get another pair of slacks—there's that lovely coral pink knitted cardigan you gave me, Maud—if I got sand-coloured slacks too…and a jersey dress…'

'Two,' said Mandy and Phil in unison, 'and you'd better have a pretty dress for the evening.'

'I'm going as a nurse, not a house guest,' argued Gemma.

'And think how dire it would be if you met some gorgeous man who wanted to take you out and you couldn't go because you hadn't anything decent to wear.'

It didn't seem very likely; Gemma, on good terms with everyone she met, had nonetheless never been overburdened with invitations from the men of her acquaintance. And why should she? She had asked herself that question years ago and come up with the sensible answer that she was neither pretty enough nor amusing enough. She was very well liked as a kind of big sister; a confidante, because she didn't keep interrupting when they eulogized about their current girlfriends, but it had seldom entered their heads to ask her out for an evening.

She had got over the hurt of it years ago, but deeply buried in her romantic heart was the hope that one day she might meet some man who would find her irresistible. With a reckless disregard of the amount of money she intended to spend, she said that yes, she would certainly buy something suitable for the evening. It would probably hang in the cupboard all the while she was in Holland, but there was no harm in pretending.

'Perhaps you'll wear your uniform,' suggested George suddenly, and everyone turned surprised eyes upon him.

'Never!' said Mandy hotly, but Cousin Maud looked thoughtful.

'There is that possibility,' she conceded.

Of course it was a possibility, said Gemma crossly, and why on earth hadn't she thought of it sooner? 'Probably I shall be able to get by with a new jersey dress and that cotton shirtwaister I had last summer.'

Phil groaned. 'Don't you dare! You must ask in the morning. Supposing he wants you to wear a uniform, would you mind?'

Gemma shrugged. 'I'm a nurse, aren't I?' she said flatly, and added mendaciously: 'I really don't mind, you know.'

Asking the professor about it had been more difficult than she had supposed. For one thing, he talked about everything under the sun except her impending job, and it wasn't until he was threading his way through the narrow streets of Salisbury that she asked: 'Am I to wear a uniform while I'm nursing your sister?'

He looked faintly surprised. 'Decidedly not; Rienieta would dislike that very much—she isn't a biddable girl.' He swung the car round a sharp corner and flashed a smile at her. 'You look—er—severe in your uniform. No, I have it wrong, that makes you sound like a gorgon and you're not that in the least—it would be better to say that it gives you an air of authority, and I'm afraid she doesn't react well to that. She's spoilt—the last of a large family, and we all dote on her.'

Gemma nodded. 'Oh, I quite understand—look at our George, he gets away with any amount of mischief...'

The professor parked the car in the market square and sat back, in no hurry to get out. 'You see now why I am anxious that you should come back with me and look after her?' He turned to smile at her, his blue eyes twinkling. 'She's a handful, but a delightful one.'

He got out of the car and went round to open her door. 'Where shall we meet and when? Will you be free for coffee or shall we make it lunch?'

'Oh,' said Gemma ingenuously, 'I didn't know—are we going to have lunch?'

'You won't be finished before then, will you? Shall we meet at the White Hart at half past twelve? I'll wait, so don't panic if you're late.'

She agreed gravely, wondering why she had ever thought of him as devious. He was nothing of the sort, he was dependable and kind, and somehow when she was with him, she didn't feel plain. She smiled up at him, suddenly happy. 'I'll get that passport first,' she told him, 'and then I must do some shopping, but I'll be there at half past twelve.'

The morning was a success. Once the business of the passport had been settled Gemma felt free to spend the money she had drawn from her account—rather more than she had intended, but she consoled herself with the thought that everything she intended buying would certainly be worn throughout the summer and probably next summer too. She arrived at the White Hart a mere ten minutes late, loaded with boxes and parcels which the professor took from her with the air of a man who had done this service many times before, before ushering her into the dining room.

They lunched with splendid appetites off cold roast beef and a great bowl of salad, and, her tongue loosened by the claret her companion had chosen and egged on by his quiet questions, Gemma talked as she hadn't talked for a long time; about her parents, who had been killed five years earlier in a car crash, and the subsequent difficulties of bringing up her brothers and sisters until Cousin Maud, coming to live with them two years back, had eased her problems. Gemma stopped rather abruptly in the middle of her paean of praise about that lady and exclaimed: 'I'm sorry, I'm talking too much.'

'No, you're not, I'm interested.' His calm voice, while allaying her fears of being a bore, made her feel that she should change the conversation, which she did rather abruptly.

'It was funny that Charlie Briggs wasn't at the fire,' she observed.

Her companion agreed. 'I take it he should have been on call and was nowhere to be found? Although from the little I saw of him I doubt if he would have been much use.'

'You're so right,' declared Gemma, her brown eyes flashing, 'and if that sounds unfair I'm sorry, but if you knew how I dislike him—' She added: 'It's strange how you dislike some people on sight.'

'And like others the moment you set eyes on them,' he offered lazily. 'I can't say I took to the young man myself. What is Matron going to do?'

They talked about the hospital for a few minutes until the professor suggested that they might finish their shopping together. 'I should like to get your cousin something. She's been very kind—cups of tea and cake…' He smiled his pleasant smile. 'What do you suggest?'

They spent another hour or so at the shops and it was only much later, sitting quietly with Maud when the others had gone to bed, that Gemma remembered that she hadn't asked the professor a single question about his home or his family.

And two days later, sitting beside him as they drove away from the village, she wondered if she would wake up suddenly and find that everything had been a dream. The few days had flashed by, she had tried on all her new clothes for the edification of her brothers and sisters, packed them neatly and then gone about her usual household chores, and during that time she had barely exchanged a couple of words with the professor. He had told her, on their way back from Salisbury, at what time they would be leaving and apparently had seen no need to remind her of it. She had eaten a hurried breakfast in the bosom of her family and had then been escorted to the front gate by all of them, to find the professor already there, leaning on his car's elegant bonnet, so that her goodbyes had been swift before he had packed her tidily into the seat beside his, disposed of her luggage in the boot, said his own goodbyes with cheerful brevity, and driven off. Now they were already through Salisbury and he had put his large, well shod foot down on the accelerator and kept it there. He was a fast driver but a careful one, taking traffic jams and the like with a massive calm which made light of them.

They were crossing from Dover by Hovercraft and driving up through France and Belgium. Bergen-op-Zoom, Gemma had discovered, was their destination, and now she was studying the map to discover just where that was.

The professor had elected to go via Andover and pick up the M3 beyond that town, which meant that he could keep up a good seventy miles an hour until they reached Chobham, where he turned off for Dorking and a cross-country route. They stopped at Seal for coffee and then presently picked up the M2 and finally the A2 into Dover. It had been a pleasant run, Gemma conceded to herself. Either the professor knew the route very well indeed or he had an excellent bump of locality, for he hadn't once evinced uncertainty as to their road, nor had he shown any sign of irritation at the small delays they had had, and he had kept up an entertaining flow of small talk which had passed the time very agreeably. Gemma, pleased with her world, stepped on board the Hovercraft and was whisked towards the coast of France. If there was a fly in her ointment it was a very small one; the professor, she was well aware, was a relaxed man by nature, but did he need to relax so completely that he should fall asleep and stay so, peacefully, for the entire crossing, and leaving her to her own devices? True, he had provided her with magazines and a refreshing drink, but it was the kind of behaviour one might expect from a husband... Perhaps she should take it as a compliment that he should stand on so little ceremony with her. She stared out, watching the coast of France coming closer with every second, and when she looked at him again it was to find him watching her.

He smiled at once as she caught his eye and said apologetically: 'So sorry—shocking manners, I'm afraid.' He was wide awake now. 'I didn't have much sleep last night—Mrs Turner's twins…'

Her eyes opened wide. 'They never arrived—why, Doctor Gibbons said they weren't due…'

'And nor were they; they stole a march on us and he was out at Giles Farm.'

'Oh, so you delivered them.' She was full of concern. 'You must be dog-tired. Couldn't we pull in somewhere after we land so that you could have another nap?'

'How accommodating of you, dear girl, but there's no need of that. I feel in splendid shape. We'll have a meal, though.'

An invitation to which Gemma readily agreed, for she was famished.

So presently, half an hour's drive from Calais, they stopped to eat enormous omelettes at a roadside café; they polished off a bowl of salad too and drank several cups of coffee before, much refreshed, they took to the road once more. They had turned away from the coast now, cutting across the country to pick up the motorway to Ghent and then on to Antwerp. The professor skirted the city, but all the same, the traffic slowed them up a little so that Gemma was relieved to hear him say: 'I'm sure you're dying for a cup of tea. We're not far from the frontier now, so we'll stop in Holland—there's a roadhouse just on the other side of the *douanes*.'

The tea came in glasses and without milk, but it

was refreshing, and Gemma drank it thankfully. She looked as fresh and tidy as when they had set out that morning; her neat coil of hair was still pinned on top of her head, her blue and white jersey dress had no creases, she looked cool and composed even though she felt neither. They had only another twenty or so miles to go and she was beginning to wonder what her patient would be like, whether she would like her, whether his family would mind her coming… She said suddenly: 'Does your mother know I'm coming? I mean, I know I'm supposed to be a surprise, but surely only to Rienieta?'

She looked at him so anxiously that he sat up in his chair and said reassuringly: 'My parents know that you are coming and very much approve of the idea—did I not tell you?' And when she shook her head: 'I'm sorry about that, but I can assure you that you will be most warmly welcomed.' He gave her a quick nod and added, 'You're worrying—don't!'

They were back in the car now, tearing down the motorway, and presently he said: 'We're just coming in to the outskirts of the town—see that medieval gate ahead of us? We go through there.'

Gemma looked about her; they were passing pleasant villas, each set in its own neat garden bright with flowers, and very shortly these became terraced houses with a shop here and there, and rising above them, the magnificent gateway; it led to the heart of the town through a narrow winding street of

more shops and which in its turn opened out on to a
square lined with old houses, a hotel or two, a great
church and a splendid town hall, but she was given
no time to see much of these, for the professor kept
straight on across the square and into another narrow street going slightly uphill, leading away from
the town again.

'You shall explore some time,' he promised her.
'My parents live a mile or two away. We're on the
road to Breda now, but we turn off presently; they
live on the edge of a small village.'

The country was so flat that Gemma could see its
houses when he pointed them out to her, and at that
distance they appeared a mere huddle of tiled roofs
dominated by two towering churches.

'Two?' asked Gemma.

'Protestant and Roman Catholic.'

'But it's such a very small village...'

'But a wide-flung parish—besides, everyone goes
to church in these parts.'

She gave him a quick look. 'I never thought to
ask—I mean, if you're RC. I'm not.'

'My dear girl, my family has been stubbornly
Protestant for some hundreds of years—and once
upon a time it wasn't easy to be that—the Spanish
Occupation, you know. But now we all get on well
together although you will find separate schools and
clubs—hospitals too.'

'Isn't that rather limiting?'

'Not really.' He grinned briefly. 'The talent seems to be fairly evenly distributed on both sides.'

The village was quaint, with a minute square across which the two churches faced each other, flanked by a café, the tiny Gemeentehuis, one or two shops and a row of very small houses. But they didn't stop here either, but took a cobbled road past one of the churches which ran into the open country again. There was a canal now, the evening light reflected in its quiet water, and the road looked as though it led to nowhere. But it did; a very small signpost pointed the way in important letters to Breda—a back way, explained the professor, which cut off quite a few miles if one knew the way well enough. 'And here we are,' he exclaimed as they passed a copse and came round a curve in the road which disclosed a white-painted, square house set in a fair sized garden. There were iron railings all round and a glimpse of outbuildings and wilder ground at the side. The professor drove through the wide open gates and drove up the straight drive to the front door where he alighted before helping Gemma out. She stood for a moment, her hand still in his, looking at the house; it had a plain face, a solid door under a weighty porch and precise rows of large square windows showing only a glimpse of curtains. For lack of a word, she described it to herself as well established.

'Like it?' asked her companion.

'Oh, yes—yes, very much.' She stopped as the

door was opened and a short, fat man held it wide. 'Ah,' said the professor, 'here is Ignaas.' And at her look of inquiry: 'He's been with us for so long that I can't remember when he wasn't here.'

He was still holding her hand in his, just as if he knew that she was nervous; perhaps Ignaas guessed it too, for his round face broke into a smile as Gemma bade him how do you do, and as for the professor, he clapped the older man on the back and made some laughing remark which changed the smile into a deep, rich chuckle as they were led into the hall, a square apartment with a polished wood floor, crimson wall hangings and some extremely solid oak furniture. Very old, thought Gemma, craning her neck stealthily as they went.

They were shown into a room at the side of the hall through massive mahogany double doors crowned by an abundance of carved and gilded woodwork. It was large and lofty and furnished with a nice assortment of richly covered easy chairs, occasional tables, display cabinets and an enormous carved pillow cupboard which took up half one wall. The windows were wide and high and curtained with swathes of crimson brocade and the white walls were hung with a vast collection of paintings, mostly portraits. Gemma's mouth hung open slightly at the sight of so much richness; it reminded her of some stately home or other she had once visited. She had never imagined that people actually lived their day-to-day lives surrounded by such treasures, but apparently they did, for there was a small boy sitting on the carpet in the centre of the room, the bricks he was playing with in tumbled heaps around him, and there was a slightly older girl sharing one of the great chairs with a corgi dog. There was a pile of knitting thrown down carelessly on one of the velvet-upholstered sofas and a young woman lying full length on the floor, her chin in her hand, reading. They all looked up at the same time and made a concerted dash for the professor, who received their onslaught with great good humour, tossing the children into the air before bending to kiss the girl.

'Gemma, this is my elder sister Gustafina and her two children—Bessel and Wijanda—we call her Nanda.' And when she had shaken hands with them all: 'You're staying?' he asked his sister, 'or is this a brief visit?'

They were alike, Gemma could see that watching them together, although Gustafina was quite a lot younger; they had the same handsome good looks and bright blue eyes, and so, for that matter, had the two children. The pair of them grinned at her shyly and their mother said: 'They like you, I think—we shall come again so that they may make friends.'

The professor offered Gemma a chair and asked idly; 'You're not staying for the evening?' His blue eyes were amused. 'Curious, Gustafina?' And when she smiled: 'Where is Mama?'

'Upstairs with Rienieta—she has been difficult.'
She smiled at Gemma. 'We are all so glad that you
could come, for she is not a good patient and my
mother finds it so difficult to be firm with her when
she is ill...' She broke off. 'There is Piet, I can hear
the car. We have to go.'

The man who entered the room was quite unlike
the husband Gemma had expected. He was short
and thickset and not in the least good-looking, although he had a pleasant face. He was a good deal
older than Gustafina, who quite obviously adored
him, and it was also obvious that he was on very
good terms with the professor. 'We are delighted,'
he told her when he was introduced, 'and we shall
hope to see more of you—we live only a short distance away, and when you find Rienieta is too much
for you then you must escape to us.'

Everyone laughed and Gemma, laughing with
them, knew that she was going to like being with
these people. Never mind if her patient was difficult,
everyone else was super; that nice old man who had
opened the door, the professor's sister and the children, and now this cheerful little man... The only
thing which worried her now was meeting Rienieta's
mother and father.

Her mother walked in at that very moment, just as
though she had answered a cue in a play, and Gemma
was surprised once more, for Mevrouw Dieperink
van Berhuys wasn't at all what she had expected; she

was short and cosily plump, with a round face, dark eyes and silver hair drawn back in a simple knot. She was wearing a soft blue dress, cut so skilfully that one forgot, looking at her, how plump she was.

She beamed at everyone in general as she came in, but it was to the professor she went first, and he went to meet her, giving her a great hug before saying over his shoulder: 'Gemma, come here and meet my mother.'

There had been no need to worry, Gemma realized; this dear little lady wasn't frightening at all. She broke at once into apologies for not being there to welcome them and then went on to ask a great many questions about their trip. 'You're in Holland for the first time?' she asked Gemma. 'You shall see something of it while you are with us and we are so very glad to have you. It is unkind to say so, but I am so very glad that there was a fire at your hospital, otherwise you would not have come.' She added hastily, 'Not that I would wish any harm to come to your patients, it must have been dreadful for them. I think that I would rather die than be pushed down one of those chutes.' She smiled charmingly. 'Ross told me.'

Gemma smiled in reply. 'They're awful,' she admitted, 'and I was terrified.' After a little pause she asked: 'Would you like me to go to my patient now?'

The dark eyes twinkled at her; the little lady wasn't in the least like her son—or her daughter for that matter, but there was something about her which reminded Gemma forcibly of the professor; probably the smile, she concluded. 'My dear child, first you shall have a drink with us and we can tell you a little about Rienieta and talk about your free time and such things, for they are important, are they not?' Her face suddenly softened and glowed. 'Here is my husband.'

A tall man in his late sixties had come into the room, kissed his grandchildren and his daughter, exchanged a few words with the professor and Piet and come to join his wife. He was a handsome man still; it was easy to see where the professor and his sister got their good looks. His voice was as deep and slow as his son's. 'Ah, our nurse from England—we are pleased to welcome you to our home, my dear. Ross took care of you on the journey?'

The two men smiled at each other and the woman between them beamed at them both and said to Gemma: 'There are more of us for you to meet, but you have brothers and sisters, too, have you not, so you will not feel nervous. Now we will sit down and drink a glass of sherry and then I will take you to see Rienieta.'

A delightful family circle, thought Gemma, sipping from delicate crystal; the children sprawled on their father's knee while the rest of them chatted, always in English, about nothing in particular. The effect was so soothing that she could have fallen asleep, and when the professor caught her eye and smiled she smiled back warmly; he was a nice man, so of course he would have a nice family—they were a bit like her own, actually, close-knit and friendly and yet casual. She wondered what they were all doing at home and glanced at the handsome gilt clock on the chimneypiece. The professor saw the look and crossed the room to sit beside her and murmur: 'Having supper, I expect, don't you? You shall telephone them presently.'

'Oh, may I? That would be super.' She looked at him thoughtfully. 'How did you know I was thinking about them?'

'Your face is easy to read.'

She couldn't think of anything to say to that, so instead she asked: 'Should I go to Rienieta now?'

'If you're ready. My sister and her husband are going presently, but Mama will take you upstairs.' He got up and Gemma got up too, said her goodbyes and followed his mother from the room, across the hall and up the stairs, looking around her as she went. In the gallery which ran round three sides of the hall, her hostess paused. 'Rienieta is our youngest,' she explained, 'and a darling child, but somehow this wretched fever has made her feel bad, but I think that she will like you and you must understand that we shall not interfere with you in any way. She needs a firm hand and Ross is quite sure that you will know exactly how best to go about getting her

well again.' She walked on, past several doors, and
turned down a short corridor. 'This is her room, and
yours is next to it, with a bathroom on the other side,
and I hope you will feel at home, Gemma. And now
I think I will go in with you and then leave you for
a little while.' She put out a pretty, beringed hand
to open the door.

CHAPTER FOUR

BUT IT WASN'T Mevrouw Dieperink van Berhuys who opened the door after all; the professor came leaping up the staircase to join them, remarking as he did so: 'It doesn't seem quite fair to leave the introductions to you, Mama—I'll take Gemma in.'

He held the door open as he spoke and she felt herself propelled by a firm hand in the small of her back, into the room—a charming apartment, all pale colours and dainty furniture, the carpet inches thick under her feet. There were a great many china trifles scattered around and some exquisite silver, and the bed was an enchanting affair with a frilled muslin canopy tied with pink ribbons. Its occupant's hair was tied with pink ribbons too—a very pretty girl whose prettiness just now was marred by a heavy frown. She spoke in Dutch and crossly, glaring at her brother from bright blue eyes.

He answered her in English. 'Hullo, Rienieta, and don't glower at me like that, *lieveling*—you know that I've been in England and couldn't come to see you before.' He crossed the room and dropped a kiss on top of her head. 'But I know all about you being ill—besides, I telephoned you, so don't look so cross, you spoilt brat.' He tugged gently at a blonde curl. 'I've brought you a present, and better than that, I've brought Gemma with me.'

'Who's she?' demanded the petulant young lady in the bed. She eyed Gemmma warily.

'A friend of mine—she lives next door to Doctor Gibbons, and I teased her and tormented her to come back with me and keep you company until you're well.' He drew Gemma to the bed and took her hand in his. 'Gemma, this is Rienieta, feeling very sorry for herself just at present, but you'll know how to deal with that, I've no doubt.'

'A nurse,' stated his sister in a frigid voice which barely concealed her opinion of the profession.

'And a very good one. Gemma comes from a large family too—she's the eldest.'

Rienieta took another look at Gemma. 'How many brothers and sisters have you?' she wanted to know.

'Five—the youngest is ten years old.'

'I'm seventeen—Ross is very old, he's thirty-seven, almost thirty-eight.'

'Yes, he told me,' said Gemma placidly. 'I'm twenty-five, but I haven't had a chance to get old yet, the family don't give me a chance.'

Her patient smiled. 'I think I shall like you,' she

decided. 'I'm sorry if I was rude, but the nurse I had was quite old and so strict and she never laughed. She had no brothers and sisters and didn't like children.'

'Poor thing,' said Gemma with sincere pity. 'It's fun being one of a large family, isn't it?'

'Yes—are you very strict too?'

Gemma considered. 'No, I don't think I am, but I'm not all that easy-going either.' Her plain face was lightened by a wide smile. 'The others do what I tell them, anyway.'

'Oh, well, I suppose I shall too. Do you play cards?'

'Like an expert—it's our favourite pastime during the winter evenings—cribbage too, and draughts and dominoes and very bad chess. Do you?'

Rienieta nodded happily. 'That is good news, for when I feel well we can play, can we not?' She turned a much more cheerful face to the professor, who had been leaning nonchalantly against the foot of the bed, not saying a word. 'You are a dear kind brother, Ross, to bring me this so nice Gemma. I shall now get well very quickly.'

He grinned down at her. 'Well, my dear, that's a good start, but remember that it's a slow business; you're allergic to all the antibiotics which would cure you in a few days, so we shall have to go to the long way round—but it won't be all that long if you do as Gemma says.' He bent to kiss her again. 'I must be on my way, I've been idle far too long. *Tot ziens.*' He nodded with casual friendliness to Gemma, murmured that his mother would be back and went out of the room, shutting the door silently behind him.

'Ross is my favourite brother,' confided Rienieta. 'He is a little large perhaps, but he is kind and amusing and almost never cross, though he has a truly dreadful temper, you know—so have I,' she added rather unnecessarily. 'He is also very handsome. You like him too?'

'He's very nice,' said Gemma sedately. 'Now tell me what you do all day and perhaps we can make bed more bearable—have you been getting up at all?'

They spent the next ten minutes discussing Rienieta's feelings on the subject of being ill and being thwarted—one would imagine most cruelly—by her parents from doing what she wanted to do and not what the doctor wished. 'And there are puppies in the stable,' she finished, 'and Mama will not let me go and see them...'

'I should think not indeed!' said Gemma in the severe tones she used to remonstrate with George. 'You see, while you have a high temperature you just have to stay quiet, but I don't see why I couldn't bring them to see you one day soon—we'll ask your parents, anyway. Once your fever has gone you'll feel better and your joints won't ache either, and then I daresay the doctor will let you go downstairs for a little while.' She got up and went to look out of the window at the pretty garden below. 'What sort of puppies are they?'

They were happily absorbed in this interesting subject when Rienieta's mother came back again, and Gemma got up once more to go with her. So far, so good, she thought, and followed Mevrouw Dieperink van Berhuys out of the room.

It seemed to her that her own room was just as beautiful as that of her patient. True, there was no canopy over the bed, which was a narrow one of the Second Empire style, but its coverlet was of thick silk lavishly embroidered with flowers, and the carpeted floor was just as cosy to her feet, and over and above the highly polished dressing table and tallboy and little bedside table, there was a small armchair drawn up to the window, with a table beside it piled high with English magazines and books. Gemma eyed it all appreciatively—even if her patient turned out to be the most difficult she had ever had, there would be compensations.

And thinking over her evening as she lay in bed later, too excited to sleep, she didn't think that Rienieta would be too difficult. She was spoilt, but then so, in a way, was her brother George—the last of a long family could expect indulgence. It was apparent that the professor's family were comfortably off, perhaps more than that; Gemma, who had never been comfortably off in her life, sighed over the wealth of silver and crystal and hand-painted china which had decked the dining table. She sighed, too, at the memory of the delicious food she had eaten and reg-

istered a resolve there and then not to eat too much—
she was already, in her own eyes, on the plump side.

She had liked the head of the family too and the
professor's younger brother, Bart, home for the evening, and another sister, Hendrina, whom everyone
called Iny. She was almost as pretty as Gustafina
and a good deal quieter. Gemma had liked her immediately and had been disappointed to find that she
didn't live at home; she was training to be a nurse
in Utrecht and had only come home, like Bart, to
meet Gemma. When she had wished her goodbye
she had said: 'Ross was quite right, you're just the
person Rienieta needs. He said you were sensible—
a no-nonsense girl, who didn't flutter her eyelashes
every time he opened his mouth.'

Gemma had been unable to think of anything to
say to that, although she had been conscious of annoyance at his opinion of her. She turned over now
in her comfortable bed and thought inconsequently
that her eyelashes were about the only thing worth
looking at in her face—long and brown and curling.
The professor couldn't have noticed.

She saw neither hair nor hide of the professor during the next three days, not that she would have had a
moment to spare for him if she had; Rienieta's fever
had returned, persistent and high, leaving her miserable and ill and extremely bad-tempered. Gemma,
caring for her with all the skill at her command, went
short of sleep and took almost no time off at all, reas-

suring the various members of the family who worried about this that she would take extra time off later on. Rienieta wasn't going to die, she wasn't seriously ill, but the very nature of her illness made her disagreeable, especially with her family, who became quite upset, but Gemma, used to dealing with fractious patients, allowed the mutterings and lowered brow to pass unnoticed while she concentrated on getting the invalid better.

It was hard on the girl, of course, for if she hadn't been allergic to antibiotics, she would have been cured by now, whereas the more conservative treatment she was having required patience, and she had very little of that. It was tiring work, but it wouldn't last for ever, as Gemma kept reassuring her patient's mother, whose pleasant round face was puckered with worry. She reassured herself as well, thinking wistfully that it would be nice to have a few hours off and see something of the quiet countryside around them.

Rienieta's mother had been kindness itself, showing Gemma the house in a snatched half hour, showing her the grounds surrounding it, making sure that she had everything for her comfort. Gemma was tempted on one or two occasions to ask about the professor; no one—in her hearing, at any rate—had mentioned him, and it seemed strange that he hadn't come to see the little sister of whom he was so fond.

Possibly he had telephoned, though, and if he had, there could be no reason for telling her.

Gemma retired to bed on the third evening quite worn out, for Rienieta had been more difficult than usual during the day, although she had seemed a little better when Gemma had settled her down for the night; indeed, creeping into her room just before she got into her own bed, she was relieved to find her patient asleep. She went back to her own room and lost no time in following her example.

She was roused an hour or two later, though; the little electric bell by her bed saw to that. As she padded to Rienieta's room she heard the great wall clock in the hall below chime one o'clock and yawned as she slid silently through the half open door.

'I can't sleep,' said Rienieta pettishly. 'I'm hot and I've been awake for hours.' She added with charming inconsequence: 'How pretty you look with your hair hanging down your back.'

Gemma held back another yawn. 'It's this flattering light, it's pretty enough to make even me passable by it. Shall I sponge your face and hands, love? And then a drink, perhaps? How about a cup of tea?'

Rienieta had cheered up a little. 'The English drink much tea, but I will drink a cup of it to please you.'

'Good, and I'll have one with you—there's something rather special about drinking tea in the middle of the night while everyone else is asleep.' Gemma was bustling gently about the room. 'Face and hands first.'

She was deft and quick and still managed to give the impression that time was of no consequence to her at all. She combed Rienieta's damp hair, shook up her pillows and switched on another little pink lamp.

'I'll be five minutes,' she promised, and stole away, down the stairs and across the hall with its dim wall lights, and through the arched door which led to the kitchens, the main one of which was a vast, old-fashioned place with its scrubbed table and high-backed chairs on each side of the Aga stove. There was plenty of up-to-date equipment too; Gemma put on the electric kettle and went to the enormous cupboard which filled the whole of one wall, in search of tea.

'It's on the second shelf, on the left,' advised the professor from the dimness behind her, and she shot round to stare a little wildly, uttering a small squeak of fright as she did so.

'Well, really!' she said, and her voice was a little loud and high. 'Frightening me like that in the dead of night—and how did you get in, anyway?'

'I have a key,' he told her mildly. 'I was in the pantry looking for something to eat.'

She reached for the tea, took it over to the teapot and carefully warmed the pot before spooning it in. Only then did she ask: 'Haven't you had any supper?'

He shook his head. 'I've been in Vienna. Father

telephoned me about Rienieta, but I was unable to
get away. I drove straight here as soon as I could—
I shall spend the night here, Mama keeps a room
ready for me, you know.' He walked towards her.
'How is Rienieta?'

He was lounging at the pantry door, watching
her, and Gemma was suddenly aware of her hastily
tugged on dressing gown and dishevelled hair, so
that she spoke more sharply than she had intended,
feeling shy. 'She's not been well at all, but I think
she's a little better—she couldn't sleep, so I came
down to make tea.'

'Splendid—may I join the party? And a little
buttered toast, perhaps?' He sounded hopeful and
vaguely wistful so that she forgot about her untidy
appearance and said in a soothing voice: 'Why, of
course—and how about a couple of boiled eggs?'

He brightened visibly. 'How kind—there's a ham
here, I'll carve a slice or two.' He paused as he turned
away. 'You, too?'

'No, thanks,' said Gemma politely; a cup of tea
would be nice, but to devour ham and eggs at half
past one in the morning between bouts of sleep
sounded like indigestion to her. Possibly the professor was made of sterner stuff.

He undoubtedly was; he devoured a huge meal,
perched on the side of his sister's bed, entertaining
her with a lighthearted account of his three days in
Vienna. He was really rather clever, thought Gemma,

studying him covertly from the chair into which she had curled herself. Rienieta was happy again; she looked hot and weary still but already she looked drowsy too. The professor's voice, keeping up a quiet monologue, was very soothing. Gemma resisted a strong desire to shut her own eyes and began, very quietly, to tidy the cups and saucers back on to the tray. Then she gently tucked her patient in once more and with a look at the professor intended to warn him not to stay too long, she trod downstairs bearing the tray. The clock chimed two resonant notes as she went and she yawned again. A whole hour of her much-needed beauty sleep gone, but it had been rather fun. Somehow the professor made life more interesting…she heard him on the staircase behind her and as he took the tray from her grasp, he said: 'I'll help you wash up…'

But in the kitchen he put the tray down on the table and left it there. 'Ria or Nel will do something about it in the morning,' he assured her, and with one quick, unexpected movement, lifted her to sit on the table beside the tray and then got up beside her. 'Tell me about Rienieta,' he begged. 'Father telephoned me each day and I spoke to Doctor Kasten, but it's your opinion I want—you see her all day and every day…' He glanced sideways at her. 'Probably you've been seeing too much of her?'

Gemma brushed the hair out of her eyes and shook her head. 'Oh, no—she's a dear girl, you know, and

she can't help being depressed—you're as aware of
that as I am. She's had a very trying time and quite
a lot of pain, but I think she's over the worst of it—
this is the third recurrence, isn't it? I hope it will be
the last—she's strong and young and very fit usually, isn't she? For what it's worth I'd say she was
on the mend.'

He flung a careless arm round her shoulders. 'And
I think you're right. She may have another bout, but
less severe. I'll have another talk to Kasten and see
if he'll consider letting her do more—she needs con-
crete evidence that she's getting better, don't you
agree? He's a good man, but old-fashioned.' She felt
his arm tighten a little. 'And you? You're happy?
You've had no time to yourself, have you—we'll
make up for that, though.'

'Well, I don't know what I'd do with it if I had it,'
remarked Gemma practically, 'though your mother
said that I might borrow a bike and explore a bit.'

He was staring at his feet, his head bent. 'You're
content with very little, Gemma.'

'Me? Am I?' She considered. 'Not really, but if
you haven't had something you don't hanker after it,
do you?' She added in a matter-of-fact way: 'I think
you have everything.'

He said at his mildest: 'No—there is just one thing
I hanker for.' He paused and she longed to know what
it was, but managed not to ask. She said instead: 'I
expect you'll get it.'

'Er—yes, I have that intention,' and he asked to surprise her: 'Have you a boyfriend, Gemma?'

'Me? Heavens, no!' She was quite astonished. 'I've never had the time,' she told him simply, 'although that must sound silly—and I'm not pretty.'

He said very quietly: 'My mother isn't pretty, but my father considers her to be quite beautiful, so do we all—and my grandmother had a cast in one eye and a little beaky nose, and my grandfather was her devoted slave.'

Gemma wriggled a bit. 'Well, they must have had something…your mother is charming. I expect charm has something to do with it.' She heard with astonishment the clock strike the half hour. 'Look, I must go to bed, and so should you. Do you have to work tomorrow?'

He got off the table and scooped her down to stand beside him. 'Yes, but not until the early afternoon.' His hand on her shoulder propelled her towards the door, where he turned the light out. 'How are your family?'

His hand felt friendly. 'They're fine—your mother allows me to telephone home, you know. George has broken Doctor Gibbons' window again.'

The professor chuckled. 'He'll grow out of it,' he told her comfortably as they went up the wide stairs. In the long dimly lit gallery which encircled the hall below he patted her shoulder in avuncular fashion, dropped a casual kiss on to the top of her head, and wished her goodnight. Gemma murmured sleepily and padded down the passage to her room, peeping in at Rienieta on the way; she was fast asleep. Gemma, on the point of entering her own room, looked back. The professor was still standing in the gallery. She waved briefly before she closed her door. He really was rather a dear.

He wasn't at breakfast in the morning. Gemma, having seen to her patient's wants, shared her meal with the lady of the house and no one else. Bart had gone back to medical school and Iny was at the hospital. Klaas, older than Bart, she hadn't met yet; he was married and living in Friesland. She glanced round the empty table and as though she had read her thoughts, Mevrouw Dieperink van Berhuys remarked: 'Just the two of us, my dear; my husband and Ross went out early. Ross has to go back to Utrecht shortly, although I daresay he will go and see Rienieta before he goes.'

'He saw her last night,' said Gemma, and unaware that her hostess knew all about it already, recounted the night's activities, vaguely put out because the professor wasn't at the breakfast table and just as vaguely glad that she would see him before he went away again.

Only she didn't. When she got back to Rienieta's room it was to find that he had already said goodbye to her and was on the point of leaving the house. Indeed, she heard the powerful roar of his car not five minutes later. For some reason she felt put out, although she concealed her feelings well enough, telling herself that she was doubtless tired.

Doctor Kasten came later in the day and pronounced himself satisfied that Rienieta had recovered from her relapse. 'The spleen is no longer enlarged,' he told Gemma, 'and the joints much less painful, although we must do another agglutination test tomorrow. Perhaps a little distraction, eh, Nurse? Shall we allow the patient to go down for an hour or so this afternoon—with all precautions, of course?'

Gemma agreed, although she had a shrewd suspicion that Rienieta, given an inch, would take an ell if she were given half a chance, and be back in bed again in no time at all. She repaired to the sickroom and delivered a homily on the subject of doing too much too soon, very much in the manner of an elder sister, and surprisingly her patient listened to her patiently and promised to do exactly as she was told.

So the day passed very satisfactorily, with Rienieta going down for her tea, dressed in her most becoming dressing gown and with her hair carefully arranged. She ate a good tea, too, surrounded by those members of her family who happened to be home for the occasion—but not the professor. Gemma, sitting a little apart from the family circle, regretted that.

Tea was almost over when there was a bustle in the hall and Bart came in and with him a young man of Gemma's age—a slim, good-looking man with dark hair worn rather long, and even though he wasn't above middle height he commanded attention, perhaps because of the elegance of his clothes—not the subdued elegance and conservative cut of the professor, but trendy and wildly expensive. He stood in the doorway, smiling with charm at everyone there, and the younger members of the party greeted him with cries of 'Leo!' and a gabble of swift talk, although the professor's parents, while greeting him with courtesy, displayed no great pleasure at seeing him. But he was, of course, invited to sit down and have a cup of tea from the fresh pot Ignaas had brought in, and he was on the point of doing this when his eyes lighted upon Gemma.

He got up again at once, crying in English: 'But no one has introduced us—it is Rienieta's nurse, is it not? I have heard of her from Bart.'

Gemma shook hands and murmured, feeling, for some reason, shy—perhaps because this young man eyed her with the kind of look she wasn't used to receiving. It was absurd, but he somehow conveyed the idea that he found her enchanting and pretty and exquisitely dressed, and all this while making the most commonplace remarks. She answered him sedately enough, aware that the new dress she was wearing was really the only pretty thing about her, but he didn't appear to notice her cool manner, but engaged her in conversation for some minutes before going over to sit with Rienieta on the big sofa by the window. It was later, when she was ushering her patient back upstairs, that he followed them into the hall on the pretext of speaking to Rienieta. Whatever it was he wanted to say only took a moment, though, and as she went on up the staircase he put out a retaining hand to stop Gemma following her. 'We must see more of each other,' he said, soft-voiced, 'when are you free?'

'I really don't know.' She wished she did with all her heart, and that same heart doubled its beat when he went on: 'I'll telephone you—I want to take you out.'

She smiled a little, wished him goodbye and ran up the stairs after Rienieta, who was loitering along very slowly indeed, and when they reached her room she turned an impish face to Gemma. 'I was listening,' she declared. 'You ought to be careful of Leo, he's a—lady killer—is that the word?'

'That's the word,' said Gemma crisply, 'and I don't quite see what I have to be careful about, do you?'

Her patient gave her a thoughtful look. 'No, you don't see, do you? Oh, well, never mind—I'm only teasing. He's fun, isn't he?'

Gemma was turning down the bed and plumping up the pillows. 'Well, I really haven't had a chance to find out,' she confessed. 'Now sit down, love, while I take your temperature—if it's OK we'll have a game

of cards before you get ready for bed, if you would
like that.'

The temperature was fine; the two of them played
beggar-my-neighbour for the next hour and then with
the small, numerous evening chores to keep her busy,
Gemma thought no more of Leo. She thought about
him later, though, when she was in bed. He had been
mentioned several times during dinner that evening
and she had been able to piece something of his life
together. He had known the family for years; his
people lived only a few miles away, he did nothing
to earn his living. She rather gathered from what
the head of the household said that he disapproved
of that—he had money, more than enough, but that,
according to old Doctor Dieperink van Berhuys, was
no reason to be idle. He was engaged to be married, too—to some girl no one had ever seen who
lived in Curaçao, so that no one took the engagement
very seriously, least of all Leo. Gemma had had the
feeling that he wasn't really approved of, although
the younger ones had voted him great fun and very
amusing. She found herself thinking about him for
quite some time, and on the edge of sleep at last,
she admitted to herself that the professor, although
a perfect dear, lacked the excitement the afternoon's
visitor had engendered in her.

He occupied rather too much of her thoughts during the next day too. It was only at the end of that
day that she allowed herself to admit to disappoint-

ment—she had actually believed him when he had said that he wanted to see her again. She was, she told herself, getting soft in the head. With great difficulty she made herself think about something else, and went to sleep.

Leo telephoned the next day in the middle of lunch, so that Ignaas, serving the meal and going to answer the telephone, had first to tell Mevrouw Dieperink van Berhuys that the call was for Gemma from Mijnheer de Vos. He stood impassive while the information was translated for Gemma's benefit, but as she made her excuses and left the table she caught him looking at her with a kind of fatherly concern. She liked Ignaas, but she had no time to think about him now. She picked up the receiver, aware of excitement, which was why her voice came out rather coldly in a bald 'Hullo.'

'Oh, she's cross,' said Leo's soft voice. 'Are they working you too hard? Ross is a slave-driver...'

Gemma wouldn't have that. 'He's not—he's kind and considerate and clever...'

'And dull...I sometimes wonder if he has ever kissed a girl—his work is his life.' And then, as though he sensed that he had offended her, he went on: 'He's a very clever man and highly esteemed in his world and I expect he's kissed dozens of girls. Am I forgiven?'

Gemma smiled at the telephone. 'Yes, of course,

only please remember that I admire the professor very much.'

'So do we all, darling. Are you free this evening?'

'Well, I'm not sure—I suppose I could be if I asked. I haven't had much time off so far, and Rienieta is better. I could leave her for an hour or so, I expect.'

He sounded amused. 'Good. I'll take you out to dine and dance.'

'Won't that make it a bit late?'

'If I promise to bring you back on the stroke of midnight?'

'Well, all right—but you'll have to wait while I ask…'

Of course no one raised any objection, only her hostess looked faintly uneasy about it. But Gemma, on top of her little world, didn't notice that. She promised to be ready at eight o'clock and went back to finish her lunch, and beyond a few polite comments on her chance to see a little of the social life outside the house, no one said anything.

A surprisingly acquiescent Rienieta made no bones about being readied for bed earlier than usual; Gemma had time to put on the pink crêpe dress her sisters had insisted that she should buy. Had they not said, half jokingly that she had to have a pretty dress just in case she met some gorgeous man? And she had. She took great pains with her plain little face, arranged her hair in its usual topknot and went downstairs a few minutes early. Mandy and Phil would have been shocked at that; they both believed in keeping a man waiting, but Gemma, unversed in female wiles, didn't dare. She reached the last tread of the stair as the big door opened from outside and the professor came in. He closed it without haste, looking at her. 'Very nice,' he said at length. 'Who's the lucky man?'

'Leo de Vos. He—he's taking me out for an hour or two.' She thought for a moment that he frowned, but the light in the hall was dim and when she looked more closely he was smiling faintly as he so often did. All the same she went on quite unnecessarily: 'I met him when he came here the other day with Bart.'

The smile was still there, but he offered no comment, so she went on a little faster: 'I don't expect you know that Rienieta came down to tea the day before yesterday, and she's been down each day since. Doctor Kasten is very pleased with her.' She moved a little uneasily because his silence bothered her. 'If you would rather that I stayed with her, I will—I don't mind a bit...'

'My dear Gemma,' he sounded very amused, 'of course you mind. Leo is a most amusing companion. I have no doubt that you will have a delightful evening.' She thought he was going to say something else, but he lapsed into silence to break it presently with: 'Have a nice time. I'm going up to see Rienieta.'

He crossed the hall and went past her and up the staircase, taking the broad, shallow steps two at a time. Gemma had the odd sensation that she had been deprived of something, although she had no idea what it might be—it was a vague, half-felt feeling and instantly dispelled by the imperious blast of a horn outside. Leo, for her, presumably.

The professor had been quite right; Leo was an amusing companion, and Gemma, simple in such matters, took his subtle compliments as gospel truth, and his sly innuendoes for the most part passed over her head. She saw no point in pretending that she wasn't enjoying herself, because she was, very much—Leo had taken care of that; he had chosen to take her to the Princeville, a smart restaurant just south of Breda, and they had dined and danced and talked—not serious talk, Leo wasn't any good at that, his conversation was gay and witty and amusing and sometimes malicious, but Gemma hardly noticed that. She basked in his admiration and felt for the first time in her life that perhaps she wasn't quite as plain as she had supposed herself to be.

It never occurred to her that he found her amusingly unsophisticated, even at times a little dull; it certainly didn't occur to her that he didn't mean a word he said. She only knew that she had met someone who treated her like a queen, had even become, miraculously, attracted to her, and because she was honest herself she made no secret of her interest in him. All the same, she tried not to let him see it too much—indeed, when he reached out to take hold of her hand across the table, she withdrew it in a matter-of-fact way which nonplussed him for the minute. He changed his tactics then, telling her about Holland, making her laugh at the odd tales and legends he told with such ease, and he didn't touch her again, not even when he drew up outside the door of Huis Berhuys and leant across to open the door for her. He didn't get out, though, but wished her an airy goodnight and without another word about seeing her again, drove away. Gemma watched him go and shivered a little; perhaps she had imagined that he liked her…she got the key from her purse and was about to open the door when it was opened for her. The professor ushered her in, looking absent-minded. He waved the book he held at her and murmured: 'I was reading and heard the car. Didn't Leo want to come in?'

She lifted a rather unhappy face to his. 'I don't know—I didn't ask him. I think he was in a hurry to get home.'

Her companion nodded. 'Probably. I hope you had a pleasant evening? Where did you go?'

She told him, still feeling not quite happy; she had been deposited at the door in a rather summary fashion, surely? Mandy and Phil, when they went out in the evening, were always ushered carefully in through their front door by their companions. Perhaps the Dutch had different views about such things. She frowned a little and the professor said comfortably: 'Rienieta is sleeping soundly—so is everyone else. Come and share my coffee before you go to bed and you can tell me all about your evening.' He smiled at her. 'I'm not *au fait* with gay nights.'

Gemma preceded him across the hall and into the pleasant cosiness of the library. 'Well, you ought to be,' she said a trifle tartly. 'There's no reason why you shouldn't be; you can take your pick of pretty girls and go where you like...'

'Most girls look exactly alike to me,' he confessed mildly, and pushed her gently into a chair. 'Be mother and pour the coffee. Perhaps I'm getting too old.'

'Don't talk rubbish,' she begged him. 'You're not in the least old.'

'Thank you, Gemma.' He settled his length in a chair close to hers. 'I like four lumps, please.'

She handed him his cup and because the silence seemed a little long, asked: 'Are you staying the night?'

'Yes. I—er—missed an engagement this evening and it seemed more sensible to go back to Vianen in the morning.' He leaned back, very much at his ease. 'Did you dance?'

'Oh, yes—Leo dances very well, you know, though I'm not so keen on this modern style.'

'Ah—he'll be taking you again, I dare say.'

She gave him a rather bleak look. 'I don't know, he didn't say.'

The professor's eyes narrowed. 'He will.' He became all at once brisk. 'Finished your coffee? Off to bed with you, then, and leave me in peace to finish this most interesting book.' He got to his feet, his smile robbing the words of abruptness. 'Dream of your splendid evening, Gemma. Goodnight.'

CHAPTER FIVE

GEMMA HADN'T EXPECTED to see the professor the next morning, but when she went along to Rienieta's room there he was, sitting on the window seat with his feet up, listening with every sign of close interest to whatever it was that his sister was talking about so earnestly. She was speaking Dutch, but when she saw Gemma she switched at once to English. 'Hullo, Gemma, I'm telling Ross that I'm quite well again...'

Gemma made some casual reply and wished the professor good morning, suppressing the strong suspicion that Rienieta hadn't been talking about herself at all, but her nurse. The professor had got to his feet, given his sister a brotherly hug, nodded cheerfully to Gemma and wandered away.

The door had barely closed behind him when Rienieta burst out: 'Well, did you have a lovely evening? Where did you go? What did you do? Did Leo admire your dress?'

'He didn't say,' said Gemma lightly.

'How horrid of him, for you looked very pretty. I should have been angry with him.' She tossed her pretty head and then smiled with great charm. 'Shall I tell you a secret?'

She was like a pretty child with her beguiling ways. Gemma found herself returning the smile. 'Well, no, love—if it's a secret, it won't be any longer if you tell it.'

The invalid frowned over this and then her brow cleared. 'It's not that kind of secret. Ross came to take you out yesterday, only he didn't know about Leo calling for you—imagine, two dates in one evening!' She giggled. 'You must be very sexy, Gemma.'

Gemma said a little absently that no, she didn't think she was, while she digested the news that the professor had come to take her out, and while she didn't feel the same excitement that she had felt at Leo's invitation, there was a pleasant glow inside her at the thought of it, dispelled at once by Rienieta saying airily: 'I expect he thought he'd better keep you sweet—you haven't had much time to yourself, have you? and you hadn't been out at all. Perhaps he was afraid that you would be tired of the job.'

Perhaps he was. Gemma shook pills from a bottle. 'No,' she said quietly, 'I'm not tired of the job, and I certainly don't expect to be taken out just to keep me sweet.'

'The trouble with you is that you're too nice,' declared her companion. 'If I were you, I would want to be amused after spending hours with me. Am I very tiresome?'

The blue eyes were anxious. 'Oh, lord, no,' laughed Gemma, 'you're not tiresome at all—why should you think that? And I'm not at all overworked, you know—I feel as though I'm on holiday.'

'Even when I ring the bell in the middle of the night just because I am fed up?'

'Even then, and that doesn't happen often, does it? You'll be as good as new in another week or two.'

'That's what Ross said, and he never tells fibs.' Rienieta asked after a pause: 'Do you like him?'

'Yes.' Gemma meant that; she did like him; he had a nice habit of turning up at the right moment. 'What would you like for your breakfast?' she asked briskly.

The professor had gone by the time she went downstairs. She would have liked to have spent an hour or two in his company, telling him about Leo and the lovely time she had had and how wonderful she had felt and how doubtful she felt now—a rather ridiculous wish, really, but that hadn't occurred to her; all she knew was that she could tell him things she wouldn't dream of telling anyone else.

There wasn't anyone at the breakfast table by the time she got there, either. Old Doctor Dieperink van Berhuys had gone to Breda where he still had a small consulting practice with two partners, and his wife had gone with him. Gemma exchanged good mornings with Ignaas who had brought in fresh coffee for her and sat down to her lonely meal.

But at least there were letters for her; a thick envelope with news from each of her brothers and sisters as well as a long, neatly written one from Cousin Maud, in which she was told to have a good time while she was in Holland. 'And,' Maud suggested, 'if you want to, when your job is finished, why don't you go to Amsterdam and have a look round? I'm sure Ross would know of some inexpensive, quiet hotel.'

Gemma smiled as she read this; Ross, she felt sure, if he felt the need to stay in a hotel in Amsterdam, would go to the Amstel or the Doelen; she doubted very much if he had ever poked his high-bridged nose into any lesser establishment. She put down Maud's letter and picked up the last envelope. From Matron, bless her, hoping that she was happy and implying, in the nicest possible way, that there would be no job for her when she got back; there was some dispute about the number of geriatric beds and the fire had given some of the more cheese-paring members of the board to press for a cut in the number of patients as well as nurses. Matron expressed the hope that Gemma might find herself a nice, well-paid job in Holland; probably she would have the opportunity of looking around for herself and inquiring at some of the larger hospitals. Utrecht or Leiden, wrote Matron knowledgeably, were renowned for their teaching hospitals and Gemma was sufficiently highly qualified to apply for any post she chose.

Gemma folded the letter thoughtfully. She saw very little chance of going to either Utrecht or Leiden and still less of seeing the inside of any hospital; she would have to look around the moment she got back to England—London was a safe bet, of course; her own training hospital would give her a job if there was one going, but then she wouldn't be home each day to help Cousin Maud. She would have to think about it.

She was about to leave the table when Ria came to tell her that she was wanted on the telephone. She tried not to hurry across the hall; it was absurd how breathless she felt at the prospect of hearing Leo's voice again. Only it wasn't Leo, it was Bart, wanting to know if she would like to go to the Annual Ball at his hospital. 'Saturday,' he told her, 'so you have two days to arrange things, and that shouldn't be difficult because Iny will be home for days off and she'll keep an eye on Rienieta. And you are to wear the pink dress you wore the other evening.'

Gemma didn't remember that he had seen her in it, but probably Rienieta had told him about it. Her head was so nicely full of excited thoughts that she quite forgot about Leo; did he think, she asked anxiously, that two evenings out in one week seemed rather a lot? She listened to his reassurances, admitted that she hadn't had much free time so far, and promised she would ask if anyone would mind.

They didn't; she was urged to accept, plans were made for Doctor Dieperink van Berhuys to drive her to Utrecht where Bart would meet her, and so much interest was displayed in what she intended to wear and how she would do her hair that she was made to feel quite important. She forbore to mention that she had only the pink dress, anyway—and as for her hair, she decided to do it as she always did, otherwise it might come adrift and spoil her evening.

Rienieta was improving steadily now; there had been almost no fever for two days, although she still had aching joints if she attempted to do too much. Gemma let her do a little more each day, playing with the puppies, playing endless games of cards, discussing clothes, and never lacking something to talk about. They got on well together, and Rienieta regaled her with tales of her family, only she never seemed to have much to say about Ross. It was surprising, mused Gemma, that he seemed such a casual yet candid person, and yet the very whereabouts of his home was a secret to her. She brushed his image aside and concentrated upon Leo, but he hadn't taken any notice of her since they had had their evening together, so she brushed him aside too, which wasn't so easy.

She spent the whole of Saturday in a state of apprehension, afraid that Rienieta would develop a temperature and have another relapse so that she would be unable to go to the ball, but she remained in quite excellent health, and Gemma, having dealt with pills, instructions for going to bed and any emergency which could possibly arise, retired to her room to dress, to reappear just as Ignaas was coming up the stairs to tell her that Doctor Dieperink van Berhuys was ready to leave. She flew to say good-night to Rienieta and Iny and skipped downstairs, where she found Rienieta's mother waiting to wish her a pleasant evening and offer, in the most tactful way, a soft white shawl.

'Too warm for a coat,' she observed tactfully, 'but you might need a wrap when you return.' Her nice little face broke into a smile. 'Don't let Bart drive too fast, my dear.' Bart was to bring Gemma back and stay the night.

Ross's father had very much the same manner as his eldest son; he was almost as placid and he drove just as fast. Gemma hardly noticed the journey; she chatted away happily, led on by his quiet questions and comments, laughing at his small jokes, so that by the time they arrived at the hospital she was in exactly the right mood for a super evening. She thanked him prettily for bringing her, expressed the hope that he would drive carefully home again, and allowed herself to be handed over to Bart, who said at once to win her heart: 'Ah, the pink dress—good!'

She went at once to tidy her hair and dispose of

the shawl and went back to the entrance hall to join him again. There were a great many people there and from what she could see of the women around her, her dress was barely adequate—still, as long as Bart found it pretty... They took to the dance floor and Gemma forgot everything else but the pleasure of dancing. They had circled the floor perhaps twice when Leo took Bart's place with a careless: 'Thanks, old chap,' and a smile for her which set her heart beating nineteen to the dozen. 'Surprised?' he wanted to know. 'I got Bart to fix it...'

'Why?'

He looked taken aback. 'Well, I thought it would be fun—besides, I thought that the van Berhuys might object.'

'Object?' She was quite bewildered. 'Why should they? You're a friend of the family.'

'Oh, rather—known them for years.' He smiled his charming smile again. 'I wanted to keep it a secret—you and me. People don't believe in love at first sight any more.'

'Don't they?' Her heart was dancing a jig. 'I can't think why not; there must be dozens of ways of falling in love, so why not at first sight?'

'A sensible darling, aren't you? We're going to have a lovely evening together and I shall drive you home afterwards.'

She looked at him with delight, then said regretfully: 'I can't come with you, Leo. I promised his

mother that I would see that Bart didn't drive too
fast.'

Leo looked annoyed, but she didn't see that, only
heard him say carelessly: 'Oh, well, we'll sort that
out later, shall we?'

The music had stopped, but he didn't let her go.
'Come and meet some of my friends,' he invited, and
caught her hand in his. There was no sign of Bart
and the place was packed now; it would be hopeless to look for him, so Gemma allowed herself to
be led across the room to a rather noisy group, the
young men long-haired and extravagantly dressed,
the girls in dresses which Gemma thought privately
weren't quite decent even if they had cost a fortune.
She smiled and murmured her way around the circle and everyone asked her a great many questions
in too loud voices while they eyed her dress with
thinly veiled amusement. Gemma saw the look and
her small chin lifted, but the situation was saved by
one of the young men, who swept her off to dance
so that the unpleasant moment passed. He danced
well but a little wildly, singing in her ear and holding her so tightly that she could hardly breathe. She
resigned herself to ten minutes or so of his company
before, surely, Leo would rescue her.

It wasn't Leo who rescued her. They had reached
the comparatively empty space at the bottom of the
ballroom when her companion said, far too loudly:

'This is the stuffed shirt end—the professors and deans and clever dicks...'

Ross was there, sitting at one of the small tables with another older man and two rather matronly women with nice faces, and although she hadn't meant to, Gemma gave him an appealing glance as they passed the table and whirled away again. He was the last person she had expected to see there, and probably he was just as surprised to see her... Her partner disappeared and the professor was in his place, dancing her quite beautifully down the ballroom.

'Hullo,' he said matter-of-factly. 'I hope I interpreted that look correctly. It was rescue you wanted, wasn't it?'

'Oh, yes, thank you,' said Gemma fervently, aware that he danced a good deal better than Bart or Leo and certainly far better than the noisy type she had just endured. 'I'm not sure who he was—a friend of Leo's...' She paused and the professor said non-committally:

'Ah, yes—I saw him. Where is Bart?'

'Bart? Well—I haven't seen him just lately...' She didn't see the rather grim expression on her companion's face. 'He's taking me home,' she added, aware somehow that the professor needed placating and not sure why. She added, because he was a man one didn't try to sidetrack: 'Leo said he would, but I said no because your mother asked me most particularly to see that Bart didn't drive too fast.'

'Ah, yes,' murmured her partner, which told her nothing at all and was the kind of annoying answer to dry up any conversation. 'Come and meet a few friends of mine,' he invited, and she found herself sitting at the little table, drinking something or other, drawn into the friendly talk of the older man, who was the dean, and the two women, one of whom was his wife. Presently another man came over to join them and the dean, making little jokes about his age, asked Gemma to dance. They circled the room sedately and she saw that the professor was dancing with the dean's wife, although she couldn't see Bart anywhere, or Leo—but somehow she didn't mind very much; this was better than having to talk to Leo's friends, even though it wasn't very exciting.

The dance ended and they went back to their table. Gemma finished her drink and hoped that the professor would ask her to dance again, but he showed no inclination to do so, and when Bart suddenly appeared and invited her to take the floor with him, she did so, wondering what it was that the professor had uttered low-voiced to his brother to make him look so defiant and sulky. She set herself to cheer him up, but her good intentions were cut short by the reappearance of Leo, who slid smoothly into Bart's place and danced her off the floor and into one of the small rooms leading out of the ballroom.

'Lord, what a crush!' he complained. 'I saw you entangled with the elderlies and sent Bart along to rescue you.' He was holding her hand, but she withdrew it gently.

'I didn't find them elderly,' she told him, 'and why didn't you do the rescuing yourself?'

He grinned like a small boy and Gemma found herself smiling back at him. 'You must have guessed by now that Ross doesn't like me overmuch—we keep out of each other's way and we're civil when we meet, of course, but he's a good deal older than I am, isn't he, and we have very little in common. Being so learned makes him a bit of a bore and rather a dull fellow.' He had taken her hand again and she let it lie.

'You're wrong, of course,' she told him quietly. 'He's not dull and he's certainly not a bore...'

'My darling girl, he shall be none of these things if you say so—now let's talk about us.' He pulled her to him and kissed her, and Gemma, who had been hoping that he would do just that, was disappointed to find that it wasn't what she had expected—oh, it was thrilling all right, but something was lacking. Perhaps she was too excited to enjoy it. She kissed him back a little awkwardly and said shyly: 'I can't think what you can see in me.'

His answer was more than satisfactory, but then it should have been, for had she but known it he had had considerable practice in such matters with other girls. But she didn't know it, so she took his words at their face value, cherishing every one of them to remember later.

They danced again presently, and Gemma, caught up in daydreams and excitement and the heady belief that Leo thought her a wonderful girl, looked for once almost pretty, so that the professor, treading a sober foxtrot with the dean's wife again, looked at her thoughtfully and while carrying on a desultory conversation with his partner, allowed his powerful brain to assess the situation. But none of this showed on his calm features. He bent his head to listen to some triviality uttered by his partner, and when he caught Gemma's eye as she flashed past them in a more up-to-date version of the dance, his faint smile betokened polite recognition and nothing more.

The end of the evening came too soon for Gemma; she had danced almost every dance with Leo, although between them she had had to endure the brittle friendliness of his companions, but that had been a small price to pay for the delight of his company. As for the professor, she had glimpsed him from time to time, and presently forgot him completely.

Leo had said nothing more about taking her home, and although she would have liked to have gone with him more than anything else, she had put it out of her mind, and supposed that he had done the same. She fetched the shawl from the mass of evening wraps and fur coats and repaired to the entrance hall to wait for Bart, but the minutes passed and the crowds thinned rapidly; she was beginning to feel anxious when Leo joined her.

'Sorry you were left alone,' he said solicitously, 'but Bart isn't feeling well—had too much to drink, I shouldn't wonder, so it looks as though I'm going to get my wish after all; someone has to take you home and there's nothing I'd like more.'

Gemma hesitated. 'Ought I to see Bart first?' she asked. 'His mother might want to know why he didn't come home—I'm not sure…'

'I've messages from him—you weren't to worry, for a start, and will you make it all right with his mother, and he'll telephone in the morning.'

It didn't sound quite like Bart. 'Oh, well, all right,' she said at length. She was still hesitating and Leo frowned a little.

'You don't seem very pleased at the prospect of my company.'

He sounded cool and she hastened to say: 'Oh, but I am, really I am, only I'm sorry about Bart.'

'He's in good hands; he'll be as right as rain in no time—he's had the sense to know that he's in no fit state to drive.' He tucked a hand under her arm. 'Let's go, shall we?'

She accompanied him happily enough to the entrance; it was hard luck on Bart, but as things turned out, convenient for her. She went through the big double doors of the hospital and walked into the professor's large and solid back.

It wasn't Leo's hand on her arm any more, but the professor's, and Leo was standing a little apart, looking sulky.

'You took a long time,' observed the professor, and although his voice was mild it held a silkiness which gave Gemma the nasty feeling that he was in a riproaring temper, but she had no need to reply, for he went on in Dutch, addressing himself to Leo. Leo answered him presently, sounding as sulky as he looked, and Gemma looking from one to the other of them in bewilderment, was relieved when the professor said in English:

'A little misunderstanding—Bart isn't fit to drive, but as I'm going home anyway, I'll take you with me.' He glanced at Leo. 'Good of you to offer Gemma a lift,' he remarked in a voice which suggested that there was nothing good about it. 'Goodnight.'

He didn't give Gemma a chance to say more than goodnight herself, but swung her round and marched her across the courtyard to where a white Jaguar XL-S was parked. The professor opened its door and ushered her in smartly and she said crossly: 'This isn't your car,' her world so awry for the moment that she would have liked to have burst into tears or given him a good thump, only with the size of him, she wouldn't have done much damage.

'Er—yes, it is. Now don't be a silly girl—get in.'

Gemma snorted. Now she was a silly girl, was she, to be ordered about and have her evening ruined,

and bullied into the bargain! She got into the luxurious seat with dignity without looking at him and then
forgot all about being dignified, for Bart was sitting
in the back. It was a handsome car, meant for two
but with space for an occasional third, and he looked
a little cramped. He said hullo in a sheepish voice,
and startled out of her own not very happy thoughts,
she exclaimed: 'Bart—Leo said you weren't feeling
quite the thing…' She looked at him anxiously, for
he was a nice boy; the twins would be like him in a
year or two… 'Shouldn't you be in bed?'

'He will be in bed soon enough,' observed the professor, easing himself into the seat beside her, 'and
he can start sleeping it off now—it's only a hang-
over, but my dear Bart, if you will drink vodka in
such quantities, that is to be expected.'

'It was a joke.' Bart still sounded sheepish.

'I know that, but a thoughtless one. It was known
that you were to drive Gemma back, was it not?'

'Yes, of course. I told Leo—probably he forgot.'

'Probably he did,' said his brother in a dry voice.

Gemma was only half listening. As the big car
slid out of the hospital courtyard and into the city
streets, she muttered in a voice she strove to keep
even, 'I can't quite see why you should have to take
me home, Professor.'

He glanced at her briefly. 'Spoilt your evening,
have I? Don't worry, Gemma, Leo always gets what
he sets his heart on—that is, almost always.'

'That's hardly the point, is it? You just—just…'

'Gummed up the works? Yes, I did.' He added impatiently: 'Why do you have to be such a child—the eldest of six and still wet behind the ears!'

This inelegant speech had the effect of rendering her speechless for several seconds until she managed in a furious voice: 'You're rude and arrogant and—and you're a bully too…'

'Anything you say,' he agreed blandly, and she reflected uneasily that although he had spoken so quietly he was probably holding a very nasty temper in check. The perverse urge to annoy him still more took hold of her, so that she went on recklessly: 'I was having a simply lovely time and I'm perfectly able to look after myself—Leo would have taken me home.' She added nastily: 'And I should have enjoyed that.'

The professor laughed. 'Vixen!' he murmured. 'I'm sorry you're so upset, but it will do no harm, you know—Leo enjoys a good chase and I promise you that I won't be there to spoil things next time. Am I forgiven?'

Gemma had never quarrelled for more than half an hour with anyone and she never bore a grudge. She said willingly enough, 'Yes, all right, but I don't want to talk about it any more.'

They were on the motorway and the Jaguar was making light of the kilometres. Just as though they hadn't had a single cross word, the professor remarked easily: 'You met a great many people this evening. How did you like the dean and his wife?'

'Nice,' pronounced Gemma. 'He's a poppet, and she was so kind—in the same way as your mother is kind. One can talk to people like that and they listen in a cosy way, but they're never inquisitive.'

He nodded. 'And what about the crowd Leo runs with?'

She stirred uneasily. 'Well, I'm not used to people like that—clever and smart and one never quite knows if they're serious or not—can you imagine them in the village at home? You see, I'm not clever or witty and I can't talk like they do—I felt an ig-ig...'

'Ignoramus,' he supplied gravely. 'But not really; they would feel the same if someone put them into the middle of a hospital ward and told them to take the temperatures. They're in their element at a night club, and you're in yours flinging old ladies down fire chutes and making tea at one o'clock in the morning without so much as a frown.' They were approaching Rosendaal and he slowed a little. 'Talking of tea, I think we shall have to revive Bart with some black coffee when we get in.'

'He'll be all right in the morning?'

'He'd better be; I've no intention of Mama finding out that he was pickled in vodka.'

It gave her a pleasant feeling, knowing that the professor stood by his brothers and sisters when they needed it after some petty misdemeanour. She said suddenly: 'I'm sorry I said all that about you just now. None of it was true—it's jolly decent of you to cover up for Bart.'

He thanked her blandly. 'But you would do the same?'

'Of course—the eldest always does.' She frowned into the motorway ahead, clearly seen in the car's headlights. 'You said pickled with vodka.'

'Just that. He was dared to drink a glass of the stuff, and he did, silly chap, between Pilseners, and then, for a joke it seems, someone laced his next few Pilseners with more of the stuff. He was out cold when I found him.'

'Found him? Did they leave him like that?'

'Yes.'

'It must have been one of those friends of Leo's—they were rather wild.'

'Probably.' Gemma waited for him to continue, but he didn't, so she went on: 'Leo said Bart had a bit of a headache and was a bit under the weather; if he'd known, he would have done something about it.'

'Oh, undoubtedly,' agreed the professor gently.

'Have you known him long?' Her head was full of Leo again.

'De Vos? All our lives—he is ten years younger than I.'

'He's great fun.' Her voice was a little high in her efforts to keep it casual.

'Indeed yes. I gather that you—er—like him.'

'I do.' She was in full spate now, longing to tell someone how she felt about Leo, and this placid man beside her, despite his unexpected, quickly damped down anger, seemed to fulfil the role of confidant to the manner born. 'You see, no one has ever treated me like that before—looked at me as though I was pretty, and told me I was even though I know I'm not, and—and telephoned me…and I never knew that he would be at the ball—it was a super surprise. I wish I had another dress, though, this one wasn't nearly grand enough.'

The professor made a small sound. He said in a kind voice: 'I thought it was charming, and so did the dean.'

She thanked him; it was the kind of remark she might have expected from him, although she could hardly say that the dean's opinion of her dress didn't matter a fig to her; it was Leo she wanted to please.

There was a companionable silence between them until she asked: 'Do you really suppose he'll ask me out again?'

'Of course he will. I should buy a new dress, if I were you—it won't be wasted.'

They were almost home. Gemma turned to look at Bart, snoring behind them; at least she would be able to say with perfect truth that he hadn't driven fast. As though he had read her thoughts, the professor said:

'I'll tell Mama that I decided to come home and

drive you both—there's no need to say more than that.'

'Very well.' He turned the car in at the gates and stopped in front of the door; there was a faint light showing through the transom above it but the rest of the house was in darkness. He got out and opened the door, then came back for her, and when she was safely inside he went back to rouse Bart.

'Coffee in the kitchen?' inquired Gemma. She spoke in a whisper, because the dim quiet of the hall made it impossible to do otherwise.

The professor nodded, his arm round Bart, who, half awake, was complaining about his head. 'Oh, do hush him,' she said urgently, and led the way across the hall.

There was coffee on the Aga; it took only a moment to find three mugs and the sugar, sit Bart down in a chair and urge him to drink up. He did it reluctantly at first, but by the time he had downed the second cup he was feeling decidedly better. 'So sorry,' he said apologetically, 'made an ass of myself.'

'No, you didn't,' said Gemma in a comforting voice. 'You weren't to know about the rest of that vodka—it was a rotten trick to play on you. Do you begin to feel better?'

She filled his cup for the third time and offered the silent professor another mugful. 'Yes, thanks, Gemma—you're a good sort not to mind.'

He sounded like one of her twin brothers and she

gave him a motherly smile and got to her feet. 'I'll get these out of the way and go to bed.'

She tidied away neatly, thanked Bart for her lovely evening with a sincerity which allowed of no sarcasm and started for the door, to find the professor beside her long before she reached it. She said goodnight as he opened it, but he followed her into the hall and she asked: 'Is something the matter? Did you want to say something about Bart?'

'Not about Bart—about you, Gemma. You have had your happy evening spoilt and you've been a darling about it. You're a gem of a girl, do you know that? I hope all your dreams come true, for you deserve them.'

Before she could reply he bent to kiss her—not at all the same kind of kiss which Leo had given her, for it was gentle and brief. She knew that long after the heady excitement of Leo's kiss had faded, she would remember this moment. She said 'Oh,' rather blankly and ran up the staircase without looking back.

CHAPTER SIX

TO HER SURPRISE, Gemma slept at once and dream-lessly, to wake at her usual time feeling quite re-freshed. Rienieta was already awake when she went along to see how she was, and they whiled away half an hour talking about the ball, Gemma doing her best to answer her companion's eager questions. Fortunately she had a good memory; she was able to give detailed descriptions of a number of the dresses there, the food she had eaten and the people she had met, and even a few of their names.

'And Bart?' asked Rienieta. 'Was he waiting for you? Papa said you looked so pretty that he would have liked to stay and dance with you—he joked, of course,' she added seriously. 'He would never go anywhere without Mama.'

'No, of course he wouldn't,' Gemma agreed, 'but how nice of him to say that.' She launched into an ac-count of Bart's prowess as a dancer, and mentioned casually that Leo had been there too.

Her patient was examining her tongue in a hand mirror. She put it back in to say: 'I—We are not surprised. Mama said yesterday that she was afraid that he would be there too—he and his friends. Were they there, Gemma?'

Gemma charted her patient's temperature with a steady hand. 'Oh, yes—rather silly I thought, not quite my cup of tea. The girls wore those lovely impossible dresses you see in *Vogue*.' She smiled at Rienieta as she shook down the thermometer. 'Your mother doesn't like Leo?'

'She understands that he is great fun...'

'But she would prefer me not to go out with him. Well, I can understand that—we haven't the same background. I'm middle class, you know, and neither clever nor smart.' She hesitated. 'I hadn't thought of it before, but I can see now that if I had someone like me working for me, I wouldn't want me to go tearing off with the upper crust.'

Rienieta's blue eyes grew round, but it was the professor's voice that answered her. He was standing in the doorway watching her and smiling a little. 'What a very muddled way of putting it, Gemma, but you don't do yourself justice; such an idea would never enter Mama's head and certainly not my father's—nor anyone else in the family, for that matter. It's no use telling you that you are far too good for de Vos, but if he has been lucky enough to win your regard then none of us, I can promise you, will lift a finger to prevent you seeing him as often as it can be arranged.'

Gemma's eyes were as round as her patient's, her face remarkably flushed. She tried to think of something to say and found that her usually sensible head was quite empty, but as it turned out there was no need to say anything at all, for he came wandering into the room, saying easily: 'I thought you might like to know that Bart is more or less himself—he looks washed out, but that can be put down to too much dancing. Are you coming down to breakfast?'

'No—yes,' said Gemma wildly. 'I hadn't thought about it—I must see to Rienieta…'

'I see no reason why she shouldn't, just this once, come down too. It will—er—distract attention…'

'Why?' asked his sister. 'What's Bart been doing? Tell, or I won't help.'

'He's done nothing, brat; he was a bit under the weather last night, so I brought him back with Gemma and stayed the night.'

'Drunk?' inquired Rienieta wisely.

'A nasty word,' reproved her brother. 'Bart doesn't get drunk—he drank something by mistake, though, and it made him feel wretched. Mama is not to know.'

'OK. Though I don't mind betting you that she'll find out. She always does, you know—you always find things out, too, don't you, Ross? Only you never tell anyone…'

'A gift.' His voice was amiable. 'Don't you wish you had it? Now, how about breakfast?'

The meal was noisy and talkative because so many members of the family were there and Rienieta, undoubtedly the family darling, was in tearing spirits. Probably we shall have tears by teatime, thought Gemma gloomily, watching her. All the same, she was almost recovered from her illness and she had had no fever for several days. Soon she would be pronounced well and she herself would go back to England. She didn't want to go, and not only because of Leo; she liked Holland and she liked the people with whom she was sharing her breakfast; she would miss them dreadfully. She looked round the table and caught the professor's eye, and when he smiled, her vague worries about leaving disappeared.

He and Bart went shortly afterwards, and Gemma, busy with her patient, had no chance to say goodbye, although she heard the car leave. The house seemed very quiet for the rest of the day and it wasn't until the end of the day, while she was helping Rienieta to bed, that Leo telephoned. His voice sounded gay in her ear as well as tender, and to begin with, apologetic.

'About last night,' he began, 'sorry about the mix-up; there wasn't much I could do, though, and I knew you'd get home safely enough with Ross.' He laughed softly as though he found that funny. 'But, lord, I was disappointed, I can tell you. You're not in disgrace or anything like that, sweethcart?'

'Disgrace? Why ever should I be?' asked Gemma, savouring the sweetheart part.

'Oh, nothing. Have you used up all your free time, or could we have a quick run this evening?'

'Not this evening.' She hoped her voice sounded firm; she would have loved to have said yes, but she had come as Rienieta's nurse and even though there wasn't much for her to do, she was still employed as such.

'Tomorrow, then?'

'Well, that would be nice, but I must ask first, and then only for an hour or so after Rienieta is in bed.'

'Splendid. I'll be outside about half past eight. They dine at seven, don't they?'

'Yes. Goodbye, Leo.'

She wore a jersey dress this time and took a cardigan and scarf with her because Rienieta had warned her that Leo drove an open sports car as well as the BMW he had taken her out in before. She was glad of the advice when she saw that the car was a Porsche—a 911S Targa. Leo didn't get out when he saw her, but leaned across to open the door, said briefly: 'Hop in, darling,' and sped out into the road almost before Gemma had settled herself.

'How about den Haag?' he inquired.

She knotted the scarf firmly under her chin before replying. 'That's too far, Leo—I said an hour.'

He looked annoyed. 'Good lord, I didn't think you meant that—why, an hour is just a waste of an evening.'

'In that case, stop, turn round and take me back again,' she said crisply.

Her words had the effect of making him laugh. 'I've never met anyone quite like you,' he told her, 'but all right, little darling, an hour it shall be.'

He was driving fast and rather recklessly. 'We'll go to my place and have a drink and I promise you I'll take you back in an hour's time.'

'Where is your place?'

'Just off the motorway, going towards Breda—quite close by. I've a few friends staying with me—I think you met some of them Saturday night…and what a dreary affair that was!'

'I enjoyed it very much.' Gemma frowned a little, for they seemed at outs with one another. 'But then I don't go out a great deal; there's nothing much in the village where I live; a few dinner parties and tennis in the summer—anyway, I haven't much time…'

'My poor darling, it must be utterly ghastly looking after the sick—and you don't have to pretend that you like it to me.'

'But I do like it. Leo, what happened to Bart Saturday evening?'

He had turned into a narrow country road and was hooting impatiently because there was a cattle lorry ahead of him. 'Bart? Oh, the young idiot drank some vodka and passed out—I didn't tell you because I didn't want to upset you.' He smiled at her and she glowed under it.

'You look lovely,' he uttered the trite words with practised charm and then turned away to curse the lorry driver in Dutch as he skidded past him. 'Shouldn't allow the fellows on the roads,' he grumbled, and then: 'Here we are.'

The house stood back from the road, smaller than Huis Berhuys and built of brick in a rather pretentious style. Gemma didn't like it much, although she was prepared to try because it was Leo's home. The evening was warm, the windows were open, showing a brightly lighted interior and allowing a good deal of noise to escape; his few friends must be enjoying themselves, Gemma decided as she got out of the car and, obedient to his nod, walked into the hall, a dark apartment with a good deal of carved furniture in it and painted leather walls. The sitting room, in contrast, was brilliantly lighted and full of people, she saw that at once as Leo drew her into it with a hand on her arm, and she had met several of them, just as he had said. She realized a little late in the day that she was too tired to join in the bright froth of chatter going on around her and which seemed to be their sole conversation, but she smiled and nodded and said hullo and accepted the glass Leo gave her—champagne. She took a sip and wrinkled her nose at its dryness, and Leo, a careless arm flung around her shoulders, asked laughingly: 'Never had it before, Gemma?'

Everyone laughed when she said seriously: 'Not often, birthday parties and things like that,' and the harmless remark sparked up a great many witty remarks about nothing much so that she allowed her gaze to wander round the room. It was furnished in a heavy style she didn't much care for, although there were some pictures on its walls she would have liked to have examined, but her eye lighted on the gilt clock above the marble chimneypiece and she said at once: 'Leo, I should like to go back, please— we've been gone an hour already.'

'Of course, darling. Just one more glass of champagne first—Cor, go out and turn the car for me, will you?' He turned back to Gemma. 'Darling, we've hardly spoken to each other, we'll have to do better than this.'

She wished silently that he wouldn't call her darling so often, it made the word meaningless. 'I'm going back to England soon,' she told him.

'Then we must arrange something…' His smile came and went. 'England's not so far away, you know.' He went on in a concerned way: 'You're getting worried about getting back, aren't you? We'll go this very moment.'

She smiled her gratitude. 'I'm sorry, it was hardly worth you coming to take me out, was it?'

He said in her ear: 'Even five minutes of your

company would be worth a whole evening's travel.'
She didn't quite believe that, but it was a nice thing to
have said of one. They left the house on a noisy wave
of goodbyes and laughter. Leo's friends laughed a
good deal about nothing much.

Leo drove straight back to Huis Berhuys; he drove
fast but much more carefully this time, and when
they got there he got out and opened the car door
for Gemma and walked with her to where Ignaas
was waiting at the house door. He waited until the
door had been closed behind her after wishing her
a restrained goodbye under the old man's eye—a
goodbye hinting at hidden devotion and suppressed
eagerness—and then got back into his car and drove
away, very well pleased with himself. It had taken
him a little while to discover that Gemma was dis-
tinctly old-fashioned; he was going to get nowhere
with her with champagne and parties. She might
be unsophisticated, but she wasn't a fool either. He
grinned to himself; his technique with girls had
never failed, and it wasn't going to now, only he
would have to work fast if she was going back to
England so soon. He began planning the next outing—lunch at a rather staid restaurant perhaps, it
might be a bit boring. He would have to tell Cor and
the others... He drove on, his mind nicely occupied.

Gemma, happily unaware of Leo's plans, thanked
Ignaas for opening the door, remarked, in the handful of Dutch words she had acquired, that it was a

nice evening and went upstairs to find Rienieta sitting up in bed with the telephone clamped to her ear.

She waved as Gemma went in, said something into the receiver and then: 'It's Ross, he wants to speak to you.'

Gemma came down from the romantic cloud she had been floating upon and took the receiver, sat down on the side of the bed and said briskly: 'Hullo, Professor.'

'Gemma? I want you to bring Rienieta to Utrecht tomorrow—she's to have a complete checkup, it's something we feel should be done; she seems cured and probably is, but as you know it's an illness which is sometimes more serious in an adult. She can stay overnight in the hospital and you will stay with her, if you will, although you won't be needed a great deal.' His voice, impersonal until now, became warm and friendly. 'It will give you a chance to see something of Utrecht.'

Gemma, her feet firmly on the ground again, said yes, how nice and at what time were they to be ready?

'I'm coming down in the morning—if I can manage to get away I shall come this evening, but I don't know yet, and I'll take you both back with me after breakfast. Father has to come up to Utrecht and he will drive you both home again.' There was a little silence. 'You haven't made any arrangements for yourself?'

'None.' Gemma was still brisk, nudging aside the thought that probably Leo would have telephoned later and made another date. Oh, well, absence made the heart grow fonder, didn't it? And what was two days? Anyway, they might be back in time for her to spend an evening with him. She said goodbye and handed the receiver back to Rienieta, who embarked on a long conversation in her own language. When she finally put the telephone down she said at once: 'I say, won't it be super? I hate hospitals, but if Ross is there and you are too—you don't mind coming? I don't suppose there'll be anything to do but just to have you with me…you're so reassuring, Gemma.'

The big blue eyes filled with tears and Gemma hurried over to the bed and put her arms round her patient's shoulders. 'Now, now, love, there's nothing to be scared about—it's just a routine check-up. I don't suppose it will take more than an hour or two and I won't be far away, I promise you.'

'You really promise?'

'Promise—cross my heart and hope to die.' She produced a clean handkerchief and handed it to the still sniffing Rienieta. 'Now, what will you wear?'

Her patient brightened. 'I've a new dress…'

'Splendid, just as long as it's easy to get out of and into. Remember you will be tired after the journey and for certain they'll want you to go to bed at once so that you're nicely rested ready for the tests and so on.'

'It's a denim pinafore with a white blouse—it has a drawstring neck and long sleeves with lots of buttons at the wrist, only there is no need to undo them.'

'Sounds ideal, but supposing we ask your mother what she thinks?' Gemma went to the door. 'Will she be in the drawing room?'

'Yes, it isn't eleven o'clock yet and she never goes to bed until then.'

'Then I'll ask her to come up again even though she's been up to say goodnight to you, but if I fetch her will you promise to go straight to sleep afterwards?'

'Cross my heart,' said Rienieta seriously.

Her mother was sitting in the small armchair she always used, knitting. She was wearing glasses a little crooked on her nose so that her round face looked endearingly youthful. She put the knitting down as Gemma went in and glanced across at her husband. 'We rather expected you, Gemma. Ignaas told us that Ross had telephoned Rienieta and wanted to speak to you—he wants her to go to Utrecht, I expect. He was talking of it…'

Gemma explained and added that Ross had said that he might arrive later in the evening, and his father put down his book to say: 'Much better if he comes tonight, then you can make an early start in the morning. I said that I would bring you back, he'll be far too busy—some lecture or teaching round, I forget which. Did he say if he's spoken to Doctor Kasten?'

'I think he must have done, because he said Doctor Kasten had telephoned him.'

The old doctor nodded. 'Good. I'll wait up; Ross is almost certain to come tonight and we shan't have time to talk in the morning.'

He smiled at her and then glanced at his wife and smiled at her too—quite a different smile, Gemma noticed; tender and loving and very faintly amused. She supposed that the professor would smile in just the same way at his wife when he got himself one.

She explained about Rienieta wanting to see her mother and the doctor got up to open the door for them. Nice, thought Gemma, following Mevrouw Dieperink van Berhuys up the staircase, to have doors opened for you and things picked up for you when you dropped them and someone to smile at you like that...it would be lovely to go through life with someone who smoothed the rough edges and cherished you. It was no wonder that the little lady sailing along ahead of her looked so happy and contented; a devoted husband and children who loved her dearly...Gemma fetched a sigh and her companion, on the point of entering Rienieta's room, turned round to ask: 'You're tired, child. Did you have a pleasant evening? But too short, I think.'

'It was delightful, thank you, *mevrouw*, but Leo

took me back to his house and there were a great many people there.'

It sounded rather silly, put like that, but her companion seemed to understand, for she nodded and smiled. 'People can be a great nuisance,' she said kindly, and opened the door.

She didn't stay long, the question of her daughter's wardrobe was quickly settled and after a few reassuring remarks she went downstairs again, leaving Gemma to settle Rienieta for the night and pack the few things she would need. It didn't take long; Gemma had finished and her patient was fast asleep and she herself in bed before she heard the sound of a car coming fast. Ross had arrived, coming into the house so quietly that she didn't hear a sound. Only much later, while she still lay awake thinking about her evening with Leo and her future and then Leo again, she heard his quiet, slow tread going down the gallery to his room. It was as though she had been waiting for that sound before she slept, for a moment later she closed her eyes with a contented little sigh.

She was up early, seeing that Rienieta had her breakfast in bed before she bathed and dressed. She herself was already dressed in the Jaeger skirt and coral cotton sweater she had bought in Salisbury; its accompanying jacket neatly laid out on her bed, ready to put on at the last moment; her hair was twisted into its usual tidy bun and she had taken pains with her face. She had taken a minimum of things for herself; night clothes, flat shoes in case she had the opportunity to go sightseeing, which she very much doubted… She went down to the kitchen where Ria gave her Rienieta's breakfast tray, and she was on her way up again with it carefully balanced, when the study door opened and the professor came out, dressed in an elegantly sober grey suit which Gemma judged must have cost him a small fortune. He looked, she considered, eyeing him over her tray, absolutely smashing. She wished him a sober good morning and he countered it with a cheerful 'Hullo' and added: 'Come down again when you've seen to Rienieta, will you, Gemma?'

He didn't smile, only stared at her rather hard, so that she clutched the tray to her and hurried on, wondering why he should look so annoyed, only that wasn't the right word; he never looked annoyed— remote was nearer the mark.

She was back within five minutes, tapping on the study door, to have it flung wide, and as he ushered her in with all the vigour of a north wind: 'For heaven's sake, Gemma,' said the professor in an exasperated voice, 'you don't have to knock on doors!' His voice was so sharp that she said forthrightly:

'And you don't have to take me up so snappily!'

'I'm sorry, and you're quite right.' His tone was silky and he didn't mean a word of it. 'Do sit down.'

Gemma perched on the edge of a large leather

chair; they were all outsize, made for large men, she found herself wondering how his mother managed.

'I am glad that I was able to speak to you yesterday evening,' he remarked, still very silky. 'I should have remembered that you would probably be out.'

She coloured faintly but met his cool gaze frankly enough. 'You didn't need to remember anything of the sort, Professor; I've been out on just three occasions and never when I considered that Rienieta might need me—however, if you find me unsatisfactory, I'll go at once. There must be some very good nurses in Utrecht,' she added helpfully.

He didn't say anything at all for such a long time that she sat a little straighter in her chair, wondering what was coming next. When he did speak she was so surprised that she could only stare at him. 'Gemma, I told you that you were a gem of a girl and I haven't changed my opinion; you have gone well beyond the bounds of duty in giving up hours of time to Rienieta—oh, I know all about the endless card games and the chess and the hours you have spent with her before she would sleep at night. You are entitled to a great deal more free time than you get and no one is going to dispute that.'

He paused and she seized the opportunity to ask: 'Then why did you look so angry just now?'

His voice was placid again. 'I have a bad temper,' he observed. 'Now and again it gets the better of me, but it's all right now.' He smiled at her while his eyes searched her face. 'About Rienieta, it may help if I tell you what we intend to do...'

She listened to his quiet voice discussing hospital procedure, tests, arrangements made for their stay, the time of their arrival; it was hard to believe that this was the man who had so recently shown all the signs of a nasty temper. He was brief and concise and presently she got up to go. He got up too. 'Have you had breakfast? Nor have I. If Rienieta is still eating hers, I'll see you in the breakfast room in a few minutes.' He opened the door for her as she went past him, put a hand on her arm. 'You look charming, Gemma—you should wear that next time you go out with Leo. Does he know that you are going to Utrecht?'

'No.'

'Would you like me to let him know? I should think you would have an hour or two to spare this afternoon while they're busy with Rienieta, so he could meet you...'

Gemma studied his face. The heavy lids prevented her from seeing his eyes, but he was smiling and she suddenly had the strangest feeling that Leo wasn't quite real, that he didn't matter at all, and if he wanted to meet her again he could find out where she was himself—there was no reason why the professor should do it for him, especially when Leo had said that they disliked each other. 'You don't like him, do you?' she asked.

The lids lifted long enough for her to see how very blue his eyes were. 'My dear girl, what has that to do with it?' he asked.

She shook her head, not quite knowing herself. 'Nothing,' she told him. 'Do you ever find your thoughts in such a muddle that you can't make head or tail of them?'

'Frequently. What has that to do with meeting de Vos?'

'I don't know—that's what I meant about being in a muddle.'

There was a gleam in his eyes, quickly quenched. 'You would like me to telephone him?'

Her 'No, thank you,' was uttered so strongly that the gleam came back again. She went back to Rienieta without saying any more.

He didn't have much to say to her at breakfast; the conversation was general and in any case Gemma ate her meal quickly and excused herself on the grounds of keeping an eye on an excited Rienieta. She went reluctantly, though she was enjoying the family chatter going on around her. The professor got on well with his parents and there was a good deal of laughter—the kind of laughter she could share; it didn't make her feel uneasy like the laughter of Leo's friends.

The professor was driving the Aston Martin. He packed his sister into the back seat and bade Gemma take the seat beside his, explaining that Rienieta would be tired enough by the time they reached Utrecht and if she were on her own, would be more likely to sleep. 'So close your eyes, Rienieta,' he begged her. 'I'll stop for coffee on the way.'

He drove with smooth speed, not saying much. Gemma, peeping at him sideways, saw that his handsome profile looked severe and wondered why. But the idle remarks he addressed to her from time to time were made in his usual good-natured manner, and when they stopped for coffee some miles north of Breda, he carried on a light-hearted conversation with his sister which quite belied the profile. They were in Utrecht soon after that, shepherded straight into the hospital and taken without delay to the private wing on the top floor, where they were met by a Ward Sister, a hovering nurse, a grave young man in a pristine white coat and another young man in a short white jacket.

The professor was greeted with respect and wished the entire party an affable good morning before introducing them briefly: Hoofd Zuster Blom, Zuster van Leen, Doctor Woolff and Doctor Hemstra. He then assured his sister that he would see her shortly, nodded to Gemma and ambled away with various people flying in front of him to open doors. He rewarded their efforts with polite thanks and Gemma found herself smiling; for an important man, and he seemed to be that in the hospital, he was singularly modest in his manner.

Rienieta had a small comfortable room at the end of a long corridor of similar rooms and Gemma had one next to it. There was to be nothing done until Rienieta had rested and had lunch—the professor had primed Gemma about that. She busied herself getting her patient nicely settled in her bed with the magazines her parents had thoughtfully provided, unpacked their few odds and ends and then went back to sit with Rienieta until Zuster Blom stuck her head round the door with the news, in very tolerable English, that Rienieta's lunch was on the way up and if Gemma cared to do so, she could go to the hospital canteen and have a meal herself.

Leaving Rienieta with a dainty meal on a tray and assuring her that she would be only a very short time, Gemma started off down the corridor, through the swing doors at the end and down the stairs as she had been told. She was shy of going to the canteen, for she had no idea whether she paid for her food there or would it be put on Rienieta's bill, and supposing no one spoke English, how could she find out? The professor might have told her, or had he forgotten that she had to eat like anyone else?

She was halfway down the first flight of stairs when she met him, coming up two at a time, to bar her way. 'Hullo,' he said casually. 'I took a chance on you being scared of the lifts, and I was right.'

'I don't even know where the lifts are,' she told

him, faintly peevish with worrying about how to get her lunch. 'I'm on my way to the canteen.'

'That's right—with me.' He had turned and started down the stairs beside her.

She stopped to look at him. 'Oh—but I told Rienieta...'

'Zuster Blom will have told her by now that you're lunching with me—we'll go back together. There's a pleasant little restaurant just round the corner from the hospital.'

He marched her down the remainder of the stairs and out of the hospital entrance and then down a narrow street which opened into a miniature square lined with old houses, most of which were antique shops. The restaurant was small and dim and fairly full, but there was a table in a corner for them and Gemma seated herself with a small sigh of pleasure. The room was panelled in some sort of dark wood and there was a large tiled fireplace and no more than half a dozen tables, each with its stiffly starched tablecloth and well polished silver and glass. It undoubtedly had the edge on the canteen.

'I thought you might be a little shy of being on your own in the canteen,' explained her companion, and Gemma, murmuring suitable thanks, found herself wishing that he had asked her for her company and not out of kindness. 'And I'm not being kind,' he continued, unerringly reading her thoughts so that she coloured faintly. 'I wanted to have lunch with you.'

'Oh,' said Gemma, and regretted her inability to give a clever answer to such a remark; Mandy or Phil would have known exactly what to say. But the professor didn't look as though he expected her to say more, only inquired if she would like sherry and ordered a Jenever for himself. 'They'll start on Rienieta at half past two. I've a full afternoon until five o'clock, so if you wouldn't mind being around? She's scared, though I can't think why, unless she managed to get hold of some medical book or other and read up on all the complications she could have had and didn't. Reassure her if you can. She has complete confidence in you, Gemma—and she likes you.'

'I'll do my best. If she gets the all clear today, will she be able to…that is, you won't want me any more?'

He looked at her over the menu he was studying. 'You want to know when you can return home? Are you so anxious to go?' His eyes narrowed. 'No, how stupid of me, you want to know how much time you have in which to be with de Vos.'

She pinkened. 'It sounds horrid put like that, but I suppose that's what I was thinking.' She added accusingly: 'How selfish you make me out to be!' She glowered at him and he made matters worse by laughing at her.

'Indeed, I had no intention—don't look like that, Gemma. Have you forgotten that I promised you that

I wouldn't stand in your way with de Vos? None of us would.' He assumed a look of concern which she didn't think was genuine. 'Why, only this morning, I offered to telephone him…'

'Yes—well, never mind that now,' she begged him hastily. 'There's really no need for you to bother yourself about me—I'm quite capable…'

'No bother,' he assured her airily. 'You have only to call upon me.' He gave her a bland smile. 'And now what would you like to eat? Have you tried our herrings—one for starters, perhaps and then how about Steak Orloff?'

They didn't talk of Leo again. The professor was a surprisingly good talker when he chose to be and Gemma found herself relaxing under his gentle flow of small talk and the delicious food. She ate it with appetite, rounding off the meal with a plate of *poffertjes* and a large bowl of whipped cream and observing when she had finished, 'That was one of the nicest meals I've ever had.' She looked around her. 'This is a delightful place.'

'There are equally delightful restaurants in all our big cities,' he assured her. 'I daresay that sooner or later you will visit them all,' and before she could challenge this remark: 'I'm afraid that we must go back to the hospital, much as I regret it…'

He was two men, she decided; the placid friendly one who had fetched the sausages for her and hung out the washing to the manner born, and this suave,

elegant host who was so clearly perfectly at home
in exclusive restaurants. It was as they were walking back down the narrow street once more that she
asked: 'What did you mean—that I should visit most
of the restaurants?'

'Just exactly what I said, dear girl, and if that is
another question burning the end of your tongue, let
me assure you in your cryptic English: Wait and see.'

They were going through the hospital doors as
he spoke. He stopped just inside them, nodded to a
group of white-coated young men and women obviously waiting for him, said: 'I shall see you later,
Gemma,' and gave her the gentlest of shoves towards
the stairs. She went at once without a word; this
would be one of his teaching rounds and she knew
better than to delay him.

Rienieta was waiting for her and a little disappointed about not seeing Ross. 'A teaching round,'
explained Gemma cheerfully. 'And now are we all
ready for the first of the tests?' She chattered on
cheerfully, bolstering up Rienieta's spirits with a
nice mixture of elder sisterly advice and professional
know-how so that, by and large, the afternoon went
smoothly enough. By five o'clock everything had
been done and dealt with and the patient was back in
her room, sharing a tray of tea with Gemma.

'I have been good?' she asked. 'I have done what
I was told to do without fuss and not made a nuisance of myself?'

'You've been quite super,' declared Gemma warmly, 'a splendid patient.'

'Then I shall ask for a new dress—I shall tell Papa that you are pleased with me and he will allow me to go to that dear little boutique and choose what I want. I should also like a handbag. I could go to Wessel's—they have the very best...'

The tests were over, but the results wouldn't be known until the next morning; Gemma was relieved that her companion's thoughts were so nicely diverted. The pair of them were deep in discussion as to the merits of calf over suede when the professor walked in.

He received his sister's rapturous greeting with tolerant affection, at once agreed that a new handbag was an absolute necessity, and endeared himself still more to her by offering to take her to Wessel's so that she might choose one. 'Let me see,' he mused, 'I'm free from ten o'clock until about midday—I'll fetch you and bring you back here so that we can learn the results of your tests and so on before Vader gets here.' He sat down and stretched his legs. 'Will that do?'

'Oh, Ross, you are my favorite brother—may I buy exactly what I want?'

'Exactly, *lieveling*. Are you tired?'

Rienieta considered the question. 'Perhaps, a little. Zuster Blom says that I must go to bed early.

Gemma must be tired too, for she has been here all the afternoon.'

Gemma disclaimed all idea of tiredness, however. 'I'm bursting with energy,' she protested. 'I've done nothing all day—I could walk for miles.'

'How providential—perhaps you will take pity on me and keep me company for dinner, and if you're so bent on walking, there is plenty to see in Utrecht and it is a pleasant evening.'

Gemma hesitated. She had hoped—still hoped, that Leo would somehow have heard where she was and come to see her, even if only for a little while. There was nothing much for her to do once Rienieta had been settled for the night and there were nurses enough if she should want anything. 'Always provided, of course, that you have no other engagement,' said the professor slowly.

'Well—no. Actually I haven't. It's very kind of you—if Rienieta doesn't mind…?'

Rienieta yawned to make her emphatic: 'I do not mind, Gemma,' even more emphatic. 'But you do not go at once? You will stay for a little while?'

'I'll be back about seven o'clock,' said her brother, and got to his feet. 'Goodnight, little sister. I'm going to telephone Mama and then I have some work to do.' He strolled to the door. 'Gemma, walk to the stairs with me, will you?'

In the corridor she asked anxiously: 'Is it about Rienieta? Is something wrong?'

'No, and I don't think anything will be—there is every sign that she is completely free of brucellosis, although we can't be positive until the result of the tests. Gemma, will you promise me something? You have been hoping that de Vos might come, have you not? Should he do so, I want you to feel free to spend your evening with him.'

She said awkwardly, taken by surprise: 'I—I don't suppose he will—it was only a silly idea of mine. How did you guess?' She looked away from him. 'Anyway, I couldn't do that. I've just said I'd go out with you, Professor.'

'My name is Ross, I told you that a long time ago, and I should consider myself a very mean-spirited fellow if I held you to your word—I'm a poor substitute for Leo.' His voice was very even.

'You're not!' said Gemma hotly. 'You're not a poor substitute for anyone, ever—you're—you're…'

'Spare my blushes, dear girl, and just give me your promise.'

She promised in a troubled little voice.

Leo arrived at five minutes to seven, as she and the professor were crossing the hospital entrance hall. It was the professor who spoke in a quite unruffled voice.

'Just in time, de Vos,' he observed. 'I was about to take Gemma out to dinner and show her something of the city, but now that you are here, I can feel free to hand her over to you for an hour or so.'

He smiled down at Gemma, who was racking her brains for something to say; it was absolutely marvellous to see Leo, of course, but wasn't the professor giving her up too willingly? She felt vaguely that she was being treated as a parcel, handed from one to the other...perhaps he was relieved to be shot of her. All the same she asked: 'Couldn't you come with us?' and didn't see Leo's quick frown.

The smile widened. 'How kind of you to suggest it, but I have a lecture to prepare and shall welcome the opportunity to do so in peace and quiet.'

He nodded casually at them both and walked back across the hall and into one of the passages leading from it. Gemma watched him go, a prey to mixed feelings. So he wanted peace and quiet, did he? Probably he was overwhelmingly relieved that she should be taken off his hands at the last minute; had merely offered to take her out of kindness. She choked on humiliation and rage, forgetting the promise she had made earlier that evening, and smiled brilliantly at Leo. 'However did you discover that I was here?' she asked.

Leo took her arm. 'I have my spies,' he told her laughingly. 'Let's go somewhere gay and eat, shall we? I'm looking forward to a wonderful evening.'

Gemma agreed quickly, aware that that wasn't quite true; it should have been a wonderful evening, but somehow the professor had spoilt it for her. He was a tiresome man, she told herself, and got into

Leo's car, carrying in her head a vivid picture of
him sitting alone in some dreary room, surrounded
by dry-as-dust books and with no one to talk to. She
had to remind herself that it was sheer imagination
on her part before she could dispel the picture.

CHAPTER SEVEN

GEMMA WAS TAKEN to an Indonesian restaurant in a
semi-basement under one of the lovely old houses
in the heart of the city. It was hung with silk paintings and lighted by paper lanterns, and Leo ordered
a variety of spicy dishes for her to sample. He was at
his most charming, displaying an unexpected interest
in Rienieta and an even greater interest in herself.
He was cheerful too, but it was as though he wanted
her to see that he had a serious side to his character
as well as the lighthearted one he usually displayed.
He listened to her brief account of her day and protested: 'My poor darling, you do have a dull time of
it—absolutely no fun at all!'

She looked uncertain. 'Well, I don't know what
you mean by fun—I've enjoyed it, actually; Rienieta
is a darling, you know, and the family are marvellous.'

'Even Ross?' Leo was half smiling at her in a tender way which made her forget everything and every-

one else. She said: 'Even Ross,' and then remembered how he had been prepared to waste his evening on her. She had been cross about it at the time, but now she felt a pang of pity for him. The picture she had conjured up of him sitting alone with his dreary lecture returned more vividly than before. Try as she might she couldn't quite make herself believe that the professor had no other interest in life but his work.

'What are you thinking about?' asked Leo, and then with narrowed eyes: 'Or who?'

She didn't answer that but said instead: 'I expect to go back to England in a week's time, perhaps less than that.'

He waved the waiter away, and Gemma, who would have liked a dessert after all that spicy food, felt faint annoyance at his action—he could at least have asked her; she couldn't imagine the professor doing that... She didn't pursue the thought as Leo exclaimed: 'I know what I shall do! I shall give a party—a summer evening party—it is a little early in the year to have one, perhaps, but that doesn't matter. We will have supper in the garden room and hang lights outside and everyone can stroll round in the garden, and later we can dance.'

A farewell treat? Gemma thought it might well be and then felt a surge of excitement as he went on: 'Of course, we must see a lot more of each other— when will you be free again?' He frowned. 'We never seem to have more than an hour or two… What about this weekend?'

'Well, nurses don't have weekends when they're on cases, not regular ones…'

He looked amused and she wondered why. 'Oh, never mind—a day perhaps, or even half a day. Surely you're able to manage that?'

She looked doubtful but said that she would try. If Rienieta was pronounced cured, she wouldn't need a nurse any more, only someone to keep a check on her temperature and observe her health for a few more days—anyone in her family could do that, but Gemma thought that the professor might expect her to stay and do it. There was a possibility, a faint one it was true, that Rienieta might become ill again, and he would want to guard against that.

Leo was watching her; he wasn't quite sure of her—not yet, but if he could get her alone for several hours it would be fun to get her to admit that she had fallen in love with him. He was beginning to regret his sudden impulse to attract her. She was a nice enough girl even though she was plain, but like most nice girls he had known, she tended to be quite unexciting; besides, she was a complete stranger to his way of life. It had been amusing at first and his friends had found it good sport… He caught her eye across the table and smiled delightfully at her. 'Let's go somewhere and dance,' he suggested, 'just for an hour.'

He took her to the Holiday Inn, but not even the champagne hc ordered or the excellence of the dance floor deterred her from asking him to be taken back to the hospital after an hour or so. Leo was too clever to show his irritation. He drove her straight there without demur, wished her exactly the right kind of goodnight, displaying just the right amount of eagerness to see her again while at the same time displaying a flattering reluctance to say goodbye. Gemma floated into the hospital, her eyes shining, her world a-glow, and the professor, watching her from the doorway of the consultants' room, noted her flushed cheeks and sparkling eyes and sighed soundlessly.

She was half way across the hall before she turned her head and saw him and stopped to say: 'My goodness, you are up late! Didn't the lecture go well?'

The professor, who never had trouble with the preparation of his lectures, indicated that it had absorbed his evening. He made no effort to move from his lounging position by the door and after a moment's hesitation, Gemma walked across to him, driven by some impulse to tell him about her evening, and at the same time tell him that she was sorry not to have spent it with him. She stopped herself in time, however, for that would have sounded silly, and said baldly: 'We went to an Indonesian restaurant. I wish you had been with us.'

'My dear Gemma, how kind of you to say that, but I hardly think de Vos would agree with you.'

'No—well, perhaps not.' She felt uncomfortable under his steady gaze. 'We went on to a place called the Holiday Inn.'

'You're back early,' he observed mildly.

'It's midnight,' she pointed out, 'and I told Rienieta that I wouldn't be away too long.' She flushed a little. 'I like her.'

'I know that. She's going to miss you—don't be in too much of a hurry to go, Gemma. I know there is no nursing to do, but you are a splendid companion for her and you're giving her back her confidence.'

'I'm glad.'

His voice was smooth. 'You have lost a good deal of free time during the last week or so, haven't you? We must see that you have a couple of days to yourself during the next week.' He smiled thinly. 'I'm sure Leo has asked you for another date.'

She smiled widely. 'Oh, yes—I told him I might have a half day, and he's going to give an evening party. Would you mind if I went to it?'

The professor's lips twisted wryly. 'Why should I mind?'

Somewhere close by the church clocks chimed the half hour and immediately after that there was the sound of quiet feet and rustling—the night nurses were going to first dinner. 'I'd better go,' said Gemma, and felt surprisingly reluctant to do so. She said diffidently: 'I'm truly sorry about this evening, though I expect you were quite glad to have the time to spare for your lecture.'

He agreed gravely, not disclosing the fact that he had scribbled the salient points of it in his abominable scrawl in ten minutes flat and spent the remainder of the evening with his mind totally engrossed in a quite different matter.

'Goodnight, then,' said Gemma.

And 'Goodnight,' said the professor, only he didn't stop there, he caught her close and kissed her so soundly that she had no breath left to do more than utter a squeak of surprise. She was already up the first flight of stairs before remarks suitable to such an occasion began to enter her bewildered head, and by then it was too late to utter them.

She awoke feeling apprehensive about meeting the professor after breakfast; it destroyed her appetite, so that the loss of it drew sympathetic glances and remarks from the nurses in the canteen, and even Rienieta, never the most observant of girls, remarked on her distraite air. 'You are worried?' she wanted to know. 'You look as though you are going to be sick.'

Gemma mumbled about the rich Indonesian food she had eaten and took care to have her back to the door when the professor arrived, but she need not have worried; he wished her a good morning in his usual casual fashion, suggested that they might as well go at once to the shops, and swept both girls into the lift and out into the street. Wessel's shop was close by and the three of them walked the short distance in the morning sunshine, and spent all of half an hour in its luxurious interior while Rienieta hesitated between a variety of handbags. Her brother, showing no signs of impatience, sat at his ease, apparently half asleep, while the two girls weighed up the advantages and disadvantages of the selection spread before them, but presently he suggested that as Rienieta couldn't make up her mind between a green suede shoulder bag and a brown calf model, it might be as well if she had both. A simple solution but a rather expensive one, thought Gemma, who would have liked either one for herself. She tore her eyes from a particularly pretty brown patent leather clutch purse, and found the professor's eyes fastened upon her so intently that in a fever of anxiety that he might feel it incumbent upon him to purchase it for her, she hurried across the shop to examine some quite dreary shopping bags with an air of nonchalance which brought a gleam of amusement to his eyes.

They had coffee before returning to the hospital, at a large, crowded café which the professor had obviously chosen in order to please his sister, who would have stayed there all the morning if he hadn't pointed out goodhumouredly that he had work to do. They gained the hospital in excellent humour, with Gemma quite recovered from her awkward feelings

at seeing him again, and went at once to discover
the results of Rienieta's tests and examination. The
consultant physician they were to see was elderly, a
shade pompous and tiresomely long-winded. He had
a few words with the professor after an exchange of
civilities and the latter came back with a cheerful:
'Well, you're cured, Rienieta! Another few days finding your feet and then back to your studies, my girl.'
He looked at his watch. 'I must be off.' He kissed her
briefly, nodded absently in Gemma's general direction, and disappeared, leaving them to drink more
coffee with Zuster Blom until Doctor Dieperink van
Berhuys arrived to drive them home.

'Well, that's that,' thought Gemma regretfully as
she followed the others to the lift. 'Whatever Ross
says, there's no reason for me to stay for more than
another few days.' She would go back home and
never see Leo again, unless of course he had anything to say to her before she went—there was the
party, and he had suggested that they must meet
again before that. She brightened at the thought and
began to plan what she would wear—something new
would have been nice and she had enough money to
buy a new outfit. On the other hand if she did that,
the washing machine would have to be put off for
months. Besides, she hadn't a job to go to and she
wasn't going to sponge on Cousin Maud. Perhaps
the clothes she had would do.

Leo telephoned that evening. Rienieta had just

gone to bed, tired and overexcited, and Gemma had gone to the library to write a letter home, preparing them for her return. She was half way through it when Ignaas came to tell her that he had put the call through to her there.

'Which day is it to be?' asked Leo. 'The party's at the end of the week and of course you're coming to that, darling, but what about tomorrow? or the day after?'

'The day after, I think—I haven't asked yet. Besides, I think Rienieta should be kept quiet for a day, and if I'm with her…I could be free after lunch.'

'For the rest of the day? Splendid. I'll take you to Amsterdam and show you round. Can you get a key?'

'Get a key? Why?'

He laughed. 'So that you can get in, my darling idiot.'

'But Ignaas never goes to bed before midnight— he told me so. He'll let me in.'

'Midnight? Be your age, Gemma—we'll probably still be in Amsterdam until two or three in the morning.'

'Then I don't think I want to…'

He was quick to lull her thoughts. 'OK, sweetheart, we'll leave in good time and you'll be back in your bed at a respectable hour.'

'Thank you, Leo. What time shall I be ready?'

'You said after lunch? Two o'clock? It's only a hundred and forty kilometres to Amsterdam and a

good road, we'll be able to get up some speed—
'bye for now.'

Gemma slept dreamlessly; life had never been so
wonderful and it looked just as wonderful the next
morning. She and Rienieta went for a leisurely cycle
ride after breakfast, round and about the country
roads running between the green fields. It was warm,
but there was a breeze too, disheveling her hair and
giving her cheeks a nice colour; she could have gone
on for hours, but mindful of Rienieta she suggested
that a visit to the stables to see how the puppies were
might be fun, and her companion agreed eagerly.
They had their coffee, brought by a willing Ignaas, at
the stables with the little beasts tumbling all around
them, and then lay on a convenient pile of hay in
the sun. They were on their way back to the house
when they met Ross, strolling across the lawn to
meet them. Rienieta greeted him with a shout of
pleasure. 'Ross, how lovely! You have never been to
see us so many times for years and years—are you
taking a holiday from your work? Are you staying?'
She went on eagerly: 'We could go out this afternoon—you and me and Gemma?'

He shook his head. '*Lieveling*, I'm on my way to
Brussels and I'm only here for lunch. What have you
been doing with yourself?'

He addressed his sister, but it was Gemma he
looked at.

'We went on our bikes,' Rienieta told him happily, 'and then we played with the puppies, and this afternoon, after I've had a rest, we're going on the lake—Gemma knows how to row...'

'And is Gemma to have no time to herself?'

His sister looked taken aback. 'I don't know.' She looked at Gemma. 'Gemma?'

'Oh, I'm quite content,' said Gemma cheerfully, 'and tomorrow I'm going out after lunch.' And even though the professor showed not a vestige of interest, she went on: 'With Leo—he's taking me to Amsterdam to see the sights. He's promised to bring me back here by midnight.'

The professor glanced at her briefly. 'I'm sure you will enjoy that,' he said formally. 'And now shall we go in to lunch?'

Gemma didn't see him alone again. The Jaguar slid away from the house directly lunch was over and he didn't look back, although he must have seen her standing outside the drawing room windows. She wished vaguely that she was going with him before allowing her thoughts to return to Leo once more.

The next day was glorious. She put on the jersey dress and hoped that Leo wouldn't notice that she had worn it before and was flattered when he cried: 'Hullo, my lovely,' and then felt completely deflated by his: 'You've worn that dress before, haven't you? Haven't you anything else?' Perhaps the look on her face warned him, for he added: 'You look lovely in it anyway.'

Her world was back on an even keel once more; she smiled warmly at him, returned his kiss a little shyly and slid into the seat beside his.

Thinking about it later, she couldn't remember what they had talked about, but they had laughed a lot and Leo had set himself to captivate her with his own particular brand of charm and gaiety. They were in Amsterdam before she realised that they were any-where near it, and she looked about her with interest as he drove through the narrow streets, bustling with life. He had a parking place, he told her smugly— the garage of someone he knew. From there it was only a short walk to the Hotel Doelen, where he had suggested that they might go to the open-air restau-rant and have tea. Gemma would have liked time to stroll through the city and look about her. There was so much to see—quaint houses, quiet canals, tree-lined and ageless, with their floating flower-shops, and fairylike bridges, but Leo hurried her along; ob-viously such things held no novelty for him.

But once they were drinking their tea, she was content enough to sit and watch the world go by and listen to her companion's amusing talk. The nagging thought that while they were sitting there she could have been looking at the Rijksmuseum, Rembrandt's house, the little Museum of Our Lord in the Attic, the royal palace and the Begijnhof, let alone take a trip through the canals on one of the sightseeing boats, clouded her afternoon a little; the sneaking idea that if it had been Ross opposite her instead of Leo, he would have made it his business to ask her what she wanted to do and see and then made sure that she was able to do both was something she firmly refused to think about. She was with Leo and that was all that mattered, and when they had finished their tea and she had hinted that she would like a quick look at the palace and see the Dam Square, she allowed herself to be squashed with an: 'Oh, lord, darling, you can't possibly want to go sightseeing—Tourists…' He shrugged, implying that they were something quite outside his world.

'I'm not a tourist,' protested Gemma, 'and I may never have another chance to see Amsterdam.'

'Don't you worry your pretty head about that.' He took her arm. 'Now we're going to stroll along to the Swarte Schaep and have a drink. We'll eat there later and then visit around…'

'Visit around?'

'You'll see.'

Their meal took a long time. By the time they had had a drink, ordered and then sat down to eat it, it had turned nine o'clock. Dusk, fretted Gemma silently, and she had seen nothing of the city, only the inside of a restaurant and a café. She wasn't going to see more than that for the next hour or so, either; they went first to Le Maxim, where they danced and watched the floor show, a colourful, noisy affair, before they took a taxi to the Bird's Club, where Leo was a member. Gemma was quite out of her depth here, admitting apologetically that it wasn't quite her cup of tea and reminding Leo that it really was time they started back if they were to be at Huis Berhuys round about midnight.

Leo laughed a little then, coaxing her to laugh too. 'Come on, darling,' he said persuasively. 'We're only just beginning to enjoy ourselves—who is to know what time you get back, anyway?'

'Well, Ignaas, for one.'

He dissolved into laughter. 'That old man—he's a servant!'

Uneasiness crept into Gemma's head. Leo hadn't talked quite like that before; perhaps he had had too much to drink. She remembered the small glasses of gin he had tossed off...

'Leo, I'd like to go back now. You promised.'

He agreed with surprising readiness, and during their walk back to the garage where he had left the car, there was nothing in his manner to bear out her suspicions—indeed, he behaved in exactly the way a girl in love would hope for, so that she felt mean for being suspicious, especially when Leo told her how much he was looking forward to their drive back.

They were south of the Moerdijk bridge, with the last village some kilometres behind them and Zeven-bergen about the same distance ahead, when the car's engine coughed, spluttered, stopped, spluttered again and died. Leo swore, pressed the self-starter and with the tiny spark of life which returned, eased the car on to the grass divider between the up and down lanes. 'Have to stay like this,' he muttered. 'I can't possibly get enough power to run her on to the shoulder. There's almost no traffic, anyway.'

'No petrol?' asked Gemma. 'Hard luck, but this is a good place to stop—anything going the other way will pass so close we shall be able to stop them easily.'

Leo glanced at her. She was taking the situation calmly enough; he hadn't planned it quite like this, but the best laid plans and so on… With luck there would be almost no traffic for some hours. The heavy stuff from the south had gone for the day and wouldn't start again until the early morning. He slid an arm along the back of the seat and said coaxingly: 'Don't hate me, Gemma. I had every intention of getting petrol on our way this afternoon and I completely forgot it.'

It didn't enter her head not to believe him. She made a comforting comment and looked at the dashboard clock. It wanted only a few minutes to midnight; she would be late back. 'Is there a garage within walking distance? There was a village…' She couldn't remember how long ago they had passed it. 'How far is it to the next town?'

'Oh, miles away,' said Leo airily, 'and that village we passed is kilometres away now. We'll have to sit it out. I don't mind, we haven't had a chance to talk…'

'All this afternoon and all this evening,' she reminded him.

He laughed softly. 'You funny girl, that wasn't
talking. There's such a lot to say—your future…
You do love me, darling?'

She surprised herself almost as much as she did
him by saying that she didn't know; she said it so
uncertainly that he could be forgiven for assuming
that he was being teased a little, but when he tried to
kiss her she said quickly: 'Please, Leo—I was sure
that I did—at least I think I was sure, and now suddenly, I don't know.'

'Perhaps this will help.' He had produced a bottle
from behind him. 'Champagne, my beauty,' and at
her surprised glance, he added convincingly: 'My
housekeeper has a birthday tomorrow, I was taking it back…'

Gemma's heart warmed at his thoughtfulness.
Perhaps she was being an idiot; after all, she was in
love with him, wasn't she? Only he hadn't said that
he loved her… She said in a practical voice: 'Then
we certainly mustn't drink it. Look, Leo, I must get
back. I'm going to walk to the next village. I might
see a petrol station on the way—one of those self-
service ones.'

'There aren't,' he said positively. 'What's more,
my dear idiot, I'll be surprised if you find anything
in Zevenbergen—and how are you going to manage
about the language?'

'Oh. Well, couldn't you go?'

'And leave you alone? Certainly not! We'll have to stay here until someone comes along.'

'Would they stop? Will that be long, do you think?' She tried not to sound anxious.

'Some hours, I should think. The commercial stuff comes up from Antwerp round about four o'clock...'

She spoke sharply. 'Well, we can't sit here all night.'

'I'm afraid we must, my sweet, so let's make the best of it.'

Gemma looked around her, but there was nothing; the motorway was white under the moon, the flat country stretched away on either side of them and there wasn't a light to be seen. Quite suddenly she didn't feel happy; Leo was wonderful and she adored him, didn't she, so why wasn't she beside herself with joy at the idea of spending a few hours alone with him—and he had said that they had to talk about her future, but all she was really thinking about was getting back to Huis Berhuys.

She said in a voice she strove to keep normal, 'Oh, dear, what are we to do?' and saw the headlights of a car coming towards them—on the fast lane, too, so that it would pass within a few feet of them and couldn't fail to see them. 'Look,' she cried, and now she didn't try to hide the relief in her voice. 'Someone's coming!'

To her surprise Leo made no attempt to get out of the car. 'You'll have to be quick,' she urged him, 'it could go past.'

It didn't. The Jaguar swept to a majestic halt beside them and the professor got out unhurriedly. 'Trouble?' he inquired, and didn't even look at Gemma.

'I'm out of petrol,' Leo told him, and she could hear the rage in his voice and wondered at it.

'I thought it might be that,' said Ross, and added something in Dutch. He looked at Gemma then.

'I'll take you back—get into my car.' He opened the door and helped her out and took her arm, led her to the Jaguar and sat her in the front seat before going back to Leo. Whatever it was he said didn't take him long; he got in beside her, reversed the car and started back the way he had come.

'I've broken the law,' he remarked conversationally, 'turning on a motorway.'

He could break all the laws he liked. 'Leo?' she asked him urgently. 'You've left him...you didn't give him any petrol...'

'There's an all-night garage a couple of minutes from here; I'll get them to go out to him.'

'But Leo said there weren't any.'

'He had probably forgotten,' he said gently, and all at once she wasn't annoyed with him any more, only anxious to explain.

'I'm glad you came—we were wondering what we

should do...' She glanced at his severe profile. 'We left Amsterdam in plenty of time.' She got no answer, so she tried again; 'Were you on your way home?'

'Yes. I called at Huis Berhuys and Ignaas was getting worried, so I decided to come this way—he was afraid that you might have had an accident.'

'Dear Ignaas,' said Gemma, and then exclaimed: 'Oh, my goodness, I never said goodnight to Leo—I do hope he gets home safely.'

'He will.' Ross's voice was bland. 'Did you have a pleasant time in Amsterdam?'

She welcomed his interest; she must have imagined the anger in his voice. She gave him an account of where they had been and added: 'Of course, I should have liked to have seen the city—the old buildings and the palace and a museum or two, but that would have bored Leo.'

'You enjoyed the night club?'

'Well, no, not exactly. I've never been to one before and it was a bit unexpected.'

Her companion gave a rumble of laughter. 'But you have had a taste of night life, haven't you?'

'Yes—but I don't think I'd mind if I didn't go again.'

They were almost there and he slowed the car. 'You are going to Leo's party?'

'Yes, if—if no one minds. He's coming to fetch me and bring me back in good time. It's rather a lot—twice in one week...'

'Ah, but time is running out, is it not, Gemma?' he asked softly, and before she could answer stopped the car outside the house.

Ignaas was waiting. He exchanged a rapid conversation with the professor, made a number of tutting noises and shook his head a good deal and went away to fetch the tray of coffee he produced, if needed, at any time of the day or night. Gemma sat opposite the professor, drinking hers and wishing she could think of something to say. Finally she came out with: 'Did you have a successful time in Brussels?'

'Brussels?' He sounded as though he had never heard of the place and she realised that she need not have attempted to make conversation; he was deep in his own thoughts. Gemma drank her coffee quickly after that, thanked him for bringing her back, apologised for the trouble it had given him, and went to bed. She was tired, but not too tired to know that something, she wasn't sure what, had cast a blight over what should have been a wonderful day. Strangely enough, when she pondered it, it had nothing to do with Leo running out of petrol.

Nobody said a word to her the next morning about her late return; questions were asked as to whether she had enjoyed herself, hopes were expressed that the party would be fun, and that was all. She spent the whole day out of doors with Rienieta, contented in the peace and quiet around her. Leo telephoned in the evening, turning last night's small adventure into a joke, not mentioning Ross at all, and yet Gemma sensed irritation behind his laughing voice. Reaction, she told herself, after last night; he must have been worried…everything would be all right at the party and perhaps they would have time for that talk.

He was in splendid form when he came to fetch her; he praised her pink dress just as though it was a new model he had never seen before, made a lot more jokes about their trip to Amsterdam, and assured her that she was going to have the night of her life.

It certainly seemed like it when they reached his house. It was crammed with girls and men, spilling into the gardens, eating supper at the little tables which had been set up in the large sunroom at the back of the house. Leo stayed with Gemma to begin with and then, when she was asked to dance, disappeared, to reappear presently to take her to a small table well away from the others. 'Supper,' he said smilingly. 'I tried to think of everything you would like to eat. We'll dance again presently, shall we, and then I'll take you round the house.'

She had only drunk one glass of champagne, but she felt a little lightheaded from it. She smiled and said yes and looked at the little dishes of food spread out between them. Everything was going to be all right, the faint unease she had been feeling for days now was fast disappearing. She accepted the glass he offered her, but before she could drink any of its contents, Cor, whom she didn't like very much but who was one of Leo's closest friends, sidled up to the table and bent to mutter in his ear. She saw Leo's faint smile as he listened.

'I'm wanted on the telephone, Gemma. I'll be back—finish that drink and have another, and try some of those bits and pieces...'

She felt very alone sitting there with the tables around her filled with people she didn't know. She ate a prawn vol-au-vent and took a sip of her drink. It tasted of nothing much and she was about to try it for a second time when the professor, materialising from nowhere, took it from her hand. 'I shouldn't,' he said mildly. 'Vodka and champagne don't mix very well. Where's Leo?'

Gemma was so surprised that she couldn't speak for a moment, then she said a little crossly because he threatened to spoil her lovely supper with Leo: 'He had to telephone. He's coming back...'

'Yes? Then take pity on me and stroll in the garden for a minute or two—he'll find you quickly enough.'

She got to her feet unwillingly. 'I didn't expect to see you here—you didn't say you were coming...'

If he found this speech ungracious he gave no sign. 'Er—no. I decided to call in briefly.' He looked around him with a hint of distaste. 'I don't much care for this sort of thing.'

They were in the garden now, a pleasant place and warm in the setting sun. The professor paused at a seat and suggested that they might sit down. 'I've had a busy day,' he confided, and bore out this remark by remaining silent for several moments. Gemma looked around her; probably Leo was looking for her, but she could hardly get up and leave the professor sitting. Besides, his silent company was soothing, although why she should need to be soothed she had no idea. She glanced sideways at him and found his blue eyes on her; even as she looked they assumed a sleepiness which threatened to overcome him at any moment. One couldn't sleep at a party; she began turning over in her mind some suitable topic of conversation.

CHAPTER EIGHT

THE PRIVET HEDGE behind them was thin and high. Gemma became aware of voices, sounding very clear in the quiet evening.

'I shall speak English,'—the voice was a woman's, 'for my French is bad and your Dutch is even worse, my dear. You are enjoying yourself?'

'But of course—such a delightful party, but tell me, what is it which necessitates Leo going away into the house with Cor? And why are they so amused together?'

Gemma wasn't really listening; she was picking nervously at the skirt of her dress, trying to think of something to talk about, since her companion remained so disobligingly silent, but the banality she was about to utter remained unsaid, for the voice, pitched a little higher now, went on: 'It is very amusing—that plain English girl with the funny name and so dull—she does not excite, you understand? Well, Leo and Cor had a bet that Leo would get her to fall for him in less than three weeks, and now today he declared that he had won and they are settling the bet.'

The speaker's unseen companion gave a little laugh. 'She is stupid enough to think that he is in love with her? How can it be possible? She has no looks and she is also plump—besides, she is good.'

Their laughter was in unison and unkind. 'And now what will he do? He surely has no interest in her?'

'Of course not. I told you, he has found it amusing, that is all. He flies to Curaçao tomorrow—he had everything planned very well...'

'He is a wicked one.' Again the unkind little laugh. 'And when this girl discovers...I should like to be there...' There was a faint rustle of skirts. 'Let us go back and see what is happening.'

Gemma listened to the sound of their retreating footsteps. The colour had drained from her face, leaving it white and pinched; not even the evening dusk could conceal its plainness now. She didn't look at her companion, not even when he stood up.

'I shan't keep you a moment,' he told her in a casual, friendly voice, just as though he hadn't heard every word of the disgraceful conversation. 'Will you stay here? I shall be back very shortly.'

Gemma nodded, still not looking at him. She felt sick; to give way to strong hysterics would have been a great relief, to shout and scream and drum her heels on the velvet turf… The professor turned on his heel and made his way to the house, shouldering his way through the noisy groups of people in the drawing room, to cross the hall and enter a small room on its other side. Leo was there, so was Cor, so too were a handful of their friends. He paused to look at them, his pleasant mouth thinned and turned down at its corners, and although he had said nothing at all, the group spread out, leaving Leo more or less alone.

The professor spoke genially. 'Ah, there you are, de Vos. I hear that you are planning to go to Curaçao tomorrow. A pity that you may have to postpone the trip—on account of this.' He stretched a powerful arm and caught Leo by the collar of his jacket and shook him like a rat, then stood him carefully on his feet and knocked him down with a well-placed fist on his jaw. He stood over him for a moment, dusting off his hands while his calm gaze roamed round the room until it lighted on Cor. His arm came out once more. 'You too,' he said gently, and knocked him down as well; then without hurry he nodded unsmilingly at the astonished faces around him and took his way to the sideboard, where he poured whisky into a glass and left the room with it in his hand.

Gemma hadn't moved. When he handed her the glass, she took it, thanking him in a high voice and tossing off its contents with a fine disregard for its potency; indeed, she had no idea what she was drinking—tap water, tea, sulphuric acid, they were all one and the same to her in her agitated state of mind.

Her companion's eyebrows rose, but he said nothing, only sat down beside her and flung a careless arm across her shoulders, and presently when she exclaimed: 'I do feel most peculiar!' he suggested that she should rest her head on his shoulder, something she was glad enough to do, and remained patiently waiting until it was sufficiently clear for her to mutter in a muffled voice: 'I have no idea what to do…'

'Quite simple,' he told her promptly. 'We're going to walk into the house and through the drawing room to the front door, looking the very epitome of gaiety.'

She lifted a still swimming head to look at him. 'I can't,' she declared, her voice peevish with shock and humiliation and sheer misery. 'And I won't.'

With no sign of impatience he reiterated: 'Yes, you will. Where's your pride? Pull yourself together, girl—and where's that phlegm peculiar to the English race? Let them all see that you don't care, that you find it amusing too, in a childish way.' He got up and pulled her to her feet. 'Now stop looking like a whey-faced orphan!'

Gemma's eyes glittered with a fine burst of temper, nicely stoked by far too much whisky—it had made her feel sick again, too, but temper, for the moment at least, was uppermost. 'Don't you call me names!' she said belligerently, and then gulped. 'I still feel very strange…'

'So much the better.' Ross tidied away an end of hair which had blown loose from her neat head and studied her forlorn face. 'Now come along. You don't need to say a word, just smile—laugh if you can; it will only be for a couple of minutes.'

They were almost at the door when her steps slowed. 'I don't think...'

'Good—thinking won't help at the moment; it's action we need.'

'But supposing we meet Leo?'

The professor allowed himself a faint smile. 'I don't think we shall.' He was ushering her into the crowded room and she muttered fiercely:

'I don't want to...'

He cut her short: 'I know what you're going to say: Set foot in this house again. Well, there's no reason why you should, in fact, I'll promise you that you shan't. Now smile.'

It was a command; Gemma did as she was told, and when he paused to exchange pleasantries with a few of the guests, she laughed too. He said his good-byes as they went, taking his time, while all the time he had her arm firmly tucked into his.

He had said a couple of minutes; it seemed like hours. The open door with the grand sweep of garden beyond became a symbol of escape, the sight of his car filled Gemma with relief. They were in it, driving through the gates and away down the narrow road, when she said urgently:

'I think I'm going to be sick.'

'Only to be expected,' his voice was brisk, 'after all that whisky you tossed off.' He pulled up and leaned across and opened her door for her. 'Shout if you want any help!'

There was a convenient ditch, its steep grass bank running down to clear water. She sank on to the grass and endured the miseries of the moment.

Ross fastened her seat belt when she got back into the car, offered her a large white handkerchief and remarked matter-of-factly that a cup of coffee would be just the thing. 'There's a café down the road, we'll stop.' He shot her a quick, all-seeing glance. 'Did you get anything to eat?'

She shook her head, remembering the daintily arranged dishes of delicious food which had been on the table where she had sat with Leo. She burst into tears and heard Ross say: 'Nor did I. I daresay we can get a *broodje*.' He drove on, taking no notice of her sniffing and snorting into his handkerchief, feeling vaguely resentful because he didn't seem to care in the least that her heart was broken and she was utterly desperate.

The café was open, almost full and poorly lighted in the deepening dusk, so that Gemma's face was hardly noticeable. She was walked inside, with Ross exchanging cheerful good evenings with the other customers as he led her to an empty table in one corner.

It was surprising what two cups of coffee and a cheese roll did for her outraged feelings, outwardly at least. She replied politely to her companion's desultory conversation, and looked around her, her face calm now, although inside her, her unhappiness was so deep and real that she could feel its weight on her chest. She had finished her second cup when the professor asked: 'Do you want to make plans? Talk? Run away?'

Her chin went up. 'I should like to go back home this very instant,' she told him forcefully, 'but I won't do that—I can't, can I? Just to walk out on Rienieta like that, and your mother and father have been so kind to me—but perhaps they would let me leave in a week's time. She could get someone else by then if she wanted to, I expect.' She paused: 'Would that be long enough?'

He knew exactly what she meant. 'To let Leo and his friends realise that you hadn't been scared away? Oh, yes, and we'll go one better than that. I'll take you out and about so that they will be forced to conclude that his boast was an empty one; that you had been having fun at his expense.' He stared at her so hard that she waited expectantly for him to go on talking, but he only smiled again.

'You're kind,' she told him, her face a little flushed, 'but wouldn't that be a bore for you?'

His mouth twitched. 'Not in the least—I enjoy the occasional evening out.'

'Yes, but not with me...'

The twitch became a smile. 'All the more reason to do so at the earliest opportunity, Gemma. Tomorrow evening—I'll call for you about seven o'clock—and wear that dress, it's pretty.'

Even in her unhappiness, his remark pleased her. 'Yes, well, thank you—if you're sure.' Her eyes, puffy with her weeping, searched his face. 'Why are you doing this?' she wanted to know.

'We're old friends,' he spoke without hesitation, 'not in terms of time, perhaps, but we've done a good deal together, haven't we? And friends help each other.'

It was a nice, uncomplicated answer, and looked at from all angles, it made sense. She nodded. 'It's only for a week,' she reflected aloud, quite failing to see the gleam in his eyes, 'then I shall go home and forget all about it.' She spoke in a wooden voice: forgetting would be hard, it would be like going back into another world. She would have to get a job quickly; perhaps it would be wiser to work in London after all—the future looked empty and dull and she swallowed the knot of despair which was threatening to choke her. She heard Ross say in a comfortable voice: 'Of course you can go home— remind me to see about a seat on a plane for you, but shall we take things a day at a time?' He lifted a finger to the boy who had served them. 'If you're ready to go?'

Somehow—Gemma wasn't sure how—he had

turned the miserable evening into a commonplace incident hardly worth mentioning. Indeed, he said not another word about it but saw her safely into Huis Berhuys, and then got back into his car and drove away with a friendly wave. She stood in the flower-scented quiet of the dim hall and listened to the whine of the car's engine getting fainter and fainter. She felt very lonely.

She didn't sleep at all; the evening's events paraded themselves remorselessly before her resolutely closed eyes, so that when she appeared at the breakfast table, she looked quite dreadfully pale, and the tears she had shed and hadn't bothered to mop had puffed her eyelids and reddened her nose. All the same, she was as neat and composed as she always was and her good morning to Mevrouw Dieperink van Berhuys was just as cheerful as it normally was. 'Rienieta is awake,' she informed that young lady's mother—'she had a very good night and she looks super this morning—she's famished too—she's just about one hundred per cent again. Shall I go to the kitchen and ask Ria to take up her breakfast?'

The lady of the house gave her a brief, smiling glance which saw everything. 'Please, my dear— how wonderful it is to have the dear child well again.' She busied herself with the coffee pot. 'Was it a good party?'

'Yes, thank you.' Gemma took the cup she was

handed and made rather a business of choosing a roll from the basket before her.

The older lady helped herself to cherry jam and went on conversationally: 'I'm told that Leo gives splendid parties, though I don't care much for his friends. Did he bring you home?'

'No. Ross did—he was at the party too.'

'Indeed?' Mevrouw Dieperink van Berhuys' face and voice expressed a convincing surprise, all the more remarkable by reason of the fact that she had had a long telephone conversation with her eldest son not half an hour previously. But Gemma didn't know that; she was busy turning over in her tired mind how best to introduce the subject of her leaving. She had her chance when her companion made some observation about her daughter's splendid progress.

'I wondered,' began Gemma, taking the bull by the horns, 'if she would be needing me much longer—she's really well now...'

'Thanks to you, Gemma. And much as we shall all be sorry to see you go, we mustn't be selfish. I don't know if you have anything in mind, but my sister—the one who lives in Friesland, you know—is coming down this weekend and she particularly asked if Rienieta might go back with her. She would have her cousins for company and ride and sail to her heart's content. What do you think about that?'

Gemma, in a black mood, had anticipated all kinds of difficulties; now there were none at all. She said now: 'I think it sounds marvellous, but I expect the doctor will decide. It's not for me…'

'He will be coming this afternoon.' Mevrouw Die-perink van Berhuys was quick to see the surprise on Gemma's face and went on smoothly: 'Yes, I know he isn't due to come for a few days, but he is going away. Could Rienieta be in the house after lunch so that he can take a final look at her?'

'Yes, of course, *mevrouw*. She wants to go on the lake and it's a lovely morning. When she's tired of that we could go for a stroll.'

The morning dragged. Gemma, bearing Rienieta company while they pottered on the lake, wandered in the gardens and went yet again to see how the puppies fared, began to feel that it would never be lunch time even while she was aware that the day was beautiful, as were her surroundings, and that normally her contentment would have been complete, but the thought of Leo nagged like a bad toothache. Perhaps it would be easier to forget him once she was back in England and working hard—she wondered if she would forget everyone else too; she would miss them all, especially would she miss Ross. The thought reminded her that she hadn't said anything about him coming to take her out that evening. She did so after lunch, still too unhappy to do more than wonder at his mother's placid acceptance of her news, and her soothing: 'That will be nice, my dear—you haven't been out nearly enough.'

'I went to a party yesterday,' Gemma pointed out. It seemed like years ago.

'Oh, a party.' The older lady's tone implied that she considered that the party in question hadn't been much of a treat. 'A great many gabbling young women,' she observed in her pretty voice, 'criticising each other's clothes and young men with long hair who talk about themselves.'

Gemma laughed despite herself. 'Oh, dear—it was a bit like that, but I thought it was just me; I don't go to grand parties like that at home.'

'There are parties and parties, Gemma. I have no doubt that you will enjoy a pleasant evening with Ross.'

And as it turned out, she did. He arrived a little early, so that when she got downstairs, wearing the pink dress and with her hair and face carefully dealt with, it was to find him sitting with his mother and father in the drawing room, but he got up to meet her as she went in and took her hands in his and held her arms wide. 'Very nice,' he commented in a voice which could have been an elder brother's, 'and delightfully punctual. Shall we go?'

He bade his parents goodbye, made some light-hearted remark about bringing Gemma back safely, and accompanied her out to the car. He drove off at once and without giving her time to speak, said: 'We're going to den Haag—or rather, Wassenaar—there's a dinner dance at Kasteel oud Wassenaar and

A GEM OF A GIRL

I happen to know that quite a few of the people who were at the party last night will be there. It's an hour and a half's drive if we get a clear run past Rotterdam. Have a nap if you would like that.'

Gemma was conscious that her day had taken a turn for the better. 'I'd rather talk, if you don't mind. You live in Vianen, don't you? Would you tell me about it? Is your practice there?'

'I don't live in Vianen itself but in a small village close by—I've consulting rooms in Utrecht and Vianen and I sometimes see patients at my home.'

She plunged rather feverishly into more questions; it was a welcome change from her unhappy thoughts. 'Don't you wish you could live at Huis Berhuys—it's so lovely there.'

He sent the car surging along the broad, straight road. 'Oh, very often, but you see eventually it will be mine and I shall live in it as head of the family, but not, I hope, for a great many years. Until then I'm very content and the hospital is a fine one, did you not think so?' He discussed it at some length, giving her no chance to ask any more questions.

It struck her then that she would never see his home; she would be leaving Holland very soon now, although he was taking her out it was to stop her being made to look a fool by Leo's friends, not because he wanted to admit her to his private life. Vague regret stirred within her as she listened politely to his description of the new wing which had just been added to the hospital; he was a good talker and she found herself interested despite her preoccupation with her own worries, and presently she forgot them sufficiently to join in a lively argument about hospital management. It lasted until they reached the outskirts of den Haag, and before she had time to feel nervous, he was slowing the car outside the hotel's imposing entrance.

He had been quite right, and she recognised several of the faces turned towards them as they were led to the table Ross had reserved. And it wasn't in a discreet corner, she noted vexedly, but well within the view of most of the crowded restaurant. She assumed what she hoped was a carefree expression and sat down. Ross must have noticed the interest they had aroused too, for his hand came down gently on hers lying on the table between them, and pressed it very slightly. Gemma took it as a gesture of encouragement, although any of those watching them so discreetly might be forgiven for thinking otherwise. He withdrew the hand almost immediately and she wanted to clutch it back again because somehow it made her feel better, but he was asking her what she would like to drink and then there was the business of choosing from the enormous menu.

Until she looked at it she hadn't realised how hungry she was—she hadn't eaten much all day, but now peckishness was temporarily outweighing unhappiness. She decided on hors d'oeuvres, followed by

salmon poached in white wine, which she ate to the
accompaniment of her companion's pleasantly amusing conversation; indeed, she found herself joining
in quite gaily, and presently forgot the carefully casual glances sent in their direction. She finished her
delectable meal with a lemon syllabub, drank down
the rest of the wine in her glass and jumped up readily enough when the professor suggested she might
like to dance. She danced well, she knew that without being conceited about it; the knowledge, coupled
with the excellent Sauternes with which Ross had
filled her glass, added a sparkle which gave the lie
to any speculation and gossip among Leo's friends.
Here, apparently, was no heartbroken girl; anyone
less heartbroken would be hard to find. Leo had been
taken for a ride, they told each other, and Ross, seeing everything without appearing to do so, was well
satisfied.

The evening flew by, and it was Gemma who
pointed out that they should really leave. 'For we
shan't be back before one o'clock as it is,' she observed, 'and I daresay you have appointments for
the morning.'

Ross had looked faintly amused and agreed so
readily that she wondered if he had been bored; he
hadn't appeared to be, but then he had such good
manners that he would never allow boredom to show.
Her conversation, she remembered uneasily, hadn't
been in the least amusing, which wouldn't have

mattered so much if she had been pretty enough for every man in the room to envy him. This reflection had the effect of rendering her almost silent during their drive back, and any remarks she did achieve were wooden observations about the band and the hotel. Even her thanks, when they arrived at Huis Berhuys, sounded stiff in her own ears, and his conventional reply did nothing to make her feel easier on that score, so that she was surprised when he got out of the car to help her out and then accompanied her indoors. 'There will be coffee in the library,' he told her, and led the way there.

She watched him pouring the coffee from a thermos jug. He looked calm and placid and not in the least tired, and he was undeniably handsome in the soft lamplight. 'Are you spending the night here?' she asked him.

He gave her her cup and sat down opposite her. 'No—I'd like to, but I've a number of patients to see at the hospital in the morning.'

She glanced at the small gilt carriage clock on its wall bracket. 'But it's awfully late.'

'The road will be almost empty at this time of night—I shall be home in an hour or so.' He smiled at her. 'I have tickets for the ballet at den Haag tomorrow evening—will you come?' And when she hesitated: 'It might be a good idea—this evening was a great success. I can imagine the telephone conver-

sations in the morning.' He added deliberately: 'Leo
will be told every smallest detail.'

Gemma swallowed. 'I—I thought he had gone
to Curaçao.'

'He has been delayed,' said the professor gently.
'A question of his front teeth…'

She gave him a puzzled look. 'Front teeth?'

'He lost them yesterday—I knocked them out.'

'You did? Oh, how very kind of you,' declared
Gemma with such enthusiasm that her companion's
eyes glinted with amusement. 'It's just the sort of
thing my brothers would have done.'

'Think nothing of it,' Ross begged. 'It gave me
great satisfaction. I hope you will forgive me when
I say that it is something I have wished to do for
some time.'

'Oh, well, yes—I gave you a good excuse, didn't
I?' She could hear her voice, brittle with false cheerfulness and ready to crack at any moment. She put
her cup down and sat looking at it until he said:
'Well, I suppose I must be going. Will you lock the
door after me?'

Gemma turned the ponderous key in its lock and
shot the bolts and listened to the squeal of the tyres
as he turned the car at the gates. Without him, her
thoughts became gloomy once more, but she was too
tired to pursue them. She went up to bed, her head a
fine muddle of smart restaurants, missing front teeth
and what she should wear to the ballet.

She had expected not to sleep, but awoke to find the sun streaming in through her bedroom window and Ria standing by the bed with her morning tea. She was one day nearer home, and hard on that waking thought came the one that she would like to stay for ever at Huis Berhuys, wrapped in its peace and security—and that was nonsense, she told herself roundly; what about George and the others and her career? She drank her tea, then jumped out of bed and went along to see how Rienieta was feeling. She was awake and excited at the prospect of a visit to Friesland, so much so that beyond a casual inquiry as to Gemma's evening out, she showed no interest in the subject.

The two of them spent the day out of doors and friends came in the afternoon to join them, and it wasn't until she went to her room to change for the evening that Gemma realized that she hadn't thought about Leo all day—she hadn't had the chance, but somewhere deep inside her she was unhappy, and that unhappiness was made worse when she remembered that she would be leaving Holland in a very few days now. It was no good brooding, she told herself, and self-pity never helped anyone. She would have to grin and bear it until time rubbed it out.

She wore a cream wild silk dress; it wasn't new, but it suited her and its very simplicity rendered it more or less dateless; she hadn't worn it when she had gone out with Leo because it was quite obviously last year's dress and he was observant of such things, but now no one was likely to notice her appearance. She was wrong, for Ross noticed; he came to meet her as she went downstairs and said at once: 'That's nice—and eye-catching.'

Gemma paused to look at him. 'Eye-catching? Oh, I thought…it's not in the least fashionable, you know. It's last year's—I thought no one would notice…' Her voice tailed away under his amused look. 'That sounds awfully rude, as though it doesn't matter what I wear when I'm with you. I didn't mean that.'

'I know what you meant, Gemma. All the same, it's attractive, and we want people to notice you, don't we? We have to keep up the good work, don't we?'

'Yes—yes, of course.' She came down off the stairs and walked to the door with him. 'I suppose you haven't heard…?' Her voice died away and she wouldn't look at him.

'If Leo has been told about our dinner together? No, but then I've been at the hospital all day. But I imagine it highly probable that he has.'

The Koninklijke Schouwburg was packed and they took their seats with only a few moments to spare, which meant that they came under the eyes of those already seated around them. Gemma, conscious of the glances cast in their direction, nonetheless assumed an unconcerned leisurely progress which earned her a whispered word of praise from her companion. 'Good girl—that was very well done,' he said low-voiced in her ear as she sat down, 'and don't look round, but that girl with the teeth who looks like a tent pole is sitting two rows behind us— you remember her?'

Gemma remembered—Lise someone or other, who had sneered at the pink dress. A little thrill of childish pleasure because Ross had called her a tent pole ran through her and she smiled up at him and was disconcerted to meet the unsmiling penetrating look in his eyes; but only for a second, the next moment he was smiling again.

She watched the performance with every sign of interest, not really seeing it at all, her thoughts busy. Surely Leo would have been told by now, and what had he thought? Would he be furious at her apparent turning of the tables on him, or might the whole thing have sparked off a real interest in her in place of the feeling he had pretended so well? Her hands clenched in her lap, as she remembered how well he had done that, and were instantly covered by Ross's large firm hand, and she threw him a grateful glance before concentrating on the stage, this time in earnest.

It wasn't until he was preparing to go after they had returned to Huis Berhuys that he mentioned casually that he had arranged her flight for her. 'I'll let you have the ticket tomorrow,' and when she looked at him questioningly: 'Mama is taking Rienieta shopping tomorrow afternoon; I'll come over for you about two o'clock.' He barely gave her time to agree and thank him for her evening before his own quiet goodnight. She bolted the door after him as she had done on the previous night and felt a faint stir of excitement at seeing him again. He hadn't said where they were going—perhaps to some other public place where Leo's friends would see them; by now surely they would have all realised that Leo's bet had misfired, but perhaps he wanted to make quite certain. Certainly his plan had helped. She no longer felt so humiliated, and Leo would never know now whether she had fallen for him or had been playing his own game. She sighed. Falling in love hadn't been at all what she had expected. She sighed again and went to sleep.

It was raining by lunch time on the following day; Rienieta and her mother went off, driven by her father in the big BMW, and Gemma went to get her raincoat and a scarf for her hair. Not knowing where she was going, she had put on the Jaeger skirt and the coral jumper and a pair of light shoes, and now she looked at herself in the glass and hoped that she would do.

She was too early, but she might as well go downstairs and wait for Ross. He was already there, sitting in the hall, reading a paper. He got up as she went towards him, cast the paper down untidily on to a chair and opened the door on to the driving rain outside. His greeting had been friendly and he made some casual remark about the weather as they got into the car. It wasn't until Gemma asked him where they were going and expressed the hope that she was suitably dressed that he said: 'I thought we would go to my house and then take a look at Vianen.' He glanced sideways at her. 'You look very nice—you always do.'

She felt grateful for his kindness; somehow he always conveyed the impression that she was the kind of girl any man would enjoy taking out, and what was more, she was beginning to believe him. She settled back beside him, already happier. 'I looked up Vianen this morning,' she told him. 'Rienieta was telling me about it, you see, and I wanted to know about the gateways and the Counts of Brederode and the medieval town hall…are there a lot of tourists there in the summer?'

'Very few, thank heavens. We'll take the motorway, I think, and come back through the country.'

'I forgot to ask your mother at what time she would like me to be back.'

'I said that we'd be back in time for dinner—there's no hurry, is there, and Rienieta's shopping expeditions are time-consuming events, no one will be home before seven o'clock. How well she looks now—you have done her a lot of good, Gemma.'

'Thank you, but I haven't done much, you know. She's a dear, and I'm glad she's quite well again.'

'So am I. She's my father's darling, being the youngest—she's everyone's darling, I think—rather like George...'

There was so much to talk about; the journey seemed to Gemma to be too short, and she was surprised when Ross said: 'We turn off here. Vianen is another kilometre or so ahead of us; the village is at the end of this lane.'

She hadn't known what to expect, certainly not the delightful house fronting the village square, its ponderous door reached by a double flight of steps, its enormous windows gleaming in the sudden burst of sunshine after the rain. It was flanked by an archway leading to a narrow cobbled lane on one side of it, and the other was hedged off by a high brick wall with a nail-studded door in its centre.

Ross stopped the car at the bottom of the steps, said: 'Here we are,' and opened her door.

'Well,' said Gemma, a little breathlessly, 'I had no idea—I mean, I thought you would have a flat or a little house. This is—is...' Words failed her and her companion smiled.

'It was my grandfather's house, and his father's before him. Over the years it has been the custom for the eldest son to take possession when he's of age. Come in.'

The door opened under his hand and they went into the long, narrow, high-ceilinged hall, with its traditional black-and-white tiled floor, its panelled walls and a number of arched doorways on either side. Before he had closed the door, a large, stout woman came sailing down the hall with cluckings of delight and cries of welcome. Reaching them, she clasped her hands across her vast waist, eyed Gemma with small, bright blue eyes, and allowed her strong features to break into a smile.

'This is my housekeeper, Ortje,' said Ross. 'She's from Friesland and married to my gardener. Her niece is the housemaid—all very cosy and convenient for all of us.' He said something to Ortje, who chuckled richly, and when Gemma put out a hand, wrung it briskly and broke into a spate of words.

'Oh, dear,' exclaimed Gemma, 'what a handicap it is not understanding a word! Please will you tell her I'm very glad to meet her?'

The professor said something else and his housekeeper shook with laughter as she led the way to one of the closed doors and threw it open. The room they entered was charming; a combination of muted colours which blended very nicely with the thick patterned carpet underfoot. The walls were patterned too with some sort of silk hanging and hung with paintings under an ornate plaster ceiling. Gemma took the chair she was offered and looked around her. 'It's quite beautiful,' she exclaimed. 'Is your consulting room here too?'

'On the other side of the hall; it can be reached

from the door at the side without coming into the house.'

'Was your grandfather a doctor too?'

'Oh, yes, and his father and grandfather before him. We will take a look round presently if you would like that and I'll take you to Vianen before tea—it's not large.'

The rest of the house was beautiful too, its rooms high-ceilinged and furnished with a restrained elegance and comfort which Gemma loved, and presently they wandered out to the car again and drove to Vianen, where Gemma was taken to see the Lekpoort and the Hofpoort and then to view the magnificent town hall while the professor gave her a brisk précis of its history. She asked him anxiously once or twice if he didn't find it tiresome to take her sightseeing, but he seemed to be enjoying it as much as she was, and later, when she had seen everything, he took her back to his house and they had their tea by the open sitting room window, taking advantage of the now brilliant sunshine. And when it was time to go, Gemma got up with a reluctance which caused the professor to hide a small satisfied smile. She wasn't sure now if it wouldn't have been better if she hadn't visited his house, for then she wouldn't have minded leaving it. And she did mind; she craned her neck for a last glimpse of it as they drove away and Ross said: 'You like it, don't you?'

'Yes. I like Huis Berhuys, but now I've seen your house, and I like it even better.'

Her companion smiled and said nothing, and Gemma, her head full of the afternoon's pleasure, was content to sit quietly until he said: 'I'm going off the motorway here and on to the Dordrecht road, we'll skirt the town and take the road to Willemstad.' He had left the motorway as he spoke. 'There's a map in the side pocket if you want to see where you are.'

She studied it carefully, asking a lot of questions and mispronouncing the names of the towns quite dreadfully. There was plenty to talk about, and they were back, she discovered, long before she wanted to be.

Most of the family were in the house when they went in. Dinner was a gay meal with a great deal of laughter and talk. Gemma looked round the table and knew that whatever else she forgot, she would never forget any of them. She caught Ross looking at her and smiled. She wouldn't forget him either. He had understood how she had felt about Leo; without his help she would never have got through the last few days. For the first time since the party, she slept deep and long.

There were two days left, she told herself when she woke up the next morning, and it didn't seem possible, and today Ross wasn't coming. He had said that he had to go to Amsterdam and didn't expect to be back until late in the evening, and after today there would be only one day left. She had been booked on a late morning flight from Schiphol and she tried not to think about it, and was succeeding very well until Mevrouw Dieperink van Berhuys told her that there was to be a family lunch party the next day and of course she would join the family. 'Such a pity Ross can't come,' said his mother, and shot a glance at Gemma's face, which, did she but know it, registered disappointment.

There were a great many guests—aunts and uncles and cousins, the latter all looking very alike, so that Gemma kept thinking that Ross had come after all. The girl cousins were pretty and there was a sprinkling of children and one very old lady with white hair and black eyes. She had a deep booming voice and held a silver-handled ebony stick which, as far as Gemma could see, she used, not to walk with, but to prod various members of her family when she wished to attract their attention. Gemma, feeling shy, was handed briskly round the family until at last she found herself standing in front of the old lady.

'Our great-aunt,' said the cousin, so very like Ross, who was escorting her. 'Barones Berhuys van Petterinck.'

His venerable relation adjusted her spectacles and took a good look at Gemma. 'Nice figure,' she pronounced in penetrating English, 'a *jolie laide*, I see— she'll pay for dressing. Come here, child, where I can see you properly.'

Gemma advanced a few steps. Her 'How do you do, Barones,' was politely uttered despite the old lady's remarks, and she was rewarded by 'Nice manners, too.' Her interrogator patted the chair beside her and waved the nephew away. 'Sit down and tell me about yourself,' she commanded, and Gemma patiently answered the sharp questions put to her until lunch was announced and she was able to slip away to her own place at the table between two cheerful young men whose conversation kept her chuckling throughout the meal.

It was a glorious afternoon; lunch eaten, the whole party scattered into small groups, the elderlies to the drawing room, where they unashamedly took refreshing naps, the younger ones out into the garden and the children to the stables to see the puppies. And because, despite everyone's niceness to her, Gemma still felt shy, she took charge of the children, still small enough to control despite her lack of Dutch. She led the party down to the charming little lake when the puppies palled, and it was here that Ross joined them. 'Got landed with the brats?' he asked cheerfully, and was drowned by the vociferous welcome from the smaller members of the party.

When it was a little more peaceful, Gemma said: 'Your mother said you wouldn't be coming.'

'To the lunch party, no. Do you find my family overpowering?'

'No, not at all. They're all charming.'

'And does that include Great-Aunt Rienieta?'

'The very old lady with the stick? She's gorgeous.'

'Was she outrageous? She's noted for her outspokenness.'

'She called me a *jolie laide*, which is so much nicer than being told that one is plain.'

Ross put his head on one side and took a long look at her. 'There is a difference, you know.' His voice was very deliberate, his eyes on her face. 'No looks, wasn't it—too plump and far too good.'

She went a very bright pink. 'There's no need...' she began.

'Oh yes, there is, even if it's only to make you see that you mustn't always believe what you hear. What you are, in actual fact, is *jolie laide*, just as Great-Aunt said, and although this may surprise you, men like plump girls—they like good girls too, Gemma, and don't you forget that.'

He turned away to toss a very small girl high in the air and sit her on his shoulder. 'We are all bidden to drink tea in the drawing room.' He added something in his own language to the moppet on his shoulder, who giggled and shrieked as they went up to the house. The children liked him; he should have married and had children of his own, thought Gemma, trying to keep up to his long stride. Before she could curb her tongue she voiced the thought out loud, then went scarlet and said: 'Oh, I do beg your pardon!'

He had stopped to look at her. 'That's exactly what Great-Aunt has told me a hundred times, and when I told her the other day that I intended to take her advice, she was for once speechless.'

All Gemma could think of to say to that was 'Oh!'

She didn't see him to speak to alone after that. He went away again after tea and they said their good-byes in the middle of a chattering group of cousins. 'I'll drive you to Schiphol,' he told her carelessly. 'The news will get around and there's always some-one coming or going there—a last gesture, don't you think?'

'There's no need...' she began.

'I have to go to Amsterdam,' he told her coolly.

He had been right again. There was someone there—Cor, standing with the beanpole, probably waiting for someone. Cor pretended not to see them, but the beanpole nodded coldly and Gemma managed to smile, terrified to look round her in case Leo was there too.

'He's not,' said Ross softly. 'I happen to know that he's in a clinic having some new front teeth put in.' 'Oh,' said Gemma, and then caught her breath as he went on: 'He'll have to be quick about it, he's getting married in Curaçao next week.'

She let out the breath she had been holding and said very crossly: 'Why did you have to tell me that now—and here, too?'

'It seemed a good place.' His voice was mild. 'If we'd been on our own you would probably have burst into tears and flung yourself on my shoulder. You can't very well do that here.'

She had to admit that there was sense in this re-mark, although she took exception to his dislike of having her head on his shoulder; he need not have said that. She said, still crossly: 'You need have no fear of that; I'm not in the habit of flinging myself at you or...' She bit her lip, remembering Leo; she hadn't flung herself at him, but she must have done something very like it, because he had felt so sure of her, hadn't he? She swallowed and looked at Ross, who was looking at her with no expression at all. She heard a voice calling her flight and was thank-ful for it, for she had no idea what to talk about any more. Now she was able to exclaim in a bright voice: 'Oh, I have to go, don't I?' She tried to sound pleased and eager.

She put out a hand and he took it. He took the other one too and pulled her to him and kissed her hard and long. Cor and the girl must be watching, Gemma thought confusedly, and kissed him back.

She joined the queue without looking back at him, and her muttered goodbye was so low that he could scarcely have heard it.

CHAPTER NINE

THE JOURNEY WENT smoothly, which gave Gemma no
reason for the feeling of gloom which slowly envel-
oped her, and it wasn't Leo who filled her thoughts;
it was the memory of Ross's hand crushing hers in
a gentle grip—and his kiss. She had been an em-
barrassment and a nuisance to him, and her heart
warmed at the remembrance of his help when she had
needed it most, and the time and trouble he had spent
on taking her out during those last few days, especially after what he had told her. She hadn't thought
about it much, but if he was about to be married, he
must be relieved to see the back of her. She felt so
forlorn at the idea that she picked up the magazine
on her lap and made herself read it until the plane
touched down at Heathrow. She went through the
Customs and boarded the bus to London without really noticing what she was doing, for nothing seemed
quite real any more; it was like having a bad dream,
only she didn't seem able to wake up from it.

It was when she was standing in the queue waiting for a bus to Waterloo station that the explanation of her gloom struck her with all the force of a thunderbolt. It was Ross, not Leo, whom she couldn't bear to leave, and it was he, and not Leo, whom she loved—had loved all the time; she knew that now with all the clarity of hindsight.

She stood there, unable to think of anything else, while the more unscrupulous of those behind her edged past to take her place in the swelling queue. She didn't notice—indeed two buses came and went before she roused herself to board the third. She had to queue again at the station for a train which wouldn't leave for the best part of an hour, but she didn't notice that either. Anyway, what did it matter if she missed a train—nothing mattered now; she was never going to see Ross again, and she didn't know how she was going to bear it.

She arrived home at last, her head an aching jumble of regrets and far-fetched ideas about meeting Ross again, although none of them really held water, and what would be the use if he was about to get married?

She went through the open gate and up the path and in through the door standing ajar. There were voices coming from the sitting room; she opened the door and went in.

Everyone was there—the entire family—and with

them, standing with his back to the empty fireplace and looking very much at home, was Ross.

Gemma dropped the bag she was carrying from suddenly nerveless fingers and gulped back the heart which had somehow got into her throat. 'Ross?' she said in a funny, dry little voice.

There was movement around her. She was aware of the family trooping out, grinning delightedly but saying nothing. When they had all gone: 'You silly darling girl,' said Ross, 'I was beginning to think that you would never know, and then at the very last moment when I kissed you goodbye...but you didn't quite know then, did you?'

'No,' whispered Gemma, 'it wasn't until I was in the bus queue. How did you get here?'

'I chartered a plane.'

Her eyes flew wide open. 'Ross—a whole plane!' She looked down at her feet and mumbled: 'I didn't know, it's so silly, but I didn't...'

'Know that you loved me and that I loved you?' he finished for her. 'I know you didn't, dear love, that's why it seemed a good idea to get here first, just in case you didn't discover it on your way here.' He added: 'My dear muddle-headed darling.' His arms, wrapped around her, felt hard and strong but tender too.

She muttered into his jacket: 'But you heard what they said—I'm plain and—and I don't excite...'

She felt him shake with laughter, but she wasn't

allowed to say any more, for he kissed her breathless and then put a hand under her chin to look into her eyes. 'You are my own beautiful girl,' he told her with satisfying conviction, 'and you excite me very much.'

'Oh, Ross,' she said again, then remembered something and pushed him away a little so that she could see his face. 'You said you'd taken your great-aunt's advice and that you were going to marry.'

'You, my dearest, who else? It's been you, ever since I first saw you, all tangled up in the washing. And why do you suppose Mama gave a lunch party for the entire family? So that everyone could meet you, of course.'

'There were so many of them, too.'

'You have quite a family yourself, my darling—we'll marry and have them all to see us wed.' He kissed her again and paused, his eyes narrowed in thought. 'Let me see, I could manage next week—a special licence could be arranged. Which day would you prefer, my darling?'

'Next week?' Gemma's voice rose to a squeak. 'But how could I possibly—besides, a special licence… and where?'

'Here, of course—with you in white silk and roses and the church crammed with our families—is there any reason why we shouldn't?'

'None at all,' declared Gemma happily, dismissing at least a dozen good reasons why it couldn't be managed—but if Ross said so…

The door opened and George's head appeared. 'Cousin Maud said we weren't to interrupt, but it's only me,' he excused himself with a beguiling smile. 'I just wondered if you're going to be married.'

'That is the idea,' agreed the professor gravely.

George eyed him thoughtfully. 'Has Gemma said she will?'

His future brother-in-law assured him that she had. 'Oh, good,' said George. 'I can come and stay with you in Holland, then?'

'Certainly. We shall be delighted to have you.'

George nodded his untidy head; of course they would be delighted. 'I suppose you'll have some babies?' and when Ross said 'Oh, yes,' in a bland voice and grinned at him, he offered: 'I'll play with them if you like—one at a time.'

'A generous offer, George. I believe that Gemma has a present for you in her case—take it with you and have a look.'

When the door had been firmly shut once more, Ross tightened his hold and pulled Gemma a little closer. 'These interruptions!' he murmured. 'How far had I got?'

'Let's play safe,' suggested Gemma, 'and start again from the beginning.'

* * * * *

LOVE CAN WAIT

CHAPTER ONE

Mr Tait-Bouverie was taking afternoon tea with his aunt—a small, wispy lady living in some elegance in the pleasant house her late husband had left her. She was seventy and in the best of health and, although a kind woman, very taken up with herself and that health. She had long ago decided that she was delicate, which meant that she never exerted herself in any way unless it was to do something she wished to do. She was his mother's older sister, and it was to please his parent that he drove himself down from London to spend an hour with her from time to time.

He was standing at the window overlooking the garden, listening to her gentle, complaining voice cataloguing her various aches and pains, her sleepless nights and lack of appetite—aware that her doctor had recently examined her and found nothing wrong, but nonetheless offering suitable soothing remarks when appropriate.

Someone came into the room and he turned round

to see who it was. It was a girl—rather, a young woman—tall, splendidly built and with a lovely face. Her hair, a rich chestnut, was piled tidily on top of her head and she was dressed severely in a white blouse and navy skirt.

She was carrying a tea tray which she set down on the table beside his aunt's chair, arranging it just so without fuss, and as she straightened up she looked at him. It was merely a glance; he was unable to see what colour her eyes were, and she didn't smile.

When she had left the room he strolled over to a chair near his aunt.

'Who was that?' he asked casually.

'My housekeeper. Of course, it is some time since you were last here—Mrs Beckett decided to retire and go and live with her sister, so of course I had to find someone else. You have no idea, James, how difficult it is to get good servants. However, Kate suits me very well. Efficient and rather reserved, and does her work well.'

'Not quite the usual type of housekeeper, surely?'

'She is rather young, I suppose. She had impeccable references—Bishop Lowe and Lady Creswell.'

Mr Tait-Bouverie accepted a cup of tea and handed his aunt the plate of sandwiches. 'Someone local?' he hazarded.

'I believe so. She lives in, of course, but her mother lives locally—a widow, so I am told. Left rather badly off, I hear—which is to my advantage, since Kate needs the job and isn't likely to give her notice. I must say, it is most convenient that she drives a car. I no longer need to hire a taxi to go to Thame to my hairdresser each week—she takes me and does the shopping while I'm at Anton's. It gives her a nice little outing...'

Mr Tait-Bouverie, watching his aunt eating sandwiches with dainty greed, wondered if shopping for food could be regarded as a 'nice little outing'.

'And, of course,' went on Lady Cowder, 'she can cycle to the village or into Thame for anything I need.'

'A paragon,' murmured Mr Tait-Bouverie, and passed the cakestand.

He left half an hour later. There was no sign of the housekeeper as he got into the Bentley. He had half expected her to show him out, but it had been Mrs Pickett, the daily from the village, who had opened the door for him and stood watching him drive away.

Kate watched him too, from the kitchen window. She had to crane her neck to do so, for although she had looked at him in the drawing room it had been a quick glance and she wanted to fill in the gaps, as it were.

Tall, very tall—six and a half feet, she guessed—and a very big man. He had a clever face with a high-bridged nose and a thin mouth, straw-coloured hair going grey and, she supposed, blue eyes. He was a handsome man, she conceded, but there was nothing of the dandy about him. She wondered what he did for a living.

She went back to her pastry-making and allowed a small sigh to escape her. He would be interesting to meet and talk to. 'Not that that is at all likely,' said Kate, addressing the kitchen cat, Horace.

She went presently to clear the tea things away, and Lady Cowder looked up from her book to say, 'The chocolate cake was delicious, Kate. My nephew had two slices. A pity he was unable to stay for dinner.' She gave a titter. 'These men with their girlfriends.'

Kate decided that she wasn't supposed to answer that.

'You asked me to remind you to ring Mrs Johnson, my lady.'

'Oh, yes, of course. It had quite slipped my mind. I have so much to think of.' Lady Cowder closed her book with an impatient frown. 'Get her on the phone for me, Kate.'

Kate put down the tray and picked up the telephone. She still found it difficult to be ordered about without a please or thank you. She supposed it was something she would get used to in time.

Back in the kitchen, she set about preparing dinner. Lady Cowder, despite assuring everybody that she had the appetite of a bird, enjoyed substantial meals. Kate knew now, after almost three months, that her employer's order for 'a morsel of fish and a light sweet' could be interpreted as Dover sole with shrimp sauce, Avergne potato purée, mushrooms with tarragon and a portion of braised celery—followed by a chocolate soufflé or, by way of a change, crème caramel.

It was of no use to allow that to annoy her; she had been lucky to get work so near her home. She suspected that she wasn't being paid quite as much as the going rate for housekeepers, but it included her meals and a small, quite comfortable room. And the money enabled her mother to live without worries as long as they were careful.

Kate had plans for the future: if she could save enough money she would start up on her own, cooking and delivering meals to order. It would need enough capital to buy a van, equipment for the kitchen and money to live on while she built up a clientele. Her mother would help, although for the moment that was out of the question—Mrs Crosby had fallen and broken her arm and, although she made light of it, it was difficult to do much with it in plaster.

When Mrs Crosby expressed impatience about it, Kate sensibly pointed out that they couldn't make plans for a bit—not until she had saved some money. If she could get a hundred pounds she could borrow the rest. It was a paltry sum, but would be an argument in her favour when she tackled their bank manager. It would be a risk but, as she reminded herself constantly, she was twenty-seven and if she didn't take that risk soon it would be too late. Being a housekeeper was all very well but it was a temporary necessity.

When her father had died suddenly and unexpectedly their world had fallen apart. He had given up his work in a solicitor's office to write a book, the outline of which had already been approved by a well-known publisher. He had given himself six months in which to write it—but within three months, with the research barely completed, he had fallen ill with emphysema and died within six weeks, leaving his wife and daughter with the remnants of the capital that they had been living on.

It had been a risk, a calculated risk which he had been sure was worthwhile, and it was no one's fault. Kate had set about getting their affairs in order and looked around for a job. A sensible girl, she had looked for work which she could do and do well— and when she'd seen Lady Cowder's advertisement for a housekeeper in the local paper she had presented herself to that lady and got the job.

She had no intention of being a housekeeper for a day longer than was necessary; she intended to start a cooked-meals service from her home just as soon as she could save enough money to get it started. But she and her mother had to live—her mother's small pension paid the rent and the running costs of the little house, but they had to eat and keep warm and have clothes. Even with the frugal way in which they lived it would take a couple of years. There were better paid jobs, but they weren't near her home. At least she could go home for her weekly half-day off, and on her day off on Sunday.

It was Sunday the next day—a warm June day with hardly a cloud in the sky, and Kate got onto her bike and pedalled briskly down to the village, thankful to be free for one day. She sighed with content as she pushed her bike up the little path to the cottage where she and her mother lived. It was the middle one of three at the top end of the village main street. It was rather shabby, and the mod cons weren't very 'mod', but the rent was low and the neighbours on either side were elderly and quiet. Not quite what they had been used to, reflected Kate, propping the bike against the back fence and going in through the kitchen door, but it was their home…

Her mother came into the kitchen to meet her. Still a good-looking woman, her russet hair was streaked with grey but her eyes were the same sparkling green as her daughter's.

'You've had a busy morning,' she said with ready sympathy. 'No time for breakfast?'

'I had a cup of tea…'

'You need more than that, a great girl like you,' said her mother cheerfully. 'I'll make a pile of toast and a pot of tea and we'll have lunch early. Come and sit down, love. We'll go into the garden presently.'

Mrs Crosby frowned a little. 'I'm not sure that this job is good for you. Lady Cowder seems a very demanding woman.'

Kate sat down at the kitchen table and Moggerty, their elderly cat, got onto her lap. The room was small but very neat and tidy and the sun shone warmly through the window over the sink. It seemed so much nicer than Lady Cowder's gleaming white tiles and stainless steel. She said mildly, 'It isn't for ever, Mother. Just as soon as we've got a little money saved I'll give it up. And it isn't too bad, you know. I get good food, and my room's quite nice.'

She pulled the breadboard towards her and began to slice bread for the toast. 'How is your arm? Isn't it next week that you're to have another plaster?'

'Yes, dear. It doesn't hurt at all, and I only wear a sling when I'm out—then no one bumps into me, you see.'

When Kate started to get up her mother said, 'No, dear, I'll make the toast. It's nice to do something for someone other than me, if you see what I mean.'

Her mother was lonely, Kate realised, although she wouldn't admit that. Kate was lonely, too—and though they had a strong affection for each other neither of them were ever going to admit to their loneliness. She said cheerfully, 'We had a visitor yesterday. Lady Cowder's nephew came to tea.'

Mrs Crosby turned the toast. 'Young? Old? What does he do for a living?'

'Youngish—well,' Kate added vaguely, 'In his thirties, I suppose. Very pale hair going grey, and one of those faces which doesn't tell you anything.'

'Good-looking?'

'Yes, but a bit austere. One of those noses you can look down. Enormous and tall.' She began to butter the toast. 'I've no idea what he does. Probably so rich that he does nothing; he was driving a silver-grey Bentley, so he can't be poor.'

'One of those young executive types one is always reading about. Make their million before they're twenty-one, being clever on the stock exchange.'

'Perhaps, but I don't think so. He looked too—too reliable.'

Mrs Crosby regretfully dismissed him as a staid married man. A pity—Kate met so few men. She had had plenty of admirers while her father had been alive but once she and her mother had moved from their comfortable home in the Cotswolds they had gradually dwindled away, much to Mrs Crosby's regret. Kate hadn't minded in the least—she had felt nothing but a mild liking for any of them. She could have married half a dozen times, but for her it was all or nothing. As she had pointed out to her mother in her sensible way, if any of the men who had professed to love her had really done so they would have made it their business to find out where she and her mother had gone, and followed them. And done something about it.

Kate, who wanted to marry and have children, could see that it wasn't very likely that she would get her wish. Not in the foreseeable future at any rate. She did her best to ignore her longings and bent all her thoughts on a future which, hopefully, would provide her and her mother with a livelihood.

Presently they went into the tiny garden behind the cottage and sat under the old plum tree in one corner.

'Once I can start cooking,' said Kate, 'this tree will be a godsend. Think of all the plums just waiting to be bottled and turned into jam. Perhaps I could specialise in some kind of plum tart...'

'Not this year,' remarked her mother.

'No, no, of course not. But by the end of next year we might have enough money to persuade the bank manager.'

Moggerty had gone to sleep on Kate's lap, and presently Kate dozed off too.

She made light of her job, but she was up early and went to bed late and quite often did the work of two. Lady Cowder saw no reason to hire more help in the house—Kate was young and strong, and didn't complain. Besides, Mrs Pickett came up from the village each morning to help with the housework. That she was elderly, with arthritis in her knees which didn't allow her to do anything much below waist level, was something which Lady Cowder found unimportant; a hefty young woman like Kate had plenty of energy...

Kate awoke feeling much refreshed, ate a splendid lunch with her mother and later that evening cycled back to Lady Cowder's house, half a mile or so outside the village. She reminded her mother that in three days' time, on her half-day off, they would take the bus into Thame and have a look at the shops. They would take sandwiches and eat them on a bench in the pleasant green gardens around the church, and later treat themselves to tea in one of the teashops.

Taking Lady Cowder's breakfast tray up to her room the next morning, Kate found her sitting up in bed with a pad and pencil. She nodded in reply to Kate's polite good morning, accepted her tray without thanks and said, with more animation than she usually showed, 'My god-daughter is coming to stay—she will arrive tomorrow, so get the guest room overlooking the garden ready. I shall arrange a dinner party for her, of course—Wednesday suits me very well...'

'My half-day off,' Kate reminded her quietly.

'Oh, so it is. Well, you will have to manage without it this week—I'll see that it's made up to you later on. I want Claudia's visit to be a happy one. We can have a few friends in for tennis, tea on the terrace, and perhaps a little supper one evening. Certainly

I shall ask friends to come for a drink one evening. We must keep her amused…'

And me run off my feet! thought Kate. She said, without visible annoyance, 'I shall need extra help.'

Lady Cowder looked startled. 'Whatever for? Surely you're capable of a little extra cooking?'

'Of course I am, Lady Cowder, but I can't make beds and dust and cook meals for dinner parties and suppers, let alone teas. Of course, I could go to the supermarket—they have excellent meals, all ready to warm up.'

Lady Cowder stared at her. Was the girl being impertinent? Seemingly not; Kate had spoken gravely and stood there looking concerned.

'No, no, certainly not. I'll get Mrs Pickett to come for the whole day.'

'She has a niece staying with her,' volunteered Kate, straight-faced. 'I think she is in service somewhere in Oxford—perhaps she would oblige for a few days.'

'Yes, yes, see what you can do, Kate.' Lady Cowder buttered toast and piled on the marmalade. Feeling magnanimous, she added, 'I dare say you can get an hour or so free in the evenings after dinner.'

Kate thought that unlikely. 'I should like to go home for an hour this evening, or perhaps after lunch while you are resting, Lady Cowder. My mother and I had arranged to go out on Wednesday, and I must tell her that I shan't be free.'

'Very well, Kate. As long as it doesn't interfere with your work.' Lady Cowder lay back on her pillows. 'You had better get on. I fancy a light lunch of cold chicken with a salad, and one or two new potatoes. Perhaps one of your jam soufflés to follow. I'll let you know later about dinner.'

Kate went back downstairs, dusted the small sitting room where Lady Cowder sat in the morning, got out the Hoover ready for Mrs Pickett and went to the kitchen to make a pot of tea and butter a plate of scones—Mrs Pickett needed refreshment before she started on her work and so, for that matter, did Kate—although a good deal of her day's work was already done.

Mrs Pickett, sweetened by the tea and scones, agreed to come for the whole day.

'A week, mind, no more than that. Sally will come up for a few hours whenever you need her. She'll be glad of a bit of extra money—the cash that girl spends on clothes… How about a couple of hours in the morning? Nine-ish? Just to make beds and tidy the rooms and clear the breakfast. You'll have your work cut out if Her Nibs is going to have parties and such. Sally could pop in evenings, too—help with laying the table and clearing away. I'll say this for the girl: she's a good worker, and honest.' Mrs Pickett fixed Kate with a beady eye. 'Paid by the hour, mind.'

'How much?'

'Four pounds. And that's cheap. *She* can afford it.' Mrs Pickett jerked her head ceilingwards.

'I'll let you know, and about your extra hours. Would you like to stay for midday dinner and clear up after while I get the cooking started?'

'Suits me. Puts upon you, she does,' said Mrs Pickett. 'Do her good to do a bit of cooking herself once in a while.'

Kate said cheerfully, 'I like cooking—but you do see that I need help if there's to be a lot of entertaining?'

'Lor' bless you, girl, of course I do. Besides, me and the old man, we're wanting to go to Blackpool in September for a week—see the lights and have a bit of fun. The extra cash will come in handy.'

Lady Cowder, informed of all this, shied like a startled horse at the expense. 'Anyone would think that I was made of money,' she moaned. She caught Kate's large green eyes. 'But dear Claudia must be properly entertained, and it is only for one week. Very well, Kate, make whatever arrangements you must. I shall want you here after tea to discuss the meals.'

Mr Tait-Bouverie took off his gloves, stood patiently while a nurse untied his gown, threw it with unerring precision at the container meant for its reception and went out of the theatre. It had been a long list of operations, and the last case hadn't been straightforward so there would be no time for coffee in Sister's office—his private patients would be waiting for him.

Fifteen minutes later he emerged, immaculate and unhurried, refusing with his beautiful manners Sister's offer of coffee, and made his way out of the hospital to his car. The streets were comparatively quiet—it was too late for the evening rush, too early for the theatre and cinemagoers. He got into the Bentley and drove himself home, away from the centre of the city, past the Houses of Parliament, and along Millbank until he reached his home—a narrow house wedged between two imposing town houses, half their size but sharing their view of the river and the opposite bank.

He drove past it to the end of the side street and turned into the mews at the back of the houses, parked the car in the garage behind his house and walked back to let himself in through the front door. He was met in the hall by a short, stout man very correctly dressed in black jacket and pin-striped trousers, with a jovial face and a thick head of grey hair.

His 'Good evening, sir,' was cheerful. 'A splendid summer evening,' he observed. 'I've put the drinks on the patio, sir, seeing as how a breath of fresh air would do you no harm.'

Mr Tait-Bouverie thanked him, picked up his letters from the console table and took himself and his bag off to the study. 'Any messages, Mudd?' he paused to ask, and braced himself as the door at the back of the hall was thrust open and a golden Labrador came to greet him. 'Prince, old fellow, come into the garden—but first I must go to the study...'

'Lady Cowder phoned,' said Mudd. 'Twice. She said she would be glad if you would telephone her as soon as you return home, sir.'

Mr Tait-Bouverie nodded absently and sat down behind his desk in the study, with Prince beside him. There was nothing in the post to take his attention and he went into the sitting room at the back of the house and out onto the small patio facing the narrow walled garden. A drink before dinner, he decided. He would ring his aunt later.

It was a pleasant little garden, with its borders stuffed with flowers and a small plot of grass in its centre. The walls were a faded red brick and covered in climbing roses, veronica and clematis. Mr Tait-Bouverie closed his eyes for a moment and wished he was at his cottage in Bosham—roomy, old and thatched, at the end of Bosham Lane beyond the avenue of oaks and holly trees, within sight and sound of the harbour.

He spent his free weekends there, and brief holidays, taking Mudd and Prince with him, sailing in the creek, working in his rambling garden, going to the pub and meeting friends there... Perhaps he could manage this weekend, or at least Saturday. He had a list next Monday and he had no free time at all until Saturday, but it was only Monday now—he had the whole week in which to arrange things to his satisfaction.

He ate the dinner Mudd set before him and went to his study to phone his aunt.

'James, I was beginning to think you would never telephone. I've tried twice to get you.' She paused, but not long enough for him to reply.

'Something so exciting. Dear Julia Travers's daughter, Claudia—my god-daughter, you know—is coming to stay for a week. Such a dear girl, and so pretty. It's all rather sudden.' She gave a little laugh. 'But I'm doing my best to plan a pleasant stay for her. I've arranged a dinner party for Wednesday evening—just a few friends, and you, of course. Do say that you can come…eight o'clock. Black tie.'

Mr Tait-Bouverie listened to this patiently for he was a patient man. A list of possible excuses ran through his head but he discarded them. He didn't want to go, but on the other hand a drive down to Thame in the middle of the week would make a pleasant break.

'Provided there is no emergency to keep me here, I'll accept with pleasure,' he told her. 'I may need to leave directly after dinner, though.'

'Splendid. I'm sure it will be a delightful evening.'

He thought it unlikely. His aunt's friends weren't his, and the evening would be taken up with time-wasting chat, but the drive back to London in the evening would compensate for that.

Lady Cowder talked for another five minutes and he put down the phone with an air of relief. A few minutes later he let himself out of his house with Prince and set off on his evening walk, Wednesday's dinner party already dismissed from his mind. He had several cases for operation lined up for the week and he wanted to mull them over at his leisure. Much later he went to his bed to sleep the sleep of a man whose day had gone well.

Kate, going to her bed, reflected that her day hadn't gone well at all. After she had given Lady Cowder her lunch and eaten a hasty snack herself, she'd got into the car and driven to Thame, where she'd spent an hour or more shopping for the elaborate food decided upon for the dinner party. When she got home she had been summoned once more—dear Claudia, she was told, would arrive before lunch on the following day, so that meal must be something special, and Kate was to make sure that there was a variety of cakes for tea. Moreover, dinner must be something extra special too.

Unlike Mr Tait-Bouverie's, Kate's day had not gone well.

Claudia arrived mid-morning, driving her scarlet Mini. She was small and slender and pretty—a chocolate-box prettiness—with china-blue eyes, a pert nose, pouting mouth and an abundance of fair curls. She looked helpless but Kate, carrying in her luggage, reflected that she seemed as hard as nails under that smiling face. She had wasted no time on Kate, but had pushed past her to embrace Lady Cowder with little cries of joy which made Kate feel quite sick.

Kate took the bags up to the guest room, fetched the coffee tray and retired to the kitchen where Mrs Pickett was cleaning vegetables.

'Pretty as a picture,' she observed. 'Like a fairy. And such lovely clothes, too. She won't stay single long, I'll warrant you.'

Kate said, 'Probably not,' adding silently that Claudia would stay single just as long as it took her to find a man with a great deal of money who was prepared to let her have her own way, and indulge every whim. And if I can see that in five minutes, she thought, why can't a man?

Her feelings, she decided, mustn't get in the way of her culinary art. She presented a delicious lunch and forbore from uttering a word when she handed Claudia the new potato salad and had it thrust back into her hands.

'I couldn't possibly eat those,' cried Claudia. 'Vegetables which have been smothered in some sauce or other; it's a sure sign that they've been poorly cooked and need disguising.'

Lady Cowder, who had taken a large helping, looked taken aback. 'Oh, dear, you don't care for devilled potatoes? Kate, fetch some plain boiled ones for Miss Travers.'

'There aren't any,' said Kate. 'I can boil some, but they will take at least twenty minutes…'

'Well, really… You should have thought of it, Kate.'

'If Miss Travers will give me a list of what she dislikes and likes I can cook accordingly.'

Kate sounded so polite that Lady Cowder hesitated to do more than murmur, 'Perhaps that would be best.'

When Kate had left the room Claudia said, 'What an impertinent young woman. Why don't you dismiss her?'

'My dear, if you knew how difficult it is to get anyone to work for one these days… All the good cooks work in town, where they can earn twice as much. Kate is a good cook, and I must say she runs the house very well. Besides, she lives locally with a widowed mother and needs to stay close to her home.'

Claudia sniggered. 'Oh, well, I suppose she's better than nothing. She looks like a prim old maid.'

Kate, coming in with home-made meringue nests well-filled with strawberries, heard that. It would be nice, she thought, serving the meringues with an impassive face, to put a dead rat in the girl's bed…

Claudia Travers wasn't the easiest of guests. She needed a warm drink when she went to her room at night, a special herb tea upon waking, a variety of yoghurts for breakfast, and coddled eggs and wholemeal bread—all of which Kate provided, receiving no word of thanks for doing so. Claudia, treating her hostess with girlish charm, wasted none of it on Kate.

Lady Cowder took her god-daughter out to lunch the next day, which meant that Kate had the time to start preparing for the dinner party that evening. She was still smarting from her disappointment over her half-day off. No mention had been made of another one in its place, and over breakfast she had heard Claudia observing that she might stay over the weekend—so that would mean no day off on Sunday, either.

Kate, thoroughly put out, started to trim watercress for the soup. There was to be roast duck with sauce Bigarade, and Lady Cowder wanted raspberry sorbets served after the duck. For vegetables she had chosen braised chicory with orange, petits pois and a purée of carrots; furthermore, Kate had been told to make chocolate orange creams, caramel creams and a strawberry cheesecake.

She had more than enough to get on with. The menu was too elaborate, she considered, and there was far too much orange...but her mild suggestion that something else be substituted for the chocolate orange creams had been ignored.

After lunch she started on the cakes for tea. Claudia had refused the chocolate sponge and the small scones Kate had offered on the previous day, so today she made a madeira cake and a jam sponge and, while they were baking, made herself a pot of tea and sat down to drink it.

As soon as Claudia left, she would ask for her day and a half off and go home and do nothing. She enjoyed cooking, but not when everything she cooked was either criticised or rejected. Claudia, she reflected crossly, was a thoroughly nasty young woman.

The cold salmon and salad that she had served for dinner the previous evening had been pecked at, and when Lady Cowder had urged her guest to try and eat something, Claudia had smiled wistfully and said that she had always been very delicate.

Kate had said nothing—but in the kitchen, with no one but the kitchen cat to hear her, she'd allowed her feelings to erupt.

Sally, Mrs Pickett's niece, arrived later in the afternoon. She was a strapping young girl with a cheerful face and, to Kate's relief, a happy disposition. She served tea while Kate got on with her cooking, and then joined her in the kitchen. Mrs Pickett was there too, clearing away bowls and cooking utensils, making endless pots of tea, laying out the tableware and the silver and glass.

Kate, with the duck safely dealt with and dinner almost ready, went to the dining room and found that Sally had set the table very correctly. There was a low bowl of roses at its centre, with candelabra on either side of it, and the silver glass gleamed.

'That's a marvellous job,' said Kate. 'You've made it look splendid. Now, when they have all sat down I'll serve the soup from the sideboard and you take it round. I'll have to go back to the kitchen to see to the duck while you clear the dishes and fetch the hot plates and the vegetables. I'll serve the duck and you hand it round, and we'll both go round with the potatoes and the veg.'

The guests were arriving. Kate poked at her hair, tugged her skirt straight and went to open the door. It was the local doctor and his wife, both of whom greeted her like old friends before crossing the hall to their hostess and Claudia who was a vision in pale blue. Following hard on their heels came Major Keane and his wife, and an elderly couple from Thame who were old friends of Lady Cowder. They brought a young man with them, their nephew. He was good-looking and full of self-confidence. And then, five minutes later, as Kate was crossing the hall with the basket of warm rolls ready for the soup, Mr Tait-Bouverie arrived.

He wished her good evening and smiled at her as she opened the drawing room door. Her own good evening was uttered in a voice devoid of expression.

Mindful of her orders, Kate waited ten minutes then announced dinner and went to stand by the soup tureen. Claudia, she noticed, was seated between the

nephew and Mr Tait-Bouverie and was in her element, smiling and fluttering her eyelashes in what
Kate considered to be a sickening manner. A pity
Sally hadn't spilt the watercress soup down the front
of the blue dress, thought Kate waspishly.

Dinner went off very well, and an hour later Kate
helped clear the table after taking coffee into the
drawing room. Then she went to the kitchen, where
the three of them sat down at the kitchen table and
polished off the rest of the duck.

'You're tired out; been on your feet all day,' said
Mrs Pickett. 'Just you nip outside for a breath of air,
Kate. Me and Sally'll fill the dishwasher and tidy up
a bit. Go on, now.'

'You don't mind? Ten minutes, then. You've both
been such a help—I could never have managed...'

It was lovely out in the garden, still light enough
to see around her, and warm from the day's sunshine. Kate wandered round the side of the house
and onto the sweep in front of it, and paused to look
at the cars parked there: an elderly Daimler—that
would be the doctor's—Major Keane's Rover, a rak-
ish sports car—the nephew's no doubt—and, a little
apart, the Bentley.

She went nearer and peered in, and met the eyes
of the dog sitting behind the wheel. The window
was a little open and he lifted his head and breathed
gently over her.

'You poor dear, shut up all by yourself while everyone is inside guzzling themselves ill. I hope your master takes good care of you.'

Mr Tait-Bouverie, coming soft-footed across the grass, stopped to listen.

'He does his best,' he observed mildly. 'He is about to take his dog for a short stroll before returning home.' He looked at Kate's face, pale in the deepening twilight. 'And I promise you, I didn't guzzle. The dinner was superb.'

He opened the door and Prince got out and offered his head for a scratch.

'Thank you,' said Kate haughtily. 'I'm glad you enjoyed it.'

'A most pleasant evening,' said Mr Tait-Bouverie.

Kate heaved a deep breath. 'Probably it was, for you. But this was supposedly my half-day off, and on Sunday, when I should have a full day, I am not to have it because Miss Travers is staying on.' Her voice shook very slightly. 'We—I and my mother— were going to spend the day at Thame, looking at the shops. And my feet ache!'

She turned on her heel and walked away, back to the kitchen, leaving Mr Tait-Bouverie looking thoughtful.

CHAPTER TWO

MR TAIT-BOUVERIE STROLLED around the garden while Prince blundered around seeking rabbits, his amusement at Kate's outburst slowly giving way to concern. She had sounded upset—indeed, he suspected that most girls would have given way to floods of tears. Knowing his aunt, he had no doubt that Kate was shown little consideration at the best of times and none at all when Lady Cowder's wishes were likely to be frustrated. He had been touched by her idea of a day's outing to Thame to look at the shops. The ladies of his acquaintance didn't look at shop windows, they went inside and bought whatever they wanted.

He frowned as he remembered that she had said her feet ached…

Back in the house, Claudia fluttered across the room to him. 'Where have you been?' she wanted to know, and gave him a wide smile. 'Are you bored?' She pouted prettily. 'Everyone here, except for Roland, is a bit elderly. I'd love to walk in the garden…'

He had beautiful manners and she had no idea how tiresome he found her.

'I'm afraid I must leave, I'm already late for an appointment.'

Claudia looked put out. 'You've got a girlfriend…?'

He answered her in a bland voice which gave no hint of his irritation. 'No, nothing as romantic, I'm afraid. A patient to check at the hospital.'

'At this time of night? It will be twelve o'clock before you get back to town.'

'Oh, yes. But, you see, people who are ill don't observe conventional hours of sleep.' He smiled down at her pretty, discontented face. 'I must say goodbye to my aunt…'

Lady Cowder drew him a little apart. 'You enjoyed your evening?' she wanted to know. 'Isn't Claudia charming? Such a dear girl and so pretty, is she not?'

'Oh, indeed. A delightful evening, Aunt. The dinner was superb. You have a treasure in your housekeeper, if she did indeed cook it. A big task for her, I should imagine—but doubtless she has ample help.'

'Oh, Kate can do the work of two,' said Lady Cowder airily. 'Of course, I allowed her to have a daily woman to help, and a young girl—she waited at table. Some kind of a niece, I believe. The best we could do at such short notice.'

'You plan more entertainments while Claudia is here?'

'Oh, yes—tennis tomorrow, with tea in the garden and perhaps a buffet supper. And on Friday there will be people coming for drinks, and I dare say several of them will stay on and take pot luck. Claudia thinks she may stay until early next week. I must think up something special for Sunday. A barbecue, perhaps. Kate could manage that easily.'

She would manage, thought Mr Tait-Bouverie, but her feet would be aching fit to kill her by then, and her longed-for day off would be out of the question.

'If Claudia is staying until Monday or Tuesday, why don't you bring her up to town on Friday evening? I'm free for the weekend. We might go to a play on Friday evening, and perhaps go somewhere to dine on Saturday. And she might enjoy a drive down to Henley on Sunday?'

'My dear, James, what a delightful idea. We shall both adore to come. I can leave Kate to look after the house—such a good chance for her to do a little extra work…'

'Oh, you're far too generous for that,' said Mr Tait-Bouverie suavely. 'Let the girl go home for a couple of days; your gardener could keep an eye on the house. I'm sure you will want to reward Kate for such a splendid dinner. Besides, why keep the house open when you can lock up and save on your gas and electricity bills?'

Lady Cowder, who was mean with her money, said thoughtfully, 'You know, James, that *is* a good idea. You have no idea how much this place costs to run and, of course, if I'm not here to keep an eye on Kate she might give way to extravagance.'

'I'll expect you around six o'clock,' said Mr Tait-Bouverie. 'And, if by chance I'm held up, Mudd will take care of you both. You'll come in Claudia's car?'

'Yes. She's a splendid driver. She does everything so well. She will make a splendid wife.'

If she expected an answer to this she was to be disappointed. Her nephew remarked pleasantly that he must leave without delay and embarked on his farewells, saying all the right things and leaving the house by a side door.

He was letting Prince out of the car for a few moments when he heard voices, and saw Mrs Pickett and her niece leaving the house from the kitchen door. They wished him goodnight as they reached him, and then paused as he asked, 'You're going to the village? I'm just leaving, I'll give you a lift.'

'Well, now, that would be a treat for we're that tired, sir.'

'I imagine so.' He opened the car door and they got in carefully.

'You will have to tell me where you live, Mrs Pickett.' He started the car and said over his shoulder, 'What a splendid dinner party. You must have worked very hard.'

'That we did—and that poor Kate, so tired she couldn't eat her supper. Had a busy time of it, with all the shopping and the house to see to as well as concocting all them fancy dishes. Now I hears it's to be a tennis party tomorrow—that means she'll have to be up early, making cakes. Missed her half-day off, too, though she didn't say a word about it.'

Mrs Pickett, a gossip by nature, was in full flood. 'It's not as though she's used to service. She's a lady, born and bred, but she's got no airs or graces, just gets on with it.' She paused for breath. 'It's just along here, sir, the third cottage on the left. And I'm sure Sally and me are that grateful,' she chuckled. 'Don't often get the chance of a ride in such a posh car.'

Mr Tait-Bouverie, brought up to mind his manners by a fierce nanny, got out of the car to assist his passengers to alight—an action which, from Mrs Pickett's view, made her day. As for Sally, she thought she would never forget him.

'I cannot think what possessed me,' Mr Tait-Bouverie told Prince as he drove back to London. 'I have deliberately ruined my weekend in order to allow a girl I hardly know to go and look at shop windows…'

Prince leaned against him and rumbled soothingly, and his master said, 'Oh, it's all very well for you to approve—you liked her, didn't you? Well, I'm sure she is a very worthy person, but I rather regret being so magnanimous.'

Lady Cowder told Kate the following morning, making it sound as if she was bestowing a gracious favour. She sat up in bed while Kate drew the curtains and put the tea tray beside her.

'There are some employers who would expect their staff to remain at the house during their absence, but, as I am told so often, I am generous to a fault. You may go home as soon as you have made sure that your work is done, and I expect you back on Sunday evening. Harvey, the gardener, will keep an eye on things, but I shall hold you responsible for anything which is amiss.'

'Yes, Lady Cowder,' said Kate, showing what her employer found to be a sorry lack of gratitude. Kate went down to the kitchen to start breakfast for the two ladies, who liked it in bed. More extra work for her.

It would be lovely to have two whole days at home; the pleasure of that got her through another trying day, with unexpected guests for lunch and a great many people coming to play tennis and have tea in the garden.

Mrs Pickett's feet didn't allow her to walk too much, so Kate went to and fro with pots of tea, more sandwiches, more cakes, lemonade and ice cream.

'It's a crying shame,' declared Mrs Pickett, 'expecting you to do everything on your own. Too mean to get help, she is. I suppose she thinks that having Sally last night was more than enough.' Mrs Pickett sniffed. 'It's the likes of her should try doing a bit of cooking and housework for themselves.'

Kate agreed silently.

That evening there was a barbecue, the preparations for which were much hindered by Claudia rearranging everything and then demanding that it should all be returned to its normal place—which meant that by the time the guests began to arrive nothing was quite ready, a circumstance which Claudia, naturally enough, blamed on Kate. With Kate still within earshot, she observed in her rather loud voice, 'Of course, one can't expect the servants to know about these things…'

Kate, stifling an urge to go back and strangle the girl, went to the kitchen to fetch the sausages and steaks.

'Now you can get the charcoal burning,' ordered Claudia.

Kate set the sausages and steaks beside each other on one of the tables.

'I'm wanted in the house,' she said, and whisked herself away.

She made herself a pot of tea in the kitchen, emptied the dishwasher and tidied the room. It was a fine, warm evening, and the party would probably go on for some time, which would give her the chance to press a dress of Claudia's and go upstairs and turn down the beds. First, though, she fed Horace, scrubbed two potatoes and popped them into the Aga for her supper. When they were baked she would top them with cheese and put them under the grill.

One more day, she told herself as she tidied Claudia's room. The drinks party the next day would be child's play after the last few days. She wished Mr Tait-Bouverie joy of his weekend guests, and hoped he was thoughtful of his housekeeper. She wasn't sure if she liked him, but she thought he might be a man who considered his servants...

The barbecue went on for a long time. Kate did her chores, ate her potatoes and much later, when everyone had left and Lady Cowder and Claudia had gone to their rooms, she went to hers, stood half-asleep under the shower and tumbled into bed, to sleep the sleep of a very tired girl.

Since Lady Cowder and her goddaughter were to go to London in the early evening, the drinks party the next day was held just before noon, and because the guests had tended to linger, lunch was a hurried affair. Kate whisked the plates in and out without waste of time, found Lady Cowder's spectacles, her handbag, her pills, and went upstairs twice to make sure that Claudia had packed everything.

'Though I can't think why I should have to pack for myself,' said that young lady pettishly, and snatched a Gucci scarf from Kate's hand without thanking her.

Kate watched them go, heaved an enormous sigh of relief and began to clear lunch away and leave the house tidy. Horace had been fed, and Harvey promised he would be up to see to him and make sure that everything was all right later that evening. He was a nice old man, and Kate gave him cups of tea and plenty of her scones whenever he came up to the house with the vegetables. He would take a look at the house, he assured her, and see to Horace.

'You can go home, Missy,' he told her, 'and have a couple of days to yourself. All that rumpus—makes a heap of work for the likes of us.'

It was lovely to sleep in her own bed again, to wake in the morning and smell the bacon frying for her breakfast and not for someone else's. She went down to the small kitchen intent on finishing the cooking, but her mother wouldn't hear of it.

'You've had a horrid week, love, and it's marvellous to have you home for two whole days. What shall we do?'

'We're going to Thame,' said Kate firmly. 'We'll have a good look at the shops and have tea at that patisserie.'

'It's expensive…'

'We owe ourselves a treat.'

They sat over breakfast while Kate told her mother about her week.

'Wasn't there anyone nice there?' asked Mrs Crosby.

'No, not a soul. Well, there was one—Lady Cowder's nephew. He's very reserved, I should think he has a nasty temper, too. He complimented me on dinner, but that doesn't mean to say that he's nice.'

'But he talked to you?'

'No, only to remark that it had been a pleasant evening.'

'And?'

'I told him that it might have been pleasant for some, and that my feet ached.'

Her mother laughed. 'I wonder what he thought of that?'

'I've no idea, and I really don't care. We'll have a lovely day today.'

A sentiment not echoed by Mr Tait-Bouverie, who had welcomed his guests on Friday evening, much regretting his impulsive action. After suitable greetings he had handed them over to Mudd and, with Prince hard on his heels, had gone to his room to dress. He had got tickets for a popular musical, and Mudd had thought up a special dinner.

Tomorrow, he had reflected, shrugging himself into his jacket, he would escort them to a picture gallery which was all the fashion and then take them to lunch. Dinner and dancing at the Savoy in the evening would take care of Saturday. Then a drive out into the country on Sunday and one of Mudd's superb dinners, and early Monday morning they would drive back.

A waste of a perfectly good weekend, he had

thought regretfully, and hoped that Kate was enjoying hers more than he expected to enjoy his. 'Although, the girl is no concern of mine,' he had pointed out to Prince.

Presently he had forgotten about her, listening to Claudia's ceaseless chatter and his aunt's gentle complaining voice. A delicious dinner, she had told him, but such a pity that she wasn't able to appreciate it now that she suffered with those vague pains. 'One so hopes that it isn't cancer,' she had observed with a wistful little laugh.

Mr Tait-Bouverie, having watched her eat a splendid meal with something very like greed, had assured her that that was most unlikely. 'A touch of indigestion?' he had suggested—a remark dismissed with a frown from Lady Cowder. Indigestion was vulgar, something suitable for the lower classes...

He'd sat through the performance at the theatre with every show of interest, while mentally assessing his work ahead for the following week. It would be a busy one—his weekly outpatients' clinic on Monday, and a tricky operation on a small girl with a sarcoma of the hip in the afternoon. Private patients to see, and a trip to Birmingham Children's Hospital later in the week.

In his own world of Paediatrics he was already making a name for himself, content to be doing something he had always wished to do, absorbed in his work and content, too, with his life. He supposed that one day he would marry, if he could find the right girl. His friends were zealous in introducing him to suitable young women in the hope that he would fall in love, and he was well aware that his aunt was dangling Claudia before him in the hope that he would be attracted to her. Certainly she was pretty enough, but he had seen her sulky mouth and suspected that the pretty face concealed a nasty temper.

The weekend went far too quickly for Kate. The delights of window shopping were followed by a peaceful Sunday: church in the morning, a snack lunch in the little garden behind the cottage with her mother and a lazy afternoon. After tea she went into the kitchen and made a cheese soufflé and a salad, and since there were a few strawberries in the garden she made little tartlets and a creamy custard.

They ate their supper together and then it was time for Kate to go back to Lady Cowder's house. That lady hadn't said exactly when she would return—some time early the following morning, she had hinted. Kate suspected that she would arrive unexpectedly, ready to find fault.

The house seemed gloomy and silent, and she was glad to find Horace in the kitchen. She gave him an extra supper and presently he accompanied her up to her room and settled on the end of the bed— something he wouldn't have dared to do when Lady

Cowder was there. Kate found his company a comfort, and, after a little while spent listening rather anxiously to the creaks and groans an old house makes at night, she went to sleep—her alarm clock prudently set for half-past six.

It was a beautiful morning; getting up was no hardship. She went down to the kitchen with Horace, fed him generously, let him out and made herself a pot of tea. She didn't sit over it but went back upstairs to dress and then went round the house, opening windows and drawing back curtains while her breakfast egg cooked. She didn't sit over breakfast either— fresh flowers were needed, preparations for the lunch that Lady Cowder would certainly want had to be made, the dining room and the sitting room needed a quick dusting... .

Lady Cowder arrived soon after nine o'clock, driven in a hired car, her eyes everywhere, looking for something she could complain about.

She had little to say to Kate. 'Dear Claudia had to drive to Edinburgh,' she said briefly. 'And my nephew had to leave early, so it seemed pointless for me to stay on on my own. You can cook me a light breakfast; I had no time to have a proper meal before I left. Coddled eggs and some thinly sliced toast—and coffee. In fifteen minutes. I'm going to my room now.'

Lady Cowder wasn't in a good mood, decided

Kate, grinding coffee beans. Perhaps the week-end hadn't been a success. Come to think of it, she couldn't believe that she and Claudia and that nephew of hers could have much in common. Although, since he had invited them, perhaps he had fallen in love with Claudia. She hoped not. She knew nothing about him—indeed, she suspected that he might be a difficult man to get to know—but he had been kind, praising her cooking, and he might be rather nice if one ever got to be friends with him.

'And that is most unlikely,' said Kate to Horace, who was hovering discreetly in the hope of a snack. 'I mean, I'm the housekeeper, aren't I? And I expect he's something powerful on the Stock Exchange or something.'

If Mr Tait-Bouverie, immersed in a tricky operation on a very small harelip, could have heard her he would have been amused.

It was some days later, chatting to one of his colleagues at the hospital that he was asked, 'Isn't Lady Cowder an aunt of yours, James? Funny thing, I hear her housekeeper is the daughter of an old friend of mine—he died a year or so ago. Nice girl—pretty too. Fallen on hard times, I hear. Haven't heard from them since they left their place in the Cotswolds— keep meaning to look them up.'

Mr Tait-Bouverie said slowly, 'Yes, I've met her. She seems very efficient, but overworked. My aunt is a kind woman, but incredibly selfish and leaves a good deal to Kate, I believe.'

'I must do something about it.' His elderly companion frowned. 'I'll get Sarah to write and invite them for a weekend.'

'Kate only has Sunday off...'

'Oh, well, they could spend the day. Have they a car?'

'Kate rides a bike.'

'Good Lord, does she? I could drive over and fetch them.'

'Why not invite me, and I'll collect them on my way and take them back on my way home?'

'My dear James, that's very good of you. We'll fix a day—pretty soon, because we're off to Greece for a couple of weeks very shortly and I dare say you've your own holiday planned. I'll write to Jean Crosby. They left very quietly, you know; didn't want to make things awkward, if you understand. A bit dodgy, finding yourself more or less penniless. Kate had several young men after her, too. Don't suppose any of them were keen enough, though.'

Mr Tait-Bouverie, overdue for his ward round, dismissed the matter from his mind. He liked Professor Shaw; he was a kindly and clever man, but also absent-minded. He thought it was unlikely that he would remember to act upon his suggestion.

He was wrong. Before the end of the week he was reminded of their plan and asked if he could spare

the time for the Sunday after next. 'Sarah has written
to Jean and won't take no for an answer, so all you
need do is to collect them—come in time for drinks
before lunch. Our daughter and her husband will be
here, and she and Kate were good friends. Spend the
day—Sarah counts on you to stay for supper.'

Mr Tait-Bouverie sighed. It was his own fault,
of course—he had suggested driving the Crosbys
down. Another spoilt weekend, he reflected, which
he could have spent sailing at Bosham.

Kate, arriving home for her day off with barely time
to get to church, since Lady Cowder had declared in
her faraway voice that she felt faint and mustn't be
left, had no time to do more than greet her mother
and walk rapidly on to church.

She felt a little guilty at going, for she was decidedly out of charity with her employer. Lady Cowder,
cosseted with smelling salts, a nice little drop of
brandy and Kate's arm to assist her to the sofa in
the drawing room, had been finally forced to allow
her to go. She was being fetched, within the hour,
to lunch with friends, and when Kate had left she'd
been drinking coffee and nibbling at wine biscuits,
apparently quite restored to good health.

'This isn't a day off,' muttered Kate crossly, and
caught her mother's reproachful eye. She smiled then
and said her prayers meekly, adding the rider that

she hoped that one day soon something nice would happen.

It was on their way home that her mother told her of their invitation for the following Sunday. 'And someone called Tait-Bouverie is driving us there and bringing us home in the evening…'

Kate came to a halt. 'Mother—that's Lady Cowder's nephew—the one I told about my aching feet.' She frowned. If this was the answer to her prayers, it wasn't quite what she'd had in mind. 'Does he know the Shaws? Professor Shaw's a bit old for a friend…'

'John Shaw and he work at the same hospital; Sarah said so in her letter. He's a paediatrician—quite a well-known one, it seems.'

'But how on earth did he know about us?'

'John happened to mention our name—wondered how we were getting on.'

'You want to go, Mother?'

'Oh, darling, yes. I liked Sarah, you know, and it would be nice to have a taste of the old life for an hour or two.' Mrs Crosby smiled happily. 'What shall we wear?'

Her mother was happy at the prospect of seeing old friends again. Kate quashed the feeling of reluctance at going and spent the next hour reviewing their wardrobes.

It seemed prudent to tell Lady Cowder that she would want to leave early next Sunday morning for her day off. 'We are spending the day with friends, and perhaps it would be a good idea if I had the key to the side door in case we don't get back until after ten o'clock.'

Lady Cowder cavelled at that. 'I hope you don't intend to stay out all night, Kate. That's something I'd feel bound to forbid.'

Kate didn't allow her feelings to show. 'I am not in the habit of staying out all night, Lady Cowder, but I cannot see any objection to a woman of twenty-seven spending an evening with friends.'

'Well, no. I suppose there is no harm in that. But I expect you back by midnight. Mrs Pickett will have to sleep here; I cannot be left alone.'

Lady Cowder picked up her novel. 'There is a lack of consideration among the young these days,' she observed in her wispy voice. 'I'll have lamb cutlets for lunch, Kate, and I fancy an egg custard to follow. My appetite is so poor...'

All that fuss, thought Kate, breaking eggs into a bowl with rather too much force, just because I intend to have a whole day off and not come meekly back at ten o'clock sharp.

Lady Cowder, not intentionally unkind, neverthe-less delayed Kate's half-day on Wednesday. She had friends for lunch and, since they didn't arrive until almost one o'clock and sat about drinking sherry for another half-hour, it was almost three o'clock by the time Kate was free to get on her bike and go home for the rest of the day.

'I don't know why I put up with it,' she told her mother, and added, 'Well, I do, actually. It's a job, and the best there is at the moment. But not for long—the moment we've got that hundred pounds saved...'

She was up early on Sunday and, despite Lady Cowder's pathetic excuses to keep her, left the house in good time. They were to be called for at ten o'clock, which gave her half an hour in which to change into the pale green jersey dress treasured at the back of her wardrobe for special occasions. This was a special occasion; it was necessary to keep up appearances even if she was someone's housekeeper. Moreover, she wished to impress Mr Tait-Bouverie. She wasn't sure why, but she wanted him to see her as someone other than his aunt's housekeeper.

Presently she went downstairs to join her mother, aware that she had done the best she could with her appearance.

'You look nice, dear,' said her mother. 'You're wasted in that job—you ought to be a model.'

'Mother, dear, models don't have curves and I've plenty—on the ample side, too...'

Her mother smiled. 'You're a woman, love, and you look like one. I don't know about fashion models, but most men like curves.'

Mr Tait-Bouverie arrived five minutes later, but, judging by the detached glance and his brisk handshake, he was not to be counted amongst that number.

Rather to her surprise, he accepted her mother's offer of coffee and asked civilly if Prince might be allowed to go into the garden.

'Well, of course he can,' declared Mrs Crosby. 'Moggerty, our cat, you know, is asleep on Kate's bed. In any case, your dog doesn't look as though he'd hurt a fly.'

Indeed, Prince was on his best behaviour and, recognising someone who had spoken kindly to him when he had been sitting bored in his master's car, he sidled up to Kate and offered his head. She was one of the few people who knew the exact spot which needed to be scratched.

Kate was glad to do so; it gave her something to do, and for some reason she felt awkward.

Don't be silly, she told herself silently, and engaged Mr Tait-Bouverie in a brisk conversation about the weather. 'It's really splendid, isn't it?' she asked politely.

'Indeed it is. Do you have any plans for your holidays?'

'Holidays?' She blinked. 'No—no. Well, not at present. I'm not sure when it's convenient for Lady Cowder.'

She hoped he wasn't going to talk about her job, and he'd better not try and patronise her...

Mr Tait-Bouverie watched her face and had a very good idea about what she was thinking. A charming face, he reflected, and now that she was away from her job she actually looked like a young girl. That calm manner went with her job, he supposed. She would be magnificent in a temper...

'Did you enjoy your weekend?' he wanted to know, accepting coffee from Mrs Crosby. 'Cooking must be warm work in this weather.' He gave her a thoughtful look from very blue eyes. 'And so hard on the feet!' he added.

Kate said in a surprised voice, 'Oh, did Lady Cowder tell you that? Yes, thank you.'

She handed him the plate of biscuits and gave one to Prince. 'I dare say he would like a drink before we go.' She addressed no one in particular, and went away with the dog and came back presently with the air of one quite ready to leave.

Mr Tait-Bouverie, chatting with her mother, smiled to himself and suggested smoothly that perhaps they should be going. He settled Mrs Crosby in the front seat, ushered Kate into the back of the car with Prince and, having made sure that everyone was comfortable, drove off.

The countryside looked lovely, and he took the quieter roads away from the motorways. Kate found her ill-humour evaporating; the Bentley was more than comfortable and Prince, lolling beside her, half-asleep, was an undemanding companion. She had no need to talk, but listened with half an ear to her mother and Mr Tait-Bouverie; they seemed to have a great deal to say to each other.

She hoped that her mother wasn't telling him too much about their circumstances. She suspected that he had acquired the art of getting people to talk about themselves. Necessary in his profession, no doubt, and now employed as a way of passing what for him was probably a boring journey.

Mr Tait-Bouverie, on the contrary, wasn't bored. With the skill of long practice, he was extracting information from Mrs Crosby simply because he wished to know more about Kate. She had intrigued him, and while he didn't examine his interest in her he saw no reason why he shouldn't indulge it.

The Shaws gave them a warm welcome, tactfully avoiding awkward questions, and the Shaws' daughter, Lesley, fell easily into the pleasant friendship she and Kate had had.

There was one awkward moment when she re-marked, 'I can't think why you aren't married, Kate. Heaven knows, you had all the men fancying you. Did you give them all the cold shoulder?'

It was Mrs Shaw who filled the too long pause while Kate tried to think of a bright answer.

'I dare say Kate's got some lucky man up her

sleeve. And talking of lucky men, James, isn't it time
you settled down?'

Mr Tait-Bouverie rose to the occasion.

'Yes. It is something I really must deal with when
I have the time. There are so many other interests
in life...'

There was a good deal of laughter and light-
hearted banter, which gave Kate the chance to recover her serenity. For the rest of their visit she
managed to avoid saying anything about her job. To
the kindly put questions she gave a vague description
of their home so that everyone, with the exception of
Mr Tait-Bouverie, of course, was left with the impression that they lived in a charming cottage with
few cares and were happily settled in the village.

Presumably, thought Mrs Shaw, who had been
told about the housekeeper's job, it wasn't quite
the normal housekeeper's kind of work. There was
talk about tennis parties and a pleasant social life
in which, she imagined, Kate took part. Not quite
what the dear girl had been accustomed to, but girls
worked at the oddest jobs these days.

Mrs Shaw, whose own housekeeper was a hard-
bitten lady of uncertain age who wore print aprons
and used no make-up, dismissed Kate's work as
a temporary flight of fancy. There was certainly
nothing wrong with either Kate's or her mother's
clothes...

Mrs Shaw, who didn't buy her dresses at high-street stores, failed to recognise them as such. They were skilfully altered with different buttons, another belt, careful letting-out and taking-in...

Mr Tait-Bouverie did, though. Not that he was an avid follower of women's fashion, but he encountered a wide variety of patients and their mothers—mostly young women wearing just the kind of dress Kate was wearing today. His private patients, accompanied by well-dressed mothers and nannies, were a different matter altogether. He found himself wondering how Kate would look in the beautiful clothes they wore.

He had little to say to her during the day; the talk was largely general, and he took care to be casually friendly and impersonal. He was rewarded by a more open manner towards him; the slight tartness with which she had greeted him that morning had disappeared. He found himself wanting to know her better. He shrugged the thought aside; their encounters were infrequent, and his work gave him little time in which to indulge a passing whim—for that was what it was.

After supper he drove Kate and her mother home. It had been a delightful day and there had been plans to repeat it.

'We mustn't lose touch,' Mrs Shaw had declared. 'Now that we have seen each other again. Next time you must come for the weekend.'

Sitting once more with Prince in the Bentley,

Kate thought it unlikely. As it was she was feeling edgy about returning so late in the evening. Even at the speed at which Mr Tait-Bouverie was driving, it would be almost midnight before she got to Lady Cowder's house.

Mr Tait-Bouverie, glancing at his watch, had a very good idea as to what she was thinking. He said over his shoulder, 'Shall I drop you off before I take your mother home? Or do you wish to go there first?'

'Oh, please, it's a bit late—if you wouldn't mind...'

The house was in darkness when they reached it, but that wasn't to say that Lady Cowder wasn't sitting up in bed waiting for her with an eye on the clock.

It was foolish to feel so apprehensive. She worked long hours, and Lady Cowder put upon her quite shamelessly in a wistful fashion which didn't deceive Kate—but she couldn't risk losing her job. She didn't need to save much more before she would be able to see the bank manager...

Mr Tait-Bouverie drew up soundlessly and got out of the car.

'You have a key?'

'Yes. The kitchen door—it's round the side of the house...'

Kate bade her mother a quiet goodnight, rubbed the top of Prince's head and got out of the car.

'Give me the key,' said Mr Tait-Bouverie, and walked silently beside her to the door, unlocked it and handed the key back to her.

'Thank you for taking us to the Shaws',' whispered Kate. 'We had a lovely day...'

'Like old times?' He bent suddenly and kissed her cheek. 'Sleep well, Kate.'

She went past him, closed the door soundlessly and took off her shoes. Creeping like a mouse through the house, she wondered why on earth he had kissed her. It had been a careless kiss, no doubt, but it hadn't been necessary...

CHAPTER THREE

KATE FOUND HERSELF thinking about Mr Tait-
Bouverie rather more than she would have wished
during the next day or so. Really, she told herself, there was no reason for her to do so. They
were hardly likely to meet again, and if they did it
wouldn't be at a mutual friend's house. She told herself that his kiss had annoyed her—a careless reward,
a kind of tip. Her cheeks grew hot at the very idea.
She dismissed him from her mind with some difficulty—but he stayed there, rather like a sore tooth,
to be avoided at all costs.

Lady Cowder was being difficult. She seldom
raised her voice but her perpetual, faintly complaining remarks, uttered in a martyr-like way, were difficult to put up with. She implied, in the gentle voice
which Kate found so hard to bear, that Kate could
work a little harder.

'A big strong girl like you,' she observed one
lunchtime, 'with all day in which to keep the place

in good order. I don't ask much from you, Kate, but I should have thought that an easy task such as turning out the drawing room could be done in an hour or so. And the attics—I am sure that there are a great many things there which the village jumble sale will be only too glad to have. If I had the strength I would do it myself, but you know quite well that I am delicate.'

Kate, offering a generous portion of sirloin steak with its accompanying mushrooms, grilled tomatoes, French-fried onions and buttered courgettes, murmured meaninglessly. It was a constant wonder to her that her employer ate so heartily while at the same time deploring her lack of appetite.

Because she needed to keep her job, she somehow contrived to arrange her busy days so that she could spend an hour or so in the attics. There was a good deal of rubbish there, and a quantity of old clothes and pots which no self-respecting jumble sale would even consider, but she picked them over carefully in the hope of finding something worth offering. It was a thankless task, though, and took up any spare time she had in the afternoons. So it was that when Mr Tait-Bouverie called she knew nothing of his visit until he had gone again.

'Really,' said Lady Cowder in her gentle, complaining voice, 'it was most inconvenient, Kate. You were up in the attics and there was no one to get us tea...'

'I left the tea tray ready, Lady Cowder.'

'Yes, yes, I know that, but poor James had to boil the kettle and make the tea himself. As you know, I have had a headache all day and did not dare to leave the chaise longue.'

The idea of 'poor James' having to make his own tea pleased Kate. Serve him right, she reflected waspishly. And there had been only thinly cut bread and butter and sponge cake for tea, since Lady Cowder had declared that her digestion would tolerate nothing richer. He would have gone back home hungry.

Kate didn't bother to analyse her unkind thoughts—which was a pity for he had gone to some trouble to do her a good turn.

Mr Tait-Bouverie had gone to see his aunt on a request from his mother, and he hadn't wanted to go. His leisure hours were few, and to waste some of them on a duty visit went against the grain—although he'd had to admit that the prospect of seeing Kate again made the visit more tolerable.

Lady Cowder had been pleased to see him, regaling him in a plaintive little voice with her ill-health, deploring the fact that Kate had taken herself off to the attics so that there was no one to bring in the tea tray.

Mr Tait-Bouverie had made the tea, eaten a slice of the cake Kate had left on the kitchen table while he boiled the kettle and borne the tray back to the

drawing room. He was a kind man, despite his some-
what austere manner, and he had listened patiently
while his aunt chatted in her wispy voice. Presently
he had striven to cheer her up.

'I'm going to Norway in a week or so,' he told her.
'I am to give some lectures in several towns there,
as well as do some work in the hospitals. I was there
a few years ago and they asked me to go back. It's a
delightful country...'

'Ah, you young people with your opportunities
to enjoy yourselves around the world—how fortunate you are.'

He agreed mildly. There wouldn't be much opportunity to enjoy himself, he reflected—the odd free
day, perhaps, but certainly not the social life he felt
sure his aunt envisaged. Not being a very sociable
man, except with close friends, he hardly thought
he would miss that.

His aunt ate the rest of the bread and butter in a
die-away fashion, while at the same time deploring
her lack of appetite.

'Perhaps a holiday would improve my health,'
she observed. 'I have never been to Norway but, of
course, I couldn't consider it without a companion.'

Mr Tait-Bouverie, a man who thought before he
spoke, for once allowed himself to break this rule.

'Then why not go? Surely a companion won't be
too hard to find?'

'The cost, dear boy...'

He remained silent; Lady Cowder could afford a dozen companions if she wished, but, as his mother had told him charitably, 'Your aunt has always been careful of her money.'

Lady Cowder glanced at the empty cakestand. 'Really, I don't know what I pay Kate for—my wants are so simple, and yet she seems unable to offer me even a simple meal.'

Mr Tait-Bouverie wished that Kate would come down from the attics; he had no more than a passing interest in her but she intrigued him. He said, half jokingly, 'Why should you pay for a companion? Take Kate with you. She seems to be a woman of good sense, capable of smoothing your path…'

Lady Cowder sat up straight. 'My dear James, what a splendid idea. And, of course, I need only pay her her usual wages. She will be delighted to have the opportunity to travel. Tell me, where would you recommend that we should stay?'

Mr Tait-Bouverie hadn't expected his suggestion to be taken so seriously. 'Kate might not wish to go to Norway…' he said. 'Though at this time of year one of the smaller villages around the fiords would be delightful. Very quiet, of course, but by no means cut off from civilisation—these places attract many visitors in the summer months. Or you could stay in Bergen—a pleasant small city with everything one could wish for.'

'Could you arrange it for me?'

'I'm so sorry, Aunt. I'm not free to do that. My trip to Norway has been arranged, of course. I suggest that you get hold of a good travel agent and get him to see to everything. That is, if you intend to go.'

'Of course I intend to, James. I'll tell Kate in the morning and she can see to the details.'

'She might not wish to go.'

'Nonsense. It's the chance of a lifetime for the girl. A free holiday and nothing to do. I hardly think it necessary to pay her her wages at all—after all, she won't need to spend any money.'

Mr Tait-Bouverie lifted an eyebrow. 'I don't think that would be legal. You wouldn't wish to be involved in a court case.'

'Certainly not. She will, of course, have to make herself useful.'

'If she agrees to go with you…'

'She can have a month's notice if she refuses,' said Lady Cowder tartly.

Mr Tait-Bouverie, his duty visit paid, took himself off home. There had been no sign of Kate, and the thought crossed his mind that he might have done her a disservice. He reminded himself that she was a young woman capable of managing her own affairs. She had only to refuse to go and look for another job.

He dismissed the whole affair from his mind but, all the same, it returned to bother him during the next few days.

* * *

Kate, bidden to the drawing room by one of the old-fashioned bells which still hung in the kitchen, took off her apron, tucked an errant russet tress behind an ear, and went upstairs. The sack? she wondered. Or, far worse, another visit from Claudia. She opened the door, went into the room and stood quietly, waiting to hear whatever news her employer had for her.

Lady Cowder stared at her. Really, the girl didn't look like a housekeeper and certainly didn't behave like one; she didn't even look interested…

'I have decided to take a holiday, Kate. I need relaxation. My palpitations must be a sign of something more serious although, as you know, I am never one to worry about myself. I intend to go abroad—to Norway. You will come with me. I need someone to take care of me, see to travel arrangements and so on. It is a pleasant surprise to you, no doubt, to have a holiday which will cost you nothing. I shall, of course, continue to pay you your wages. You may consider yourself very fortunate, Kate.'

Kate said quietly, 'Are you asking me to go away with you, Lady Cowder?'

'Well, of course—have you not been listening?'

'Yes, but you haven't asked me if I wish to go, Lady Cowder.'

Lady Cowder turned a shocked gaze upon her. 'You are my housekeeper, Kate. I expect you to do what I wish.'

'If I am asked,' said Kate calmly. 'And I would prefer not to go, Lady Cowder. I am sure you will have no difficulty in finding a suitable companion.'

'And you expect to remain here, being paid for doing nothing?'

Kate didn't answer, and Lady Cowder spent a few moments in reflection. She didn't want to give Kate the sack—she was hard-working, a splendid cook and hadn't haggled over her wages. Nor was she a clock-watcher, everlastingly going on about her rights. To engage a companion, even for a month, would cost money—something Lady Cowder couldn't contemplate without shuddering...

There was only one solution. She said, in the wispy voice she used when she wanted sympathy, 'Please consider my offer, Kate. It would be for a month, and I am prepared to pay you the normal wages of a companion—considerably more than you get at present. Of course, when we return your wages will revert to the present amount.'

'What exactly would my wages be, Lady Cowder?' asked Kate pleasantly.

Lady Cowder closed her eyes and assumed a pained expression. She was thinking rapidly. Mrs Arbuthnott, a friend of hers, had just engaged a new companion and her salary seemed excessive, although Lady Cowder had been assured that it was the standard rate. Surely half that amount would be sufficient for Kate;

that would still be almost twice as much as her present money.

Lady Cowder opened her eyes and told Kate.

Twice as much, thought Kate, and if she could save all of it she would soon have the money she needed. She said quietly, 'Very well, Lady Cowder, I will come with you. When do you intend to go?'

'As soon as possible, while I still have my health and strength. Go to Thame tomorrow morning and see the travel agents. I wish to fly—first class, of course—and stay at one of the smaller towns situated close to the fiords. A good hotel, not isolated, with all the amenities I am accustomed to.'

'You want me to bring back particulars of several places so that you may choose?'

'Yes, yes. And some possible dates—within the next two weeks.' Lady Cowder sank back against the cushions. 'Now bring me my coffee. I could eat a biscuit or two with it.'

Kate, watching the coffee percolate, weighed the doubtful delights of travelling with her employer against twice as much money for a month. She didn't expect to enjoy herself, but it would mean that she would be able to give up this job sooner than she had expected. It would also mean careful budgeting; her mother would have to manage on her pension while Kate was away so that every spare penny of her wages could be saved.

'The chance of a lifetime,' Kate told Horace, of-

fering him a saucer of his favourite cat food. 'I shall become a famous cook and live happily ever after.'

She told her mother when she went home for her half-day.

'Darling, what a stroke of luck…' Mrs Crosby got a pencil and the back of an envelope and began to do sums. The result was satisfactory and she nodded and smiled. Then she frowned. 'Clothes—a hotel—you'll need clothes…'

'No, I shan't, Mother. There's that mole-coloured crêpe thing I had years ago. That'll do very well if I have to change for the evening. Lady Cowder wouldn't expect me to be fashionable, and no one will know us there.' She thought for a moment. 'There is also that black velvet skirt—if I borrow your silk blouse, that'll do as well. I'll only need skirts and blouses and sweaters during the day, and the navy jacket and dress will do to travel in.'

'One or two summer dresses?' suggested Mrs Crosby. 'It's July, love, it could be very warm.'

'I'll take a couple of cotton dresses. But I'm a bit vague about the weather there—for all I know it might even be getting cooler! I should have asked at the travel agents, but there was so much to discuss. I'm to drive us to Heathrow and leave the car there, and the flight should be easy enough. We're to be met by a taxi at the airport and taken to the hotel in Bergen that Lady Cowder has chosen. She wants

to spend a day or two there before we go to Olden;
there's a modern hotel there. It's a small village on
the edge of a fiord. I do wonder if Lady Cowder is
going to like it. A whole month...'

'Let's hope she will get to know some of the
people staying there. She plays bridge, doesn't she?
Hopefully so will they; that will give you some free
time. I can't think why she can't go alone. She's elderly, but she's quite fit, and there would be plenty
of help at the kind of hotels she stays at.'

'I'd much rather have been left to caretake—
but don't forget all the extra money, Mother. And a
month goes quickly enough.'

'Money isn't everything,' observed Mrs Crosby.

'No, but it does help...it *is* a stroke of luck.'

Something she had to remind herself of during the
next ten days, for Lady Cowder's orders and counter-
orders were continuous. Her entire wardrobe had to
be inspected, pressed, packed—and then unpacked,
because she had changed her mind as to what she
would or would not take. Kate's patience was sorely
tried.

The ten days went quickly and Kate, busy from
early morning until late at night, had little time to
think her own thoughts. All the same, from time
to time she thought about Mr Tait-Bouverie. She
had to admit to herself that she would have liked to
know more about him. 'Not that he would remem-

ber me,' she said to herself as she repacked Lady Cowder's cases for the third time.

Mr Tait-Bouverie hadn't forgotten her. The thought of her wove through his head like a bright ribbon, disrupting his erudite ponderings over the lectures he was to give at the various hospitals to which he had been invited in Norway. Only by an effort was he able to dismiss her from his mind as he stepped onto a platform and embarked on the very latest advances in paediatrics. It would not do, he told himself firmly; the girl was disrupting his work as well as his leisure hours. He even dreamed of her...

Surprisingly, the journey to Bergen went smoothly. Kate drove to Heathrow, deaf to Lady Cowder's back-seat driving while she went over in her mind all the things she had to see about in order to get them safely to the hotel in Bergen. She guided her employer safely onto the plane, assured her for the tenth time that the car had been safely parked, that she had the tickets in her handbag, that the plane was perfectly safe and that they would be met at the airport in Norway.

Lady Cowder assumed the air of an invalid once on board, and asked wistfully for a glass of brandy— as she felt faint. She murmured, 'My heart, you know,' when the stewardess brought it to her, and she smiled bravely at the two passengers on the other

side of the gangway. She then sank back with her eyes closed, and stayed that way until they were airborne and lunch was served.

'Perhaps you would prefer just a little soup?' suggested the stewardess.

'How kind,' murmured Lady Cowder. 'But I believe that a small meal might give me the strength I shall need when we land.'

Kate listened to all of this nonsense with some amusement, tinged with dismay. A month of this and it would be she who would be the invalid, not Lady Cowder.

Lady Cowder was helped off the plane with great care, Kate following burdened with scarves, handbags and books. Once they were alone, Lady Cowder said sharply, 'Well, don't just stand there, Kate—find whoever it is who is to meet us.'

This was easily done, seeing that he was standing with a placard in his hand with Lady Cowder's name on it. A pleasant man, he went with Kate to collect their luggage, settled Lady Cowder in the back of the car and held the door open for Kate.

'Get in front, Kate,' said Lady Cowder. 'I need to be quiet for a time. I'm exhausted.'

Kate did as she was told, thinking thoughts best left unsaid, then cheered up in response to the driver's friendliness.

There was so much to see as he drove; her spirits rose as he pointed out anything which he thought

might interest her and by the time they reached Bergen, she was ready to enjoy every minute of their stay there. He indicated the fish market, the shops, and the funicular to the top of the mountain behind the town, then asked how long they would be staying.

'Only two days. I don't suppose I'll have time to see everything, but I'll do my best.'

An optimistic remark, as it turned out.

The Hotel Norje, in the centre of the town, was everything anyone could wish for—even Lady Cowder gave her opinion that it was comfortable. She had a splendid room overlooking the Ole Nulle Plass— a handsome square opening into a park—and an equally splendid bathroom.

'You may unpack at once,' she told Kate, 'and phone for tea. You had better have a cup before you go to your room. I shall rest for an hour or so and dine later.'

Kate poured tea for both of them, unpacked Lady Cowder's luggage and disposed of it in cupboards and drawers, only too aware that in a couple of days she would have to pack it all again. She did it silently and competently, then went down to Reception to collect her room key.

Her room was on the floor above Lady Cowder's. It was nicely furnished, but lacked the flowers, bowl of fruit and comfortable chairs. There was no bathroom either; a small shower cubicle was curtained off in one corner. Kate unpacked what she would need

for a day or so, showered, got into the mole crêpe
and went back to her employer.

'Go and get your dinner. You can tidy the room
while I'm in the restaurant, and wait here. I shall
probably need some help with getting to bed; I'm
utterly exhausted.'

Kate, her tongue clenched between her splendid
teeth, went down to the restaurant. Obviously Lady
Cowder didn't intend to eat with her housekeeper.

Not that Kate minded—she was hungry, and ate
everything set before her—soup, cod, beautifully
cooked, and a dessert of cloud berries and cream.
She sat over her coffee, oblivious of the admiring
glances cast at her. Despite the sombre dress, her
lovely face and magnificent person made a striking picture. Indeed, several people wished her good
evening as she left the restaurant, and she answered
them with her serene smile.

She paused at the reception desk to ask about
sending letters to England, accepted a free postcard,
wrote on it then and there and left it for the receptionist to post, with the promise of paying for the
stamp in the morning. She would have liked to have
phoned her mother, but she had only a small amount
of English money. She would have to go to a bank in
the morning and change some of it.

Lady Cowder greeted her crossly. 'What a very
long time you have been, Kate. Had you forgotten

that I was waiting for your return until I could go to dinner?'

Kate, mellowed by good food and the friendly glances she had received, said cheerfully, 'You could have come down to the restaurant, Lady Cowder— there was no need to wait for me.'

Quite the wrong answer. 'See that someone brings me a warm drink when I return, and tidy the room and bathroom. I sent the chambermaid away. I can't find my travelling clock; you had better look for it.'

Kate found the clock, tidied the bathroom and sat down in one of the easy chairs to wait. She was going to earn every penny of that extra money, she reflected, but it would be worth it. She spent some time thinking about her plans for the future, and then allowed her thoughts to dwell on Mr Tait-Bouverie. She was sorry for him, having an aunt as disagreeable as Lady Cowder. She wondered if his mother was like her. Perhaps that was why he wasn't married. To have a mother like that was bad enough, to be married to a woman of the same nature would be disastrous.

Her musings were cut short by Lady Cowder's return. She declared that she must go to bed immediately—which didn't prevent her from wanting this, that and the other before Kate was at last told that she might go.

In her room at last, Kate took a quick shower and got into bed. Her last thought was one of thankful-

ness that Lady Cowder was going to have her breakfast in bed and didn't wish to be disturbed until ten o'clock. A splendid chance to nip out directly after she had had breakfast and take a quick look at the town.

Kate woke early and got up at once. It was a grey morning, but that didn't deter her from her plan. She went downstairs and found several other people breakfasting. They greeted her pleasantly and waved her towards the enormous centre-table loaded with dishes of herrings, cheese, bacon, eggs and sausages. It seemed that one helped oneself and ate all one wanted. She piled her plate, asked for coffee, and sat down at a table by herself, only to be invited to join a group of young men and women close by. They were on holiday, they told her, on their way to the north of the country. When she told them that she knew nothing of Norway, they told her where to go and what to see.

'You are alone?' they asked.

'No. I'm travelling with an elderly lady—I'm her housekeeper in England.'

'So you are not free?'

'No. Only for an hour or two when it is convenient for her.'

'Then you must not lose time. The shops will be open soon, but the fish market is already busy. Go quickly and look there; it is a splendid sight.'

It was an easy walk down the main shopping street, and well worth a visit. It wasn't just the fish, although they were both colourful and splendid, it was the flower stalls, bulging with flowers every colour of the rainbow. Kate went from one to the other and longed to buy the great bunches of roses and carnations, thinking how delightful it would be to buy a whole salmon and take it back home. Impossible, of course. She caught sight of a clock and hurried back in time to present herself in Lady Cowder's room.

There was no reply to her civil good morning.

'Go down to the desk and arrange for a car to drive us out to Troldhaugen—Edward Grieg, the composer, lived there—we will return here for lunch. Make sure that the driver is a steady man.'

Kate, not sure how she was to do that, decided to ignore it and hope for the best. Their driver turned out to be a youngish man who spoke excellent English and was full of information. Kate listened to every word, but Lady Cowder closed her eyes and asked Kate to give her the smelling salts.

They had to walk a short distance to the house, something which they hadn't known about. Lady Cowder, in unsuitable shoes, declared that the walk would tire her, but rather grudgingly agreed to Kate having a quick look.

There were other tourists there with their guides, but Kate, given a strict ten minutes, didn't dare linger.

All the same, when she returned to the car, she

was expected to give an account of what she had seen. Kate suspected that when they returned to England and Lady Cowder met her friends again she would wish to recount her activities in Norway. A little knowledge of Grieg's house and Kate's impressions of it would be useful in conversation...

Kate didn't escape for the rest of that day. Lady Cowder had little desire to stroll around looking at the shops; certainly the fish market had no attraction. She intended to take the funicular to the top of Mount Floyen.

'It would, of course, be much nicer to go by car, but that would take time and probably not be worth the journey. Besides, I'm told everyone goes by the funicular.'

Kate held her tongue, afraid that if she ventured an opinion they might not go at all.

It was raining when Kate got up the next morning. It rained a great deal in Bergen, the friendly receptionist told her, but that didn't deter her from putting on her raincoat and tying a scarf over her head and hurrying out as soon as she had breakfasted. This was their last day in Bergen, and the chances were that Lady Cowder would refuse to go out at all.

The funicular was out of the question, so were the various museums. If she walked very fast she could get a glimpse of the Bryggen, with its medieval workshops and old buildings. She started off down the main street towards Torget and the Bryggen, head down against the rain, only to be brought to a sudden halt against a vast Burberry-covered chest.

'Good morning, Kate,' said Mr Tait Bouverie. 'Out early, aren't you?'

She goggled up at him, rain dripping from her sodden scarf.

'Well, I never...!' She gulped and added sedately, 'Good morning, sir.'

Since he made no move to go on his way, she added politely, 'You don't mind if I go on? I haven't much time.'

He gripped her arm gently. 'To do what, Kate?'

'Well, Lady Cowder doesn't like to be disturbed until ten o'clock, so I want to see as much as I can before then.' She added hopefully, 'I expect you're busy.'

'Not until midday. Where are you going?'

She told him, trying not to sound impatient.

'In that case—' he lifted a hand at a passing taxi '—allow me to make up for the delay I have caused you.'

He had bundled her neatly into the taxi before she could draw breath.

'It is a little after half-past eight; you have more than an hour. Tell me, how long have you and my aunt been here?'

'We're here for two days; we go to Olden later today—for three weeks.'

'I shall be surprised if my aunt remains there for so long. It is a delightful little place, but, beyond the hotel, there isn't much to do. There are ferries, of course, going to various other small villages around the fiords, but I doubt if she would enjoy that.' The taxi stopped. 'Here we are, let us not waste time.'

For all the world as though I didn't want to see the place, thought Kate crossly, getting out of the taxi and ignoring his hand.

She said coldly, 'Thank you for the taxi, Mr Tait-Bouverie. I'm sure you have other plans…'

He took her arm. 'None at all, Kate.' He led her down a wide passage lined with old wooden houses. 'Let us have a cup of coffee and you can recover your good humour.'

'I have only just had breakfast,' said Kate, still coldly polite. A remark which was wasted on him. The wooden houses, so beautifully preserved, housed small offices, workshops and a couple of cafés. She found herself sitting in one of them, meekly drinking the delicious brew set before her.

'They make very good coffee,' observed Mr Tait-Bouverie chattily.

'Yes,' said Kate. 'It's very kind of you to bring me here, but really there is no need…'

A waste of breath. 'Your mother is well?' he asked.

'Yes, thank you. The plaster is to come off very shortly.' Kate finished her coffee and picked up her gloves. 'I'd better be getting on. Thank you for the coffee, sir.'

Mr Tait-Bouverie said pleasantly, 'If you call me "sir" just once more, Kate, I shall strangle you!'

She gaped at him. 'But of course I must call you "sir," Mr Tait-Bouverie. You forget that I'm in your aunt's employ—her housekeeper.'

'There are housekeepers and housekeepers, and well you know it. You may cook divinely, dust and sweep and so on with an expert hand, but you are no more a housekeeper than I am. I am not by nature in the habit of poking my nose into other people's business—but it is obvious to me, Kate, that you are housekeeping for a reason. Oh, I'm sure you need the money in order to live, but over and above that I confess that I am curious.'

Kate said coolly, 'I'm sure that my plans are of no interest to you, s—Mr Tait-Bouverie.'

'Oh, but they are. You see, I can think of no reason why you should work for my aunt. I dare say she underpays you, certainly she works you hard. She may be my aunt, but I should point out that my visits to her are purely in order to reassure my mother, who is her younger sister and feels that she must keep in touch.'

'Oh, have you a mother?' Kate went pink; it was a silly question, deserving a snub.

'Indeed, yes.' He smiled faintly. 'Like everyone else.'

He lifted a finger and asked for more coffee and, when it had been brought, settled back in his chair. 'Are you saving for your bottom drawer?' he asked.

'Heavens, no. Girls don't have bottom drawers nowadays.'

'Ah—I stand corrected. Then why?'

It was obvious she wasn't going to escape until she had answered him. 'I want to start a catering business. Just from home—making simple meals to order, cooking for weddings and parties—that sort of thing.'

'Of course. You are a splendid cook and manager. Why don't you get going?'

It was a relief to tell someone about her schemes. For a moment she hesitated at telling this man whom she hardly knew and would probably not meet again on equal terms. But she felt reckless. Perhaps it was being in foreign places, perhaps it was the caffeine in all the coffee she was drinking.

'I'm saving up,' she told him. 'You see, if I can go to the bank and tell the manager that I've a hundred pounds he might lend me the money I need.'

Mr Tait-Bouverie looked placid, although he doubted very much if a bank manager would see eye to eye with Kate. A hundred pounds was a very small sum these days: it might buy dinner for two at a fashionable restaurant in London, or two seats for the latest play; it might be enough to pay the electricity bill or for a TV licence, but one could hardly regard it as capital.

He said in a kind voice, 'Do you have much more to save?'

'No. That's why I've come with Lady Cowder. She has said she will double my wages if I act as her companion while she is here.'

He nodded. 'I have often wondered, what do companions do?'

'Well, they are just there—I mean, ready to find things and mend and iron—and talk, if they're asked to. And buy tickets and see about luggage and all that kind of thing.'

'Will you get any time to yourself?' He put the question gently and she answered readily.

'I'm not sure—but I don't think so. I mean, not a day off in the week or anything like that.'

'In that case, we have just fifteen minutes to take a quick look around while we're here. There's a rather nice shop along here that does wood carvings and some charming little figures—trolls. Have you bought a troll to take home?'

She shook her head. 'Not yet...'

He bought her one, saying lightly, 'Just to bring you luck.'

They went back to the hotel by taxi presently, and when it stopped, Kate asked, 'Are you coming in? Shall I tell Lady Cowder you're here?'

He said unhurriedly, 'No, I must go to the hospital very shortly and later today I'm going to Oslo. No need to say that we met, since there is no chance of my aunt seeing me.'

Kate offered a hand. 'Thank you for taking me to the Bryggen and giving me coffee. Please forget everything I told you. I shouldn't have said anything, but I don't have much chance to talk to anyone. Anyway, it doesn't matter, does it? We don't meet—I mean, like this.'

He smiled down at her lovely face, damp from the rain. All he said was, 'I do hope you enjoy your stay in Norway.'

She didn't want to go into the hotel; she would have liked to have spent the day with him. The thought astonished her.

CHAPTER FOUR

LADY COWDER WAS sitting up in bed eating a good breakfast.

'They tell me it is raining,' she informed Kate. 'There seems no point in staying here. Go down to the desk and arrange for a car to take us to Olden. I wish to leave within the next two hours.'

It was a complicated journey—Kate had taken the trouble to read the various leaflets at the reception desk—involving several ferries, and quite a distance to go. But there would be no need to get out of the car, she was assured, unless they wished to stop for refreshment on the way. It would be prudent, decided Kate, to get the clerk to phone the hotel at Olden. She asked for the bill, asked if coffee could be sent up to Lady Cowder's room in an hour's time, and went back upstairs. There was all the packing to see to...

The rain stopped after they had been travelling for an hour, and by the time they reached Gudvangen there was blue sky and sunshine.

'Tell the driver to take us to a hotel for lunch,'
said Lady Cowder.

He took them up a hair-raisingly steep road.
'Nineteen hairpin bends,' he told them proudly, 'and
a gradient of one in five. A splendid view is to be
had from the top.'

'But the hotel?' queried Lady Cowder faintly. She
had been sitting with her eyes closed, trying not to
see the sheer drop on either side of the road.

'A splendid hotel,' promised the driver. As indeed
it was. Once inside, with her back to the towering
mountains and the fiord far below, Lady Cowder did
ample justice to the smoked salmon salad she was
offered. The driver had taken it for granted that he
would have his lunch with his passengers, so he and
Kate carried on an interesting conversation while
they ate.

Olden, it seemed, was very small, although the
hotel was modern and very comfortable. 'There are
splendid walks,' said the driver, looking doubtfully at
Lady Cower. 'There are also shops—two or three—
selling everything.'

Lady Cowder looked so doubtful in her turn that
Kate hastily asked to be told more about the hotel.

Presently they took the ferry, after another hair-
raising descent to the village below, and crossed the
Sognefjord to Balestrand to rejoin the road to Olden.
Quite a long journey—but not nearly long enough for
Kate, craning her neck to see as much as possible of

the great grey mountains crowding down to the fiord. She was enchanted to see that wherever there was a patch of land, however small, squashed between the towering grey peaks, there were houses— even one house on its own. Charming wooden houses with bright red roofs and painted walls.

'Isn't it a bit lonely in the winter?' she asked.

The driver shrugged. 'It is their life. The houses are comfortable, there is electricity everywhere, they have their boats.'

Olden, when they reached it, was indeed small— a handful of houses, a small landing stage and, a little way from the village, the hotel. Reassuringly large and modern, its car park was half-full. Lady Cowder, who had had little to say but had somehow conveyed her disapproval of the scenery, brightened at the sight of it.

Certainly their welcome lacked nothing in warmth and courtesy. She was led to her room, overlooking the fiord, and assured that a tray of tea would be sent up immediately, together with the dinner menu.

Kate unpacked, went down to the reception desk to make sure that their driver had been suitably fed and went to find him. He had been paid, of course, but Lady Cowder had added no tip, nor her thanks. Kate handed him what she hoped was sufficient and added her thanks, knowing that Lady Cowder would want an account of everything Kate had spent from the money she had been given for their expenses. She would probably have to repay it from her own wages but she didn't care—the man had been friendly; besides, he had told her that he had five children.

Her room, she discovered, was two floors above Lady Cowder's and at the back of the hotel, its windows looking out towards the mountains. It was obviously the kind of room reserved for such as herself: companions, Ladies' maids, poor relations. It was comfortable enough but it had no shower, and the bathroom was at the end of the passage to be shared with several other residents. She didn't mind, she told herself—and felt humiliation deep down.

She was to eat her dinner early and then return to Lady Cowder's room and wait for her there, occupying herself with the odd jobs: buttons to sew on, odds and ends to find, things to be put ready for the night.

She enjoyed dinner; the dining room was elegant and the food good. The brown crêpe hardly did justice to her surroundings, but she forgot that in the satisfaction of discovering that there were several English people staying at the hotel. Moreover, they looked to be the kind of people Lady Cowder might strike up a passing acquaintance with. Kate, straining her ears to catch their conversation, was delighted to hear that they were discussing bridge, a game her employer enjoyed.

She finished her coffee and went back to Lady Cowder's room, and listened with outward serenity to that lady's grumbles about a crumpled dress.

Alone, she tidied up, fulfilled the odd jobs she had been given to do, arranged for Lady Cowder's breakfast to be brought to her in her room and then went to look out of the window.

The sky had cleared and the last of the evening sun was lighting the sombre mountains, making the snow caps that most of them wore glisten. But if the mountains were sombre, there was plenty of life going on beneath them. Passengers were going aboard a ferry, and she wished that she was going with them to some other small village, probably isolated except for the ferries which called there. Not that she sensed any loneliness amongst the people she had met so far—indeed, they seemed happy and perfectly content.

Who wouldn't be, she reflected, living in such glorious surroundings? As far as she could discover, communications were more than adequate; the driver had told her more in a couple of hours than any guide book could have done. She watched the ferry until it was out of sight round a distant bend in the fiord, and then she drew the curtains—Lady Cowder's orders.

Her employer was in a good temper when she returned. 'So fortunate,' she observed. 'There are several English people staying here, only too glad to make up a table for bridge. They tell me that this hotel is most comfortable; I am glad I decided to come here.'

After the first few days Kate agreed with her. A bridge table was set up each afternoon and she was

free for several hours to do as she liked. She spent
the first afternoon walking to the village, which was
cheerfully full with visitors, its one shop bustling
with tourists. It sold everything, she discovered,
not only souvenirs but clothes and shoes, household
goods and food. She bought cards to send home,
walked to the end of the village and then retraced
her steps, stopping to admire the smart men's outfit-
ters displaying the latest male fashions—wondering
when they would be worn in such a small commu-
nity.

A ferry had just come in, and she spent some time
watching the cars landing and the passengers coming ashore. There were plenty of people waiting to
board, too, and she wanted very much to know where
it was going. In a day or two, she promised herself,
when she felt more at home in her surroundings, she
would find out.

After that afternoon she got bolder. She went a
little further each day, stopping to ask the way, discovering that English seemed to come as easily to the
Norwegians as their own tongue. Greatly daring, she
took the bus to Loen, a pretty village some kilometres away from Olden. She had no time to explore it,
for Lady Cowder had told her that she must be in the
hotel by five o'clock, ready to carry out her wishes,
but at least, she told herself, she had been there.

She had suggested that Lady Cowder might like
to hire a car and visit some of the neighbouring vil-

lages herself, only to be told that it wasn't for her to suggest what they should do.

'I should have thought,' said Lady Cowder, sounding reproachful, 'that you were more than grateful for the splendid time that you are having. Heaven knows, there is little enough for you to do.'

It wasn't a companion that Lady Cowder needed, thought Kate. A lady's maid would have been nearer the mark. Kate, who had a kind heart, felt sorry for her employer, being so incapable of doing the simplest thing for herself. Perhaps she had had a husband who'd spoilt her and seen to it that she never had to worry about anything.

'Very nice, too,' said Kate, addressing a handful of sheep peering at her from their pasture, which was sandwiched between two frowning mountains. 'But who on earth is likely to wrap me in carefree luxury?'

She walked on past the sheep, and along a narrow road running beside the fiord. She wished her mother could have been with her. Never mind the mundane tasks she was given to do, the indifference of her employer, the small—perhaps unintentional—pinpricks meant to put her in her place a dozen times a day; she was happy to be in this peaceful land. Just as long as the bridge parties continued each afternoon, life would be more than tolerable.

It was the following morning, when she went as usual to find out what Lady Cowder wanted her to do be-

fore she went down to breakfast, that she found that
lady in a bad temper. She ignored Kate's good morning, and told her to pull the curtains and fetch her a
glass of water.

'The Butlers are leaving today.' She spoke with
the air of a martyr. 'There is no one else in this place
who is willing to make up a table for bridge. I shall
die of boredom.' She looked at Kate as though it
was her fault.

'Perhaps there will be some other guests…'

'I have enquired about that—something you might
have done if you had been here. There are no English
or Americans expected. I intend to leave here. There
is a good hotel at Alesund; the Butlers have stayed
there and recommend it. Go downstairs to the reception desk and tell them that we are leaving tomorrow.
Then phone the hotel and get rooms.'

She handed Kate a slip of paper with the name
of the hotel and the phone number on it. 'I require a
comfortable room; I hardly need remind you of that.
Get a room for yourself. Those with a shower are
cheaper, and it doesn't matter if it isn't on the same
floor as mine. Now hurry along and do as I ask instead of standing there, saying nothing.'

Kate went down to talk to the clerk at the reception desk. Why had they come all this way? she
wondered. Lady Cowder could have played bridge
just as easily at home. She set about the business of
smoothing Lady Cowder's progress through Norway.

Alesund was a large town, built on several islands, and the hotel was, fortunately, to Lady Cowder's liking. It had all the trappings she found so necessary for her comfort—a uniformed porter at its door, bell boys to see to the luggage, a smiling chambermaid and willing room-service. Her room, the lady was pleased to admit, was extremely comfortable—and there was a number of Americans and English staying at the hotel.

Kate unpacked once again, listened to a list of instructions without really hearing them, and went to find her own room, which was two flights up with a view of surrounding rooftops. It was comfortable, though, and she had her own shower. She hung up her few clothes and went down to make sure that Reception knew about Lady Cowder's wishes. She found some information leaflets, too, and took them back with her to read later.

Hopefully they would stay here for the rest of their time in Norway—they had been only nine days at Olden; there were still more than two weeks before they returned to England. Kate prayed that there would be an unending flow of bridge players for the next few weeks. Certainly, there were several Americans in the foyer.

She went back to Lady Cowder to tell her this, and was told to order tea to be sent up.

'And you can get yourself tea, if you wish,' said Lady Cowder, amiable at the prospect of suitable company.

* * *

Mr Tait-Bouverie, finding himself with several days of freedom between lectures, reminded himself that his aunt might be glad to see him. It was his duty, he told himself, to keep an eye on her so that he could assure his mother that her sister was well. At the same time he could make sure that Kate was having as good a time as possible.

It annoyed him that he was unable to forget her while at the same time remaining unwillingly aware of her. He reminded himself that his interest in her was merely to see if she would achieve her ambition and branch out on her own. She was a competent girl, probably she would build up a solid business cooking pies and whatever.

He drove himself to Olden, to be told at the hotel there that Lady Cowder had given up her room and gone to Alesund. So after lunch he drove on, enjoying the grand scenery, queueing for the ferries as he came to them, going unhurriedly so that he had the leisure to look around him. He had been on that road some years earlier, but the scenery never failed to delight him.

It was four o'clock by the time he reached the hotel at Alesund and its foyer was nearly full. He saw Kate at once, standing with her back to him, reading a poster on a wall. He crossed to her without haste, tapped her lightly on the shoulder and said,

'Hello, Kate.' He was aware of a deep content at the sight of her.

Kate had turned round at his touch and for a moment her delight at seeing him again was plain to see. Though only for a moment. She wished him good afternoon in a quiet voice from a serene face. She asked at once, 'Have you come to see Lady Cowder? I'm sure she will be delighted to see you…'

'Are you delighted to see me?'

She prudently ignored this. 'She plays bridge until five o'clock every afternoon.' She glanced at her watch. 'I'm just waiting here until she's ready for me.'

'Your free time?' He wanted to know.

'Yes, every afternoon unless there's something…' She paused. 'I've seen quite a lot of the town,' she added chattily. 'Walking, you know, one can see so much more…'

He had a mental picture of her making her lonely way from one street to the next with no one to talk to and no money to spend. He put a hand under her elbow and said gently, 'Shall we sit down and share a pot of tea? If you'll wait here while I get a room and order tea…'

He sat her down in a quiet corner of the lounge alongside the foyer and went away, to return within minutes followed by a waitress with the tea tray, a plate of sandwiches and a cakestand of tempting cream cakes.

'Be mother,' said Mr Tait-Bouverie. Kate, he could see, was being wary, not sure of herself, so he assumed the manner in which he treated his childish patients—an easy-going friendliness combined with a matter-of-fact manner which never failed to put them at their ease.

He watched Kate relax, passed the sandwiches and asked presently, 'Do you suppose my aunt intends to stay here for the rest of her holiday?'

'Well, as long as there are enough people to make up a four for bridge. I think she is enjoying herself; it's a very comfortable hotel and the food is excellent, and so is the service.'

'Good; I shall be able to send a satisfactory report to my mother. What happens in the evenings?'

He watched her select a cake with serious concentration.

'I believe there's dancing on some evenings. I—I don't really know. I dine early, you see, and then go and wait for Lady Cowder to come to bed.'

'Surely my aunt is capable of undressing herself?' He frowned. 'And why do you dine early? Don't you take your meals together?'

Kate went pink. 'No, Mr Tait-Bouverie. You forget—I'm your aunt's housekeeper.' She saw the look on his face and added hastily, 'I don't take my meals with Lady Cowder in her own home.'

'That is entirely another matter. So you don't dance in the evenings?'

She shook her head. 'I'm having a lovely holiday,' she told him earnestly.

A statement of doubtful truth, reflected Mr Tait-Bouverie.

It was two minutes to five o'clock. 'I must go,' said Kate. 'Thank you for my tea.' She hesitated. 'I dare say you would like to surprise Lady Cowder?'

'No, no. I'll come up with you. Is she in her room?'

'There is a card room on the first floor. I go there first…'

She sounded so unenthusiastic at the thought of his company that Mr Tait-Bouverie found himself smiling, then wondered why.

It had struck five o'clock by the time they reached the card room. Lady Cowder was sitting with her back to the door, but she heard Kate come in. Without turning round, she said, in the rather die-away voice calculated to win sympathy from her companions, 'You're late, Kate, and I have such a headache. I dare say you forgot the time.' She glanced at her three companions. 'It is so hard to get a really reliable…' She paused, because they were all looking towards the door.

Mr Tait-Bouverie, a large hand in the small of Kate's back propelling her forward, spoke before Kate could utter.

'Blame me, Aunt. I saw Kate as I arrived and kept her talking. I was surprised to find that you had left Olden, and she explained—'

'My dear boy,' said Lady Cowder in a quite different voice. 'How delightful to see you. Have you come all this way just to see how I was enjoying myself? I hope you can stay for a few days.'

She got up and offered a cheek for his kiss, then turned to the three ladies at the bridge table. 'You must forgive me. This is my nephew; he's over here lecturing and has come to see me.'

He shook hands and made all the usual polite remarks, aware that Kate had returned to stand by the door, watching, ignored. She might have been a piece of furniture.

'We shall see you this evening?' asked one of the ladies.

'Certainly. We shall be dining later.' He turned to his aunt. 'At what time do you and Kate have dinner, Aunt?'

Lady Cowder looked uncomfortable. 'I dine at half past eight, James.' She smiled brightly at her bridge companions. 'I'm sure we shall all meet presently.'

She said her goodbyes and went to the door. Mr Tait-Bouverie, following her, slipped a hand under Kate's elbow and smiled down at her.

The three ladies were intrigued; his Aunt was outraged. Alone with him presently she said, 'You forget, James, Kate is my housekeeper.'

He agreed placidly. 'Indeed I do; anyone less like a housekeeper I have yet to meet.'

'And it is quite impossible to dine with her...'

Mr Tait-Bouverie's blue eyes were hard. 'Can she not manage her knife and fork?' he enquired gently.

'Yes, of course she can. Don't be absurd, James. But she hasn't the right clothes.'

'Ah,' said Mr Tait-Bouverie, and added reflectively, 'You and my mother are so different, I find it hard to remember that you are sisters.'

Lady Cowder preened herself. 'Well, we aren't at all alike. I was always considered the beauty, you know, and your mother never much cared for a social life. It has often surprised me that she should have married your father. Such a handsome and famous man.'

'My mother married my father because she loved him and he loved her. I see no surprise in that.'

Lady Cowder gave a little trill of laughter. 'Dear boy, you sound just like your father. Isn't it high time you married yourself?'

'I think that perhaps it is,' said Mr Tait-Bouverie, and wandered away to his own room.

Kate, summoned presently to zip up a dress, find the right handbag and make sure that Reception hadn't forgotten Lady Cowder's late-night hot drink, was treated to unusual loquacity on the part of her employer.

'My nephew has plans to marry,' she observed, already, in her mind's eye, seeing Claudia walking down the aisle smothered in white tulle and satin.

'He is, of course, a most eligible man, but dear Claudia is exactly what he needs—pretty and well dressed, and used to his way of life. The dear girl must be in seventh heaven.'

She surveyed her reflection in the pier-glass, nodded in satisfaction and glanced briefly at Kate. Not really worth a glance in that brown…

Mr Tait-Bouverie, dining presently with his aunt, behaved towards her with his usual courtesy, but refused to be drawn when she attempted to find out if he had plans to marry soon.

As they drank their coffee he asked idly, 'Where is Kate? Off duty?'

'Waiting for me in my room. I'm sure she is glad to have an hour or so to herself.' Lady Cowder added virtuously, 'I never keep her up late.'

They went presently to the small ballroom where several couples were dancing to a three-piece band. When he had settled his aunt with several of her acquaintances, James excused himself.

'But it's early, James,' his aunt protested. 'Do you care to dance for a while? I'm sure there are enough pretty girls…'

He smiled at her. 'I'm going to ask Kate to dance with me,' he told her.

Kate, leaning out of the window to watch the street below, withdrew her head and shoulders smartly at the knock on the door. Lady Cowder occasionally sent for her, wanting something or other, so Kate called, 'Come in,' and went to the door to meet the messenger.

Mr Tait-Bouverie came in quietly and shut the door behind him. 'If you could bear with a middle-aged partner, shall we go dancing?'

Kate stopped herself just in time from saying yes. Instead she said sedately, 'That's very kind of you to ask me, sir, but I stay here in the evenings in case Lady Cowder should need me.'

'She doesn't need you; she is with people she knows. I have told her that we are going to dance.'

'And she said that I could?'

Mr Tait-Bouverie, a man of truth, dallied with it now. 'I didn't hear her reply, but I can't see that she can have any objection.'

Kate had allowed common sense to take over. 'Well, I can. I mean, it just won't do.' And then, speaking her thoughts out loud, she added, 'You're not middle-aged.'

'Oh, good. You consider thirty-five still youthful enough to circle the dance floor?'

'Well, of course. What nonsense you talk…' She stopped and started again. 'What I should have said…'

'Don't waste time trying to be a housekeeper, Kate.'

He whisked her down to the ballroom at a tremendous pace and danced her onto the floor.

It had been some years since Kate had gone dancing, but she was good at it. It took only a few moments for her to realise that Mr Tait-Bouverie was good at it, too. Oblivious of Lady Cowder's staring eyes, the glances from the other guests, the brown dress, she allowed herself to forget everything save the pleasure of dancing with the perfect partner—for despite his vast size he was certainly that. He didn't talk, either, for which she was thankful. Just dancing was enough...

The music stopped and she came down to earth. 'Thank you, sir, that was very nice. Now, if you will excuse me...'

'Kate, Kate, will you stop being a housekeeper for at least this evening? You aren't *my* housekeeper, you know. The band's starting up again—good. And did I ever tell you that I shall wring your neck if you call me "sir"? I should hate to do that, for you are a magnificent dancer—big girls always are.'

Kate drew a deep breath. 'How very rude,' she told him coldly. 'I know I'm large, but you didn't have to say so...'

'Ah, the real Kate at last. Did I say big? I should have said superbly built, with all the curves in the right places, and a splendid head of hair.'

Kate had gone very pink. 'I know you're joking, but please don't. It—it isn't kind...'

'I don't mean to be kind. You see, Kate, I want to see behind that serene face of yours and discover the real Kate. And I'm not joking, only trying to get to know you—and it seems to me that the only way to do that is to stir you up.'

The music stopped once more and he took her arm. 'Let us take a walk.'

'A walk? Now? But in an hour Lady Cowder will go to bed.'

'We can walk miles in an hour. Go and get a jacket or shawl or something while I tell her.'

Kate gathered her wits together. 'No, no. Really, I can't! I'd love to, but I really mustn't.'

For answer he took her arm and trotted her across the room to where his aunt sat.

'I'm taking Kate for a brisk walk,' he told her. 'I'm sure you won't mind, Aunt. It's a pleasant evening and we shan't be gone long. Do you need Kate again before you go to bed?'

'Yes—no...' Lady Cowder was bereft of words for once. 'I dare say I can manage.'

'I'll knock when I come in, Lady Cowder,' said Kate in her housekeeper's voice. 'But if you would prefer me not to go, then I'll not do so.'

Lady Cowder looked around her at several interested faces.

'No, no, there's no need. Go and enjoy yourself.' She added wistfully, 'How delightful it must be to be young and have so much energy.' She smiled around her, and was gratified by the approving glances. She was, she told herself, a kind and considerate employer, and Kate was a very fortunate young woman. Poor James must be feeling very bored, but he was always a man to be kind to those less fortunate than himself.

They walked the short distance to the harbour, which thrust deep into the centre of the town, and walked around it. It was still light and quite warm, and there were plenty of people still about. Mr Tait-Bouverie sauntered along beside Kate, talking of this and that in a pleasantly casual manner, slipping in a question here and there so skilfully that she hardly noticed what a lot she was telling him.

On their way back to the hotel he observed, 'Since I'm here with a car I'll drive you to the nearest two islands tomorrow. You're free in the afternoon?'

Kate said cautiously, 'Well, I am usually—but if Lady Cowder wants to go anywhere or needs me for something...'

'Like what?'

'Well—something; I don't know what.'

He said softly, 'You don't need to make excuses if you don't want to come with me, Kate.'

She stopped and looked up at him. 'Oh, but I do, really I do. You have no idea...'

She paused, and he finished for her. 'How lonely you are...?'

She nodded. 'I feel very ungrateful, for really I have nothing much to do and I don't suppose I'll ever have the chance to come here again.'

'But you are lonely?'

'Yes.'

He began to tell her about the islands. 'Unique,' he told her. 'Connected by tunnels under the sea, and the islands themselves are charming. There is a small, very old church with beautiful murals; we'll go and look at it.'

At the hotel she wished him goodnight. 'It was a lovely evening,' she told him. 'Thank you.'

He stared down at her upturned face. He knew as he watched her smile that he was going to marry her. He could see that there would be obstacles in his path, not least of which would be Kate's wariness as to his intentions once he declared them. But he had no intention of doing that for the moment. First he must get behind that calm façade she had adopted as his aunt's housekeeper and find the real Kate. He was a patient man and a determined one; he had no doubt as to the outcome, but it might take a little time.

He said with cheerful friendliness, 'Goodnight, Kate. I'll see you tomorrow around two o'clock.'

Kate paused on her way to her room, wondering if she should knock on Lady Cowder's door—and then decided not to. She had said that there was no need, hadn't she? Besides, Kate hated the idea of the cross examination to which she would be subjected.

She stood under the shower for a long time, remembering her delightful evening. It was strange how Mr Tait-Bouverie seemed to have changed. He was really rather nice. She got into bed and lay thinking about tomorrow's trip. She would have a lot to write home about, she thought sleepily.

She was on the point of sleep when she remembered that Mr Tait-Bouverie was going to marry Claudia. If she hadn't been half-asleep already the thought would have upset her.

Lady Cowder wasn't in a good mood in the morning. Kate was sent away to press a dress which should have been done yesterday. 'But, of course, if you aren't here to do your work, what can one expect?' asked Lady Cowder, adopting her aggrieved, put-upon voice. Kate said nothing, seeing her chances of being free in the afternoon dwindling. She was aware that her employer disapproved of her nephew having anything to do with her, and would interfere if she could.

Kate had reckoned without Mr Tait-Bouverie, who took his aunt out for a drive that morning, gave her coffee at a charming little restaurant and drove to the top of Mount Aksla so that she might enjoy the view over Alesund.

'You're playing bridge this afternoon?' he wanted to know. 'Supposing I take Kate for a short drive? I want to visit a rather lovely old church, and she might as well come with me.' He added cunningly,

'It is very good of you to allow her to have the afternoons free. She seems to have explored the town very thoroughly.'

Lady Cowder smiled complacently. 'Yes, she may do as she likes between two and five o'clock each day and, heaven knows, I am the easiest mistress any servant could wish for. Take her with you by all means; this holiday must be an education to her.'

Mr Tait-Bouverie swallowed a laugh. His aunt had had a sketchy education—governesses, a year in Switzerland—and had never made any attempt to improve upon it. Whereas he knew from what Kate's mother had told him during one of his seemingly casual conversations, that Kate had several A levels and would have gone on to a university if her father hadn't wanted her at home to help research his book.

'Just so,' he said mildly, and drove his aunt back to the hotel.

Kate, brushing and hanging away Lady Cowder's many clothes, was quite startled when that lady came into her room.

'I have had a delightful morning,' she announced. 'And I have a treat in store for you, Kate. Mr Tait-Bouverie has offered to take you for a drive this afternoon. I must say it is most kind of him, and I hope you will be suitably grateful both to him and to me. Now go and have your lunch and come back here in case I need anything before I go to lunch myself.'

Kate skipped down to the restaurant, gobbled her food and hurried to her room. She wondered what Mr Tait-Bouverie had said to make Lady Cowder so amenable. Perhaps she could ask him; on the other hand, perhaps not. He was making a generous gesture and probably wasn't looking forward to the whole afternoon in her company. What on earth would they talk about for three hours?

She got into the jersey dress she hadn't yet worn. It was by no means new, but it fitted her and the colour was a warm mushroom—it toned down her bright hair nicely. Her shoulderbag and shoes had seen better days, too, but they were good leather and she had taken care of them. She went downstairs, wondering if Mr Tait-Bouverie had left a message for her at the desk. She had told him that she was usually free soon after two o'clock, but now that she saw the time she saw that she was much too early. It would never do to look too eager. She turned round and started back up the stairs.

'Cold feet, Kate?' asked Mr Tait-Bouverie, appearing beside her, apparently through the floor. 'I'm ready if you are.'

She paused in mid-flight. 'Oh, well, yes. I'm quite ready, only I'm too early.'

'I've been waiting for the last ten minutes,' he told her placidly. 'It's a splendid day; let us cram as much into it as we can.'

Kate was willing enough. She was led outside to

where his hired Volvo stood, ushered into it, and, without more ado, they set off.

'Giske first,' said Mr Tait-Bouverie, driving away from the town and presently entering a tunnel, 'I hope you don't mind the dark? This goes on for some time—more than a couple of miles—but it is used very frequently, as you can see, and is well maintained. Giske is rather a charming island—it's called the Saga island, too. We'll go and see that church, and then drive over to Godoy and have tea at Alnes. It's quite a small village but there's a ferry, of course, and in the summer there are tourists...'

His placid voice, uttering commonplace information, put her quite at her ease. She wasn't sure if she liked the tunnel very much—driving through the mountain with all that grey rock and presently, as he pointed out to her, under the fiord—but he was right about Giske. It was peaceful and green, even with the mountains towering all round it. There were few cars, the sun shone and the air was clear and fresh.

Kate took a deep breath and said, 'This is nice.'

The little church delighted her, so very small and so perfect, with ancient murals on its walls and high-backed pews. It was quiet and peaceful, too; she could imagine that the peace went back hundreds of years. Mr Tait-Bouverie didn't say much but wandered round with her, and when she had had her fill he took her outside to the little churchyard with its gravestones bright with flowers.

'It's something I'll remember,' said Kate, getting back into the car.

They drove on to Godoy then, through small villages, their houses beautifully kept. And when they reached Alnes they had tea at the small hotel opposite the ferry. By now Kate had forgotten to be wary and become completely at ease.

Mr Tait-Bouverie watched her lovely face and was well content, taking care not to dispel that.

CHAPTER FIVE

KATE, MAKING A splendid tea, was happy to have someone to talk to, to answer her questions, who was apparently as happy as she was. After a couple of weeks
of no conversation—for Lady Cowder only gave orders or made observations—it was delightful to say
what she thought without having to make sure that it
was suitable first, and, strangely enough, she found
that she could talk to Mr Tait-Bouverie.

'We should be going,' he told her presently. 'A
pity, for it is such a pleasant day.' He smiled at her
across the table. 'There's another very long tunnel
ahead.'

'Longer than the other one?'

'Yes. But there's plenty of time; we are quite near
to Alesund.'

'It's been a lovely afternoon,' said Kate, getting
into the car, wishing the day would never end. In
a little over an hour she would be getting into the
brown crêpe dress, ready to eat her solitary dinner.

She frowned, despising herself for allowing self-pity to spoil the day. Besides, there was still the drive back…

The tunnel took her by surprise; one moment they were tooling along a narrow road edged with thick shrubs, giving way to trees as they climbed the mountain beyond, the next they were driving smoothly between grey rock. True, the tunnel was lighted, and there was a stream of traffic speeding past them, but, all the same, she caught herself wondering how many minutes it would be before they came out into daylight again.

Mr Tait-Bouverie said soothingly, 'It takes less than five minutes, although it seems longer.' He added, 'You don't like it very much, do you? I should have asked you about that before we left the hotel. There are any number of other places to visit.'

'No, oh, no, I've loved every minute—and really, now we are in the tunnel, I truly don't mind. I wouldn't like to drive through it alone, though.'

He laughed. 'You're honest, Kate. Even if you don't exactly enjoy it, it's something you will remember.' He glanced at the dashboard. 'We're exactly halfway.'

The sudden sickening noise ahead of them seemed to reverberate over and over again through the tunnel—a grinding, long drawn-out noise accompanied by shouts and screams. And the lights went out.

Mr Tait-Bouverie brought the car to a smooth halt

inches from the car ahead of him as other cars passed him, unable to slow their pace quickly enough, colliding inevitably. He could have said the obvious; instead he observed calmly, 'A pity about the lights,' and reached for the phone beside his seat.

Kate, who hadn't uttered a sound, said now in a voice which shook only very slightly, 'I expect someone will come quickly,' and thought what a silly remark that was. 'Were you phoning for help? You were speaking Norwegian?'

'Yes, and yes. Now, Kate, perhaps we can make ourselves useful. I'm sure everyone with a phone has warned Alesund, but the more helpers there are the better. Come along!'

He reached behind him and took his bag from the back seat. 'How lucky that I've my bag with me. I don't care to leave it at the hotel. Stay where you are; I'll come round and open your door, then follow me and do as I say. You're not squeamish, are you?'

It didn't look as though she would be given the chance to be that. She said meekly, 'I don't think so.'

'Good; come along, then.'

They didn't have far to go—a van had gone out of control and slewed sideways so that the car behind it had crashed into it, turned over and been pushed by another car against the wall, presumably with such force that the lighting cables had been damaged.

There were a great many people milling around, some of them already hauling people from damaged cars. Mr Tait-Bouverie, holding Kate fast by the hand, spoke to a man kneeling beside a woman whose leg was trapped under the wheel of a car.

'I'm a doctor; can I help?'

He had spoken in Norwegian and the man answered him in the same language, shining his torch on Mr Tait-Bouverie and then on Kate. 'English, aren't you? God knows how many there are trapped and hurt. I've told people to go back to their cars. There is a nurse somewhere, and several men giving a hand.' He glanced at Kate again. 'The young lady?'

'Not a nurse, but capable. She will do anything she is asked to do.'

'Good. Can she help the nurse? Over there with those two children? This young woman—if you could look at her? Tell us what to do—most of us have some knowledge of first aid....'

'Off you go,' said Mr Tait-Bouverie to Kate. 'I'll find you later.'

I must remember, thought Kate rather wildly, picking her way towards the nurse, to tell him that he is a rude and arrogant man.

Then she didn't think about him again; there was too much to do.

The nurse, thank heavens, spoke excellent English. Kate tied slings, bandaged cuts and held broken arms and legs while the nurse applied splints made of umbrellas, walking sticks and some useful lengths of wood someone had in their boot.

She was aware of Mr Tait-Bouverie from time to time, going to and fro and once coming to kneel beside her to find and tie a severed artery. The nurse had told her to apply pressure with her fingers while she fetched the doctor and Kate knelt, feeling sick as blood oozed out despite her efforts. Mr Tait-Bouverie didn't speak until he had controlled the bleeding. 'Bandage it tightly with anything you can find.'

He had gone again. Kate, feeling queasy, took the clean handkerchief she saw in the patient's pocket and did the best she could.

It seemed like hours before she heard the first sounds of help arriving. It had only been minutes—minutes she never wished to live through again. Even though help was on the way it took time to manoeuvre the cars out of the way so that the ambulances and the fire engines could get through. Everyone was quiet now, doing as they were told, backing out of the tunnel whenever it was possible, making more room.

She was suddenly aware that there was a man crouching beside the old lady she was trying to make comfortable.

'You are a nurse?' he asked in English.

'No. Just helping. I'm with a doctor—a surgeon, actually. Mr Tait-Bouverie.'

'Old James? Splendid. He's around?' He didn't wait for an answer, but began to question the old lady. He looked up presently. 'Concussion and a broken arm. She's worried about her handbag. She was thrown out of her car...'

'Which car? I'll look for it.'

It was an elderly Volvo, its door twisted, its bodywork ruined. Kate climbed in gingerly and it creaked under her weight. The bag was on the floor, its contents spilled. She collected everything she could see and began to edge out backwards.

'There you are,' said Mr Tait-Bouverie. He sounded amused. 'Even if you are back to front, I'm glad to see that you're none the worse for all this.'

He stopped and lifted her neatly the right way up, out of the car.

Kate said coldly, 'Thank you, Mr Tait-Bouverie. There was no need of your help.'

'No, I know, but the temptation was too strong.' He looked her over. 'You look rather the worse for wear.'

She started back to the old lady. 'Well, I am the worse for wear,' she told him tartly, and thought vexedly that he looked quite undisturbed—his jacket over his arm, his shirt-sleeves rolled up. His tie was gone—used for something or other, she supposed. He still looked elegant.

Kate, conscious that her hair was coming down, her hands were filthy and scratched and her dress stained and torn, turned her back on him.

He was there, beside her, exchanging greetings

with the Norwegian doctor while she handed over the handbag and listened to the old lady's thanks.

'You're off now?'

'Yes. I must take this young lady back to my aunt.'

'Come to dinner while you're there. We'd love to see you again. How long are you here? Oslo, I suppose, and Bergen and Tromsö?'

'Tromsö tomorrow,' said Mr Tait-Bouverie, 'and back to England four days later.'

Kate had heard that, and was conscious of an unpleasant sensation under her ribs. Indigestion, she told herself, and shook hands politely when Mr Tait-Bouverie introduced her.

'This is not a social occasion, I am afraid, but I am delighted to meet you—may I call you Kate? Perhaps next time you come to Norway… Ah, here are the ambulance men.' He smiled goodbye, and turned his attention to his patient.

Mr Tait-Bouverie took Kate's hand. 'A hot bath and a quiet evening,' he observed as they made their way through the throng. Kate didn't reply. She would be lucky if she had time for a quick shower; Lady Cowder wasn't going to be pleased at having been kept waiting for more than an hour…

It took some manoeuvring to get out of the tunnel; cars were being backed, a way was being cleared by the police. It was all very orderly, even if it took some time. The road, when they at last reached it, had been closed to all but traffic leaving the tunnel.

'It's all very efficiently organised,' said Kate.

Mr Tait-Bouverie glanced sideways at her. Her beautiful face was dirty and her hair, by now, a hopeless russet tangle hanging down her back. He gave a sigh and kept his eyes on the road.

He had been in love several times, just as any normal man would be, but never once had he considered marriage. He had assumed that at sometime, somewhere, he would meet the girl he wanted for his wife, and in the meantime he immersed himself in his work, happy to wait. Now he had found her and he didn't want to wait. He would have to, of course. He wasn't sure if she liked him—certainly she wasn't in love with him—and circumstances weren't going to make the prospect of that any easier. Circumstances, however, could be altered...

They talked about the accident presently. 'It is a miracle that it didn't turn into a major disaster...'

'You mean if fire had broken out or there had been panic? Everyone was calm. Well, nearly everyone.' Kate added honestly, 'I would have liked to have screamed, just once and very loudly, only I didn't dare.'

'Why not?'

She looked away from him out of the window. 'You wouldn't have liked that—I mean, you knew you would go and help. I dare say you would have left me in the car to scream all I wanted to, but you had enough on your plate.'

'I wouldn't have left you alone, Kate. To be truthful, I rather took it for granted that you would help, too, in your calm and sensible way.'

Kate fought a wish to tell him that she had felt neither of these things—that sheer fright had stricken her dumb. She had felt neither calm nor sensible, only terrified. Although she had to admit to herself that having him there, quiet and assured, knowing exactly what to do, had given her a feeling of safety. Strange to feel so safe and sure with him...

Soon they reached the hotel, and he got out and opened her door and walked with her into the foyer. There were a lot of people there, gathered to hear news of the accident, and they stared and then crowded round them, anxious for details.

'You were there?' someone asked. 'We felt sure that you were. The young lady...?'

'Is perfectly all right', said Mr Tait-Bouverie placidly. 'But she does need a bath and a rest.'

He took her to the desk and the three receptionists there hurried to him.

'Miss Crosby needs a bath, a change of clothing and a rest. I'm sure she'd like a tray of tea before anything else.' He looked at Kate. 'What is your room number? There is a bathroom?'

'Well, no,' she mumbled awkwardly. 'But the shower's fine. I'm perfectly all right.'

'Of course you are, but you will do what I say. Doctor's orders.'

He turned back to the desk. 'Will you send a chambermaid with Miss Crosby to fetch a change of clothes from her room, and then go with her to my room so that she may have a most essential warm bath? Perhaps she will let me know if Miss Crosby is bruised or scratched and I'll deal with that later. She is to stay with her, and I think that she might have dinner there. In the meantime let me have another room, will you?'

He said to Kate in what she could only call a doctor's voice, 'While you are finding something to wear I'll get what I need from my room. And here is the chambermaid. Go with her, and after your dinner go back to your room and go to bed.'

Kate found her voice. 'Lady Cowder...?'

'Leave her to me.' He smiled then, and she found herself smiling back and wanting to cry. 'Goodnight, Kate.'

She lay in the warm bath and snivelled. She didn't know why; she hadn't been hurt, only scratched and bruised, and was tired from the heaving and shoving and lifting she had done. But it was nice to have a good cry, and the chambermaid was a kindly soul who found plasters to put on her small cuts and grazes and presently saw her onto the bed and urged her to have a nice nap.

Which, surprisingly, she did, to wake feeling quite

herself again and to eat with a splendid appetite the dinner that the good soul brought to the room.

Kate had half expected to have a visit from Lady Cowder—or at least a message—but there was nothing. She ate her dinner and, still accompanied by the chambermaid, went back to her own room. In a little while she went to bed. It was a pity that Mr Tait-Bouverie was going to Tromsö tomorrow; she would have liked to thank him properly for his kindness. She spared a sleepy moment to wonder what he was doing...

He was walking briskly through the town, not going anywhere special, thinking about the afternoon and Kate. His aunt had been vexed at the news that she would have to manage without Kate that evening, declaring plaintively that the news of the accident had been a great shock to her, that she felt poorly and would probably have a migraine.

To all of which Mr Tait-Bouverie had listened with his usual courtesy, before suggesting that an early night might be the answer.

'I'll say goodbye now, Aunt,' he had told her. 'For I'm leaving early in the morning. I shall be back in England shortly, and will come and see you as soon as you return.'

'I shall look forward to that, James. I believe that I shall invite Claudia to stay for a while—she is such a splendid companion, and so amusing.' When this had elicited no response, she had added, 'How delightful it will be to see your dear mother again. She wrote to say that she will be returning soon. There is so much for us to talk about.'

Mr Tait-Bouverie considered his future with the same thorough care with which he did his work. Complicated operations—the kind he excelled in—needed careful thought, and there would be plenty of complications before he could marry his Kate. At least, he reflected, he would know where she was…

Kate hadn't expected sympathy from Lady Cowder and she received none. 'So very inconvenient,' said that lady as Kate presented herself the following morning. 'You have no idea of the severity of my headache, and all the excitement about the accident… It was most generous of my nephew to give up his room for your use, though really quite unnecessary. However, he has always done as he wishes.'

Kate, perceiving that she was expected to answer this, said quietly, 'Mr Tait-Bouverie was very kind and considerate. I'm very grateful. I hope I shall have the opportunity of thanking him.'

'He wouldn't expect thanks from you,' said Lady Cowder rudely. 'Besides, he left early this morning for Tromsö. He will be back in England before us.'

Kate felt a pang of disappointment. Perhaps she would see him in England but on rather a different footing—the accident in the tunnel would have faded into the past, obliterated by a busy present. Thanking him would sound silly. She wondered if she should write him a polite note—but where would she send it? Lady Cowder could tell her, but she was the last person to ask. It was an unsatisfactory ending to what had been, for her, a very pleasant interlude, despite the fright and horror of the accident in the tunnel.

At least, Kate reflected, she had behaved sensibly even while her insides had heaved and she had been terrified that fire would break out or, worse, that the tunnel would fall apart above their heads and they would all be drowned. A flight of imagination, she knew. The tunnel was safe, and help had been prompt and more than efficient. It had been an experience—not a nice one, she had to admit—and despite her fright she had felt quite safe because Mr Tait-Bouverie had been there.

Waiting for Lady Cowder that afternoon, she wrote a long letter to her mother, making light of Lady Cowder's ill humour, describing the hotel and the town, the food and the people she had spoken to, enlarging on the beautiful scenery but saying little about Mr Tait-Bouverie's company. She wrote about the tunnel accident too, not dwelling on the horror of it, merely observing that it had been most fortunate that Mr Tait-Bouverie had been there to help.

She wrote nothing about her own part in the affair, hoping that her mother would picture her sitting safely in the car out of harm's way.

* * *

Her circumspection was wasted. Mrs Crosby, reading bits of the letter to Mr Tait-Bouverie, observed in a puzzled voice, 'But where was Kate? She doesn't say...'

They were sitting at the kitchen table, drinking coffee with Moggerty on Mr Tait-Bouverie's knee. He had arrived that afternoon, having driven down from London after a brief stop at his home. He'd been tired by the time his plane got in, and had hesitated as to whether it wouldn't be a better idea to go and see Kate's mother the following morning. But if Kate had written, the letter would have arrived by now and Mrs Crosby might be worried. He had eaten the meal Mudd had had ready for him and driven himself out of town, despite Mudd's disapproving look.

He was glad that he had come; Mrs Crosby had had the letter that morning and had been worrying about it ever since. He had been able to reassure her and tell her exactly what had happened. 'Kate behaved splendidly,' he told her. 'She's not easily rattled, is she?' He smiled a little. 'She didn't like the tunnel, though—too dark.'

Mrs Crosby offered Prince a biscuit. 'I'm glad she was able to help. Did Lady Cowder mind? I mean, Kate had to miss some of her duties, I expect.'

Mr Tait-Bouverie said soothingly, 'My aunt quite understood. Kate had her bath and her cuts and bruises were attended to, and she had an early night.'

'Oh, good. I shall be so glad to see her again, though it was most kind of Lady Cowder to take Kate with her. It's years since she had a holiday, and she does have to work hard.' She paused. 'I shouldn't have said that.'

Mr Tait-Bouverie offered Moggerty a finger to chew. 'Why not? Being a housekeeper to my aunt must be extremely hard work. You see, people who have never had to work themselves don't realise the amount of work other people do for them.'

'Well, yes, I dare say you're right. Are you not tired? It was very kind of you to come all this way... When do you start work again?'

'Tomorrow, and I knew that once I got started it would be some days before I could come and see you.'

'I'm very grateful. Kate's all right, isn't she? I mean, happy...?'

He said evenly, 'We had a very happy afternoon together. We went dancing one evening...she is a delightful dancer...'

'She was never without a partner at the parties she went to—that was before her father became ill. What was she wearing? She didn't take much with her— she didn't expect... Was it a brown dress?'

'I'm afraid so,' said Mr Tait-Bouverie gravely. 'She is far too beautiful to wear brown crêpe, Mrs Crosby.'

'She hadn't much choice,' said Mrs Crosby rather tartly.

'It made no difference,' he assured her. 'Kate would turn heads draped in a potato sack.'

Mrs Crosby met his unsmiling gaze and smiled. Not an idle remark calculated to please her, she decided. He really meant it.

He went away presently, with Prince at his heels eager to get into the car beside his master.

Mrs Crosby offered a hand. 'Don't work too hard,' she begged him. 'Though I suppose that in a job like yours you can't very well say no…'

He laughed then. 'That's true, but I do get the odd free day or weekend. I hope I may be allowed to come and see you from time to time?'

'That would be delightful.'

She watched him drive away, wondering if his visit had been made out of concern for her worry about Kate or because he really wanted to see her—and Kate—in the future. 'We shall have to wait and see,' she told Moggerty.

Kate quickly discovered that she was to pay for the few hours of pleasure she had had with Mr Tait-Bouverie. Lady Cowder declared that she was tired of bridge, and on fine afternoons a car was hired and she and Kate were driven around the countryside—Kate sitting with the driver since Lady Cowder declared that Kate's chatter gave her a headache.

Kate ignored this silly remark, and was thankful to sit beside the driver, who pointed out anything interesting and, before long, told her about his wife and children.

After several days of this the weather changed and, instead of going out in the afternoons, Lady Cowder stayed in one of the hotel lounges, playing patience or working away at a jigsaw puzzle while Kate sat quietly by, ready to help with the patience when it wouldn't come out, or grovel around the floor looking for lost bits of the puzzle.

Now she had only a brief hour each morning to herself, so the days stretched endlessly in long, wasted hours.

It was only during the last few days of their stay that this dull routine was altered, when Lady Cowder decided to shop for presents. She hadn't many friends—bridge-playing acquaintances for the most part—and for those she bought carved wood-work. But Claudia was a different matter.

'Something special for the dear girl,' she told Kate. 'She is so pretty; one must choose something to enhance that. Earrings, I think—those rather charming gold and silver filigree drops I saw yesterday. Of course, they are of no value; James will see that she has some good jewellery when they marry...'

She shot a look at Kate as she spoke, but was answered with a noncommittal, 'They would be charming. I'm sure Claudia will be delighted to have them.'

'Such a grateful girl. You might do better to copy her gratitude, Kate.'

Kate, with a tremendous effort, held her tongue!

The journey back to England went smoothly— largely because Kate had planned it to be so. All the same, it was tiring work getting Lady Cowder out of cars, into the plane and out of it again and then into her own car. She had complained gently the whole way home so that Kate had a headache by the time they stopped in front of Lady Cowder's house.

That was when her long day's work really started. Safely home again, Lady Cowder declared that she was exhausted and must go to bed at once.

'You may bring in the luggage and unpack, Kate, but before you do that bring a tray of tea up to my room. I'll take a warm bath and go to bed, I think, and later you may bring me up a light supper.' She sighed. 'How I envy you your youth and strength— when one is old…'

Seventy wasn't all that old, reflected Kate, receiving an armful of handbags, scarves and rugs. And Lady Cowder lived the kind of life which was conducive to looking and feeling a lot younger than one's years. She saw Lady Cowder to her room, got her bath ready and went downstairs to unload the boot.

Lady Cowder was in bed by the time Kate had put the car away and brought the luggage indoors.

'You might as well unpack my things now,' said

Lady Cowder, sitting up against her pillows as fresh as a daisy.

'If I do,' said Kate in her quiet voice, 'I won't have time to get your supper.' She added woodenly, 'I could cut you a few sandwiches…'

Lady Cowder closed her eyes. 'After my very tiring day I need a nourishing meal. Leave the unpacking, since you don't seem capable of doing it this evening. A little soup, I think, and a lamb chop with a few peas— if there are none in the freezer, I dare say you can get them from the garden. Just one or two potatoes, plainly boiled. I don't suppose you will have time to make a compote of fruit; I had better make do with an egg custard.' She opened her eyes. 'In about an hour, Kate.'

Only the thought of the extra wages she had earned, enough—just—to make up the hundred pounds to show the bank manager, kept Kate from picking up her unopened bags and going home.

She went to the kitchen, put on the kettle and made tea, then a little refreshed but still angry, she phoned her mother.

'I can't stop,' she told her. 'There's rather a lot to do, but I'll see you on Wednesday. I'm to go to Thame for some groceries on Thursday; I'll go to the bank then.'

Her mother's happy voice did much to cheer her up—after all, it had been worth it; the rather grey future held a tinge of pink. In a few months she would be embarking on a venture which she felt sure would be successful.

* * *

Later she carried a beautifully cooked meal up to
Lady Cowder's room.

'You may fetch the tray when I ring,' said that
lady. 'Then I shan't need anything more. I'll have
breakfast as usual up here. Poached eggs on toast,
and some of that marmalade from the Women's In-
stitute. In the New Year you can make sufficient for
the whole year; I cannot enjoy any of these marma-
lades from the shops.'

Kate said, 'Goodnight, Lady Cowder,' and received no answer. She hadn't expected one. She
hadn't expected to be asked if she were at all tired
or hungry, nor had she expected to be thanked for her
services during their stay in Norway. But it would
have been nice to have been treated like a person
and not like a robot.

She ate her supper, unpacked her things, had a
very long, too hot bath and then went to bed. She
was tired, but not too tired to wonder what Mr Tait-
Bouverie was doing. She told herself sleepily not to
waste time thinking about him and went to sleep.

She was kept busy the next day; after a month's emp-
tiness the house was clean, but it needed dusting and
airing. Stores had to be checked, tradesmen phoned,
the gardener had to be seen about vegetables, and
Horace to be made much of. He had been well looked

after but he was glad of her company again, and followed her round the house, anxious to please.

Lady Cowder, catching sight of him following Kate up the stairs, said irritably, 'What is that cat doing here? I thought he had been got rid of. I'm sure I told Mrs Beckett to have him put down before she left...'

'It's most fortunate that she didn't, Lady Cowder,' said Kate in the polite voice which so annoyed her employer. 'For he is splendid at catching mice. All those small rooms behind the kitchen which are never used...he never allows one to get away.'

She uttered the fib with her fingers crossed behind her back. It was a fib in a good cause—Horace was a sympathetic companion and someone to talk to. That he had never caught a mouse in his life had nothing to do with it...

'Mice?' said Lady Cowder in horror. 'You mean to tell me...?'

'No, no. There are no mice, but there might be without Horace. A cat,' she went on in her sensible way, 'is of much more use than a mousetrap.'

Lady Cowder agreed grudgingly, annoyed to feel that Kate had got the better of her without uttering a single word which could be described as impertinent or rude.

Kate went home on her half-day, taking her extra wages with her, and she and her mother spent a blissful afternoon making plans for the future.

'I'll need a thousand pounds to start,' said Kate. 'I'll start in a small way, and then get the money paid off to the bank and get better equipment as we expand. I'll stay with Lady Cowder until I've drummed up one or two customers—the pub, perhaps, and that bed and breakfast place at the other end of the village. Once I can get regular customers I can branch out—birthday parties and even weddings...'

'It's something you can go on doing if you marry,' observed her mother.

'Yes, but I don't know anyone who wants to marry me, do I?' For some reason Mr Tait-Bouverie's face rose, unbidden, beneath her eyelids and she added, 'And I'm not likely to.'

She took care to laugh as she said it and her mother smiled in return—but her eyes were thoughtful. Mr Tait-Bouverie would make a delightful son-in-law, and he might fall in love with Kate. It didn't seem likely, but Mrs Crosby was an optimist by nature.

Before Kate went back that evening she arranged to call in the next day on her way to Thame. She wasn't to use the car—Lady Cowder considered that Kate could cycle there and back quite easily with the few dainties which she had set her heart on.

'I quite envy you,' she'd told Kate in the wistful voice which made Kate clench her teeth. 'Young and strong with the whole morning for a pleasant little outing.'

Kate said nothing. The bike ride was one thing,

but shopping around for the special mushrooms, the oysters, the lamb's sweetbreads, the special sauce which could only be found at a delicatessen some distance from the shopping centre was quite another. But she didn't mind; she was going to find time to go to the bank…

Kate got up earlier than usual, for Lady Cowder expected the morning's chores to be done before she left, but still Kate left the house later than she had hoped for. It would be a bit of a rush to get back in time to get Lady Cowder's lunch. She stayed at her home only long enough to collect the hundred pounds, which she stowed in her shoulderbag and slung over her shoulder. It would never do to get it mixed up with the housekeeping money in the bike's basket, every penny of which she would have to account for.

It was a dull day, but she didn't mind that—this was the day she had been working and waiting for. Now she could plan her future, a successful career… It was a pity that Mr Tait-Bouverie's handsome features kept getting in the way.

'Forget him,' said Kate loudly. 'Just because he was kind and nice to be with. Remember, you're a housekeeper!'

She bowled along, deciding what to do first— the bank or the shopping. Would she be a long time at the bank? Would she be able to see the manager at once? Perhaps she should have made an appointment. Another mile or so and she would be on the outskirts of Thame. She would go to the bank first...

She parked her bike and had turned round to take her shopping bag and the housekeeping money from the basket when she was jostled by several youths. They did it quite roughly, treading on her feet, pushing her against the wall, but before she could do anything they chorused loud apologies—presumably for the benefit of the few pedestrians in the street—and ran away.

They took her shoulderbag with them, neatly sliced from its straps.

It had all happened so quickly that she had no chance to look at them properly. There had been four or five of them, she thought, and she ran across the street to ask if anyone passing had seen what had happened. No one had, although they admitted that they had thought the boys had bumped into her accidentally.

So she went into the bank, calm with despair, and explained that her money had been stolen. Here she was listened to with sympathy, given an offer to phone the police, and told with polite regret that an interview with the manager would be pointless until the money was recovered. When a police officer arrived there was little he could do, although he assured her that they would certainly be on the look-out for the youths.

'Although I doubt if you'll see your money back, miss,' she was told.

She gave her name and address, assured him that she was unharmed and, since there was nothing else to be done about it, got on her bike and did her shopping. A pity that they hadn't taken the housekeeping money instead of her precious savings.

She didn't allow herself to think about it while she shopped. Her world had fallen around her in ruins, and she would have to start to rebuild it all over again. Disappointment tasted bitter in her mouth, but for the moment there were more important things to think of. Lady Cowder's lunch, for instance…

She cycled back presently, her purchases made, wondering how she was going to break the news to her mother. She would have to wait until Sunday. She rarely got the chance to use the phone unless it was on Lady Cowder's behalf, and she saw no hope of getting enough free time to go home until then. And she had no intention of telling Lady Cowder.

Back at the house, she was reprimanded in Lady Cowder's deceptively gentle voice for being late. 'It is so essential that I should have my meals served punctually,' she pointed out. 'I feel quite low, and now I must wait for lunch to be served. You may pour me a glass of sherry, Kate.'

Which Kate did in calm silence before going down to the kitchen to deal with the mushrooms and oysters. But before she did that she poured herself a glass of the cooking sherry—an inferior brand, of course, but still sherry.

She tossed it off recklessly and started on her preparations for lunch, not caring if she burnt everything to cinders or curdled the sauce. Of course, she didn't; she served a beautifully cooked meal to an impatient Lady Cowder and went back to the kitchen where she sat down and had a good cry.

CHAPTER SIX

KATE FELT BETTER in the morning. The loss was a set-back, but with the optimism born of a new day she told herself that a hundred pounds wasn't such a vast sum and if she could save it once, she could save it a second time.

Her optimism faded as the day wore on; Lady Cowder was demanding, and for some reason sorry for herself. She declared that the journey home had upset her and went round the house finding fault with everything.

It was a blessing when the vicar's wife called after lunch to confer with her about the Autumn Fair. Lady Cowder prided herself on patronising local charity, and made no bones about telling everyone how generous she was in their cause.

She spent a pleasant afternoon telling the vicar's wife just how things should be done. Kate, bringing in the tea tray, heard her telling that lady that she would be delighted to supply as many cakes and biscuits as were needed for the cake stall and the re-freshment tent.

'As you know,' said Lady Cowder in her wispy voice, 'I will go to any amount of trouble to help a worthy cause.'

Kate, with the prospect of hours of cake baking ahead of her, sighed.

The vicar's wife was only a passing respite, though; by the following morning Lady Cowder was as gloomy as ever. Thank heavens, thought Kate, that I can go home tomorrow.

Lady Cowder fancied a sponge cake for her tea. 'Although I dare say I shall eat only a morsel of it.' She added sharply, 'Any of the cake which is left over you may use for a trifle, Kate.'

Kate stood there, not saying a word, her face calm, and wearing the air of reserve which annoyed her employer. 'I'll have the turbot with wild mushrooms for dinner. Oh, and a spinach salad, I think, and a raspberry tart with orange sauce.' She glanced at Kate. 'You're rather pale. I hope you aren't going to be ill, Kate.'

'I'm very well, thank you,' said Kate, and went away to make the sponge cake. She hoped it would turn out like lead, but as usual it was as light as a feather.

She thought of Mr Tait-Bouverie as she worked. It was silly of her to waste time over him, but at least it stopped her thinking about her lost money.

* * *

Mr Tait-Bouverie stood at the window, looking at his aunt's garden. He wasn't sure why he had felt the urge to pay her a visit and had no intention of pursuing the matter too deeply. He had almost convinced himself that the feelings he had for Kate were nothing more than a passing infatuation, but when the door opened and she came in with the tea tray he had to admit that that was nonsense. Nothing less than marrying her would do, and that as soon as possible.

However, he let none of these feelings show but bade her a quiet good afternoon and watched her arrange the tray to please his aunt. She had gone delightfully pink when she'd seen him, but now he saw that she looked pale and tired. More than that— unhappy.

She left the room as quietly as she had entered, not looking at him again, aware of Lady Cowder's sharp eyes, and he went to take his tea cup from his aunt and sit down opposite her.

'I'm sorry to hear that you found the journey home tiring. Kate looks tired, too. Perhaps you should have broken your trip and stayed in town for a night.'

'My dear boy, all I longed to do was get here— and indeed the journey was so fatiguing, getting to the airport and then the flight. You know how nervous I am. And then standing about while the luggage is seen to and the car fetched—and then the long drive here.' She added sharply, 'Kate isn't in the least tired. She's a great strapping girl, perfectly able to cope—and after a month's idleness, too. I'm glad to see that she hasn't taken advantage of your kindness to her at Alesund.'

Mr Tait-Bouverie gave her a look of such coldness that she shivered.

'Of course, I'm sure she would do no such thing,' she said hastily. 'Such a reserved young woman.' Anxious to take the look of ferocity from her nephew's face, she added, 'You will stay to dinner, won't you, James?'

Mr Tait-Bouverie, making plans, declined. After his absence from London, he pointed out, he had a backlog of work. He urged his aunt to take more exercise, volunteered to let himself out of the house and went round to the kitchen door.

Kate was sitting at the table. The ingredients for the raspberry tart Lady Cowder fancied for dinner were before her, although she was making no attempt to do anything about it.

Seeing Mr Tait-Bouverie had been a bit of a shock—a surprisingly pleasant one, she discovered. She had put down the tea tray and taken care to reply to his pleasant greeting with suitable reserve, but the urge to fall on his neck and pour out her troubles had been very strong. She reflected that she must like him more than she thought she did, not that her feelings came into it.

'But it would be nice to have a shoulder to moan on,' she observed to Horace, who was sitting cosily by the Aga.

'I don't know if you have a shoulder in mind,' said Mr Tait-Bouverie from the door. 'But would mine do?'

She turned her head to look at him. 'You shouldn't creep up on people like that; it's bad for the nerves.'

Indeed, she had gone very pale at the sight of him.

He came right into the room and sat down at the table opposite her.

'Did I shock you? I'm sorry. Now tell me, Kate, what is the matter? And don't waste time saying nothing, because neither you nor I have time to waste.'

'I have no intention...' began Kate, and stopped when she caught his eye. She said baldly, 'I went to Thame on Thursday to shop, you know, and I had the money—the hundred pounds—with me to take to the bank. I was going to see the manager. I was mugged by some boys. They took my bag with the money inside.' She paused to look at him. 'Fortunately the housekeeping money was in the basket on my bike, so I was able to do the shopping.'

She managed a small smile. 'I'm a bit disappointed.'

He put out a hand and took hers, which was lying on the table, in his. 'My poor Kate. What a wretched thing to happen. Of course, you told the police...?'

'Yes. They said they'd do their best—but, you see, no one really saw it happen. People were passing on the other side of the street but not looking, if you see what I mean.'

'You told my aunt?'

She gave her hand a tug but he held it fast. 'Well, no; there's no point in doing that, is there?'

'Your mother?'

'It's my free day tomorrow. I shall tell her then.'

'What do you intend to do?'

'Why, start again, of course. I'd hoped that I would be able to leave here quite soon, but now I'll stay for at least a year—if Lady Cowder wants me to.' Her voice wobbled a bit at the thought of that, but she added, 'A year isn't long.'

Mr Tait-Bouverie got up, came round the table, heaved her gently out of her chair and took her in his arms. He did it in the manner in which she might have expected a brother or a favourite uncle would do. Kind and impersonal, and bracingly sympathetic. It cost him an effort, but he loved her.

It was exactly what Kate needed—a shoulder to cry on—and she did just that, comforted by his arms, soothed by his silence. She cried for quite some time, but presently gave a great sniff and mumbled, 'Sorry about that. I feel much better now. I've soaked your jacket.'

He handed her a beautifully laundered handkerchief. 'Have a good blow,' he advised. 'There's nothing like a good weep to clear the air. What time are you free tomorrow?'

'I usually get away just after nine o'clock, unless Lady Cowder needs something at the last minute.'

'I'll be outside at half past nine to take you home. It might help your mother if I'm there, and it might be easier for you to explain. She's bound to be upset.'

'Yes.' Kate mopped her face and blew her pink nose again. 'That would be very kind of you, but are you staying here for the night? I didn't know—I must make up a bed...'

'I'm going back home now.' He gave her a kind and what he hoped was an avuncular smile. 'I'll be here in the morning. Perhaps we can think of something to help your mother over her disappointment. Now cheer up, Kate; something will turn up...'

'What?' asked Kate.

'Well, that's the nice part about it, because you don't know, do you? And a surprise is always exciting.' He bent and kissed her cheek. 'I must go. See you in the morning. And, Kate—sleep well tonight.'

She nodded. 'I think I shall. And thank you, Mr Tait-Bouverie, you have been so kind.' She smiled. 'You're quite right; there's nothing like a good weep on someone's shoulder. I'm grateful for yours.'

She sat at the table for several minutes after he had gone. He had offered no solution, made no hopeful suggestions, and yet she felt cheerful about the future. Perhaps it was because he had been so matter-of-fact about it, while at the same time accepting her bout of weeping with just the right amount of calm sympathy. Breaking the news to her mother would be a great deal easier with him there.

He had kissed her, too. A light, brotherly kiss which had made her feel…she sought for the right word. Cherished. Absurd, of course.

She got up and began to prepare Lady Cowder's dinner, then made herself a pot of tea, gave Horace his evening snack and sat down again to wait for Lady Cowder's ring signalling her wish for her dinner to be served.

It was a fine morning when Kate woke from a good night's sleep. A pity her nicest dress had been ruined in the tunnel she thought as she got into a cotton jersey dress. It had been a pretty blue once upon a time, but constant washing had faded it. As she fastened its belt she wished that she had something pretty and fashionable to wear, and then told herself not to be silly; Mr Tait-Bouverie wouldn't notice what she was wearing.

He did, however, down to the last button, while watching her coming round the side of the house from the kitchen door, the sun shining on her glorious hair, smiling at him shyly because she felt awkward at the remembrance of her tears yesterday.

He wished her good morning, popped her into

the car and drove off without waste of time. 'Your mother won't mind Prince again?' he wanted to know.

'No, of course not; he's such a dear.' She turned round to look at him sitting at the back, grinning at her with his tongue hanging out.

'You have slept,' observed Mr Tait-Bouverie.

'Yes, yes, I did. I'm sorry I was so silly yesterday—I was tired…' She glanced at his rather stern profile. 'Please forget it.'

He didn't answer as he stopped before her home, but got out and opened her door and let Prince out to join them. By the time he had done that Mrs Crosby was at the open door.

'What a lovely surprise. Hello, darling, and how delightful to see you again, Mr Tait-Bouverie. I hope you've come to stay? There's coffee all ready—we can have it in the garden.'

She beamed at them both and stooped to pat Prince. 'You'll stay?' she asked again.

'With pleasure, Mrs Crosby. You don't mind Prince?'

'Of course not. He shall have some water and a biscuit.' She turned to Kate. 'Go into the garden, dear, I'll bring the tray…'

Mr Tait-Bouverie carried the tray out while Kate fetched the little queen cakes her mother had made, all the while talking over-brightly about Norway—indeed, hardly pausing for breath, so anxious was she not to have a long silence which might encourage her mother to ask about her trip to Thame.

In the end, Mrs Crosby managed to get a word in. She couldn't ask outright about the bank manager, not in front of their guest, but she asked eagerly, 'Did you have a successful trip to Thame, dear?'

'I've some disappointing news, mother,' began Kate.

'Won't they lend you the money? Wasn't it enough, the hundred pounds?'

'Well, mother, I didn't get the chance to find out. I was mugged just outside the bank. The police don't think that there is much chance of getting the money back—it was in my bag.'

Mrs Crosby put her cup carefully back into the saucer. She had gone rather pale. 'You mean, there is no money…?'

'I'm afraid not, Mother, dear. It's a bit of a blow, isn't it? But we'll just have to start again.'

'You mean,' said Mrs Crosby unhappily, 'that you must go on working like a slave for too little money for another year? More, perhaps.'

She picked up her cup and put it down again because her hand was shaking. 'Did you know about this?' she asked Mr Tait-Bouverie.

'Yes, Mrs Crosby. I saw Kate yesterday evening and she told me.'

Mrs Crosby said, 'I can quite understand what a relief it must be to have hysterics. Kate, dear, I am so very sorry. After all these months of work—and you've never once complained.' She looked at Mr Tait-Bouverie. 'This is rather dull for you. Let's talk about something else.'

He said in his calm way, 'If I might make a suggestion, there is perhaps something to be done…'

He had spent a large amount of the previous evening on the telephone after he'd returned home, but first of all he had gone in search of Mudd, who had been sitting in the comfortable kitchen doing the crossword.

'Mudd, do I pay you an adequate wage?'

Mudd had got to his feet and been told to sit down again. 'Indeed, you do, sir; slightly more than is the going rate.'

'Oh, good. Tell me, would you know the—er— going rate for a housekeeper? One who runs the house more or less single-handed and does all the cooking.'

'A good plain cook or cordon bleu?' asked Mudd.

'Oh, cordon bleu.'

Mudd thought, named a sum and added, 'Such a person would expect her own quarters too, the use of the car, two days off a week and annual holiday.'

Mudd looked enquiringly at Mr Tait-Bouverie, but if he hoped to hear more he was to be disappointed. He was thanked and left to his puzzle while Mr Tait-Bouverie went to his study and sat down at his desk to think. The half-formed plan he had allowed to simmer as he drove himself home began to take shape. Presently, when it came to the boil, he had picked up the phone and dialled a number.

Now he returned Kate's look of suspicion with a bland stare. 'No, Kate, it isn't something I've thought up during the last few minutes. It is something I remembered on my way home last night. An old lady—an extremely active eighty-something—told me some time ago that her cook would have to go into hospital for some time and would probably be away for several months. It seems the poor woman should have been there much earlier, but her employer was unable to find someone to replace her. She lives in a village south of Bath—a large house, well staffed… Kate, will you tell me what wages you receive?'

She told him, for she saw no reason not to.

'I believe that you are underpaid by my aunt. Did you know that?'

'Oh, yes. But I needed a job badly, and someone we knew offered us this cottage at a cheap rent. I know I'm not paid enough, but where would I find another job where we could live as cheaply as we do here?'

'Exactly. But if you could get work where you lived rent-free and were better paid, it might be a good idea to take a calculated risk. You would be able to save more money—no rent, nor gas or electricity. I'm a bit vague about such things, but surely there would be more scope for saving?'

'But it would be temporary. I might be out of work again…'

He raised his eyebrows. 'With Bath only four miles away?' He smiled. 'Faint-hearted, Kate?'

She flared up. 'Certainly not; what a horrid thing to say.' She added quickly, 'I'm sorry. That was ungrateful and horrid of me.'

She looked at her mother. Mrs Crosby said quietly, 'We have nothing to lose, have we? I think it's a marvellous idea, and I'm grateful to James…' She smiled across at him. 'You don't mind? You see, I feel that you are our friend…for thinking of it and offering us help.'

Kate got up and went to stand by his chair, and when he got up, too, held out her hand. 'Mother's right; you're being kind and helping us, and I don't deserve it. I feel awful about it.'

He took her hand in his and smiled down at her. 'I hope that I may always be your friend, Kate— you and your mother. And as for being kind, I don't need to trouble myself further than to write to this old lady and let you know what she says. She may, of course, have already found someone to her taste.'

All of which sounded very convincing in Kate's ear. As he had meant it to.

Kate took her hand away reluctantly. 'What do you want us to do? Write to this lady asking her if she will employ me?'

'No, no. I think it best if I write to her and discover if she has found someone already. If she has, there is no more to be said—but if she is still seeking someone, I could suggest that I know of a good cook who would be willing to take over for as long as is needed.' He looked at Mrs Crosby. 'Would that do, do you suppose?'

'Very well, I should think. We'll try and forget about it until we hear from you, then we shan't be disappointed.' She smiled at him. 'We can never thank you enough, James. I've said that already, but I must say it again.'

He went away soon after that, leaving them to speculate about a possible future. 'James is quite right,' said Mrs Crosby. 'If we can live rent-free think of the money we'll save. Even if the job lasts for only a few months we might have enough to get started, with help from the bank.'

'It's a risk.'

'Worth taking,' said Mrs Crosby cheerfully, and clinched the matter.

Kate heard nothing from Mr Tait-Bouverie for the best part of a week and then suddenly there he was, standing in the kitchen doorway, wishing her good afternoon in a cool voice.

Kate paused in her pastry making, aware of pleasure at seeing him.

'Are you staying for dinner?' she wanted to know. 'Because if you are I'll have to grill some more lamb chops.'

'No. No. I merely called in on my way back from Bristol. I have been sent by my aunt to tell you that I am here for tea.'

'I have just taken an apple cake out of the oven. Does Lady Cowder want tea at once?'

'I do have to leave in half an hour or so, if that is not too much trouble?'

He came further into the kitchen. 'I heard from the old lady I told you about. She will be writing to you. It will be for you to decide what you want to do, Kate.'

She smiled widely at him. 'You have? She will write? That's marvellous news. Thank you, Mr Tait-Bouverie. If this lady wants me to work for her I'll go there as soon as I've given notice here.' She added uncertainly, 'If she would wait?'

'Oh, I imagine so,' said Mr Tait-Bouverie easily. 'I don't suppose another week or so will make any difference.'

He strolled to the door. 'I'm sure everything will get nicely settled without any difficulties.'

He had gone before she could thank him.

* * *

The letter came the next day. Kate was asked to present herself for an interview on a day suitable to herself during the next week, and she wrote back at once, suggesting the following Wednesday afternoon.

Getting there might be a problem—one solved by asking the son of the owner of the village shop to give her a lift into Oxford, where she could catch a train. It would be a tiresome journey, and to be on the safe side she told Lady Cowder that she might be back late in the evening.

Kate, hurrying down to the village to start her journey on Wednesday afternoon, felt mean about leaving Lady Cowder in the dark—then she remembered how that lady hadn't scrupled to underpay her...

Rather to her surprise, she was to be met at Bath and driven to her prospective employer's house, which was at a small village some four miles or so away. The man who met her was elderly and very polite, although he offered no information about himself.

'Mrs Braithewaite is elderly, miss, as you perhaps know. You are to see her first for a short interview and then have a talk with Cook. You are to return to Thame this evening?'

'Yes. I hope to catch the half-past-six train to Oxford, if possible.'

'I shall be taking you back to Bath. You should be finished by then.'

He had no more to say, and sat silently until he turned in at an open gate and drew up before an imposing Queen Anne house set in a large garden. Its massive front door was flanked by rows of large windows, but Kate followed her companion round the side of the house and went in through a side door.

The kitchen at the end of the stone passage was large and airy and, she noted, well equipped with a vast Aga and a huge dresser, rows of saucepans on its walls and a solid table. There were chairs each side of the Aga and a tabby cat curled up in one of them. There were three people there—an elderly woman, sitting on one of the chairs, and two younger women at the table, drinking tea.

They looked up as Kate was ushered in, and the elder woman said, 'You're young, but from all accounts you're a good cook. Sit down and have a cup of tea. Mrs Braithewaite will see you in ten minutes. I'm Mrs Willett. This is Daisy, the housemaid, and Meg, the kitchenmaid. Mr Tombs, the butler, will see you before you go.'

Kate accepted a cup of tea, thanked the man who had driven her from the station and got a quick nod from him. 'I'm the chauffeur and gardener; Briggs is the name.'

'I'm very grateful for the lift.'

He shrugged. 'It's my job. You don't look much like a cook, miss.'

She was saved from answering this by Mrs Willett, who got to her feet with some difficulty, saying, 'Time we went.'

They went along a lengthy passage and through a door opening into the entrance hall. They crossed this and Mrs Willett knocked on one of the several doors opening from it. Bidden to come in, she stood aside for Kate to go in and then followed her to stand by the door.

'Come here.' The old lady sitting in a high-backed chair by the window had a loud, commanding voice. 'Where I can see you. What's your name again?'

'Kate Crosby, Mrs Braithewaite.'

'Hmm. I'm told you can cook. Is that true?'

'Yes. I can cook.'

'It's a temporary job, you understand that? While Mrs Willett has time off to go to hospital and convalesce. I have no idea how long that will be, but you'll be given reasonable notice. Dependants?'

'My mother.'

'There's Mrs Willett's cottage at the back of the house. She's willing for you to live there while she's away. Bring your mother if you wish. I take it you have references? I know Mr Tait-Bouverie recommended you, but I want references as well.'

Kate had a chance to study the old lady as she spoke. Stout, and once upon a time a handsome woman, even now she was striking, with white hair beautifully dressed. She wore a great many chains and rings and there was a stick by her chair.

'I'm a difficult person to please,' went on Mrs Braithewaite. 'I'll stand no nonsense. Do your work well and you will be well treated and paid. You can start as soon as possible. Arrange that with Mrs Willett.'

Mrs Willett gave a little cough which Kate rightly took to be a signal to take her leave.

She thanked Mrs Braithewaite politely, bade her good day and followed Mrs Willett out of the room.

'There, that's settled, then,' said the cook in a relieved voice. 'You've no idea how many she's interviewed, and me just dying to get to hospital and be seen to.'

'I'll come as soon as I can. I have to give notice where I'm working at present. I'll write to you as soon as I've got a date to leave, shall I?'

'You do that, miss. What's your name again? Not married, are you?'

'No. Would you call me Kate?'

'Suits me. I'll tell the others. Come and see the cottage, and there's time for another cup of tea before Briggs takes you back. And you've still got to see Mr Tombs.'

The cottage was close to the house—a small, rather sparsely furnished living room opened into a minuscule kitchen and a further door led to a bathroom. The stairs, behind a door in the sitting room wall, led to two bedrooms, each with a single bed, dressing table and clothes cupboard.

Kate said, 'We have our own furniture where we are at present. We'll store it, of course, but would you like us to bring our own bed linen—and anything else to replace whatever you would like to pack away? We're careful tenants...'

Mrs Willett looked pleased. 'Now that's a nice idea, Kate. Bring your own sheets and table linen. I'll put anything I want to store away in the cupboard in the living room.'

'There's just one other thing—we have a cat. He's elderly and well-behaved.'

'Suits me, so long as he doesn't mess up my things.' Mrs Willett led the way back to the house. 'Mr Tombs will be waiting to see you...'

Mr Tombs was an imposing figure of a man. Middle-aged, with strands of hair carefully combed over his balding pate, he wore a severe expression and an air of self-importance. He fixed her with a cold eye and expressed the wish that they would suit each other. 'The kitchen is, of course, your domain, but all household matters must be referred to me,' he told her pompously.

Later, in the car being driven back to her train, Briggs said, 'You don't have to worry about Mr Tombs; his bark's worse than his bite.'

'Thank you for telling me,' said Kate. 'But I shan't

have much to do with the house, shall I? And the kitchen, as he said, is to be my domain.' She added, 'I think I'm quite easy to get on with.'

That sounded a bit cocksure. 'I mean, I'll try to fit in as quickly as possible, and I hope that someone will tell me if I don't. I shall do my best to do as Mrs Willett has done.'

'No doubt. We're all that glad that Mrs Willett can get seen to. She's waited long enough.'

Presently he left her at the station and she got into the train and spent the journey back making plans. They would have to start packing up, and the furniture would have to be stored, but they would be able to take some of their small possessions, she supposed. There was the question of telling Lady Cowder, too.

Kate spent a long time rehearsing what she would say. By the time she reached Oxford she was word-perfect.

Jimmy from the village had promised to meet her, and he was waiting.

'Any luck?' he wanted to know.

'Yes, I've got the job—but don't tell a soul until I've given in my notice, will you?'

'Course not. Coming back here when the job's finished?'

'Well, I don't know. Perhaps, if we can have the cottage back again.'

He left her at her home with a cheerful goodnight

and she quickly went indoors to tell her mother. 'I can't stop,' she told her. 'I'll tell you all about it on Sunday. I've got the job. I'll have to give in my notice tomorrow.'

She kissed her mother, got on her bike and pedalled back to Lady Cowder's house. It was late now, and she would be hauled over the coals in the morning in Lady Cowder's gentle, complaining voice. She let herself in, crept up to her room and, once in bed, lay worrying about the morning. She expected an unpleasant interview and the prospect allowed her only brief snatches of sleep.

Her forebodings looked as if they were going to come true, for when she took in Lady Cowder's tea that lady said, 'I wish to speak to you after breakfast, Kate. Come to my sitting room at ten o'clock.'

Kate, outwardly her usual quiet, composed self was very surprised to find Lady Cowder looking uneasy when she presented herself. She didn't look at Kate, but kept her eyes on the book on her lap.

'Yesterday I had a long talk with my god-daughter, Claudia—Miss Travers. As you know, I am devoted to her. She told me that her mother is going to live in the south of France and is dismissing her staff at her home here in England. Claudia is upset, since their housekeeper has been with them for some years and is, in her opinion, too elderly to find another post. Claudia asked me—begged me—to employ this woman.

'Claudia is a sensible girl as well as a strikingly pretty one—she pointed out that it will be easier for you to obtain a new post than their own housekeeper, and suggested that you might consider leaving. She is quite right, of course.' Lady Cowder looked up briefly. 'So be good enough to take a week's notice as from today, Kate. I will, of course, give you an excellent reference.'

Kate restrained herself from dancing a jig; indeed, she didn't allow her surprised delight to show. Lady Cowder's discomfiture was very evident, and Kate added to it with her calm, 'Very well, Lady Cowder. Have you decided what you would like for lunch today? And will there be your usual bridge tea this afternoon?'

'Yes, yes, of course. I have no appetite—an omelette with a salad will do.'

Kate shut the door quietly as she went, and then danced all the way down to the kitchen, where she gave Horace the contents of a tin of sardines and made herself coffee. She couldn't quite believe this sudden quirk of fate, but she was thankful for it. It was a good sign, she told herself; the future was going to be rosy. Well, perhaps not quite that, but certainly pink-tinged.

She would have to write to Mr Tait-Bouverie and tell him that his help had borne fruit. She knew where he worked as a consultant, for her mother had asked him, and she would send a letter there.

She composed it while she assembled Lady Cowder's coffee tray. She wasn't likely to see him again, she reflected, and felt decidedly sad at the thought. 'Which is silly,' she told Horace, 'for we quite often disagree, although he can be very kind and—and safe, if you know what I mean. Only I wish he wasn't going to marry Claudia...'

She wrote the letter that evening and gave it to Mrs Pickett to post when she went home. It had been surprisingly difficult to write; things she wanted to tell him and which would have sounded all right if she had uttered them looked silly on paper. She considered the final effort very satisfactory, and had stamped it with the feeling that she had sealed away part of her life instead of just the envelope. She had no reason to feel sad, she reminded herself, and the concern she felt for his forthcoming marriage to Claudia was quite unnecessary—in fact, rather silly.

Mr Tait-Bouverie read the letter as he ate his breakfast the following morning. Reading its stiff contents, he reflected that Kate must have had a bad time composing it. It held no warmth but expressed very correctly her gratitude, her wish for his pleasant future and an assurance that she would endeavour to please her new employer. No one reading the letter would have recognised the Kate who wrote it—but, of course, Mr Tait-Bouverie, with a wealth of memories, even the most trivial ones, tucked away in his clever head, knew better. He read it again and then folded it carefully and put it into his pocket. Kate might think that thcy would never meet again but he knew better than that.

CHAPTER SEVEN

THERE WAS A great deal to do during the next few days, but Lady Cowder rather surprisingly told Kate that she might go home each evening after she had served dinner and cleared away the dishes. Kate had arranged to go straight to her new job, and her mother would follow within the week, after seeing their furniture put into store and returning the cottage key to its owner.

The owner of the village store had turned up trumps with an offer to drive Mrs Crosby to her new home with most of the luggage and Moggerty, so that Kate needed only her overnight bag and a case.

It was all very satisfactory, although her remaining days with Lady Cowder were uneasy, partly because Claudia had arrived unexpectedly, bringing with her the woman who was to replace Kate. She was a thin, sour-faced person with a sharp nose and grey hair scraped back into a bun. She followed Kate round the house on a tour of inspection, answering Kate's helpful remarks with sniffs of disapproval.

'I'll not have that cat in my kitchen,' she told Kate. 'The gardener can take it away and drown it.'

'No need,' said Kate, swallowing rage. 'Horace is coming with me, and may I remind you that until I leave I am still the housekeeper here.'

Miss Brown drew herself up with tremendous dignity, then said, 'I am sure I have no wish to interfere. It is to be hoped that your hoity-toity ways don't spoil your chances of earning a living.'

With which parting shot she took herself off to complain to Claudia, who in turn complained to Lady Cowder. That lady, who was guiltily aware that she had treated Kate badly, told her god-daughter with unexpected sharpness to tell Miss Brown to be civil and not interfere with Kate.

'Kate has been quite satisfactory while she has been with me, my dear, and she will be going to another job in two days' time.'

The next morning when Kate took up Lady Cowder's breakfast tray she waited until that lady had arranged herself comfortably against her pillows before saying quietly, 'Miss Brown doesn't want Horace in the house, Lady Cowder. May I take him with me?'

'The kitchen cat? I suppose so, if he'll go with you. Can he not be given to the gardener or someone? They'll know what to do with him.'

'They'll drown him.'

Lady Cowder gave a shudder. 'Really, Kate, must

you tell me these unpleasant things just as I am about to have breakfast?'

When Kate said nothing and just stood there, Lady Cowder said pettishly, 'Oh, take the cat by all means. It is most unfair of you to cause this unpleasantness, Kate. It is perhaps a good thing that you are leaving my employ.'

She wasn't an unkind woman, although she was selfish and self-indulgent and lazy, so she added, 'Take the cat to your home this afternoon. Miss Brown can get our tea.'

Kate said, 'Thank you, Lady Cowder,' and went back to the kitchen to tell Horace that he would shortly have a new home. 'Where you will be loved,' she told him cheerfully, so that he lost the harassed expression he had had on his whiskery face ever since he had encountered Miss Brown.

Kate took him home later and, being an intelligent beast, knowing upon which side his bread was buttered, he made cautious overtures to Moggerty, explored the garden without attempting to leave it and settled down in the kitchen.

'Nice company for Moggerty,' observed Mrs Crosby.

Two days later Kate left Lady Cowder's house. It was still early morning, and Lady Cowder had bidden her goodbye on the previous evening. She had

given Kate an extra week's salary, too, at the same
time pointing out that her generosity was due to her
kind nature.

'My god-daughter told me that I am being unnec-
cssarily generous,' she pointed out to Kate. 'But as
you will no doubt agree, I have been most liberal in
my treatment of you, Kate.'

Kate would have liked to have handed the money
back, only she couldn't afford to. Lady Cowder, waiting for grateful thanks and assurances of her generosity, frowned at Kate's polite thanks.

'Really,' she told Claudia later. 'Kate showed a
lack of gratitude which quite shocked me.'

'Well, I told you so, didn't I? Brown wants to
know at what time she should serve lunch…and I
must go back home this afternoon.' She added carelessly, 'Have you heard anything of James lately?'

Lady Cowder looked thoughtful. 'No, I have been
seeing quite a lot of him during the last month or so,
but not recently. He's in great demand and probably
working hard.'

Mr Tait-Bouverie was indeed working hard, but he
still found time to think about Kate. He was aware
that he could have made things much easier for Kate
and her mother by driving them to their new home
himself, but he had kept away. His Kate, he reflected
ruefully, was suspicious of any help which smacked

even slightly of charity. Besides, she was quite capable of putting two and two together and making five...

He would have to wait until she was settled in before paying a visit, so he took on even more work and at the weekends, if he happened to be free, went down to Bosham with Prince and spent the day sailing. He had a dear little cottage there; Kate would like it, and he would teach her to sail.

He came home late one evening after a long day at the hospital, and Mudd, meeting him in the hall, observed gravely that in his opinion Mr Tait-Bouverie was overdoing it.

'With all due respect, sir,' said Mudd, 'You are wearing yourself out; you need a wife.'

Mr Tait-Bouverie picked up his case and made for his study. 'Mudd, you're quite right. Will it make you happy if I tell you that I intend to take a wife?'

Mudd beamed. 'Really, sir? When will that be?'

'As soon as she'll have me, Mudd.'

Kate, getting ready for bed in Mrs Willett's cottage, presently laid her tired head on the pillow. It had been a crowded day; not least of all her arrival, her rather solemn reception by Mr Tombs followed by a brief five minutes with Mrs Braithewaite and then tea with the rest of the staff and finally going to bed in the cottage.

Mrs Willett had left that very afternoon to go straight to the hospital, leaving everything very neat and tidy, and all Kate had to do was go to bed, close her eyes and sleep until her alarm clock went off at half past six the following morning. But despite her tiredness, she allowed her thoughts to stray towards Mr Tait-Bouverie. She wondered sleepily what he was doing and wished that she could see him again.

'You are more than foolish,' said Kate loudly to herself, 'you are downright silly. Forget him.'

So she went to sleep and dreamed of him.

During the next day, and those following it, Kate made several discoveries. Mrs Braithewaite was old and crotchety, and she expected perfection, but she never failed to thank those who worked for her. Kate, used to Lady Cowder's demands, was thankful for that. The rest of the staff, even Mr Tombs, were friendly, anxious to put her at her ease and show her where everything was kept. Mr Tombs expressed the wish that she would find her stay with them a happy one, and that she was to consult him if any problem should arise.

As to her work, she was kept busy enough running the house, being careful not to upset Daisy or Meg or the two cleaning ladies who came each day— and besides that she had the stores to order, menus to discuss with Mrs Braithewaite and the cooking

to do. She was free each afternoon for a couple of
hours and free, too, once dinner had been served to
Mrs Braithewaite and the rest of the staff had had
their supper.

Her mother had followed her within a few days
and the little cottage, decorated with a few of their
personal ornaments and photographs, had taken on
the aspect of home. Up early in the mornings, feed-
ing Horace and Moggerty, taking tea to her mother
and drinking her own by the open door leading to
the little garden beyond the cottage, Kate was happy.
It wasn't going to last; she knew that. But while it
did she was content.

Well, almost content. Despite her best efforts, she
found her thoughts wandering far too often towards
Mr Tait-Bouverie. She hadn't expected to hear from
him again, but all the same she was disappointed.
Unable to forget the matter, she asked her mother,
one day, in what she hoped was a casual manner if
she thought he might find the time to phone them.
'Just to see if we've settled in,' Kate explained.

'Most unlikely,' her mother had said firmly. 'A
busy man like him. After all, he has done all he could
for us but that doesn't mean to say that he has to be
bothered with us. He helped us and that's that, Kate.'

Mrs Crosby glanced at Kate's face, unwilling
to agree that she had been disappointed, too. She
had thought, quite wrongly, it seemed, that Mr Tait-
Bouverie had had more than a passing interest in

Kate. Well, she had been wrong; he had done an act of kindness and that was that. She went on cheerfully, 'I've been looking in the local paper—he was quite right, there are several hotels advertising for cooks or housekeepers. You'll get a job easily enough when we leave here. I shan't like that, will you? You're happier here, aren't you, Kate?'

'Yes, Mother. It's a nice job and Mrs Braithewaite is rather an old dear. I know she's strict but she's not mean. Compared with Lady Cowder she eats like a bird, although Mr Tombs tells me that she entertains from time to time on a lavish scale.'

Kate and her mother had been there just over two weeks when Kate, going off duty for her afternoon break, walked out of the kitchen door and saw Mr Tait-Bouverie. He was sitting, very much at his ease, on the stone wall by the door but he got down and came to meet her. His, 'Hello, Kate,' was casual in the extreme, which had the immediate effect of damping down her delight at seeing him.

She bade him a good afternoon in a severe manner and started to walk across the wide cobbled-stone yard, and he fell into step beside her. 'Pleased to see me, Kate?'

Of course she was, but she wasn't going to say so. She didn't answer that but observed in her calm way, 'I dare say you have come to see Mrs Braithewaite—you did mention that you knew her.'

'Of course I know her; she's one of my aunts. Are you going to invite me to your cottage?'

Kate stood still. 'Certainly not, Mr Tait-Bouverie. You know as well as I do that it's not possible.'

'You mean old Tombs will take umbrage?' He loomed over her, too close for her peace of mind. 'He taught me to ride my first bike. I used to stay here when I was a small boy.'

Kate was momentarily diverted. 'Did he? Did he, really? How old were you?'

She remembered suddenly that she must remain aloof. Grateful and friendly, of course—but aloof… 'You will excuse me if I go? I have only an hour or so, but I have several things that I want to do.'

He nodded. 'Wash your hair, rinse out the smalls, bake a cake. Stop making excuses, Kate; I asked if you were glad to see me?'

She stood there, rather tired from her morning's work, her hair not as tidy as it might be. He studied the curling tendrils of hair which had escaped, and only with difficulty stopped himself from taking the pins out and letting the whole gleaming mass fall round her shoulders.

Kate had her eyes fixed on his waistcoat; that seemed the safest place. She said quietly, 'Yes, I'm glad to see you, Mr Tait-Bouverie.'

'Good. Has our friendship advanced sufficiently for you to call me James?'

'No! I mean—that is, it wouldn't do.'

'It will do very well indeed when we're alone.'

'Very well,' said Kate. 'I'll tell Mother that I have seen you, we—she talks about you from time to time.'

'I've visited your mother. While you were slaving over a hot stove I was drinking coffee in the cottage with her.' He saw her look. 'When I come here I look up the entire household. Tombs would be upset if I didn't spend half an hour with him, and I like a word with Daisy and Meg, and old Briggs. We had a pleasant chat, your mother and I. She is full of plans for your future.'

Kate nodded. 'Yes. You were quite right—there are plenty of jobs in Bath. When I leave here we'll find something there. Just as soon as—as it's possible, we'll look for somewhere to live and I can start…'

'That is still what you have set your heart on doing, Kate?'

She said soberly, 'Yes. Then we shall have a life of our own, won't we?'

'What if a man should come along and sweep you off your feet and marry you?'

'I'd like that very much, but since it isn't likely to happen…'

'Will you promise me to tell me when it does?'

He spoke lightly and she smiled at him. 'All right,

I do promise.' She added hesitantly, 'Lady Cowder told me that you are to be married.'

'Did she, indeed? She is, of course, quite right.' He held out a hand. 'I'm going to have a chat with Briggs. I'm glad that you are happy here, Kate. Goodbye.'

She offered her hand and wished that he would never let it go. But he did, and she said a quiet goodbye and went on her way to the cottage. He had said goodbye, she reflected. She wouldn't see him again and this was hardly the time to discover that she was in love with him.

Her mother was in the small garden behind the cottage, with Horace and Moggerty curled up together beside her.

'You're late, darling,' she said. And then, when she saw Kate's face, 'What's the matter?' she asked. 'Something has upset you?'

'I met Mr Tait-Bouverie as I left the house. He—he was wandering around talking to everyone. He said he'd been to see you.' Kate took a slow breath. 'He said goodbye.'

'Yes, dear. He's going back to town this afternoon. We had coffee together—what a nice man he is, and so interested in our plans. He's off to America in a couple of days. He certainly leads a busy life.'

Indeed he led a busy life, Kate agreed silently. A life in which there was no place for her. He would become more and more successful and marry Claudia, who would arrange his social life for him, and see that he met all the right people. She would be good at that, ignoring his work and having no interest in it. He would be unhappy... Kate sighed—such a deep sigh that her mother gave her a thoughtful look.

'You're happy here, Kate? I know it isn't for long, but if all goes well we should be able to start on our own before the winter. I intend to get a job—part-time—so that I can look after us both while you get your catering started.'

That roused Kate from her unhappy thoughts. 'No, Mother, you're not to go out to work. There'll be no need—we can manage on the money I'll borrow from the bank. With luck I'll get one or two regular customers—hotels in Bath and small cafés—and we'll manage.'

They would too, Kate reflected. She would make a success of her cooking and catering and she and her mother would live in comfort for the rest of their lives. She would also forget Mr Tait-Bouverie...

As it happened that wasn't difficult to do, for the following morning she was summoned to Mrs Braithewaite's sitting room. She had seen very little of her since she had arrived to work for her, but she hadn't expected to—Mr Tombs relayed his mistress's requirements from day to day, and only occasionally had Kate been bidden to the old lady's presence.

'Not the sack,' thought Kate aloud, assuming her calm housekeeper's face and tapping on the door.

The old lady was sitting by the window, guarded from draughts by numerous shawls and scarves. She said tetchily, 'Come in, do, Kate. I hope you have your notebook and pen with you. There is a great deal to discuss.'

Kate advanced into the room and stood where her employer could see her. She said, 'Good morning, madam,' and produced her notebook and pencil without comment. Presumably a special dinner...

'It is my birthday in two weeks' time,' said Mrs Braithewaite. 'I shall be eighty-three years old and I intend to celebrate the occasion. I shall give a buffet luncheon for—let me see—about sixty or seventy persons. I do not require you to cook those tiresome morsels on biscuits, and bits and pieces. You are to do ham on the bone, and a whole salmon, of course—two, perhaps? Cheese tartlets, a good round of cold beef, chicken... I expect you to embellish these and add anything else suitable. Sweets, of course, something which can be eaten elegantly without trouble—possibly ice cream, which you will make yourself. What have you to say to that?'

'May I add suitable accompaniments to the main dishes, madam? And may I make out a menu and let you decide if it suits you?'

'Do that. I want it this evening, mind. If you need

extra help in the kitchen, say so. Tombs will see to that.'

Mrs Braithewaite was suddenly impatient. 'Go along, Kate, you must have work to do.'

Tombs was waiting for her in the kitchen. 'This is to be a great occasion,' he told her solemnly. 'Mrs Braithewaite has many relations and friends. You will let me know if you need help, Kate, and please come to me for advice if you should need it.' His tone implied that he was quite sure that she would.

Kate thanked him nicely, aware that he was doubtful as to her capabilities when it came to such an undertaking. She had no doubts herself. She went back to her work and that afternoon she went over to the cottage, told her mother and sat down to assemble a suitable menu.

She presented herself later in Mrs Braithewaite's sitting room and handed her a menu and two alternatives.

Mrs Braithewaite adjusted her lorgnettes. 'What is a toad-in-the-hole?' she wanted to know.

'A morsel of cooked sausage in a very small Yorkshire pudding. They can be eaten in the hand.'

The old lady grunted. 'The salads seem adequate. See that there is enough of everything, Kate. And desserts—sorbets, of course, ice creams, Charlotte Russe, jellied fruits, trifle... Very well, that should suffice. Send Tombs to me, if you please.'

So for the next two weeks Kate had more than

enough to do, keeping her too busy to think about anything other than food. There was an enormous freezer in the kitchen, so she was able to prepare a great deal of food in advance, and, although Mrs Braithewaite had said nothing about it, she baked a cake—rich with dried fruit, sherry and the best butter. She had wisely consulted Mr Tombs about this, and he had given it his blessing. Indeed, the kitchen staff had been consulted as to its decoration, to be undertaken at the last minute.

Kate's days were full; it was only when she laid her tired head on the pillow that she allowed her thoughts to dwell on Mr Tait-Bouverie. She supposed that he would come to the luncheon if he was back in England, but she was hardly likely to see him. She was unlikely to stir out of her kitchen.

Tombs had assembled casual help from the village to do the waiting, and she would remain in the kitchen and make sure that the food was transported safely upstairs to the big drawing room where trestle tables were to be erected, suitably swathed in white damask and decorated with the flowers that the gardener was cherishing for just such an occasion.

Mr Tait-Bouverie was back in England. His aunt's invitation was waiting for him when he returned from a weekend at Bosham, where he had spent a good deal of time thinking of good reasons why he should go and see Kate. Now the reason was most conveniently there.

He accepted with alacrity and Mudd, removing the well-worn and quite unsuitable garments which Mr Tait-Bouverie delighted in wearing when he was at Bosham, reflected with satisfaction that such an occasion would make it necessary for his master to be clothed in the superfine suiting—exquisitely tailored—the pristine linen and one of the silk ties which Mudd found fitting for a man of Mr Tait-Bouverie's standing.

'Just for luncheon, sir?' he wanted to know. 'Will you be staying overnight?'

'No, no, Mudd. I'll drive back here during the afternoon. It's a Saturday, isn't it? I'll go down to Bosham and spend Sunday there.'

Mudd nodded gloomily. He would do his best with the unsuitable garments, but that was all they would ever be in his eyes. He asked hopefully, 'You will be wearing the grey suiting, sir?'

Mr Tait-Bouverie, thinking about Kate, nodded absently. 'I'll need to leave the house early tomorrow morning, Mudd. Breakfast at seven o'clock?'

Mudd, his feelings soothed by the prospect of sending his master well-dressed to his luncheon date, assured him that breakfast would be on the table at exactly seven o'clock.

'Dinner will be ready in half an hour, sir.'

'Good; I'll be in the garden with Prince.'

He wandered around with Prince, enjoying the twilight of the early autumn evening, allowing his thoughts to dwell on the satisfactory prospect of seeing Kate again. He would have to go carefully…she was a proud girl, and stubborn. His pleasant thoughts were interrupted by Mudd, coming to tell him that Lady Cowder was on the phone.

'Dear boy,' cooed his aunt, 'you're back in England. Tell me, are you going to your aunt's luncheon party? Her birthday—just imagine, eighty-three and giving a party. I have been invited, of course, although we scarcely know each other. I mean, she is on your father's side of the family, isn't she? Of course, I have accepted, and begged to bring dear Claudia with me. May we beg a lift from you? And if you would be kind enough to drive us back after the party…?'

Mr Tait-Bouverie was a truthful man, but sometimes a lie was necessary. Certainly it was now—to spend several hours in Claudia's company was something he had no wish to do.

'Impossible, I'm afraid,' he said briskly. 'I shall be going, but only if I can fit it in with my work. Surely Claudia can drive you there and back? That is, if she accepts the invitation. She will know no one there, I presume?'

'She knows you,' said Lady Cowder, and gave a little titter. When he didn't have anything to say to that, she added, 'Oh, well, I thought I might ask you; I forget how busy you are. I do hope that we will see you there and have time for a chat. Claudia is always talking about you.'

Mr Tait Bouvrie said, 'Indeed,' in a cold voice, and then, 'Forgive me if I ring off; Mudd has just put dinner on the table.'

'Oh, how thoughtless of me, James. Tell me, before you go, how is your dear mother?'

'In splendid health.' And when he had no more to add to that, Lady Cowder rang off herself.

He was eating his breakfast the next morning when his mother phoned. 'James, I do hope I haven't got you out of bed? I'm back…I know I'm not supposed to be here until tomorrow, but there was a seat on the plane and I thought I'd transfer. Can I come to your place and tidy up before I go home?'

'Mother, dear, stay just where you are—I'm on my way to work, but Mudd shall fetch you at once. You'll stay here as long as you like. I'll be home later today and Mudd will look after you. Did you leave everyone well in Toronto?'

'Splendid, dear. The baby's a darling. I'll tell you all the news when I see you.'

'Go and have breakfast or coffee, my dear; Mudd will be as quick as he can.'

He put down the phone and found Mudd at his elbow. 'Mrs Tait-Bouverie is back, Mudd. Will you take the Rover and fetch her from Heathrow? Take

Prince with you…no, on second thoughts he had better stay at home. It's Mrs Todd's day for cleaning, isn't it? She'll keep an eye on him. Mother is sure to have a great deal of luggage.'

'Mrs Todd has already arrived, sir. I will inform her of what has happened and go immediately to the airport.'

Mudd spoke with his usual dignity, refusing to be hassled by the unexpected. Mr Tait-Bouverie swallowed his coffee and prepared to leave his house. 'Splendid, Mudd. And think up one of your dinners for this evening, will you?'

'I have already borne that in mind, sir,' said Mudd.

There was a hint of reproach in his voice, and Mr Tait-Bouverie said at once, 'You're a paragon, Mudd. I would be lost without you.'

Mudd, aware of his worth, merely inclined his head gravely.

Mrs Tait-Bouverie was sharing a sofa with Prince when her son got home that evening. He was tired; his outpatients clinic had been larger than usual, and he had interrupted his ward round in order to see a badly injured child brought into the accident room.

His mother offered a cheek for his kiss. 'You've had a long day, James.'

'Yes, Mother, but it's so nice to come home to you…'

'You should be coming home to your wife.'

He sat down opposite to her and picked up the glass Mudd had put on the table beside his chair. 'Something I hope to do.'

Mrs Tait-Bouverie put down her glass of sherry. 'James, dear, you've found her…?'

'Yes.' He glanced at his mother—a tall woman, a little given to stoutness, but still good-looking, and with a charming smile. She dressed beautifully to please herself and was always elegant.

He went on, 'She has a lovely face, and quantities of russet hair. She is tall, as tall as you, and she has a delightful voice. She is cook-housekeeper to Aunt Edith Braithewaite.'

'Why?' asked his mother.

'Fallen on hard times after her father died. She lives with her mother.'

'Not one of those beanpole girls playing at earning her living?'

'No, no. She has no money.' He grinned suddenly. 'And she has what I believe are described as "generous curves".'

His mother accepted a second glass of sherry. 'She sounds exactly right for you. Has she agreed to marry you?'

'Certainly not. I imagine that she is unaware that I'm in love with her. Certainly she treats me with a cautious politeness, which is a bit disconcerting.'

'When shall I see her?'

'We are invited to Aunt Edith's birthday luncheon.

She will be in the kitchen, of course. We must contrive a meeting.'

'When is this luncheon to be?'

'Ten days' time. Will you stay until then?'

'No, my dear. I'd like to go home and make sure that everything is all right. Have you managed to go there at all?'

'Twice. It's too far for a day's drive; I managed weekends. Everything was all right. You could easily stay here, and I'll drive you up to Northumberland after the party.'

'I think I'd like to go home first. I'll get Peggy to drive me down. Did you see her while you were there?'

'Yes. She seems very happy. I'm to be an uncle again, I hear.'

'Yes. Isn't that splendid? Your sisters have given me several grandchildren, James. It's time you did the same.'

He smiled at her. 'All in good time, my dear. Here is Mudd to tell us that dinner is on the table.'

Two weeks wasn't long in which to plan and prepare the kind of luncheon Mrs Braithewaite insisted upon giving. Kate sat up late at night, writing copious notes and then assembling everything she would need. A good deal could be prepared well ahead of the day, but catering for seventy people was a challenge. Luckily the staff, led by a self-important Mr

Tombs, were delighted with the idea of such a social gathering and went out of their way to help Kate—Tombs going so far as to drive her into Bath so that she could choose what she needed for herself and then stow it away in the huge freezer until she needed it.

All the same, even with so much willing help, there was a lot to do. Kate enjoyed it, though. Cooking for Lady Cowder had been a thankless task, but now, as she made tartlets and pork pies, cooked the hams to an exact pinkness, coated chicken breasts in a creamy cheese sauce, made lobster patties and crisp potato straws, she felt satisfaction.

On the day previous to the luncheon she stayed up until the small hours, making bowls of mouthwatering trifle, puréeing fruit to mix with gelatine and turn out into colourful shapes. And the cake... She had baked that days ago; now she iced it, decorated it with the roses she had fashioned so carefully and set a single candle amongst them.

Mr Tombs had advised that. 'Mrs Braithewaite hasn't enough breath to blow out one candle, let alone eighty-three,' he had told her seriously.

The great day dawned with a clear sky, although there was an autumnal nip in the air. Luncheon was to be served at one o'clock, and Kate and her helpers were up and about before the sun was up. The tables had to be set up, draped with damask, decorated with flowers and set with plates and cutlery, glass and napkins.

They ate a hasty breakfast and Kate assembled what she would need for dinner that evening. There were to be guests staying on—ten people, close family of Mrs Braithewaite—and she had been warned to send up a four-course meal. Rack of lamb with suitable accompaniments, a sorbet, Charlotte Russe and, for starters, mushrooms in a garlic and cream sauce. For the kitchen staff she had wisely made a vast steak and kidney pudding which could be cut into and kept warm if need be.

The guests began to arrive at around noon and Mr Tombs, Daisy and Meg went upstairs to take coats and hand around sherry. Kate, a little nervous now, put the finishing touches to the cake and put on a clean pinny. Now was her chance to nip up to the drawing room where the buffet had been arranged and make sure that everything was just as it should be.

She paused on the threshold and sighed with satisfaction. The tables were loaded with food but they looked elegant. The flowers were perfect and the hams on their vast dishes, surrounded by dishes of various salads, looked mouthwatering. The cake, of course, was to be brought in at the end of luncheon, to be cut by Mrs Braithewaite and handed round with champagne. Kate nodded her bright head, well satisfied.

Mrs Tait-Bouverie, just that minute arrived and strolling round the hall while James put the car away, paused to look at her. Even from the back Mrs Tait-Bouverie knew who she was. There weren't many heads of hair like hers—besides, James had described her very accurately. Mrs Tait-Bouverie wandered a little nearer, and when Kate turned round to go she was pleased to see that he had been quite right about Kate's looks, too. A beautiful creature and plenty of her, thought his mother. She said pleasantly, 'May I take a peep, or is it to be a surprise at one o'clock?'

Kate smiled at her. 'Well, yes, I suppose it should be. Mr Tombs said that no one was to go into the room until then. I'm the cook, and I came to make sure everything was as it should be.'

Mrs Tait-Bouverie surveyed the colourful display. 'It looks magnificent. Caterers, I suppose?'

'Well, no,' said Kate matter-of-factly. 'It's all been done here. We all helped.'

'But who did the cooking?'

'I did—only I couldn't have done it without everyone's help. I'd better go—and if you don't mind I'll shut the door...'

Which she did, and with a polite murmur went back to the kitchen. Mrs Tait-Bouverie strolled back to the entrance to meet her son.

'I've been talking to your Kate,' she told him. 'She's everything you said of her, my dear, and I sus-

pect a lot more besides. She had no idea who I was.
You'll go and find her before we leave?'

'Yes. There should be plenty of opportunity. The
house is packed with people; we had better join
them.'

CHAPTER EIGHT

MR TAIT-BOUVERIE FOLLOWING his mother, entered the smaller drawing room, where his aunt was sitting receiving her guests. A slow business, as she insisted on opening each present as it was offered to her. She greeted Mrs Tait-Bouverie with a peck on the cheek and turned to James.

'So you found the time to come?' she observed, and added slyly, 'Your Aunt Cowder is here with that girl…wanted to know where you were.'

He bent to kiss her cheek and she added wistfully, 'I should like to see you married, my dear.' She chuckled. 'Not to Claudia, of course.'

He said, 'Since it's your birthday, I believe it very likely that you will have your wish granted.'

He offered his gift, suitably wrapped and beribboned, and, leaving his mother with the old lady, wandered off to greet family and friends.

It wasn't long before Lady Cowder saw him.

'James, how delightful. You managed to get here,

after all.' She pecked his cheek and added archly, 'Claudia is so looking forward to seeing you.'

Claudia, James saw at a glance, was dressed to kill—her make-up had been applied by a skilled hand and her blonde hair had been arranged in a fashionable tangle which, while in the forefront of the current mode, did nothing for her... Mr Tait-Bouverie shook hands, said everything necessary for good manners, and excused himself, giving his aunt a vague reply when she wanted to know when he would be returning.

'Of course, he knows everyone here,' said Lady Cowder soothingly to Claudia, and wished uneasily that the girl would at least disguise her peevishness with a smile.

The last of the guests having arrived, drinks were handed round, a toast was drunk to their hostess and Tombs announced that luncheon was being served from the buffet.

This was a signal for a well-mannered rush to fill plates while Tombs carved the hams and Daisy and Meg and the girls pressed into service from the village saw to it that everyone was served.

When that was done everyone settled down to eating and gossip, having their plates replenished from time to time and drinking the excellent wines Mrs Braithewaite had provided. That lady was seated in some state at a table at one end of the room while an ever-changing stream of people came and went to exchange a few words with her. Everyone was, in fact, fully occupied, and Mr Tait-Bouverie had no difficulty in slipping away unseen.

The house was quiet once he had left the drawing room, gone down the staircase and through the baize door at the back of the hall to the kitchen. He opened its door quietly and paused to enjoy the sight of Kate, fast asleep in one of the shabby armchairs by the Aga.

She had kicked off her shoes and slept like a child, her mouth slightly open, confident that she had the place to herself for an hour or more. The last of the food had been carried upstairs and there was nothing for her to do until Tombs came to tell her to make the tea which some of the guests, at least, would undoubtedly want. So she slept dreamlessly, aware of a job well done.

Mr Tait-Bouverie trod silently across the kitchen and sat down in the equally shabby chair opposite her, quite happy to wait. He had dismissed a strong wish to kiss Kate awake, and contented himself with watching her tired, sleeping face.

Presently she opened her eyes, stared at him unbelievingly for a moment and, Kate being Kate, asked, 'Was I snoring?'

Mr Tait-Bouverie stayed where he was. 'No,' he said placidly. 'What time did you get up this morning, Kate?'

'Me? Four o'clock—I had to finish icing the cake. How did you get here?'

'I came down the stairs. Shall I make us a pot of tea?'

'That would be lovely...' She stopped and sat up straight. 'I'm sorry, Mr Tait-Bouverie, did you come with a message, or want something? I'm sorry I fell asleep.'

He perceived that any rash ideas he might have had about asking her to marry him would have to be ignored for the moment. A pity, for he saw her so seldom, and now, with plenty of time in which to tell her of his feelings, he would have to waste it making tea. He smiled at the thought.

'No, no, everything is going splendidly upstairs. I came to see if you were still quite happy here.'

He got up, opened up the Aga and put the kettle on, found a teapot and the tea and two mugs, whistling quietly as he did so—a sound which Kate found reassuring and in some strange way comforting.

'A very successful birthday party,' said Mr Tait-Bouverie. 'Have you had lunch?' And when she said that she had not, he asked, 'Breakfast?'

'Well, I didn't have any time...'

'As a small boy,' said Mr Tait-Bouverie in a voice so soothing it would have reduced a roaring lion to tears, 'I was taught to boil an egg, make toast and butter it—my mother being of the opinion that if I could master these arts I would never starve.'

He had found the bread and the eggs and was busy at the Aga. 'Is your mother well? I must go over to the cottage and see her before we leave.'

Kate's tired brain fastened on the 'we'. 'Oh, you came with Claudia, I expect.'

The fragrant smell of toast made her twitch her pretty nose, and she didn't see his quick glance.

'No. I came with my mother. She's back from Canada, and came down from Northumberland. She and Aunt Edith are close friends.'

He placed a plate of well-buttered toast on the table and dished up an egg. 'Come and eat something.' When she had sat down at the table he poured the tea, a strong brew capable of reviving anyone not actually dead.

Kate ate her egg, polished off the toast and, imbued with new energy by the tea, got to her feet.

'That was lovely, thank you very much. I mustn't keep you, Mr Tait-Bouverie.' She popped a crumb into her mouth. 'I'm very grateful, but I mustn't keep you. It was most kind...' She stopped herself saying it all again.

She didn't quite look at him, and it was an effort to remember that she was the cook and must behave accordingly.

He made no attempt to leave. 'You have made your plans for the future?' he wanted to know. 'I am told that Mrs Willett will be returning in another few weeks, but I'm sure you will find something in Bath until you are ready to start on your own.'

'Yes. I shall start looking round in a week or two. Bath seems a very pleasant place. Mother has been there—to look round, you know. I'm sure I'll find something.'

They were standing facing each other and she said again, 'Don't let me keep you—you're missing the party.'

When he didn't move, she added, 'It's a success, I hope? Mrs Braithewaite was so anxious that it should go off well. I hope she had some lovely presents—it's quite an achievement to be eighty-three and still have so many friends to wish one well...'

She spoke in her cook's voice, saying anything which came into her head, because if she didn't she might fling herself at him and pour out all her hopes and fears and love for him. She added, 'I must start the clearing up...'

'Of course. I'm glad you are happy here, Kate. I must go back upstairs and have a word with friends I haven't seen for some time.'

She nodded and answered his goodbye in a voice as cheerful as his own. It was pure chance which had caused them to meet again, she told herself when he had gone, and chances like that seldom happened twice.

Claudia was there, upstairs in the drawing room, looking, according to Daisy, quite lovely. Kate began to stack dishes, put away uneaten food and set out cups and saucers for the tea that the staff would undoubtedly be wanting later.

As for Mr Tait-Bouverie, he crossed the courtyard behind the house and paid a visit to her mother.

She greeted him warmly. 'Is it any good offering you coffee?' she asked. 'I expect you've had it already. Is the party a success?'

'Indeed, it is. A magnificent banquet; Kate can be proud of herself.'

'It was hard work,' Mrs Crosby said eagerly. 'But you see, James, that she could make a career out of her cooking, once she can get started?'

'If that is indeed what she wants.' He took the mug of coffee she offered him. 'Mrs Crosby—you're tired, or not feeling well...'

She said far too quickly, 'I'm fine.' And then, catching his eyes, 'Well, it's just this silly little pain; it comes and goes. Even when it's not there I know that it is, if you see what I mean.' She smiled. 'It's nothing; really, it isn't...'

'Does Kate know?'

'No, of course not. She has had enough to think about for the last two weeks—up at dawn and going to bed at all hours. I'll go and see a doctor when the festivities are over.'

'This pain,' said Mr Tait-Bouverie. 'Tell me where it is, Mrs Crosby.'

She told him, because suddenly he wasn't James

but a kind, impersonal doctor asking her questions in a quiet voice.

'I would not wish to alarm you, Mrs Crosby,' he told her. 'But I think that you should go to a doctor and allow him to examine you.' He smiled suddenly. 'Nothing serious, I do assure you, but from what you tell me I should suspect a grumbling appendix, which nowadays can be dealt with in a few days. Do you have a doctor?'

'No. I expect I can find one in Bath.'

'Allow me to arrange a check-up for you—I've a colleague in Bath who will see you. I'll phone him this evening and let you know when he can see you.'

'If it's necessary. I don't want Kate worried.' She added, 'You're very kind. You help us so often.'

'I'll let Kate know and reassure her.' He put down his mug. 'I must go back to the party.' He stood up and took her hand. 'Mrs Crosby, if you or Kate need help will you let me know? Phone my house. Even if I'm not there, my man will see that I get your message.'

He loosed her hand, scribbled in his pocket book and took out the page. 'Here is the number.'

Mr Tait-Bouverie wasn't a man to waste time. At home that evening he phoned his colleague in Bath, made an appointment for Mrs Crosby and picked up the phone to tell Kate.

She was making a last round of the kitchen, mak-

ing sure that everything was ready for the morning.
Daisy and Meg had already gone to their beds and
the helpers from the village had long since gone. Mr
Tombs had bidden her goodnight, expressed himself
satisfied with her efforts and gone upstairs to check
windows and doors and lock up. He had looked at
her pale face and said kindly, 'You did a good job,
Kate. Mrs Braithewaite was pleased.'

Kate was on the point of leaving the kitchen when
the phone rang. She went to answer it, wondering
who it could be, for it was used almost solely to
order groceries and receive calls from tradespeople.
Mr Tait-Bouverie's voice, very calm in her ear, took
her by surprise so that she had no breath for a moment. When he said her name for a second time she
said, 'Yes, it's me.'

'You're tired, but this is most important. I went
to see your mother this afternoon. I'm not sure, but
from what she tells me she may have a threatening appendicitis. Nothing to worry about, provided
it's nipped in the bud. I've arranged for a Dr Bright
in Bath to see your mother on Monday afternoon.
He'll examine her, and if he thinks it's necessary
he'll have her in hospital and take her appendix out.
It's a simple operation and she will be quite fit in a
few weeks.'

He was silent, and Kate said angrily, 'Why wasn't
I told? How ill is Mother? I had no idea, and now
you're telling me all this just as though it's not im-

portant, as though she's got a cold in the head or cut her hand...'

'Forgive me, Kate. You are always so sensible and practical, and I thought that I could tell you without wrapping it up in soft talk and caution.'

'Well, you're wrong. I've got feelings like everyone else—except you, of course. I don't suppose you feel anything except pleasure in nailing bones together and dancing with Claudia. You don't know about loving...' She gave a great sniff and hung up, then snatched up the phone again, appalled at what she had just said. 'No, no. I don't mean a word of it...'

The line was dead, of course.

To find a quiet corner and have a good cry was out of the question; Kate locked the door behind her and went to the cottage. Her mother gave her a guilty look as she went in and Kate said at once, 'Mr Tait-Bouverie has just been phoning me, Mother.' She spoke cheerfully and managed a smile, too. 'I had no idea that you weren't feeling well—I should have seen for myself...'

'Darling, you had more than enough to think about. Besides, I'm not really ill. What did James say?'

Kate told her. 'I expect there'll be a letter in the post on Monday morning. I'll ask Mrs Braithewaite if I can have the afternoon off and we'll catch the bus in after lunch. A Dr Bright is going to see you, and if he thinks he should he'll refer you to the hospital. We can't make any plans for the moment until we know what's to happen.'

Kate put her arms round her mother. 'I'm sorry, Mother, dear—it was very brave of you not to say something.'

'This birthday party was important, Kate. Once you start on your own you may find it useful; a lot of the guests are local people, and news gets around in the country.'

'None of that matters while you're not well, mother. I'm going to make us a warm drink and you're going to bed. We'll know more on Monday.'

There was a letter on Monday morning, giving the time and the place where Mrs Crosby was to go and, what was more, Tombs himself took Kate aside after breakfast and informed her that Mrs Braithewaite, having been appraised of Mrs Crosby's indisposition, had ordered Mr Briggs to drive them both to Bath and bring them back.

Kate stared at him, her eyes wide. 'Mr Tombs, however did Mrs Braithewaite know? I've certainly not told her—I intended to do so this morning…'

'As to that, Kate, I am quite unable to say,' he told her severely, mindful of Mr James's express wish that the source of the arrangement should be kept secret.

'I've talked to my aunt, Tombs,' Mr Tait-Bouverie had continued. 'And she has agreed to sending Briggs with the car, so not a word to a soul.'

Tombs had assured him that he would be as quiet as the grave.

So Kate and her mother were driven in comfort to see Dr Bright, a youngish man, who examined Mrs Crosby and then told her in his pleasant voice that she should go into hospital as soon as possible and have her appendix out.

'Which hospital?' asked Kate. 'You see, we don't actually live here...'

'Ah—as to that, I think things could be arranged. You are acquainted with Mr Tait-Bouverie, are you not? He is an old friend and colleague of mine—and an honorary consultant at our hospital; there should be no trouble in finding a bed for you for a week or ten days—and you are an emergency, Mrs Crosby. I should like you to come tomorrow and be seen by the surgeon there—also a colleague of Mr Tait-Bouverie—and he will decide when he will operate. The sooner the better. The operation is simple, but nonetheless necessary.'

When Mrs Crosby hesitated, Kate said, 'You are very kind, Doctor. If you will tell me where Mother has to go and at what time...?'

'Would you wait while I arrange a bed?' said Dr Bright, and ushered them back into the waiting room, to emerge in ten minutes or so.

'Bring Mrs Crosby to the hospital at two o'clock tomorrow afternoon. She will be seen then, and admitted.'

He shook hands with them both, said that he would be seeing Mrs Crosby again very shortly, and went back to his surgery and lifted the phone.

Kate was surprised at the amount of willing help she was offered when she told Mr Tombs the result of their visit to the doctor. She had expected him to grumble, even make it difficult for her to go with her mother to the hospital the next day, but he had been helpful. She was to go with her mother directly after lunch and stay until she was quite satisfied that Mrs Crosby was comfortable, and she had seen the surgeon.

'But dinner,' said Kate. 'I may not be back in time to cook it.'

'You have the morning,' Mr Tombs reminded her. 'Prepare a dish which Daisy or Meg can warm up. They are quite capable of cooking the vegetables. Unless Mrs Braithewaite asks for a special dessert, you will have time in the morning to make a trifle. She is partial to trifle.'

Kate thanked him and started to cook that evening's dinner, and make a steak and kidney pie for the staff supper. She made two; one would do for the next day. She had seen her mother safely back to the cottage and left her to pack a case and get ready for the next day. She hated leaving her alone, but Mrs Braithewaite had been kind so far, and so had Mr Tombs, but she was still the cook with a job to do.

* * *

Briggs took them to Bath the following day. Tombs had taken Kate aside while she was getting the breakfast and told her that Mrs Braithewaite had herself suggested it. 'And when you are ready to return, she wishes you to telephone to me and I will instruct Briggs to fetch you from the hospital,' said Tombs at his most pompous.

It was a surprise, too, when Mrs Crosby was taken to a small room opening out of the women's surgical ward. Kate said anxiously to the sister, 'Is there some mistake? I mean, Mother's on the NHS—we can't afford to pay—and this is a private room, isn't it?'

Sister smiled. 'It is the only bed we have free,' she explained. 'And of course you won't have to pay for it. Your mother will be here for a week or ten days at the most. Is there someone to look after her when she goes home?'

'Me,' said Kate. 'I'm a cook; we have a little cottage close to the house. I can manage quite well as long as Mother can be left while I work.'

'It should be perfectly all right.' Sister patted Kate's arm. 'You mustn't worry; I'm sure Dr Bright told you that it is a simple operation, and only needs a short stay in hospital. I'll leave you to get your mother settled in and then, if you will come to my office, I dare say Mr Samuels will see you. He's the surgeon who will operate.'

He was quite a young man, Kate discovered, and

he told her that he would operate on the following day. Possibly in the afternoon. 'I'll get someone to let you know, then if you wish to see your mother you will be able to do so.'

'I'm not sure if I can get away. You see, I'm a cook and there's dinner to prepare. I've been given a lot of free time already...' Kate added anxiously, 'If I phoned, would someone tell me if everything was all right? I'll come if I possibly can...'

'Don't worry if you can't come,' he assured her. 'We'll keep you informed, and I'm sure Sister will let you visit whenever you can manage it.'

So Kate bade a cheerful goodbye to her mother and phoned Mr Tombs, who told her to wait at the hospital entrance until Briggs came to fetch her. 'I trust everything is satisfactory, Kate?' he added.

Kate said that, yes, it was, and thanked him once again. 'Everyone is being so helpful,' she told him.

Mr Tait-Bouverie would have been pleased to hear that. He had spent time and thought and hours on the phone, persuading and explaining, shamelessly taking advantage of his consultant's post at the hospital. Because he was well liked by his colleagues—and Tombs hid a lifelong devotion to him—he had succeeded in his plan. Only Mrs Braithewaite had demanded to know why he should be taking so much trouble over her cook's mother.

'I'm sure Kate's mother is a very pleasant per-

son,' she had stated. 'But, after all, Kate is the cook,
James.'

'She is my future wife.' Mr Tait-Bouverie heard
the old lady gasp. 'So, dear Aunt Edith, will you do
as I ask?'

'Does she know?'

'No.'

Mrs Braithewaite chuckled. 'She is an excellent
cook and a very pretty girl, and it's time you settled down. Come and see me when you have the
time, James; I dare say you have some scheme in
that clever head of yours.'

'Indeed, I have. And I'm free tomorrow.'

'I shall expect you!'

The operation was a success. Kate was called to answer the phone just as she had sent Mrs Braithewaite's
lunch up on Daisy's tray. Sister was reassuringly
cheerful. 'Your mother is back in bed and sleeping
peacefully.'

'I thought it was to be this afternoon.' Kate did
her best to keep the wobble out of her voice; it was
silly to want to cry now that everything was all right.

'Mr Samuels decided to do your mother at the end
of his morning list.' Sister had hesitated before she
spoke, but Kate was in no state to notice.

'Please give Mother my love when she wakes up,
and I'll come when I can. Would this evening be
too late?'

'Come when you can,' said Sister comfortably. 'Your mother will probably be asleep, but if you visit her you'll feel better, won't you?'

Kate put down the phone. She was crying, although she had tried her best not to. Everything was all right, Sister had said, but she longed to be with her mother—just for a minute or two. Just to make quite sure…

Mr Tombs came to a silent halt beside her, and she blew her nose and sniffed back the tears. 'That was the hospital, Mr Tombs. Mother is back in her bed and everything is fine. Sister said so.'

'We are all relieved at the good news,' said Tombs, looking suitably serious. 'I will inform Mrs Braithewaite and I suggest that you go and have your dinner with the rest of the staff, Kate.'

He went on his dignified way and Kate went back to the kitchen, to be cheered by the kind enquiries she had from Daisy and Meg and the daily woman from the village. She couldn't eat her dinner, and only drank the strong tea Daisy gave her, her head filled with rather wild plans to go to Bath and see her mother. This evening, she reflected, once dinner had been served, she would get a taxi. No one would object to that, and she would be back before Tombs locked up for the night.

She got up and went along to the fridge; preparations for dinner needed to be made and Mrs Braithewaite wanted scones for her tea.

Tombs came looking for her. 'I have informed Mrs Braithewaite of your mother's operation, Kate. I am to tell Briggs to drive you to the hospital at half past seven this evening.'

Kate put down the dish of Dover sole she was inspecting. 'He will? I may go with him? How very kind of Mrs Braithewaite. I was going to ask you if it would be all right for me to get a taxi once dinner had been served, Mr Tombs.'

She smiled, wanting to cry from sheer relief. 'I'll have everything quite ready if Daisy or Meg won't mind dishing up.'

'They are glad to help you, Kate. If you wish to telephone the hospital you have my permission to do so.'

There wasn't much time once Kate had cooked dinner, so she hurried over to the cottage, tore into a jumper and skirt and shabby jacket, tied a scarf over her hair and, anxious not to keep Briggs waiting, went quickly to the other side of the yard where he would be ready.

'Sorry I'm late, Mr Briggs,' she told him breathlessly. 'It's been a bit of a rush.'

'Just you sit and catch your breath, Kate. It's a nasty old night—going to rain; chilly, too. Your ma's in the best place, I reckon.'

Certainly, Kate thought as she got out at the hospital entrance, it looked cheerful, with lights shining from every window. She paused to poke her head through the car window. 'I'll not be long, Mr Briggs. Will you be here, or shall I meet you somewhere? The car park?'

'You come here, Kate.'

He drove away when she had gone inside.

Kate went to the reception desk and waited impatiently while the girl phoned the ward. She was to go up, she was told. She could take the lift, or the stairs were at the back of the hall.

She raced up the stairs two at a time and then paused to calm down before she pushed open the ward doors. A nurse came to meet her and led her through the ward and into the short corridor onto which her mother's room opened.

'Your mother's fine, but tired,' said the nurse, and smiled and left her.

Mrs Crosby, comfortably propped up with pillows, was rather pale but almost her usual cheerful self. She said happily, 'Kate, dear, how lovely. How did you get here?'

'Briggs brought me, Mother. How lovely to have it all over and done with. Are you comfortable? Does it hurt? Are you being well looked after?'

'I'm being treated like a film star, and I'm only a bit sore. I'm to get out of bed tomorrow.'

Kate embraced her parent rather gingerly, and pulled up a chair.

'So soon? Do you want anything? I'm not sure if I can come tomorrow, but I'll be here on Friday—it's

my day off, and I can get the bus. Do you want any
more nighties? What about books? Fruit? I couldn't
bring flowers; there wasn't a shop open.'

She took her mother's hand in hers. 'Mother, dear,
I'm so glad that they discovered your appendix before it got too bad. I'll ask if I can see the surgeon
and thank him.'

'Yes, dear, such a nice man. But it's James we
have to thank. He knew what to do.'

'Yes, yes, of course. I'll write and thank him,
shall I?'

She remembered what she had said to him on the
phone and blushed hotly. It would be a difficult letter to write. And it would serve her right if he tore
it up without reading it.

She didn't stay long; her mother was already half-
asleep. She bent and kissed her, and went back down
the ward and tapped on Sister's office door.

Sister was there, sitting at her desk, and so was
Mr Samuels. Mr Tait-Bouverie was there too, lounging against the windowsill.

Kate stopped short in the doorway. She said 'Oh,'
uncertainly and then, 'I'm sorry—I didn't know…'

'Come in, Miss Crosby,' said Sister briskly.
'You've visited your mother?' When Kate nodded,
she added, 'Well, since Mr Samuels is here I expect
he'll tell you that everything is just as it should be.'

Kate transferred her eyes to his face, careful not

to look at Mr Tait-Bouverie after that first startled glance.

'Your mother is doing well. Nothing to worry about. A nasty appendix; we caught it just in time. She'll be up and about in no time.' He smiled nicely. 'Of course, you know Mr Tait-Bouverie, don't you? Lucky he got the ball rolling, so to speak.'

Kate cast a look at Mr Tait-Bouverie's waistcoat. 'Yes, I'm very grateful. Thank you very much, Mr Samuels. And Sister. I'm being taken back—someone's waiting for me—I'd better go. I'll come again as soon as I can.'

Mr Tait-Bouverie hadn't uttered a word. Now he said quietly, 'I'll drive you back, Kate.'

'No.' Kate spoke loudly and too quickly before she could stop herself. She felt her face grow hot. 'What I mean is,' she added lamely, 'Mr Briggs is waiting for me.'

'He went straight back to my aunt's house. If you're ready?'

He stood up and went to the door, and she saw that there was nothing else to do but go with him. Mr Samuels was smiling, and so was Sister...

She thanked them both once more, shook hands and went past Mr Tait-Bouverie, who was holding the door open for her.

Halfway down the stairs she stopped. 'You arranged everything, didn't you? Mother being oper-

ated upon so quickly, having a private room, Briggs
driving us to and fro…'

'Yes.' He had stopped beside her, his face impassive.

'I didn't mean a word of it,' she burst out. 'All that
about you not having any feelings. I—I was taken
by surprise and frightened for Mother, but that's no
excuse.' She took a couple of steps down. 'You don't
have to take me back; I feel awful.' She stopped
again and added fiercely, 'You must know how I
feel, calling you all those awful things, and you still
helped Mother. If you never want to speak to me
again I'd quite understand.'

He said placidly, 'What a silly girl you are, Kate.'
He made it sound like an endearment. 'True, I have
satisfaction—not pleasure—in nailing bones together, as you put it. And I do enjoy dancing—but
not with Claudia. And, contrary to your opinion of
me, I do know how to love.'

They had reached the bottom of the staircase.
Kate's tongue ran away with her. 'If you're going to
marry Claudia you ought to enjoy dancing with her,'
she said foolishly.

'Why, yes, I suppose I should,' he agreed. 'Now
come along; the car is round in the consultants' car
park.'

She went with him, silent now. He had called her
a silly girl and she supposed that she was—and if
that was what he thought of her, she had indeed been

silly to fall in love with him. She got into the car and answered his casual observations about her mother in a stiff little voice.

At the house he got out of the car with her, walked her to the kitchen door, opened it, bade her a cheerful goodnight and waited until she had gone inside before walking to the front door.

Tombs, on the look-out for the car, was waiting to open it for him. Mr Tait-Bouverie greeted him with a gentle thump on the back. 'I have just returned Kate to the kitchen,' he told him. 'Mrs Crosby is doing very well. Is my aunt in the drawing room?'

'Yes, Mr James, and there's coffee and sandwiches. You're no doubt hungry...'

Mrs Braithewaite was sitting by the fire, swathed in a shawl and with her feet on a stool. She looked decidedly elderly sitting there, but there was nothing elderly about her voice.

'Come in, James. I must say, this is a fine time of day to call on me. I should be in bed...'

He bent and kissed her cheek. 'Aunt Edith, you know, and so do I, that you're never in bed before midnight.'

'An old woman of my age...' she began, and then went on, 'Oh, well since I'm here...pour yourself a whisky and you can give me one, too...'

He poured a small drink for her, added ice and gave himself a more generous drink. 'You shouldn't be drinking spirits at your age,' he told her mildly.

'At my age I'll drink anything I like!' she told him. 'Sit down; where's Kate?'

'I would suppose that she has gone to her home.'

His aunt chuckled. 'Was she surprised to see you? Did you sweep her off her feet?'

'Oh, she was surprised. But it hardly seemed the right moment to behave with anything but the utmost circumspection.'

'Oh, well, I suppose you know best. How's your mother?'

'Very well. Aunt Edith, when is Mrs Willett returning?'

'Hah! I might have known you had some scheme up your sleeve. In two weeks; it seems she has made great progress. She will come back here, of course, and your Kate will have to go.'

'Splendid. It will be too far to take Mrs Crosby up to Mother's. I intend to offer her the cottage at Bosham. When Kate leaves here, she will join her there...'

'Will she? She might not want to, James. Aren't you taking a lot for granted?'

'Possibly. It's a calculated risk, isn't it? But she will have nowhere else to go.'

'You're a prize catch, James—good looks, money, well liked, well known in your profession, comfortable ancestral home, even if it is in the north, fashionable house in town, cottage at Bosham. I'm surprised that Kate hasn't flung herself into your arms.'

'Kate doesn't care tuppence for any of that,' said Mr Tait-Bouverie. 'She's proud—the right kind of pride—and she's in love with me and won't admit it because she has this bee in her bonnet about Claudia, Lady Cowder's god-daughter. She has this idea that I'm on the point of marrying the girl. The last thing I would ever do. Lady Cowder has put it about that we are to marry, and Kate believes her.'

'But surely you told Kate?'

He shook his head. 'No. There is a great deal that I have to tell Kate, but only at the right moment.' He sat back in his chair. 'And now tell me, how do you feel? All the excitement of your birthday party must have shaken you up a little.'

He drove himself back to London presently, and he thought of Kate every inch of the way.

CHAPTER NINE

Mrs Crosby made an uneventful recovery, and, although Kate was unable to visit her everyday, twice during the following week Briggs took her in the car in the evening when her work was done. She spent her days off in Bath, seeing her mother in the morning and afternoon. Mrs Crosby was out of bed now, walking about, and looking, truth to tell, better than she had done for some weeks—and she listened to Kate's plans with every appearance of interest.

'Mrs Willett is coming back in a week's time,' Kate told her. 'So I shall be leaving very soon now. I've been looking in the local paper; there are several jobs I thought I'd try for. Whichever one I'm lucky enough to get will have somewhere where you and Moggerty and Horace can live with me. Once we're settled I'll go to the bank—there's enough money saved for me to ask them for a loan. Isn't it exciting?'

Her mother agreed, reflecting that Kate didn't look in the least excited—nor did she look happy.

The temptation to tell her of Mr Tait-Bouverie's visit was very strong, but she resisted it. Not that he had said much, only that she and Kate weren't to worry about their future.

'I can't think why you're doing this for us,' Mrs Crosby had told him.

He had smiled a little. 'Oh, but I think you can, Mrs Crosby. If you will leave everything to me…' he had said.

She had nodded. Before he'd taken his leave of her he had bent and kissed her cheek.

Mr Tait-Bouverie, home late from the hospital, was greeted by Mudd with the promise of dinner within half an hour—and the information that Miss Claudia Travers had telephoned. 'She wishes you to join a few friends at the theatre tomorrow evening, sir, and would you phone her back as soon as you returned.' Mudd managed to sound disapproving. 'I informed her that you would probably be late home.'

'Splendid, Mudd. Come into the study, there's a good fellow…'

Once Mudd was seated opposite him, with the desk between them, Mr Tait-Bouverie said, 'Mudd, the mother of the young lady I intend to marry has been ill. I think it would be a good idea if she were to convalesce at the cottage at Bosham. Mrs Squires sees to the place when we're not there, doesn't she? Do you suppose she would go each day and cook

and clean and so on while Mrs Crosby is there? It
may be necessary for you to go down from time to
time and make sure that everything is as it should
be. She will be joined by her daughter very shortly.'

'You won't be going down yourself, sir?'

'Oh, very probably, but I can't always be sure of
getting away.'

'You mentioned that you would be getting married,' said Mudd.

'Yes, indeed—once I can persuade Miss Crosby
that she wishes to marry me.'

Mudd looked taken aback. Mr Tait-Bouverie had
been the target of numerous young ladies for a number of years, all of them ready to fall into his lap at
the drop of a hat. Here was a young lady who needed
persuading. Mudd reflected that she must be someone out of the ordinary. As long as she didn't interfere in his kitchen...

'I shall notify Mrs Squires of your wishes, sir,'
said Mudd. 'If you could give me a date? She will
need to make beds and air the place and get in food.'

'It might be as well if you go down yourself and
make sure that everything is just so, Mudd. Thursday
week—eight days' time.' Mr Tait-Bouverie was lost
in thought. 'If I can manage a day off I'll drive you
down early in the morning and leave you there, then
go on to Bath and collect Mrs Crosby, bring her to
Bosham and drive you back here with me.'

'Miss Crosby?' ventured Mudd.

'She won't be free for another day or so. I'll fetch her then.'

Mudd went away then to prepare the dinner, leaving Mr Tait-Bouverie sitting there with Prince's great head on his knee, lost in thought. When the phone rang he lifted the receiver and heard Claudia's shrill voice. 'James, didn't you get my message? Why haven't you telephoned me?'

Mr Tait-Bouverie said smoothly, 'Yes, I had your message, Claudia. I'm afraid that it is a waste of time including me in your social activities—indeed, in any part of your life. I feel that our lives are hardly compatible. I'm sure you must agree.' Because he was a kind man he added, 'I'm sure that you have a host of admirers.'

Claudia snapped, 'Yes, I have, and they're all young men,' and slammed down the receiver.

Mr Tait-Bouverie put down the phone, quite unmoved by this reference to his age. 'When I'm seventy,' he told Prince cheerfully, 'our eldest son will be the age I am now.'

Prince rumbled an answer and blew gently onto his master's hand, waiting patiently for Mudd to come and tell them that dinner was on the table.

Mrs Crosby was to leave hospital the following day and Kate had packed a case of clothes to take to her. Mr Tombs had told her that she might have the time off to take them during the evening. 'But see that you are back in good time,' he had told her. 'One must not take advantage of Mrs Braithewaite's generosity.'

So Kate, carrying the case, got into the car with Briggs and made her way to her mother's room. 'Will you be all right?' she asked Briggs anxiously. 'Where will you wait? I may be half an hour at least...'

'Don't you worry your head, Kate, you come back here when you're ready.'

Her mother was sitting in a small armchair, and it struck Kate that she looked guilty—but she looked excited too.

She kissed her parent and asked, 'What's the paper and pencil for? Are you making lists?' She opened the case. 'I brought your tweed suit and a woolly, and your brown shoes; you won't need a hat. I'll unpack them and leave the case to put your nightie and dressing gown in when I come to fetch you.'

She glanced up, saw her mother smiling at someone behind her and spun round. Mr Tait-Bouverie, immaculate as to person, pleasantly remote as to manner, was standing just inside the door. He shut it quietly and said, 'Hello, Kate.'

Kate said, 'Hello.' And then, 'Why are you here again?'

He put his hands in his trouser pockets and leaned against the door. He looked enormous. 'Your mother is going to convalesce at my cottage at Bosham. She will be well looked after by Mrs Squires, who takes care of the place for me. You will be able to join her as soon as you leave Mrs Braithewaite's.'

Kate stared at him. 'High-handed,' she said at length. 'That's what you are—arranging everything behind my back.' She rounded on her mother. 'You knew about this, but you didn't tell me…'

'Well, darling, it seemed best not to, for I thought you would object.'

'Of course I object. I can take care of you at the cottage…'

'I understand that you will be leaving there within the next few days,' observed Mr Tait-Bouverie pleasantly. 'Have you found somewhere else to go?'

When she didn't answer he added, 'Kate, your mother will need a little while to get absolutely fit. The cottage is empty; a short while there will give you time to find another job. No one will bother you, you can go job hunting knowing that your mother is in good hands.

'I knew that you would dislike the idea simply because it was I who instigated it, but you will see nothing of me. Stay there until you have found something to your liking and move out when you wish to. I am sure that you agree with me that your mother's health is more important than any personal feelings you may have.'

Beneath the pleasant manner was a hint of steel. He had, reflected Kate crossly, managed to make her look selfish. She said stiffly, 'Very well. If you think that is the best thing for Mother, we accept your offer. It is most kind of you, if you're sure that it will be quite convenient? I'll ask for my free day and take Mother to Bosham. But Mr Tombs will want a day's notice, so if Mother could stay here for another day?'

'No need. I'll drive her there myself tomorrow morning, see her safely in and go on back to town. You will be free very shortly, I take it?'

'Yes.' She saw that wasn't going to be enough and added, 'Mrs Willett comes back in two days, and I'm to go three days later.'

Mr Tait-Bouverie, who knew all that already, nodded. 'Splendid.' He went to Mrs Crosby and took her hand. 'I'll be here for you about ten o'clock tomorrow. You've been a model patient.'

He went away quietly with a brief nod to Kate, who watched him go with her heart in her boots. Nothing could have been more polite and thoughtful than his manner towards her—and nothing, she reflected bitterly, could have been so uninterested. She thought fleetingly of Norway—they had been friends then. Of course, he would never understand that it was loving him that made it so difficult to accept his kindness, knowing that he didn't care for her in the least.

Her mother's voice roused her. 'Isn't it marvellous?' she wanted to know. 'It gives us a breathing space, doesn't it, darling? There's just one thing— would you be able to send on some more of my clothes? I've only got one of everything in the case, haven't I? And the nightie and the dressing gown here.'

'I'll ask Mr Briggs to bring me back. If I go home now I can pack a few things and bring them straight here. I'll bring the rest with me when I leave. Mother, what about Horace and Moggerty?'

'Oh, James said he'd deal with that…'

'How, Mother?'

'I've no idea, but if he says he will do something he does it, doesn't he?'

All the same, thought Kate, I'll have to make sure. She emptied the case, told her mother that she would be back as soon as possible and sped down to the hospital entrance. Mr Briggs was nowhere to be seen, but Mr Tait-Bouverie was. He took the case from her, took her arm and popped her into his car before she had time to utter a remark.

'Mr Briggs,' she managed. 'I must see him—he's got to bring me back—Mother's clothes—you don't understand…'

'Briggs has gone home. I'll drive you back and wait while you pack whatever your mother needs. No need for you to come back here; I'll see that she gets them.'

She could think of nothing to say as he drove her back. She would have to apologise; she had been absolutely beastly to him. If he had been angry it would have been easier… She tried out one or two suitable

speeches in her head but they didn't sound right—
but until she had told him that she was sorry it was
hard to behave with the same friendliness which he
had shown. It would be much easier if she didn't love
him so much...

He went with her to the cottage and sat patiently
with the cats on his knee while she flung things into
the case. As well as clothes she grabbed her mother's modest make-up, more wool for her knitting, a
writing pad and more shoes. She carried it down to
the sitting room and found him asleep. Somehow
the sight of him made it easy; there was no need for
speeches.

'I'm sorry,' she said. 'I've been horrible to you,
and you've shown us nothing but kindness, and I feel
awful about it. I hope you'll forgive me.'

He had opened his eyes and was watching her. He
wasn't smiling, and he looked politely indifferent. He
said coolly, 'You have made such a colossal mountain out of a molehill that you can't see the wood for
the trees, Kate. Rather a mixed metaphor, but really
true.' He got up. 'Is this all that your mother needs?
Have you any message for her?'

'No, thank you. There's a note in the case.'

Kate watched him walk to the door. He had said
that he wouldn't be going to Bosham while they were
there—she wouldn't see him again and he hadn't
said that he'd forgiven her, had he? She swallowed
back tears and wished him goodbye in a polite voice.

He didn't answer that, but said, 'Don't worry about the cats; some arrangement will be made for them.'

He had gone before she could assure him that she would take them with her when she went.

When she was sure that he had gone she sat down at the table in the kitchen. Horace and Moggerty came and sat with her, and presently she got up and fed them, made a pot of tea, drank it and went to bed. She was still the cook, and had to be up and about by seven o'clock.

Although she was tired she slept badly, but once her day had begun she worked her way through it in her usual calm and unhurried way. It was as they were finishing their midday dinner that Tombs, who had been called away, returned and told her that he had received a telephone call from Mr Tait-Bouverie to say that Mrs Crosby was installed in the cottage at Bosham and was well.

'I have ascertained the telephone number, should you wish to speak to your mother. You may use the kitchen telephone, Kate, after six o'clock.'

It was almost eight o'clock before she found the time to do so. She smiled at the sound of her mother's cheerful voice. It had been a lovely drive to Bosham, said Mrs Crosby, they had stopped and had coffee on the way and the cottage was delightful, and so comfortable. Mrs Squires had been waiting for them with James's man, Mudd.

'Such a nice person, Kate, and so efficient. I have a lovely room, and Mrs Squires is sleeping here until you come. James and Mudd went off just before tea, back to London. Mudd told me that James has a house there.' Mrs Crosby was bubbling over. 'Kate, he's thought of everything. The local doctor is coming to make sure that I am well, and he's left me his phone number.'

'I'm glad everything is so delightful, Mother. Take care, won't you? I'll be with you in four days. I'll find out the best way to travel. Train to Chichester, I expect, and then a bus…'

'Oh, I dare say,' said Mrs Crosby airily. Much later it struck Kate that her mother had shown very little interest in her journey. It was going to be an awkward one, what with the luggage and the cats…

Mrs Willett, well again and eager to resume her place in the household, took over the cooking from Kate at once. 'You'll need to pack up,' she pointed out. 'I must say you've kept the cottage very nice, and Mr Tombs told me that Mrs Braithewaite was very satisfied with your work.'

Kate replied suitably and, given a free afternoon, began the task of packing the two suitcases she would have to take with her—watched with deep suspicion by Horace and Moggerty, who got into the cases each time she opened them. 'You're coming with me,' she assured them, and wondered where all of them would finally end up. Chichester sounded nice; if they could find a small house there... She would have to go to the bank, too, and if she could get the money she wanted she would begin the slow process of building up the home catering business. Kate sighed. There was a lot to do before she could get started. 'But at least we've saved more money than we expected to,' she told the cats, 'and if I can get a part-time job to start with...'

The last day came. She was to leave in the early afternoon and take a train from Bath—an awkward journey, but she had worked it out carefully. She had her breakfast, made sure that the cottage was exactly as Mrs Willett wanted it to be, and, bidden by Tombs, went to say goodbye to Mrs Braithewaite.

'You're a good cook,' said that lady. 'They say the way to a man's heart is through his stomach,' she chuckled. 'I wish you well, Kate.'

Kate thanked her. She wanted to point out that it wasn't only men she intended to cater for—birthday parties, family gatherings, even weddings were what she aimed for—but there was no point in saying so. She said goodbye in her quiet manner and went down to the kitchen. They would be having their morning coffee, and she could do with a cup.

So, it seemed, could Mr Tait-Bouverie, sitting

there with a mug in one hand and a hunk of cake in the other. He put both down as she went in, watched the surprised delight in her face with deep satisfaction and got to his feet.

'Good morning, Kate. I'll drive you down to Bosham; I'm on my way there now.'

She had wiped the delight from her face and found her voice.

'I've booked a taxi...'

'Tombs has cancelled it. I'll go and say goodbye to my aunt while you have your coffee and then collect your things and the cats from the cottage.'

Mrs Willett chimed in. 'That's right, dear, you sit down for five minutes. Mr James will let you know when he is ready.'

Kate sat. There really wasn't much else she could do without making a fuss. There would be time enough to tell him what she thought of his high-handed actions once they were in the car.

Once they were on their way, with the cats on the back seat and the luggage in the boot, she found it difficult to begin. She mulled over several tart comments as to his behaviour, but they didn't sound right in her head and would probably come out all wrong if she uttered them.

'I'm waiting,' said Mr Tait-Bouverie.

'Waiting for what?'

'The tart reprimand I feel sure is quivering on your lip. Oh, and quite justified too. I have no business to interfere with your life, I ride roughshod over your plans, I turn up without warning and order you about. I am, in short, a tiresome fellow.'

Which was exactly what she had intended to say herself. She thought how much she loved him even when he annoyed her. He had been kind and helpful and, more than that, they had been friends. He might be going to marry Claudia—although how he could love the girl was something she would never know—but she thought that he liked her...

'Well, you do arrange things, don't you?' she said. 'I mean without saying so, but I expect that's because you're used to doing it at the hospital. I've been ungrateful and snappy. I'm sorry.'

'Good. We understand each other. Try calling me James.'

'No,' said Kate. 'How can I do that when I've cooked dinner for you?'

'Do you mean to tell me that when my wife cooks my dinner she will refuse to call me James?'

'Of course not. This is a silly question.' She added, 'Can Claudia cook?'

'Most unlikely, but Mudd, my man, is capable of that.'

She didn't see his smile.

It wasn't any good; she couldn't go on being vexed with him. Anyway, it was a waste of time for he had an answer for everything. Presently she found herself telling him of her plans, comfortably aware that he was listening—indeed, was making helpful suggestions.

She was quietly happy, even though she knew that the happiness wouldn't last. Each time they had met she had told herself that she wouldn't see him again, but there had always been a next time. These few hours together really would be the last. He had said that he wouldn't be going down to the cottage while they were there, and why should he? He had his own busy life and his marriage to plan. Her heart gave a painful twist at the thought.

She was enchanted by Bosham when they reached it, and when he stopped outside the cottage she stuck her head out of the window to take a better look.

'It's yours? It's lovely. Couldn't you live here always? It's not very far to London, is it?'

'No, but it's too far to travel there and back every day. Besides, I have a very pleasant house in London.'

He had got out and opened her door and she stood outside beside him, looking around her. It was, in Kate's opinion, quite large for a cottage, but it had a thatched roof and a number of small windows, and a solid door in a porch. Although summer was long over there were chrysanthemums and late roses, and a firethorn against one wall, vivid scarlet against the grey stone.

The door had opened and Mr Tait-Bouverie took her arm and urged her up the short path. Mudd was

there, waiting for them, bidding them good day and
casting a sharp eye over Kate. Very nice too, he considered, and ushered them into the narrow hall.

'Mrs Crosby is in the sitting room,' he informed
them. 'Mrs Squires will serve lunch in half an hour,
sir. I will see to the luggage and the cats.'

Mr Tait-Bouverie gave Kate a small shove. 'The
sitting room's there, on the left. Go on in. I'll come
presently; I must speak to Mudd.'

So Kate went in through the half-open door and
found her mother waiting for her.

'Kate, dear. Oh, how lovely to see you. I've not
been lonely for one moment. Mrs Squires is marvellous, and there's so much to do—and Mudd came
this morning, and Prince too. You're all right? Mrs
Braithewaite was pleasant? And the others? And did
you have a good trip?'

Kate hugged her mother. 'Mother, you look marvellous. Are you all right? Was the doctor pleased
with you? Are you eating well and sleeping?'

'Yes to that, my dear. I never felt better. I still get
a bit tired, but that's normal. Another two weeks
and I shall be better than I've been for a long time.'

Kate took off her coat, looking around her. The
room was low-ceilinged and quite large, with a wide
hearth with a brisk fire burning. The walls were
cream, and there was a number of pictures. She
would look at those later. The furniture was exactly
right—deep armchairs, a wide sofa on either side

of the hearth, and little lamp-tables—antiques, just
as the bow-fronted cabinet against one wall was antique. There was a beautiful sofa-table with a bowl
of chrysanthemums on it, and a charming little desk
in one corner.

'It's perfect,' said Kate.

Mr Tait-Bouverie came in then, with the cat bas-
kets, and Prince prancing beside him. To Mrs Crosby's expressed worries that Prince would eat the cats
up Mr Tait-Bouverie said placidly, 'They'll be quite
safe,' and let them out. Prince sat, obedient to his
master's quiet voice, while Horace and Moggerty
prowled cautiously round the room and presently
climbed into a chair and sat, eyeing Prince, who lay
down, put his head between his paws and went to
sleep.

They drank their sherry, then, and Mrs Crosby
and Mr Tait-Bouverie carried on a pleasant conversation about nothing much—and if they noticed that
Kate had very little to say they didn't comment upon
it.

They had lunch presently, but they didn't linger
over it; Mr Tait-Bouverie had to return to London,
taking Mudd and Prince with him, so that the cottage seemed suddenly very empty. Kate, watching
the car disappear down the lane, reflected that he had
said nothing about seeing them again. He had bidden her mother a cheerful goodbye, and when Kate
had begun to thank him for driving her down and

waved her thanks aside with a brief goodbye which
had left her downcast. She deserved it, of course;
she had said some awful things to him. She went
red just remembering.

The rest of the cottage was just as perfect as the
sitting room. Her bedroom wasn't over large, but
the bed and the dressing table were dainty Regency,
and the curtains and bedspread were pale pink and
cream. The pink was echoed in the little armchair by
the window and the lamps on either side of the bed.
Her mother's room was larger and just as pretty. 'The
loveliest room is at the back,' said Mrs Crosby. 'It's
large with its own bathroom; I peeped in one day.'

Her mother was happy. After the places they had
been living in, this must remind her of the house
she had had when Kate's father had been alive. Kate
would have to find work quickly and postpone her catering once more; with a decent job they could afford
to live in a better house. There was the money she
had saved—some of it could be used to pay rent...

'I shall go to Chichester tomorrow,' said Kate.
'And find an agency.'

'Darling, you've only just got here. James assured
me that there was no hurry for us to leave. It's too
late in the year for him to sail and he has a great deal
of work, he told me.'

'Did he say when he was getting married?' asked
Kate casually.

Her mother hesitated. 'Well, no, dear, not exactly.'

Kate said quickly, 'I'll feed the cats. They seem to have settled down nicely. Mrs Squires won't mind if I go into the kitchen?'

'Of course not, Kate. Now you're here, she said she would just come for a couple of hours in the mornings and then for an hour or so to see to the dishes after lunch. She'll be glad not to have to come out in the evening now it's getting dark early.'

It seemed a suitable arrangement. 'I'll come whenever you want me,' Mrs Squires told Kate the next day. 'If you're wanting to go away and don't like to leave your mother, just you say.'

'Thank you, I might be glad of that. I must go and look for a job. I thought Chichester...'

'As good a place as any,' said Mrs Squires. 'There's a good agency in the High Street, and plenty of hotels and big houses in and around the town.'

Kate didn't go to Chichester. The weather was bright but chilly, and her mother wanted to explore Bosham. 'I'm quite able to walk,' she declared. 'And it is such a delightful little place. Besides, I want to hear your plans. If you could find somewhere cheap where we could live, you could start cooking...but do you have to go to the bank first?'

Mrs Crosby spoke with an overbright cheerfulness which caused Kate to give her a thoughtful look. Kate had had a wakeful night. She must face the future with common sense and set aside her dreams

of starting a catering business. Seeing her mother
so happy in the charming little cottage, living the
kind of life they had led when her father had been
alive, she realised that she must plan and decide on
a different future.

She said now, 'There's plenty of time to make
plans, and it's a good day for a walk. Shall we go
down to the harbour?'

Her mother's face lit up.

They had a very happy day, exploring the little
village at their leisure. There weren't many people
and they spent a pleasant half-hour having coffee in
a small café empty of other customers. 'A bit quiet,'
said the owner, 'but it's busy enough at the weekend—they come down to overhaul their boats and
do a bit of painting and such. Staying long, are you?'

'A week or so,' said Kate cautiously.

'Very nice it is at Mr Tait-Bouverie's cottage.
Keeps it nice, he does, and always has a friendly
word. Got a lot of friends here.' She added, 'Mrs
Squires is my sister-in-law.'

On the way back Kate said, 'Perhaps we had
better be a bit careful what we say in front of Mrs
Squires, but I suppose in a small place there's always
a bit of gossip.'

That night, lying in bed wide awake, Kate thought
about their future. She discarded the idea of finding work in Chichester—it was too near the cottage
and Bosham, and there would be the risk of meeting

James when he spent his weekends there. He would have Claudia with him... She wouldn't be able to bear seeing them together. She would have to think up a good reason for moving away where she would never see him again.

Tomorrow, she promised herself, she would get a copy of *The Lady* and look for a job—preferably in the north or along the east coast. She would have to give her mother a good reason for that, too. She could see now that there would be little chance of her starting up on her own, not for several years.

Not that it mattered any more—the future unrolled before her with no James in it. She thrust the thought aside and concentrated on a possible move to a job which would be suitable. There was her mother to consider, and the cats. They would need a roof over their heads and a decent wage. If she abandoned her catering plans there wouldn't be the need to scrape and scrimp. They would go out more, buy new clothes—enjoy life!

Having made these suitable arrangements, Kate had a good cry and fell asleep at last.

She awoke very early and, rather than lie there thinking of the same unhappy things, she got out of bed and looked out of the window. It was a grey morning and still not light. A cup of tea would be nice, and she might go to sleep again. She didn't wait to put on her dressing gown but crept barefoot down the stairs and into the kitchen.

Mr Tait-Bouverie was sitting at the kitchen table, the teapot beside him, a slice of bread and butter in his hand. He looked up as she paused in the doorway and said, 'Good morning, Kate,' and smiled at her.

Kate's heart beat so loudly and so fast that she thought he must surely hear it. She drew a difficult breath. 'How did you get in?'

He looked surprised. 'I have a key.'

'Is something the matter? Do you want something?'

'Nothing is the matter. I do want something, but that can wait for the moment. Would you like some tea?'

She nodded. 'Yes, please.'

He got up and fetched another mug from the dresser. 'Then run upstairs and get a dressing gown and slippers. You look charming, but you distract me.'

Kate said, 'Oh,' and fled back to her room and wrapped herself tightly in the sensible garment she had had for years. It concealed her completely, and would never wear out. At least it covered the cheap cotton nightie she was wearing.

She went back downstairs, feeling shy. Mr Tait-Bouverie's glance slid over her person with the lack of interest of someone reading yesterday's newspaper, so that she felt instantly comfortable. She sat down by the Aga and, since she longed to look at him, she kept her eyes on Prince, snoozing comfortably between Moggerty and Horace.

Presently she asked the question which had been on the tip of her tongue. 'Is Claudia with you?'

He looked amused. 'No.'

'She knows you are here?'

'No. Why should she?'

'Well, if it was me,' said Kate, throwing grammar to the winds, 'I'd want to know.'

'Well, shall we throw Claudia out of the window, metaphorically speaking? She's no concern of mine. I can't think why you've dragged her into the conversation.'

'We weren't having a conversation. And how can you talk like that about her when you are going to marry her?' She added defiantly, 'Lady Cowder said so.'

'One of my least likeable aunts. I have no intention of marrying Claudia. I don't like her, Mudd doesn't like her, Prince doesn't like her...'

'Then why are you here?'

'Because I have something to say to you. On several occasions I have tried to do so and each time I have been thwarted. Now you are in my house, in my kitchen, and I shall speak my mind.'

Kate got up. 'I said I was sorry, and I am. I didn't mean any of the things I said...'

'Well, of course you didn't.' He had come to stand

very near her, and when she would have taken a prudent step back he folded his great arms around her, wrapping her so close that she could feel his heart beating under her ear.

'I've been in love with you for a very long time now, my darling, and I have waited for you to discover that you loved me, too—and that hasn't been easy. Such a hoity-toity miss, hiding behind her cook's apron…'

'Well, I am a cook,' said Kate into his shirt-front, and then, because she was an honest girl, she said, 'But I do love you, James.'

He put a gentle finger under her chin, smiling down at her. He kissed her then, slowly and with the greatest of pleasure, for this was the moment he had waited for. Kate kissed him back and then paused to ask, 'Mother! What about Mother…?'

'Hush, my love. Your mother and I have had a little talk. She is happy to live here with Mrs Squires to look after her. We shall come down whenever I'm free. You won't mind living in London? I have a house there, a pleasant place.'

Kate reflected that she would live in a rabbit hutch as long as she was with James. 'It sounds very nice,' she said.

'Oh, it is.' Hardly a good description of the charming little house overlooking the river.

Something in his voice made her ask, 'James, are you rich?'

'I'm afraid so. Don't let it worry you, my love.'

Kate stared up at him. 'No, I won't—it doesn't matter in the least, does it?'

'No.'

'Although, of course…' began Kate.

Mr Tait-Bouverie kissed her silent. 'Will you marry me, Kate?'

'Well, yes—of course I will, James.' She smiled at him. 'Ought we to sit down and discuss it? The wedding and so on?'

'With all the will in the world, my dearest girl, but first of all…'

He bent his head to kiss her, and Kate, in a happy world of her own, kissed him back.

* * * * *

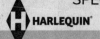
Read on for an exclusive sneak preview of
INTERVIEW WITH A TYCOON by Cara Colter…

KIERNAN WAITED FOR it to happen. All his strength had
not been enough to hold the lid on the place that contained
the grief within him.

The touch of her hand, the look in her eyes, and his
strength had abandoned him, and he had told her all of it:
his failure and his powerlessness.

Now, sitting beside her, her hand in his, the wetness of
her hair resting on his shoulder, he waited for everything to
fade: the white-topped mountains that surrounded him, the
feel of the hot water against his skin, the way her hand felt
in his.

He waited for all that to fade, and for the darkness to take
its place, to ooze through him like thick black sludge freed
from a containment pond, blotting out all else.

Instead, astounded, Kiernan became *more* aware of
everything around him, as if he were soaking up life through
his pores, breathing in glory through his nose, becoming
drenched in light instead of darkness.

He started to laugh.

"What?" she asked, a smile playing across the lovely
fullness of her lips.

"I just feel alive. For the last few days, I have felt alive.
And I don't know if that's a good thing or a bad thing."

His awareness shifted to her, and being with her seemed to fill him to overflowing.

He dropped his head over hers and took her lips. He kissed her with warmth and with welcome, a man who had thought he was dead discovering not just that he lived but, astonishingly, that he wanted to live.

Stacy returned his kiss, her lips parting under his, her hands twining around his neck, pulling him in even closer to her.

There was gentle welcome. She had seen all of him, he had bared his weakness and his darkness to her, and still he felt only acceptance from her.

But acceptance was slowly giving way to something else. There was hunger in her, and he sensed an almost savage need in her to go to the place a kiss like this took a man and a woman.

With great reluctance he broke the kiss, cupped her cheeks in his hands and looked down at her.

He felt as if he was memorizing each of her features: the green of those amazing eyes, her dark brown hair curling even more wildly from the steam of the hot spring, the swollen plumpness of her lips, the whiteness of her skin.

"It's too soon for this," he said, his voice hoarse.

"I know," she said, and her voice was raw, too.

Don't miss this heart-wrenching story, available September 2014 from Harlequin® Romance.

HARLEQUIN® Romance

Resisting Mr. Off-Limits!

Owner of Obsidian Studios, Garrett Black
might be scarred both inside and out, but
with the Hollywood Hills Film Festival fast
approaching, there's no time for distractions.
Especially not those as tempting as event
coordinator Tori Randall....

Who cares if he's gorgeous? Tori's frustrated
by this brooding CEO's aloof attitude and near
impossible demands. Even if Garrett wasn't
her boss, she'd never risk her heart to another
emotionally closed man. Normally she'd run in
the opposite direction...so why does she feel
so compelled to stay?

Her Boss by Arrangement
by
Teresa Carpenter

*Available September 2014 from
Harlequin Romance, wherever
books and ebooks are sold.*

HARLEQUIN®
Romance

You can't help who you fall for...

The arrival of Dominic Brabant is like something out of a movie. Walking into Suzanna Zelensky's shop in his buttoned-up suit, he can't help but make an impression. She can't control the erratic beating of her heart—but this stranger's here for more pressing matters...her home is top of his redevelopment list!

Zanna soon discovers you can't help falling in love with the wrong person...but ending up in her rival's arms might be the best decision she's ever made!

In Her Rival's Arms

by

Alison Roberts

Available September 2014 from Harlequin Romance, wherever books and ebooks are sold.

www.Harlequin.com

HR74306